A BOOKS
BY THE BAY
MYSTERY

Writing
All Wrongs

ELLERY ADAMS

BERKLEY PRIME CRIME, NEW YORK

BERKLEY
PRIME
CRIME

An imprint of Penguin Random House LLC
375 Hudson Street, New York, New York 10014

WRITING ALL WRONGS

A Berkley Prime Crime Book / published by arrangement with the author

BERKLEY® PRIME CRIME and the PRIME CRIME design are trademarks
of Penguin Random House LLC.
For more information, visit penguin.com.

ISBN: 978-0-425-27084-4

PUBLISHING HISTORY
Berkley Prime Crime mass-market edition / November 2015

PRINTED IN THE UNITED STATES OF AMERICA

10 9 8 7 6 5 4 3 2

Cover illustration by Kimberly Schamber.
Cover design by Rita Frangie.
Interior text design by Tiffany Estreicher.

Penguin
Random
House

A Killer Plot

Written in Stone

The Last Word

A Deadly Cliché

Praise for the *New York Times* Bestselling
Books by the Bay Mysteries

Lethal Letters

"This charming series gets better with each book . . . The author does not disappoint . . . The book is well plotted and will keep cozy mystery readers guessing." —MyShelf.com

"There is a lot more than just a mystery to solve in this one . . . Adams did a fantastic job of bringing it all to life."
—Debbie's Book Bag

"[A] charming series that never shies from darker themes, even while entertaining with delightful characters, a beautiful setting, and a love of all things literary."
—Kings River Life Magazine

Poisoned Prose

"A true whodunit . . . Adams's latest, like its predecessors, is rich with coastal color, an intriguing heroine, and a fine balance between the story line and the changing personal lives of the Bayside Book Writers. Like the good storyteller she is, Adams excels at varying her plots and developing her characters, and *Poisoned Prose* confirms her bona fides in the genre and the stature of this superior series."
—*Richmond Times-Dispatch*

"An excellent series with fun dialogue, likable characters, and themes that will resonate with readers long after the book is closed." —Kings River Life Magazine

"Another fantastic story from this fantastic storyteller. You cannot go wrong with a book by Ellery Adams!!! I highly recommend each and every one!!!"
—Escape with Dollycas into a Good Book

continued . . .

To my favorite Coastal Carolinians,
Mead and Deborah Briggs, with love

Draw your chair up close to the edge of the precipice and I'll tell you a story.

—F. Scott Fitzgerald

Chapter 1

*Marriage—a book of which the first
chapter is written in poetry and the
remaining chapters in prose.*

—BEVERLEY NICHOLS

"No one ever told me that marriage was murder," Olivia
Limoges complained while pouring cream into her
coffee.

Dixie Weaver, Olivia's longtime friend and proprietor of
Grumpy's Diner, put her hand on her hip and smirked. "You
haven't been married long enough to be comparin' the holy
state of matrimony to a capital offense." She pursed her lips,
which glistened with frosted pink gloss. "It's only been three
months. What could be wrong?"

"Me. I'm what's wrong." Olivia stirred her spoon around
and around, creating little whirlpools in the mug. "I've lived
by myself all my life, Dixie. And though the chief and I spent
a great deal of time together before we were married, he often
slept at his house so he'd be close to the station. He kept things
at my place—clothes and toiletries—but now his stuff is
everywhere. It multiplies when I'm not watching, I swear."

Dixie shot a quick glance around the dining room. Her
customers were either eating or chatting amiably over cups

of coffee, and no one appeared to need her. "What did you think would happen? That he'd go on livin' out of a drawer? The man's your husband now, 'Livia."

Olivia shook her head in exasperation. "That's not the problem. It's not about his things or the way he leaves globs of toothpaste in the sink. It's not about how he snores like a freight train when he sleeps on his back or how he'll finish the milk but won't add it to the shopping list. I can handle that stuff. It's having him around all the time that's hard. I'm not used to having someone around *all* the time. Only Haviland." She looked down at her standard poodle with affection and he gazed up at her, his caramel-brown eyes smiling.

Dixie gave the poodle's neck a fond pat. "You can't hold the chief up to Captain Haviland's standards. The poor guy is only human. And a damned fine human at that."

"I know." Olivia's voice crackled with anger. "He's a far better person than I am. He has no idea why I've been so moody. I'd just love to have my house to myself for a few days. Is that so strange?"

Dixie frowned. "Do you want your house to yourself? Or your life to yourself? 'Cause that's how this works. You're either together or you're not. You need to figure this out, hon. Aren't you headin' out on your delayed honeymoon in two days?"

Olivia nodded.

Dixie pointed at the television set mounted high behind the counter. Permanently tuned to The Weather Channel, the television's volume was muted, but the screen was visible from most of the Andrew Lloyd Webber–themed booths. The locals were always interested in the forecast. This was especially true for the fishermen, dockhands, and day laborers who filled the diner before the sun had risen. They'd order Grumpy's early bird special—a hearty breakfast of eggs, sausage, toast, and hash browns—and drink cups of black coffee while watching the forecast. The tourists liked to keep tabs on the weather too. They'd plan their days based on what they saw while savoring Grumpy's maple pecan pancakes or three-cheese omelets.

"You're still leavin' on Tuesday?" Dixie asked. "Even though the tropical storm will hit Palmetto Island tonight?"

Olivia shrugged. "Rose is a category-two storm. I'm not discounting its potential for making a mess, but even if Palmetto Island loses power, which is quite likely, we'll be fine. We'll do jigsaw puzzles, read by lantern light, and sit out on the deck with glasses of wine. If we want to have a honeymoon before the rest of the Bayside Book Writers join us, then we need to check in to our rental house as scheduled."

A customer in the *Evita* booth signaled for the check. Dixie nodded in acknowledgement and then wagged her finger in warning at Olivia: "If there's trouble in paradise before the honeymoon, then this trip could make things worse. You'd best not pack your problems in your suitcase."

Having delivered her advice, Dixie skated across the linoleum floor. When she reached the *Evita* booth, she executed a graceful one-hundred-and-eighty-degree turn, causing her diaphanous tutu to float around her legs like a surfacing jellyfish, and handed her bemused customer the check.

After that, Dixie cruised around the dining room refilling coffee cups, clearing dirty plates, and collecting credit cards. Olivia watched her pensively. Even with the extra height lent by her roller skates and her blond hair, which had been sprayed into place until it resembled a shellacked soft-serve cone, Dixie was barely five feet tall. For someone with diminutive stature, her personality was large and loud. She spoke her mind without fear of consequence, and Olivia had always found that to be one of Dixie's most admirable qualities.

"She's right, Haviland. I need to deal with my issues before we leave. If not, our honeymoon will feel like a prison sentence."

*   *   *

"Have you seen the storm footage?" Rawlings asked Olivia later that night. "Rose is raging up the Cape Fear River. How do you think our rental house weathered the high winds?"

Olivia speared a piece of flounder and swirled it around the puddle of butter, lemon juice, and fresh dill on her plate. "It's probably seen worse. Hurricanes Floyd and Isabel, for example. Still, I can get by without electricity for a day or two."

Rawlings laughed. "I can't picture you eating pork and beans out of a can."

"As long as we can heat up grits in the morning and soup or pasta for lunch and supper, we won't suffer." She examined the food on her plate. "I guess it wouldn't hurt to ask one of the sous chefs at The Boot Top Bistro to pack us a hamper."

"There you go again." Rawlings made a clicking noise with his tongue. "Abusing your power."

"Me?" Olivia poked Rawlings with her fork. "What about you? Taking a vacation weeks before the season's officially over."

Rawlings studied the back of his hand with exaggerated concern. "It's September. Things are calm now that the season's over. Sure, they'll be a few more drunk and disorderlies and a scattering of reckless driving citations, but in another two weeks, things will be quiet, verging on dull."

Maybe that's my problem, Olivia thought. *I've been involved in so many of Rawlings's cases—the serious and scary ones. Maybe I don't know how to be with him when things are peaceful.*

"Where did you go just now?" Rawlings asked, calling Olivia back to the moment.

"I'm afraid I've been analyzing us," Olivia confessed. "I've been wondering why I've been restless since we exchanged vows. After all, you're the anchor I was looking for—the person I needed to save me from drifting. So why do I feel like cutting the mooring line? Just for a day or two?"

Such candor would have rankled other men, but not Rawlings. He gave Olivia a warm smile and covered her hand with his. "You're not the only one having trouble adjusting. I haven't put my house on the market, have I? I like to go over there and putter around. I like to paint in that garage. The lighting's crap, the floors are hard, and it's cold as a meat locker. But it's my space. I've used every tool on the pegboard, built furniture on that workbench, and spent endless hours trying to turn a blank canvas into art. I can block out the world there."

"I guess this whole house has been my garage," Olivia said.

Rawlings nodded. "And now I'm here. Every night. Every morning. You've lost your garage moments—that time when no one's watching. That's when you spill coffee all over your shirt and don't bother changing. Or sing along to some cheesy rock ballad at the top of your lungs. Or eat junk food like a varsity football player. Garage time."

Olivia grinned. "You haven't had much of that lately either."

"I know. I felt like I was supposed to be here. With you." He gave her hand a squeeze. "But we're both accustomed to time to ourselves, so let's take it when we need it. When we get back from our trip, we'll figure out how to do that."

"Okay," Olivia said, feeling lighter than she had in weeks. "Have you thought about what you want to pack?"

"A little. The whole station thinks we're nuts to combine a honeymoon with the Legends of Coastal Carolina Festival, but what do they know? Three days celebrating the history and lore of our coast sponsored by the Department of Tourism. There's something for everyone at this festival. Writing workshops, history lectures, ghost stories around a bonfire, hobnobbing with celebrities, amazing barbecue—who *wouldn't* want to go?"

After pouring more white wine into Olivia's glass, he added a splash to his own. "The guys hassled me most about our spending part of the week with the Bayside Book Writers."

Olivia arched a brow. "What's wrong with that?"

"They think it's weird that we're not planning on spending the week in bed."

"That's because most of them are twenty years younger than us." Olivia scoffed. "Did you mention that we're bringing a thousand-piece jigsaw puzzle along?"

Rawlings wiped his mouth with his napkin. "I omitted that detail. In order to maintain my manly man status, I focused on pirate reenactments and the fact that Silas Black would be on the island scouting locations for his hit TV series. When they heard Mr. Black was also the headliner at the festival, they stopped giving me grief and begged me to get paraphernalia from his show—preferably autographed."

"Harris is ecstatic over the idea of rubbing shoulders with Silas Black. He's read all of his novels and is a huge fan of his show. What's it called again?"

"*No Quarter*," Rawlings said. "You and I might be the only people in Oyster Bay who aren't parked in front of the television from nine to ten every Sunday night. It's all anyone talks about at the station on Monday mornings."

Olivia cleared their dishes and began to rinse them in the sink. "I'm not surprised. After all, the series was partially filmed in New Bern and Ocracoke. Personally, I'm for it because the film industry stimulates the local economy." She paused in the act of loading a plate into the dishwasher. "However, I read something in the *Gazette* several months ago about the liberties Mr. Black has taken with our region's history." She tried to remember the details. "Something about how vicious he made the pirates. And there was criticism about his use of violence—that he's crossed the line with his graphic rape and torture scenes."

"Sounds like most of the programs on the premium cable channels."

"That's why I stick to *Masterpiece Theatre*," Olivia said. Satisfied that all the plates were neatly aligned, she closed the dishwasher door.

Rawlings took Olivia's place at the sink. This was a nightly ritual. Olivia handled the dishes while Rawlings cleaned the pots and pans. "According to water cooler gossip, Mr. Black is attempting to ingratiate himself with the inhabitants of Palmetto Island by financing the recovery of a shipwreck near Frying Pan Shoals. Apparently, the tropical storm preceding Rose carried the ship into shallower waters. Mr. Black hoped it would be a schooner from North Carolina's golden years of piracy, but it's a Civil War blockade-runner."

Olivia passed the dish towel to Rawlings. "So let me get this straight. Not only are we attending the Legends of Coastal Carolina Fest, but we're also going to be sharing an island with television people, underwater archaeologists, pirate reenactors, novelists, fans of the crime genre, and our friends?"

"Don't forget the conservationists. The Society for the Protection of the Loggerhead Turtle has been protesting a land development proposal for weeks. To raise money for their cause, they're hosting a moonlight march around the island. I think the walk takes place the same night that the festival starts. The pirates sail in the following day."

Olivia picked up both wineglasses and pointed her chin toward the back deck. Rawlings opened the door and Haviland shot outside, barking in anticipation. He raced down the stairs and over the rise of dunes, the sea oats parting as he ran. Olivia drew in a deep breath of salt-laced air, and a breeze tinged with a metallic scent lifted her hair off her forehead.

"I can smell the storm," she said.

Rawlings stared out over the water, his gaze fixed to the south, where they'd soon be traveling. Eventually, he turned to look at the lighthouse, standing proudly on its bluff. "Not too long from now, we'll be seeing another lighthouse. The oldest in North Carolina." He smiled wistfully. "I climbed to the top dozens of times when I was a boy. It's what I remember most about the island. That, and the spit of land called Cape Fear. I always thought it was a strange name for a place of such incredible beauty. A place, for those not traversing the dangerous waters surrounding it, that was anything but fearful."

"Leona showed me some old maps of the island when I stopped by the library last week," Olivia said. Overhead, a scattering of stars tried unsuccessfully to burn through the cloud cover. Their soft, gauzy light made them look more like pearls than stars.

Not a helpful light. No good for a sailor navigating in the dark, Olivia thought. Aloud, she said, "Cape Fear used to be a sharper point. It jutted out into the ocean like a stingray tail. If you stood on its tip, you could see a virtual highway of ships in motion. Leona also showed me the area's shipwreck map. There are tons of wrecks around the island, Sawyer. Schooners, steamers, blockade-runners, fishing trawlers, pleasure boats. The Graveyard of the Atlantic, indeed."

Olivia watched the waves, which curled onto the shore with a languid murmur, but she knew that within the next twenty-four hours, they would change. The water would surge forward in jagged peaks, sand roiling under its surface, white froth, like the mouths of a thousand rabid animals, crashing against the beach.

"With all those wrecks, it's no wonder our coast has been the source of so many ghost stories," Rawlings said. "I'm sure we'll hear some choice tales this weekend."

"I like ghost stories," Olivia said, her gaze sliding to the lighthouse keeper's cottage. Once, its rooms were haunted by Olivia's child self. A quiet, lonely girl with long legs, freckles, and sun-bleached hair.

I'm not alone anymore, Olivia thought and smiled at Rawlings.

Haviland returned and sat on his haunches next to Olivia. His eyes seemed tuned to the shimmering path on the water created by the lighthouse beacon. Rawlings looked at it too. As if to himself, he whispered:

> *So from the world of spirits there descends*
> *A bridge of light, connecting it with this,*
> *O'er whose unsteady floor, that sways and bends,*
> *Wander our thoughts above the dark abyss.*

Olivia squeezed his hand until he turned away from the sea and met her gaze. "We can save both the ghost stories and unsettling poetry for our trip," she said, feeling a sudden chill. "Let's go in."

"All right. No more Longfellow." Rawlings stood up, collected the wineglasses, and entered the house. After casting a final glance at the water, Olivia called for Haviland and then shut the door. The sound of the waves was diminished but not gone.

As Olivia lay in bed, they lulled her to sleep. She dreamed of shipwrecks. Of wooden carcasses. Large black smudges in a black sea. In her dreams, the sails were raised. And they rippled as if still being filled by a ghostly wind.

Two days later, Olivia parked her Range Rover in the ferry terminal lot.

Rawlings jerked his thumb at the back of the car. "I'm going to track down a luggage cart. There's no way we can haul all of this gear on board by ourselves."

Olivia shot him a wry grin. "It's just a few staples."

"A pair of suitcases, grocery bags, a packed cooler, and

a waterproof bin filled with books, flashlights, and jigsaw puzzles. Staples, eh?"

Olivia shrugged. "The electricity's out across the island. Just because we're without modern conveniences, doesn't mean we can't be comfortable. And well fed. Michel packed us a special honeymoon hamper." She shook her head in distaste. "I feel stupid using that word. It should be relegated to greeting cards or travel brochures."

Rawlings laughed. "Henceforth, I shall refer to this time together as a marital retreat. Better?"

Olivia tossed a balled-up napkin at him. "No! We'd better hurry. Our ride leaves in fifteen minutes."

Later, Olivia stood on the ferry's lower deck, holding the end of Haviland's leash tightly as the crew cast off. Rawlings was nowhere in sight. He'd left to explore the rest of the boat the moment the ferry eased away from the dock, his eyes gleaming like a boy's.

When the ferry entered the channel, Olivia noticed a concrete platform sitting squarely in the busy waterway. The potentially dangerous obstacle seemed overtly out of place. Curious, Olivia approached a deckhand and pointed at the platform. "Excuse me. What is that?"

"Quarantine pad, ma'am," the man answered. "From the old days. Ships had to dock at the quarantine station before they could continue to any port. Folks were terrified of catchin' diseases like yellow fever or small pox. They had no way to fight 'em, so they did their best to keep 'em out. That platform has been there since the late 1800s and probably saved thousands of lives. There were buildings at the station too, but they burned. Every one. All that's left is the pad."

"Isn't that hunk of concrete a hazard for ships? Especially at night?"

The man issued a noncommittal grunt. "It's on all the nautical charts. Has a light on it now too. The Coast Guard added it after a lady was killed in a boating accident. Sad business, that." He swept his arm in a wide arc, incorporating the surrounding waters. "There's all kinds of hazards here, ma'am. Everywhere you look. Shallows, sandbars, shoals. Hidden bits of reef that'll tear your hull in two—you don't take to these waters without a healthy dose of fear. Even the most seasoned captains say a prayer before they head out for Cape Fear."

"I grew up with fishermen. I've learned that it's unwise not to respect the ocean." Olivia glanced around the ferry deck. She guessed there were fewer occupants on board than usual. "Did Rose make a big mess?"

The man followed her gaze. "Nothin' serious. Trees down. Power outages. Some of the roads flooded, but in a day or two, we'll have forgotten about Rose." He grinned, displaying a row of tobacco-stained teeth. "A storm has to work much harder than that to impress us." He lifted his chin to indicate a fellow crew member coiling a length of rope on the port side. The man's face was weathered by years of working outdoors, and his thick hands and forearms were scarred by rope burns.

"What brings you to Palmetto Island?" the crewman asked. "The Coastal Carolina Festival?"

Olivia nodded. "Yes. My husband grew up hearing tales of buried treasure from his grandfather, and he's trying to turn those stories into a book."

"Silas Black sure made a bundle off our history," the crewman grumbled and then instantly brightened. "But they say he might film episodes of his show on the island. Even hire some local folks as extras. I'd sure get the ladies' attention if I was on TV. They're not real impressed when I tell 'em that I work on the ferry, but if I could say I was a pirate on Black's show? I'd be like a rooster in the henhouse."

He laughed and Olivia joined in. Raising her head, she saw Rawlings leaning over the rail of the upper deck, waiting to catch her eye. He waved for her to join him.

"I think you'd make a fine pirate. Good luck," Olivia told the friendly crewman and whistled at Haviland to heel.

On the top deck, Olivia and Rawlings watched brown pelicans dive-bomb into the water. A particularly swift bird off the port side captured a fish, and it glinted like a silver coin in his bill, and then, in a flash, it was gone, disappearing down the bird's throat. Out in the open, Olivia shivered. The air had a crisp edge to it. It was ocean air. Air that swirled around the humped backs of whales. Air sliced by freighter bows and shark fins. It spoke of the end of tourists and the beginning of gray skies and deserted beaches.

Another ten minutes passed before Olivia spotted the island's lighthouse. It wasn't as tall as Oyster Bay's, but there was something profoundly comforting about the solid pillar of white standing guard over the harbor. Olivia kept her eyes on the old structure until the ferry docked.

As she, Rawlings, and Haviland disembarked, Olivia noticed that signs advertising the Coastal Carolina Fest had been stapled to every pylon. Each poster featured a skull-and-crossbones motif and a list of festival highlights. At the end of the dock, a black banner flapped in the wind.

"Has the arrival area changed much since you were here last?" Olivia asked Rawlings.

"That was a million years ago, so yes." He pointed at a large building at the end of the pier. "This marina wasn't here. That hotel had a different name, and the houses surrounding the docks were small and modest. The boats were mostly fishing vessels or skiffs, not these luxury powerboats or yachts. And there were no slips. Just a long dock for loading and unloading." He shrugged. "It's the same as Oyster Bay, I guess. When you and I were young, our town was as yet still undiscovered. Palmetto Island was meant to attract tourists much earlier than Oyster Bay, but it wasn't nearly as developed as it is now." He gestured at the hotel. "It's all marshland behind there. No good for building, but the perfect habitat for alligators. If I didn't see at least one gator while visiting my grandparents, I was crushed."

Olivia glanced down at Haviland. "Did you hear that, Captain? Alligators. You have to wear this collar all the time."

Haviland sniffed the air, his black nose quivering. His eyes darted wildly around and he pranced on the pads of his feet in anticipation.

"I think he picked up a scent coming from that seafood restaurant," Rawlings said.

Olivia gave the poodle's head an affectionate pat. "We'll check out the eateries later, Captain. We need to rent a golf cart first."

Rawlings told Olivia to join the queue in front of the rental shack while he tracked down their luggage.

Just as Olivia and Haviland got in line behind a couple in their early twenties, the young woman let out a dramatic gasp and tugged on her boyfriend's arm. "OMG, there's Leigh Whitlow! See? She's in that golf cart behind the hotel. I can't believe she's really *here*!"

The boyfriend cast a disinterested glance at a slim woman with fair skin and glossy dark brown hair. "Who?"

"Seriously? Do you live under a rock?" The woman nudged her boyfriend. "That's Silas Black's girlfriend. *Everyone* knows who she is."

The boyfriend shrugged. "If she was a tavern wench on *No Quarter*, then I'd recognize her. That woman looks kind of used up. You sure Black is banging *her*?"

What a gem, Olivia thought, glaring daggers at the back of the young man's skull.

"Hello? I know my celebrities." The woman pretended to be offended, but she was too fascinated by Leigh Whitlow to maintain the act. "She is *so* thin. I think she looks great for someone in her forties. Shoot, she might even be *fifty*."

The boyfriend pushed his sunglasses onto his forehead and focused on the dark-haired woman in the golf cart. "She has to work to hold on to her man," he said. "He could probably have his pick of a hundred babes, so keeping him interested must be a full-time job."

Olivia would have loved nothing more than to push the jackass boyfriend right off the dock, but she knew she'd be stuck listening to him for at least another ten minutes. The line was moving at a snail's pace, and there was no sign of Rawlings.

"There are rumors that Black is fooling around behind Leigh's back," the young woman said. "Some chick on his staff. A history geek. Can you imagine? Cheating on Leigh Whitlow with a nerd? Everyone knows that Leigh is one-hundred-percent psych-ward crazy. That's why Silas won't leave her. She'd kill any woman who dared to get between them. Oh man, I am *so* glad we decided to come to this festival for extra credit. And I'm even happier that we decided to come earlier so we could rub shoulders with celebrities, aren't you?"

The boyfriend was no longer listening. A trio of giggling high school girls had caught his attention and he was eyeing them appreciatively.

"If that nerd girl is on the island, there's going to be a bloodbath," the young woman gleefully predicted as the line finally moved forward. Having turned to the right in order to keep the large man standing in front of her from blocking her view of Leigh Whitlow, the young woman was completely unaware of the flirtatious glances being exchanged between her boyfriend and the three girls. "I mean it, Rob. If you came here hoping to learn about crime and violence for your creative writing paper, you might just get your wish. Leigh Whitlow's thrown jealous rages before. She drove Silas's convertible into a lake this summer and threatened a cute fan who got too cozy with him at some book event in Chicago."

The line moved again, but the young woman didn't budge. She was riveted by Leigh Whitlow's slightest movement—every impatient flick of the famous woman's dark brown tresses, how she splayed her nails or adjusted the rings on her fingers, and the way she stared straight ahead, her jaw set in a hard line.

"When will you finally lose it?" the young woman murmured, clearly reveling in Leigh's discontent. "When will your jealousy finally push you over the edge?"

At that moment, Rawlings came up alongside Olivia. Noticing her pinched expression, he whispered, "Is anything wrong?"

Before she could answer, a man approached Leigh's golf cart and made a shooing motion, indicating that he wanted her to scoot over to the passenger seat so that he could take the wheel. Scowling fiercely, Leigh complied, and the pair drove off in a cloud of sand-colored dust.

"Not yet," Olivia said in answer to Rawlings's question. "But the day is still young."

Chapter 2

*Regardless of how many boats you send
to other shores or how many ships
arrive upon your shores, you yourself
are an island separated by its own
pains, secluded in its happiness.*

—KAHLIL GIBRAN

The house Olivia had rented was far too big for one man, one woman, and a poodle. She hadn't selected it for its spaciousness or because it had been recently renovated, but because it was located at the end of a private road and featured expansive wraparound decks overlooking the Atlantic Ocean.

Rawlings pulled his overloaded golf cart to a stop by the side door. Turning to Olivia, he whistled. "Is this Jay Gatsby's beach bungalow?"

Olivia parked her cart behind Rawlings's and told Haviland to jump down. "It's called Lifesaver, actually." She pointed at a plaque affixed to the left of the front door. "The rental agent said that all the houses on the island have names."

Rawlings frowned. "'Lifesaver' doesn't exactly inspire confidence. I'm envisioning people strapping on floatation devices while a storm surge rushes up the beach and floods the ground floor."

Laughing, Olivia gathered up the grocery bags. "The

agent told me all sorts of facts about this place. For example, the house was built on the former site of the Cape Fear Lifesaving Station. Once upon a time, men lived on the island year-round. Their job was to watch the shoals night and day in case a ship ran into trouble. Their vigilant gazes saved many a sailor."

Rawlings took the key from Olivia and unlocked the door. "I imagine their conditions were less plush than ours."

Haviland immediately pushed past Rawlings into the roomy kitchen and rushed off to explore the rest of the house. Olivia could hear his claws clicking on the hardwood floors.

"What happened to ladies first?" Rawlings called out in mock censure. He then turned to Olivia with an impish grin. "Why don't you organize the food while I unload the rest of our *staples*. Unless you'd like to step back outside so I can carry you over the threshold. How about it?"

In reply, Olivia grabbed a crab-shaped pot holder from a hook near the stove and tossed it at him. Rawlings caught the crab, stuffed it down his shirt, and headed for the golf carts.

Olivia decided to leave the groceries on the counter and search the cabinets for flashlights or battery-powered lanterns instead. The kitchen was well stocked with both.

Next, she walked into the sunlit living room and was pleased to discover a stack of firewood and a basket of kindling positioned next to a fireplace opposite a large sectional sofa. Someone had left a battery-operated DVD player on the coffee table, and Olivia found a dozen board games in the corner cupboard. In addition to the games was a treasure trove of books on Palmetto Island. Some were pictorial histories while others were academic tomes concentrating on the island's unique ecosystem or maritime history. Finally, there was an illustrated collection of ghost stories and, topping the pile like a Christmas tree star, a Nicholas

Sparks novel. Olivia assumed the Sparks novel held pride of place because the movie based on the book had been filmed across the Cape Fear River.

Olivia continued her tour by glancing into the dining room and sunroom. The air in the house felt slightly stale, so Olivia cracked a dozen windows. By the time she was done, Rawlings had finished unloading the golf carts. "There are two bedrooms on this floor. Does that mean Haviland is sleeping downstairs?"

"Not likely," Olivia said. "He's probably staking his claim on the master suite as we speak."

Taking her suitcase from Rawlings, Olivia climbed the stairs to find Haviland industriously sniffing the curtains on the wall next to the king-size bed.

"A fireplace in the bedroom?" Rawlings came into the room behind Olivia. "Who needs electricity?" Humming contentedly, he began to unpack.

Eager to check out the view from the beach, Olivia decided to organize her things later. "I think Haviland and I will go treasure hunting," she said, slipping on her old tennis shoes.

"I'm going to take a self-guided golf cart tour—see how much things have changed since I was a kid." Rawlings produced a paper map of the island. "Judging from this, the changes are significant. But I want to know if any of my old haunts still exist." His expression turned wistful. "I hope it's not all different. It's hard to come face-to-face with what the passage of time does to a place. In my memory, it's a place of adventure, mystery, and beauty. A Robert Louis Stevenson island." He glanced at Olivia. "Do I sound ridiculous?"

"No," she said. "You sound like the romantic you are. But I hope you find some of your boyhood landmarks unchanged. They're symbols of your past, so they're important." She followed Rawlings back to the kitchen. "Happy hunting."

"You too," he said. "Who knows? Maybe Tropical Storm

Rose deposited rare coins or priceless jewelry on the beach for you to find."

Olivia shrugged. "More often than not, the items with no monetary value are the most interesting. You know that I have pickle jars filled with such things. Shotgun casings, wheat pennies, belt buckles, buttons. Mulling over the story behind each object is what I like most about beachcombing."

After promising to return in time for cocktails, Rawlings pushed a baseball cap over his salt-and-pepper hair, grabbed a bottle of water, and hopped into a golf cart.

Haviland released a series of questioning barks as the chief reversed the cart, but the moment Olivia showed the poodle the familiar backpack containing a folding trench shovel, trowel, and sieve, he stopped barking and wagged his tail instead.

Shouldering her new Bounty Hunter Legacy—a wedding gift from the Bayside Book Writers—Olivia struck out for the beach.

Signs of Rose's passing were noticeable. The beach was strewn with palmetto fronds and clumps of sea grass. The waves had carved sluiceways from the shoreline to the dunes, and a precise pattern of ripples covered the sand. The design was an indication that the sand had been battered by wind and salt water for hours without pause.

Olivia wanted to walk out on Cape Fear Point first, so she kept her metal detector turned off as she and Haviland left their beach and approached the raked and debris-free area designated for the guests of Land End Lodge.

No one was on the boardwalk skirting the dunes behind the cedar-sided clubhouse, and Olivia didn't run into a single person as she turned away from the picturesque lodge and made for the spit of land jutting out into the Atlantic Ocean.

Cape Fear Point was not dissimilar in shape to the Point near her house in Oyster Bay, but there was something far more humbling about standing alone where powerful ocean currents rose up to meet the sky. The two entities were so close that their magnitude was nearly overwhelming. Olivia felt infinitely small as she listened to the waves smash against the sandbar. The deadly shallows of Frying Pan Shoals stretched before her, and it was easy to imagine ships breaking apart against the finger of land. It would be challenging enough to avoid the dangers on a calm day. During a storm, with the wind raging and water pouring from the sky and rising up from the sea, Olivia didn't see how anyone safely navigated around the island.

Olivia recalled how Rawlings had described the peacefulness of this spot, but she didn't feel at all peaceful. She felt uneasy. Gooseflesh erupted along her arms, and she was suddenly cold. It was as though a shadow had fallen over her despite the fact that she stood directly in the path of the afternoon sun.

Olivia was not a superstitious person, but she could almost hear the voices of drowned men on the wind. The crashing of the waves grew louder, roaring in her head like thunder. As she began to retreat, to return to the wider stretch of beach, she couldn't help but wonder if the recent storm had stirred up more than shells and seaweed. Perhaps the old bones of hundreds of doomed seamen had shifted as well.

She jumped when Haviland let out a sharp bark. Having spotted a willet, he'd sprinted back the way they'd come. More than ready to leave Cape Fear behind, Olivia returned to the part of beach that seemed remarkably solid in comparison to the vulnerable point sticking out into the ocean.

Chiding herself for being silly, Olivia unshouldered her metal detector, slipped on her headphones, and listened to a series of chirps and beeps as she and Haviland headed to the west.

Land End Lodge was barely out of sight when the detector made a high-pitched shriek, signaling the discovery of a metal that wasn't tin.

"Haviland!" Olivia shouted. "Come dig!"

The poodle was thrilled to oblige and plunged his front paws into the sand while Olivia worked with the trench shovel. After ten minutes of digging, alternating with frenzied bouts of shifting sand through her sieve, Olivia exclaimed, "We found something, Captain!"

She carried what appeared to be a copper coin to the water's edge and rinsed it in the salt water. Scraping caked sand off its surface with her thumbnail, she frowned when the face on the coin became clear. It was a man's face—not the embossed profile seen on many coins, but the frontal view of a bearded man barring his teeth. His ears were pierced with large hoops, and his hair was bushy and wild, as were his thick brows. His eyes were dark, angry holes.

Though Olivia assumed she'd found play money or a token from a children's pirate treasure chest, she was surprised by the hostility of the pirate's expression, by the force of rage and hatred in the voids where his eyes were meant to be.

The coin's reverse depicted a ship and a word too faded to read, and Olivia immediately felt silly for having reacted so strongly to a child's coin. But the moment she gazed down at the pirate's face again, she found herself wanting to be rid of her discovery. Without hesitating, she threw it as hard as she could and heard a satisfying plop as it hit the water.

She filled in the hole she and Haviland had made and decided to try again farther up the beach. She'd barely gone five hundred feet when she spotted the shapes of two dogs racing straight for them.

"Haviland. Heel," she commanded.

Though Haviland tended to make overtures of friendship with all dogs, Olivia knew it was best to be wary. Not every dog—or their owners for that matter—were as well mannered as Haviland.

"Easy boy," she murmured, but Haviland's ears were

pricked, and his tail bobbed in anticipation. He couldn't wait to meet the new arrivals. Judging from their coloring, their long, lean bodies, and the speed with which they flew over the sand, Olivia believed them to be greyhounds.

A man appeared over a dune rise. Cupping his hands on either side of his mouth, he shouted. Though his words were swallowed by the waves before Olivia could catch them, the greyhounds instantly froze.

The man jogged toward them and the dogs watched him over their shoulders, torn between curiosity and obedience.

"Come!" the man shouted sternly.

Responding to the authoritative tone, the dogs turned and ran to their owner.

The man waved at Olivia and headed toward her. His pace was relaxed, and his dogs trotted by his side, their pink tongues lolling and their tails whipping back and forth.

Olivia also continued her forward progress, and as the two groups drew close, she felt there was something familiar about the man. His tousled brown hair and tortoiseshell glasses struck a chord with her.

"Professor Billinger?" she called out.

The man shielded his eyes. "Ms. Limoges? Is that you?"

"It's okay, Haviland," Olivia said. "You can introduce yourself."

The poodle pranced forward, and within seconds, he and the two greyhounds were circling around one another, snorting and grunting, dizzy with excitement.

Taking Olivia's hand and holding on to it with obvious delight, Professor Billinger said, "I can't believe it. *You. Here.* On this tiny island. Have you come for the festival?"

"I have." Olivia smiled. She was happy to see Emmett Billinger. A professor of history at the University of North Carolina, Emmett had helped Olivia and the Bayside Book Writers more than once when they'd gotten involved in a criminal investigation. And though Olivia always enjoyed her infrequent encounters and lively phone conversations with Emmett, she hadn't spoken to him in six months. Suddenly, she realized that she'd failed to reply to an e-mail he'd sent back in June.

"Are you looking for pirate treasure?" Emmett asked. "Because Caesar, Calpurnia, and I can help you dig it up."

Tall and slim like Olivia, Emmett was handsome in a bookish way. He had the salubrious glow of one who spends his free time outdoors, and Olivia knew that Emmett loved to bike, fish, and sail. Just shy of fifty, he had a youthful, vivacious air about him. Olivia liked his face, seeing in it a contrary mixture of boyish zeal and the quiet wisdom of a man who's devoted his life to the pursuit of knowledge.

"I can't believe I've never met them before." Olivia held out her palm for the greyhounds to sniff. "They're beautiful."

Emmett beamed like a proud parent. Like Olivia, he had no children and doted on his greyhounds. "And I finally get to see the magnificent Captain Haviland in person. It looks like he and my two have become fast friends."

The dogs romped along the waterline, nudging one another and releasing high-pitched yips. Olivia and Emmett followed at a more leisurely pace. After insisting on carrying the metal detector, Emmett told her about a former colleague who was also a Civil War treasure hunter.

"He was arrested for trespassing. The poor guy was so intent on sweeping a particular field because he was positive that a minor battle had been fought there that he nearly had his hat shot off by an angry farmer." Emmett gestured at the abandoned stretch of shoreline. "You'll have most of the beach to yourself until the mobs arrive for the festival. How's the novel coming, by the way? Have you decided to add a mystery element to it?"

"Actually, I tossed that manuscript in the trash," Olivia said. When Emmett looked genuinely distraught, she put a hand on his arm and gave him a reassuring smile. "It's a good thing. Really. I'm now writing about the people I knew when I was young. The lighthouse keeper, the woman who ran the roadside fruit stand, a shrimp boat captain, a blind artist. It's become a collection of short stories written in my true voice. The novel was too contrived." She dropped her hand. "Are you one of the festival guest speakers? I don't recall seeing your name in the program."

"I'm a last-minute substitution," Emmett explained. "The gentleman specializing in the haunted landmarks of the North Carolina coast suffered a heart attack. Not a serious one, thank goodness, but he wasn't up to making the trip. And since I'm now on the faculty at UNC-Wilmington, it was nothing for me to drive down." He shook his head ruefully. "I won't be as entertaining as the original speaker, but I do know the area's ghostly history."

Olivia was instantly intrigued. "In that case, I'll be in the audience."

Emmett was clearly pleased by her remark, but then his face clouded over. "The organizers should have asked George Allen. He's in his nineties and has lived on the island all his life. I've heard old George tell the most unforgettable tales. His voice is rich and deep, and his eyes are the same blue as the ocean."

"It sounds like you know him well."

Emmett nodded. "I grew up in Riverport, right across the Cape Fear River, and spent most of my weekends and summers traipsing around this island after my father. He was a botanist, and this place"—he swept his arm in a wide arc—"was his Garden of Eden. It was a lonely boyhood, but on occasion, back before any of these houses were here, old George would take me fishing. For the price of bait, he'd share his stories. For a long time, he was my only friend."

"Too bad you and Chief Rawlings never bumped into

each other. His grandparents summered here," Olivia said. "I've mentioned the chief to you before, right?"

"Once or twice," Emmett said.

Olivia glanced at her wedding band. "He and I were married a few months ago."

Emmett's disappointment was obvious, but he had the good grace to smile and offer his congratulations. "I don't know why I feel like sulking over your happy news, but I do. I guess I saw us as the last two people on earth who'd grow old puttering around our houses with our dogs, too set in our bachelor ways to compromise. I'll have to bear the torch on my own, I suppose."

Olivia grinned. "Perhaps I could soften the blow by inviting you to our rental house for cocktails. It's called Lifesaver. Do you know it?"

Emmett's eyes widened. "Everyone does. The views are spectacular. You don't have a generator, do you? My cell phone battery is dead."

"We're fresh out of electricity, but we have an ample supply of liquor, food, and jigsaw puzzles."

"All the essentials," Emmett said. After a brief hesitation, he asked, "Are you sure I won't be a third wheel?"

Olivia shook her head. "Not at all. And bring Caesar and Calpurnia. The dogs can take a group nap in front of the fireplace."

She and Emmett stood on the beach and watched the three dogs play. Their game involved sporadic bursts of running combined with erratic splashing in the shallows. When they finally calmed down, Emmett returned Olivia's metal detector and said, "If you find a red Matchbox car with a lightning bolt on the roof and hood, let me know. I lost mine somewhere on this beach in 1975. It was my favorite car." He winked at her, whistled for his dogs, and promised to put on some shoes before showing up for cocktails.

* * *

As darkness fell over the ocean, the air sweeping in from the Atlantic bore an autumnal chill. Olivia pulled on a cardigan and fed more kindling into the fire.

"Better ration that," Rawlings warned. "We can't just walk into the woods to gather more."

Emmett, who'd been flipping through one of the Palmetto Island books, showed Rawlings a black-and-white photograph. "Look at this. Can you believe there used to be a lumber mill on the island? Thousands of dogwood trees were cut down and milled. Kind of ironic, considering it's our state tree."

Rawlings handed Emmett a glass of wine and gestured toward the sunroom. "Olivia dug up a Scrabble board. Between the two of you, I'm hopelessly outmatched, but I'm willing to pretend that losing doesn't bother me. Plus, there's enough food here to feed the archaeology team I saw motoring to the shore from the shipwreck site this afternoon."

Michel's hamper contained a full charcuterie including slices of salami, prosciutto, pancetta, barbecued bacon, and rosemary ham. In addition to the meats, there was an assortment of crackers, a loaf of fresh bread with a golden-brown crust, a bowl of almonds mixed with dried cranberries, an olive medley, a jar of habanero pickles, another jar of marinated tomatoes, a container of stone-ground mustard, and two types of homemade jams. To round out these predominantly salty flavors, Michel had packed a bunch of succulent red grapes, sweet potato cheese straws, and lemon-raspberry thumbprint cookies for dessert.

"I really need to make a trip to Oyster Bay," Emmett said. "If your head chef can put this feast in a picnic hamper, then I can only imagine what he's able to create with a commercial kitchen at his disposal."

Emmett shared his opinions of the various island eateries and, after easily winning the first game of Scrabble, talked about what it was like to spend so much time in the marshes and maritime forest.

"I wore waders half the year," he joked, though the humor never reached his eyes. "In all honesty, I was a lonesome kid. My father was far more interested in the forest's oak canopy or the salt shadow cast by the red cedar trees than in tossing a baseball around. And this island has multiple faces. During a summer day on the beaches, it's a paradise. But go deeper into the forest or the wetlands and you'll find snakes, alligators, and ravenous insects. The oak trees practically blot out the light in some areas, so the woods can take on a sinister feel."

Rawlings poured more wine into Emmett's glass. "I felt that way at times too. I stayed with my grandparents at the inn, but whenever I could, I'd wander off by myself. The farther I was from the beach and the hotel, the stranger the place felt. Once, I saw a white deer in the woods. It had blue eyes that seemed to look right through me. I thought it was the ghost of a deer, but my grandparents told me it was just a trick of the light. Did you ever see a white deer?"

The hopefulness in Rawlings's face was so keen that Emmett shook his head with genuine regret. "I'm surprised that I didn't. After listening to George Allen's stories, I thought I saw all kinds of things, but they were just boyhood fancies." His gaze slid to the dancing flames. "By the time I was twelve, I'd learned all I could about the island's history. So many people tried to make a living here. So many failed. From the first attempt at colonization in the late sixteen hundreds to pirates on the run, to dozens of entrepreneurs over the past century, this island has drawn people, but it doesn't let them stay. My father used to say that people don't belong here. That each time people create too deep a footprint, the island fights back."

Olivia remembered the sensation she'd experienced on Cape Fear Point. She looked out the window in the direction of Frying Pan Shoals but could see nothing except for darkness.

"Did you know there once was a second lighthouse? It

was called the Cape Fear Lighthouse, and it wasn't far from this point. A mighty tower rising one hundred and sixty feet in the air. Its light could be seen for nineteen miles," Emmett continued as Rawlings cleared the Scrabble board. "George Allen was its keeper until they tore it down. He saw dozens of ships sink. Heard people cry as they were flung into the sea. He ruined any chance of my becoming an open-water sailor, that's for sure," Emmett added in an attempt to lighten the mood. "I stick to lakes and calm harbors."

While Rawlings deliberated over his Scrabble tiles, Olivia decided that she'd very much like to meet George Allen. Though she'd already written a story about a lighthouse keeper, she thought he'd make an unforgettable character as he was now: a walking history book. A living monument shaped by nearly one hundred years of being in the same place.

He must have witnessed so many wondrous and terrible things, she thought.

"Could you introduce me to Mr. Allen?" she asked Emmett before focusing on the word Rawlings had just built. After examining her letters, she began placing tiles off the *F* in "motif."

"Sure," Emmett said affably. "The man loves to tell his stories, especially to attractive women. He also likes to talk to people like the chief. People who knew the island before it became an exclusive vacation destination." Tilting his head, he studied Olivia's word. "'Faqir'? Nicely done. Isn't that a seventeen-point play?"

Evening passed to night and Olivia found that she was enjoying herself immensely. By the time she, Rawlings, and Emmett finished the Scrabble game and started playing poker with a deck of cards and box of chips Rawlings discovered in the corner cupboard, they were beyond tipsy.

Several hands later, after Rawlings had established that he was the superior gambler, Olivia looked around and saw that the food was gone, the wine was depleted, and the candles on the mantel had burned low.

"I think the dogs and I should roll on home," Emmett said, following Olivia's gaze.

Olivia glanced over to where the poodle and the two greyhounds were curled up on the hearth rug. Haviland had his back pressed against Calpurnia's. Caesar's front paws were draped over Haviland's, and his nose was inches away from the poodle's.

"Time to go," Emmett whispered and his greyhounds reluctantly got to their feet. Stretching and yawning, they looked back at Haviland and then at Emmett, as if silently berating him for interrupting their cozy nap.

"Thank you for a wonderful evening," Emmett told Olivia and Rawlings at the door. "I'd resigned myself to heating up a can of soup and correcting student research papers, but you saved me from such a fate." He paused in the threshold. "How do you feel about my operating a golf cart while under the influence, Chief?"

Rawlings shrugged. "Not my jurisdiction. Just try to stay on the road."

Emmett coaxed his dogs into the back of the golf cart and then thanked his hosts once more. Olivia left the stoop, descended the stairs to the driveway, and peered down the unlit road.

Without electricity, the entire island seemed to have been transported back in time. Except for the rush of the waves, the night was preternaturally still. There was no rhythmic whirring of air-conditioning units or strains of music coming from the neighboring houses. There was no traffic noise. It was as though they were the only creatures awake and stirring.

"Watch out for alligators," Olivia teased Emmett once he had the golf cart running and had switched on its feeble headlights.

"The most dangerous things on this island walk on two legs," Emmett said and, having delivered this enigmatic remark, drove away.

Chapter 3

There is something haunting in the light of the moon; it has all the dispassionateness of a disembodied soul, and something of its inconceivable mystery.

—JOSEPH CONRAD

Over the next two days, Olivia and Rawlings walked on the beach, explored the island, and worked on their individual writing projects. On Thursday, just as they were reading the lunch menu tacked to the corkboard outside The Crab Pot, the seafood restaurant overlooking the marina, electricity was restored to the island.

"They can turn off that generator now," a woman entering The Crab Pot said. "I didn't want to eat with that racket in the background anyway."

The man holding the door for her rolled his eyes. "You always find something to complain about. You're bound to be disappointed by the food, the waitstaff, the décor, and the brand of toilet paper in the ladies' room."

"Oh, stuff it, Hank," the woman said before disappearing into the restaurant.

Rawlings and Olivia exchanged glances.

"You sure you want to follow that act?" Rawlings asked.

"Why not?" Olivia said. "That'll be us in a few years."

Mumbling something about an annulment, Rawlings pushed Olivia inside and then waited for Haviland to enter next.

"We don't allow pets in the dining room," the hostess informed them amiably. "But I can seat you on the back deck. You'll have a nice view of the docks."

Olivia and Rawlings were given a table next to Leigh Whitlow, who was working her way through a pitcher of margaritas while sending texts on her cell phone. A reply clearly upset her, for she released a torrent of murmured expletives after reading it. She then slapped the phone on the table and gulped down her margarita.

She was in the midst of refilling her glass when her phone rang.

"For Chrissakes!" Leigh slurred and reached for the device.

The woman who'd preceded Olivia into the restaurant scowled at her husband. "First we have to eat with a dog, and now *this*?" She flicked her wrist at Leigh. "I want to change tables, Hank."

"I'm supposed to be relaxing, remember? Doctor's orders," Hank said. "Though if my doctor spent twenty-four hours in my shoes, he might offer to euthanize me, free of charge." He signaled for the waiter. "A whiskey sour, please."

Olivia and Rawlings ordered their food—grouper tempura for Olivia and braised short ribs for Rawlings—and then discussed their plans for the afternoon.

"Emmett arranged for me to meet George Allen tomorrow," Olivia said. "In the meantime, I'd like to check out the maritime museum."

Their waiter arrived with glasses of iced tea and a bowl of water for Haviland. After thanking the young man and waiting for him to walk over to Leigh's table, Rawlings pointed at the lighthouse and said, "I thought I might paint the old beacon."

"I'll kill them both if he makes a move on her." Waving the server away, Leigh's eyes blazed with anger as she hissed into her phone. "I won't be treated this way. You know that I'm not bluffing."

The woman at the other table put down her fork. "I will *not* have my lunch ruined because other people don't know the meaning of etiquette."

Leigh shot the woman a hostile glance and then yelled into the phone. "He owes me! I've been with him from the start. Back when he had to beg people to buy his books. I set up his signings and made hors d'oeuvres for his launch parties. I've given him my best years! And we have no children! We don't even have joint custody over a dog!"

"Hank! *Do something!*" the woman prodded.

Ignoring his wife, Hank focused on his whiskey sour.

Leigh pulled some bills out of her wallet and got to her feet. She was still speaking into the phone when the waiter appeared, balancing a heavy tray on his shoulders.

"Oh!" Leigh cried. Pretending to catch her heel on a crack in the wood, she stumbled into the waiter. A bowl of seafood risotto and a platter of steamed clams and mussels landed on Hank and his wife.

The woman screamed. Her banshee cries startled Haviland, and he began to bark. In the midst of the sudden din, Hank threw back his head and laughed.

Feigning shock and dismay, Leigh apologized to the waiter and slipped a twenty into his apron pocket. She then blew Hank a kiss and sashayed inside the restaurant.

Olivia shushed Haviland while the waiter did his best to clear away the ruined lunches. Within the space of ten minutes, Olivia and Rawlings were enjoying their delicious meals alone.

"The woman who was gulping down the margaritas is Leigh Whitlow," Olivia said and went on to tell Rawlings what she'd overheard about Silas Black's girlfriend. "Though the stories of her rash behavior could be products of the Hollywood gossip machine, it's obvious that she's not a happy woman."

"She's angry," Rawlings said. "And it sounds like she's been reckless before." He gazed at the boats bobbing gently in their slips. Beyond the marina, the ferry was coming in from the mainland, its decks crowded with passengers. "It's a small island for such a big anger," he added.

They finished their lunch in silence, each lost in their own thoughts, and then parted ways in front of the marina store.

At the maritime museum, Olivia asked the docent for permission for Haviland to accompany her. "I'd be glad to pay for his admission," she offered.

The woman, a matronly type named Rosemary, flashed Haviland a warm smile. "Would you mind waiting five minutes? There's another party inside, and if you'd give them time to get ahead, you'll have the place to yourself. Perhaps you'd like to browse in the gift shop while you pass the time?"

She's a wily one, Olivia thought with admiration, and ended up purchasing a ship in a bottle kit for her niece and a toy periscope for her nephew. Judging by the threadbare carpet and faded silk plants in the lobby, the museum needed every cent the gift shop brought in, and Olivia made a mental note to tell Laurel to stop by and pick up some goodies for her sons.

A few minutes later, Rosemary gave Olivia leave to proceed into the first exhibit hall. Olivia looked at the dugout canoe encased in glass, read the plaques on the fishing techniques of the Cape Fear Indians, and then moved into the second hall, which focused on early explorers. Olivia saw what Emmett had meant when he'd said that the island rebelled against inhabitation. The initial attempt at colonization had been a total failure, and though the story lacked the drama of the disappearance of the Lost Colony of

Roanoke, the pioneers who'd tried to make a life on Palmetto Island had faced nothing but adversity.

Olivia studied one of the earliest photographs taken of the island. The beach, lined by palmetto trees and lush undergrowth, was beautiful, but there was also something hostile about the landscape. It was as though the plants and trees had formed a wall to keep invaders out. Assuming anyone made it past the dangerous shoals, of course.

Proceeding to the next display case, Olivia examined a map of the island and realized that most of it was still undeveloped. The marshlands and roaming tributaries, which formed the majority of the island, had been a wildlife sanctuary for nearly a century.

"No wonder the naturalists are protesting," Olivia said to herself and then turned to Haviland. "We're going on the moonlit walk, Captain. I want to see what they're fighting for."

Just then, Olivia heard raised voices coming from the next room. She moved to the doorway and peeked into the space. A man she immediately recognized from the festival brochures stood in front of a wall case containing an assortment of pirate weapons. He wore black jeans and a black *No Quarter* sweatshirt.

"Cutlasses, doglock pistols, and cannons. *That's* what creates excitement." Silas Black spoke to a short, balding man in a sweater vest. The man's cheeks were flushed. "I even had a crate of blunderbusses made for next season. Viewers want action, Sherrill. It's *all* about the action."

"You asked for my opinion, Mr. Black, and I'm telling you that there isn't a shred of evidence that Stede Bonnet committed rape or murder." The man dabbed at his forehead with a handkerchief. "He was known as the gentleman pirate. Gentlemen don't make a habit of rape and murder."

Silas grabbed the arm of the young woman standing beside him. "Amy is a Rhodes scholar. She's studied the lesser-known, or shall we say, darker side of history. She has plenty of evidence that Bonnet was no gentleman."

The man with the sweater vest hemmed and hawed. "Not after he became a pirate, no. Bonnet broke the law, but he wasn't a bloodthirsty barbarian either."

"You curators are all the same," Black said derisively. "Not one of you would have lasted five minutes in the times you so painstakingly preserve under glass. Your neat little cases and tidy plaques can't capture what life was like back then. It was dirty, rough, and violent. That's why you have so many of these." Black gestured at the pirate weapons case. "*These* are what people come to your sad little museum to see. Don't you want to add to your collections? To get a fresh coat of paint in these rooms? To update the awful lighting? Don't you realize that working with me is far more profitable than working against me? Think about it before this place falls down around your ears!" Black shouted and then strode out of the room.

Amy waited until Black's footsteps faded before speaking in a soft, honeyed voice. "Sorry about that, Mr. Sherrill. What Mr. Black was trying to say is that he'd like to highlight the history of the island by including Stede Bonnet in next season's story arc. If you'd give us permission to use—"

"I've seen Mr. Black's show," Mr. Sherrill interrupted. "And while I appreciate how his novels and his television show have made coastal North Carolina history extremely popular, I cannot condone the deliberate misrepresentation of a man's character." He gestured at a pen-and-ink drawing of a man wearing a coat, waistcoat, breeches, and a wig. "Bonnet had a library on his ship, not a torture chamber."

"Viewers don't want to see books in a show about adventurers," Amy said gently. She handed Mr. Sherrill a business card. "Please call if you change your mind. I'm sure any involvement in *No Quarter* would be beneficial for the museum."

"I'm afraid that I don't share your confidence, Miss

Holden," Sherrill said. "In fact, I'm surprised by your willingness to assist Mr. Black. You're supposed to be a scholar. Someone who has devoted years of study to local history. You should be writing a book about it. Instead, you're *rewriting* it to suit a television program. Or is it just to impress this Black fellow?"

Amy's composure never faltered. "Ours is strictly a professional relationship. And for the record, I did write a book. No one would publish it. I was lucky to land a job as a consultant for *No Quarter*. I didn't want to be trapped on this island or in some tiny museum in another coastal town. It's fine for people like you and George Allen, but I'm young. I want to write my own history." She pointed at the card. "You know how to reach me if you change your mind."

Olivia was about to enter the room when she hesitated. If the curator was already angry, he might not react well to seeing a dog in his museum.

She watched the agitated man approach the drawing of Stede Bonnet. "It'll be a cold day in hell before I loan Black a single artifact. There's no honor among thieves."

The following afternoon, the rest of the Bayside Book Writers joined Olivia and Rawlings for the official opening of the Legends of Coastal Carolina Festival. Short speeches were made, during which the attendees were introduced to Marjorie Tucker, the island's librarian, and to Mr. Sherrill. It was clear from the perplexed looks exchanged by the festival organizers that after Mr. Sherrill told the audience members about some of the more intriguing items in the museum's collection, he was supposed to turn the microphone over, but he rambled on and on. He spoke of the shipwrecks around the island, of the pirates who'd visited its shores, and of the book he'd written.

Eventually, one of the volunteers politely interrupted the

curator and reminded him that they'd yet to review the festival's activities. "I'm sure the attendees would like to hear from our guest of honor now. Silas Black? Would you kindly tell us what we can look forward to tomorrow?"

After sending a quick glare at Black, Mr. Sherrill scuttled off the stage.

Olivia watched the little man go, and though she listened to what the famous writer and television director had to say, her mind was fixed on a scene from the previous day.

Later, the Bayside Book Writers gathered in Lifesaver's living room to rehash the festival opening over glasses of prosecco. After they discussed which events they'd attend, Olivia shared the conversation she'd overheard between Amy Holden and Mr. Sherrill at the maritime museum. "So what do you think the curator meant?" Olivia asked her friends. "Was he calling Silas Black a thief?"

"What would Black have stolen?" bartender and soon-to-be young adult author Millay Hallowell puzzled. "It's not like he smashed and grabbed an antique pirate sword."

Harris Williams, part-time software designer and the newest member of the Oyster Bay Police Department, looked at her. "Are you a fan of *No Quarter*?"

Millay used the end of her scarf to buff the steel studs on her leather bracelet. "Not really, but I feel like people take cheap shots at Black just because he's successful. Not many writers manage to turn their own books into popular TV shows. The curator is probably jealous. He mentioned that he'd self-pubbed a local history book like ten times."

"People are going to envy you too, Millay," said Laurel Hobbs, assistant editor of the *Gazette* and mother to twin boys. "I can't believe that your first book is being released on Thursday. Are you ready?"

Millay shrugged. "At this point, I don't know what else to do. Harris created a killer website and book trailer for me, I've built a decent following on Facebook, and the early reviews are good, so I guess I'm ready. Still, I'm attending Silas Black's Q&A session to see if he has any pointers."

Rawlings, who had a copy of Black's latest novel on his lap, tapped the cover. "His books didn't become widely popular until after the TV show became a hit. I hope your book takes wing right away, Millay."

"Whatever happens, you've done something very few people can do. You took an idea, molded it into a well-written story, landed an agent, and signed a three-book deal with a major publishing house." Olivia raised her glass in salute. "You're my hero."

Embarrassed by the attention, Millay fidgeted with her bracelet again. "The rest of you aren't far behind. Chief, adding a crime element to your book is going to make it more saleable. And if you ever finished your women's fiction, Laurel, you could probably sell it based on your success as a journalist. And Harris? If you'd stop playing video games, your sci-fi novel would be done by now." She glanced at Olivia. "You have an excuse because you started a whole new project last summer. It was the right call too."

"Following your lead won't be easy," Harris said. "Ever since I started working as a research consultant for the chief, I've been toying with the idea of making some alterations to my main character. Instead of his walking loudly and carrying a big photon stick, I'm starting to envision him as a futuristic geek who solves problems using his amazing brain."

"Your leading lady could use some more gray cells," Millay said. "And less latex. Besides, I doubt latex suits make the best choice for interstellar exploration missions."

Harris shot Millay a lecherous grin. "I love it when you talk sci-fi."

Millay pressed her spiky boot heel into the top of Harris's

foot. "Watch it, or I'll narc on you to Emily. With her being in Texas, it's up to me to keep you in line."

"How's the long-distance thing going?" Laurel asked Harris.

"I miss her like crazy," Harris replied. "And I'm not sure what our next move is. She has a job and family there, but you guys, my jobs, and my house are in Oyster Bay. And I love hanging with the cops by day and being a kick-ass game designer by night. The problem is that neither Emily nor I want to give up the lives we're leading."

Rawlings gave Harris a paternal slap on the back. "You'll figure it out."

Harris stared at his hands. "How can you be so sure?"

"Because Emily makes you happy," Rawlings said. "You're smart enough to know what your future would be like without her in it, so you'll figure it out."

"Speaking of smart, who was that handsome man you were talking to at the end of this evening's panel?" Laurel asked Olivia. "I heard someone call him 'professor.'"

"That's Emmett Billinger," Olivia said. "You've all heard his name before. He's helped us numerous times over the years. I'll make sure to introduce everyone at some point this weekend."

Laurel finished her wine, set her glass on the coffee table, and then wagged a finger at Rawlings. "Look out, Chief. That professor likes your wife. He lit up like a lamp when she got close."

Olivia rolled her eyes. "All right, people. Lace up your shoes. It's time for us to raise money for turtles and learn what Emmett meant when he said that the island is a different place by night."

Several hundred people had congregated around the base of the state's oldest lighthouse waiting for Jan Powell, the head of the Palmetto Island Conservancy, to lead them in the moonlit tour through parts of the maritime forest. No one seemed to mind that the walk took place at nine instead of midnight or that the coy moon kept hiding behind a patch of watery-looking clouds. The night air smelled fresh and clean, and an ocean breeze rippled the oak tree canopy at the edge of the forest.

Jan, a formidable-looking woman with a bullhorn in one hand and a clipboard in the other, kicked off the event with a speech about the value of the island's undeveloped areas.

"The only way we can maintain the delicate balance created by nature is to *defend* nature!" Jan bellowed into the bullhorn. "The only way to protect the land between Allen's Creek and the Cape Fear River is to buy it! If Silas Black and his team of developers outbid us, they'll fill in the marshes, cut down the trees, build houses, and forever alter the ecosystem. Do we want more cookie-cutter mansions, or do we want to protect endangered animals?"

"Animals!" the majority of the crowd shouted in reply.

"Animals won't feed our families!" a man called from the periphery of the group. "I've been laid off for two years! If someone will pay me to fill in that marsh, I'll fill it in. Show me the damn bulldozer!"

This was followed by both cries of agreement and screams of indignation from the conservancy supporters.

"Things might get ugly," Rawlings said, adopting his cop stance. He spread his feet, hip width apart, and scanned the area from left to right. Olivia saw his hand reach for his gun holster, and there was a moment's confusion when he realized that he wasn't wearing his utility belt.

Suddenly, there was a surge at the front of the throng. People began shoving one another until a woman shrieked, "Look what you've done!"

The crowd parted and an old man, supported by another man, who had to be his son, wobbled toward a bench near the fence.

"Someone threw a rock at George Allen!" a woman yelled. "I think it was the guy in the flannel shirt!"

The shrill sound of a whistle cut through the angry din, which had doubled in volume following the accusation, and half a dozen policemen fanned out along the crowd's perimeter.

One of the cops took the bullhorn from Jan. "That's enough, folks." His voice floated over their heads. "If you're going on the walk, start walking. Follow Mike; he's wearing the reflective vest. Go on. Get moving." The officer waited a heartbeat before continuing. "If you're not walking, you should leave. Now."

"We have the right to free speech!" someone shouted.

"That you do," the officer agreed. "And you had a chance to exercise that right at last night's town hall meeting. The land sale won't be decided here. So unless anyone *else* would like to throw rocks at the island's oldest resident, you should go on home."

A group consisting mostly of men peeled off from the crowd. Olivia watched them move away, adjusting their baseball caps or spitting tobacco juice into the grass. Their jeans, canvas jackets, and leather boots were worn and frayed at the edges. They were working-class men without work.

"Those men need a purpose," she said to Rawlings. "Being unemployed hurts their pride."

Rawlings followed her gaze. "I heard quite a bit about this conflict between conservation and development while I was sketching today. The two sides have clashed before. The last time, the land in question was purchased by the state and donated to the conservancy, but the land currently for sale is privately owned. I sure hope the owner is keeping a low profile. This is an extremely volatile situation."

Olivia looked to where George Allen sat on the bench. She didn't want to join the walkers until she'd asked after his welfare, so she told Rawlings and the rest of the Bayside Book Writers to go ahead without her.

She approached the man who had to be George's son, who was dabbing his father's forehead with a wad of napkins. "Excuse me," Olivia said softly. "Can I offer any assistance? Get you some water, maybe?"

George managed a slight shake of the head. "I'm all right, Miss. I've got a hard noggin."

"You ready to go home, Pop?" George's son was paler than his father. The hand holding the napkins trembled.

Olivia turned to him. "May I take your father's other arm?"

"Thank you, but Boyd can manage," George answered in a whisper-thin voice. "I'm nothing but a bag of bones. You go on your walk. But keep your distance from the others if you want to learn about this place. If you listen to the island, you might hear something they don't. If you really look at her, she might show you things you won't forget."

"I'd like that," Olivia said. "I'd also like to listen to your stories, Mr. Allen. Emmett Billinger told me that you're the best storyteller he's ever met."

George smiled wearily, deepening the lines and wrinkles etched into every inch of his skin. "Emmett's a good boy. He teaches our history so it will never be lost. That's what matters, Miss. To never lose our stories."

"Come on, Pop. Let's get you to bed." Boyd flicked his gaze at Olivia. "The professor told us about you, and you're welcome to stop by tomorrow morning. Pop doesn't sleep much at night, so he tends to nap in the afternoon. We live behind the gift shop." He pointed at the renovated lighthouse keeper's cottage.

Olivia thanked both men, wished them a good night, and hurried to catch up to her friends.

She could see the slowest walkers ahead on the road, the beams of their flashlights throwing shadows across the ground. In the distance, Olivia was able to pick out Laurel's white sweater. She also saw Rawlings, Harris, and Millay, but decided to heed George Allen's advice and linger behind.

It didn't take long before the live oaks sprang up on either side of the road and the canopy of leaves obscured the moonlight. In the night, their twisted limbs and gnarled joints looked like rheumatoid fingers. The vines curling up their trunks resembled swollen veins.

As the copse of oaks grew thicker, Olivia switched on her own flashlight and kept her free hand in her coat pocket. The air, which was cool and salty, whispered through the tree leaves. Over the subtle sawing of insects, Olivia heard the sound of something moving through the undergrowth deeper in the woods. She listened as the snapping of twigs grew louder, followed by the crash of a creature racing through the trees.

Olivia froze. The animal was too big to be a raccoon or an opossum.

"A fox," she told herself. "It's probably a fox."

She increased her pace, remembering how George Allen had told her to look and to listen. She was hearing the island. She was seeing the crooked oak limbs, the jagged leaves of holly bushes, and the wisps of Spanish moss hanging from the trees like the brittle hair of a witch. If the island meant to show her its true nature, as George suggested, then its true self was wild. Untamable.

Rounding a bend, Olivia discovered that she'd caught up to the other walkers.

"There you are!" Laurel exclaimed in a dramatic whisper. "We thought you might have been captured by a pirate reenactor."

"She should be so lucky," Millay said dourly. "Who goes on a nature walk at night? I can't see squat. Trees, bushes, and more trees. I keep waiting for an alligator to pop out and scare the crap out of someone, but the most excitement we've had was when a lizard darted over some woman's shoe and she nearly jumped in the creek."

Rawlings glanced upward. "This walk has taught me plenty about the importance of setting. This place has a tangible atmosphere. The second you leave the beach and enter the forest, the island turns primeval."

"It feels haunted. It's like a cemetery without the headstones," Harris said. "You heard what Mr. Sherrill said about the thousand watery graves surrounding the island. Well, some of those people must have washed ashore. Maybe they never left. Maybe they're still here, in these woods, right over—umph!"

Millay had shoved him off the path. "You're going to be haunted by a killer case of poison ivy if you don't zip it. I want to hear how the old man is doing."

"He seems to be okay. His son took him home to bed. I'm going to . . ." She stopped as more crashing noises came from the woods.

"It's just me!" Jan announced officiously. "I circled around by another path so I could lead us back to the lighthouse." She scrutinized the five friends. "You're visitors to our island paradise, aren't you?"

They all nodded.

Jan held out her clipboard. "Have you had a chance to sign our petition yet? Or make a donation? We can use all the help we can get. We're running out of time."

"We all donated when we first arrived at the lighthouse," Olivia answered for the group. "But we don't feel comfortable signing a petition until we've reviewed the facts."

"Then allow me to tell you the conservancy's side of the argument as we walk. Is that okay?"

Olivia agreed, and Jan began a passionate recitation detailing how the sale and development of the tract of land known as Allen's Creek would forever alter the natural habitat. She'd just begun to list the animals whose territory would be transformed when she suddenly trailed off. She opened her mouth wide, but no sound came out.

"What is it?" Olivia asked and then followed Jan's horrified stare.

Behind them, Laurel made the noise Jan couldn't produce. She screamed in surprise and revulsion and clung to the sleeve of Harris's jacket.

Olivia came to an abrupt halt next to Jan, gaping at what she saw in the small clearing directly in front of them. Here, the moonlight spilled on a carpet of ferns. A ring of oaks stood like crooked sentinels around the body of a deer.

A white deer.

Its fur gleamed in the pale light like a patch of winter snow. Other than its pink ears and nose, it was completely white. Olivia had never seen anything like it.

When she got closer, however, she saw that she'd been mistaken. Another color marred the pure white. There was a bright red trail of blood running from a wound in the deer's breast. And there was red staining the white arrow shaft protruding from the wound.

Jan's hand flew over her mouth. "We're cursed," she whispered, her face taking on the deer's natural pallor. "Cursed," she repeated fearfully.

And then, like a spooked animal, she bolted.

Chapter 4

A fallen lighthouse is more dangerous than a reef.

—CHINESE PROVERB

The sight of the dead deer paralyzed most of the walkers, including Rawlings. He stood without moving, spellbound by how the deer's fur shone like moonlight on snow.

Millay snapped her fingers in front of the chief's face. "Hey! Shouldn't we call someone? What was that cop's name? The one who kept things from getting out of control back at the lighthouse."

"Peterson," Rawlings said, the glassy look vanishing from his eyes. "He might still be on the island. If not, I assume the police have their own boat, because there isn't a law enforcement station on this side of the Cape Fear River." He turned away from the deer. "I saw that animal when I was a boy. No one believed me. But here it is."

Harris shot Olivia a concerned glance and then held up his phone. "It's not the same deer, Chief. According to this website, the average life span of a wild deer is ten years. They can live as long as twenty, but that would be pretty unusual for this doe, seeing as she's a true albino. She even has pink eyes."

Laurel shuddered. "This moonlit walk has gone from mysterious to downright creepy."

Harris continued to examine his phone screen. "Only about one in every thirty thousand deer is a true albino." He looked at Rawlings. "If you saw a similar deer all those years ago, then the gene has been passed down for several generations. Makes sense, considering the insular habitat of these deer. What doesn't make sense is why anyone would kill such an amazing animal. And who goes around shooting crossbow bolts at night?"

Olivia squeezed Rawlings's arm. "You need to call Peterson right now. I'm sure he'd prefer to hear about this from another cop."

Harris pulled up the number for the Riverport Police Department and handed the phone to Rawlings. While the chief spoke to the officer on duty, the rest of the Bayside Book Writers retreated several feet. It was impossible to escape the cries of horror and dismay from the onlookers, however, so they stood in silence, gazing deeper into the woods where a small pool sparkled like sea glass in the pale light.

After what seemed like hours, Officer Peterson and a second officer arrived via golf cart.

"Step aside, folks," Peterson commanded while taking in the scene.

Peterson stared at the felled animal for several seconds, in which the conservancy supporters breathlessly waited for a reaction, and then turned to the crowd. "It's time for everyone to go home. We'll take it from here."

"Excuse me." A man worked his way to Peterson's side. "My name's Brett Collins, and I'm involved with the Palmetto Island Deer Initiative. We maintain the island's population." He pointed at the dead doe. "She can't be from here. All of our white-tailed deer wear lightweight collars and have ear tags. We can track every one of them."

Rawlings studied the man with interest. "It's deer-hunting

season throughout much of the state. Is hunting prohibited on the island?"

"Yes," Brett said. "We used to allow a certain amount of culling, but now we're injecting a specific number of does with a contraceptive. There's no need for hunting with this method of population control."

"I heard the program was suspended because one of your tagged deer was found off island," the other Riverport officer said. "A hunter could have read about that in the paper and decided to come over here and perform some old-fashioned population control."

Brett reddened. "She's not one of ours, I tell you. We've never had albinism in our population."

"I used to come here every summer when I was a kid," Rawlings told Brett. "I saw a doe just like her when I was eleven or twelve."

Brett shook his head in bewilderment. "You couldn't have. That's just a legend. A campfire story."

"Well, this story's over for tonight," Peterson said. "You and I can sort out what to do with her, Mr. Collins."

"What about the hunter?" a woman cried. "Aren't you going to track him down and arrest him?"

"We'll drive around the island to make sure no one with a crossbow is still out there," Peterson replied. "If we find the guy, we'll take him into custody. As for the rest of you, you don't need to put yourselves in the hunter's line of sight. Head straight to the lighthouse, and from there, go home."

After a brief hesitation, the shocked and angry nature lovers continued up the path toward the old lighthouse.

Rawlings and Peterson exchanged business cards, and then the Bayside Book Writers followed the rest of the walkers.

"Did you tell him about Jan?" Olivia asked Rawlings.

Rawlings nodded. "He promised to check on her before leaving the island."

More than ready to leave the gnarled trees behind, Olivia

increased her stride. "Jan was scared. She bolted after seeing that deer." She slowed long enough to glance at Rawlings. "Are you familiar with the legend Brett Collins mentioned?"

"No," Rawlings said. "But I'd be very interested in hearing it. Maybe it's in the collection of ghost stories at the rental house. I'll look when we get back."

Olivia was relieved to see the lighthouse rising into the sky up ahead. "If we can't find the legend in one of those books, I'll ask George Allen in the morning. I have a feeling he knows all about this island. And its ghosts."

Early the next morning, Olivia stopped by the island's general store to buy pastries for the Allens. At quarter to seven, the roads were empty and the air was brisk and damp, but the sky was streaked with golden light, signaling the onset of a clear autumn day.

At the Marina Market, Olivia was pleasantly surprised to find freshly baked muffins, bear claws, and butter croissants. After purchasing several of each, she drove to the Allens' tiny cottage and knocked on the door.

A curtain twitched in the room to the right of the door, and a few seconds later, Boyd was inviting her inside.

"We've got a fire going." He indicated the living room. "Pop gets chilled real easy."

With the curtains closed, it took a moment for Olivia's eyes to adjust to the dimness. "I hope these will warm him up," she said, proffering the bag of pastries.

Boyd peered into the bag and smiled. "Bear claws are his favorite. He hasn't had a breakfast treat for ages. Make yourself at home. I'll put these on a plate and get us some coffee. How do you take yours?"

"Just a splash of milk, thank you," Olivia whispered, for George Allen appeared to be dozing in a tattered recliner near the woodstove.

Olivia took the other chair near the stove and surveyed the room. It was a masculine space with navy walls, dark wood furniture, and shelves crowded with old books, magazines, and newspapers. There was little adornment other than framed photographs of George and a pretty woman Olivia assumed was George's wife and Boyd's mother. There were several of Boyd too. The child version of Boyd, whose expression was so carefree and filled with humor that Olivia barely recognized him as the man who'd invited her inside, posed in front of a Christmas tree, unwrapped a birthday gift, and played on the beach.

As she continued to study the photographs, Olivia was drawn to a black-and-white image of George as a young man. He stood on a dune, arms folded across his chest. A tall lighthouse filled the sky behind him. Though George didn't smile, his face was infused with pride.

"They blew it up," said a hoarse voice, and Olivia turned to find George Allen watching her. In the gloom, his eyes were the blue of deep water, but his gaze was intelligent and alert. An ugly purple bruise darkened his forehead where he'd been struck by the rock the previous night.

Olivia hated the sight of the old man's injury. She longed to take his hand, but instead, she leaned forward and said, "Blew what up, sir?"

"That lighthouse. They packed her full of dynamite and made her tumble. I spent so many years in that tower. A lifetime of the same view." George stared into the middle distance. "I kept that light shining day and night. It never faltered. Not until the day they shut her down."

Boyd entered the room and set a plate on his father's lap. "Look what the lady brought you, Pop. Your favorite." He smiled at Olivia again. "I'm sorry, I forgot your name."

Olivia told him while accepting a chipped coffee mug from Boyd's hands. "Your father and I have something in common. We both lived in a lighthouse keeper's cottage. My father wasn't a keeper, but a fisherman. Our lighthouse in

Oyster Bay was automated long before we moved into the cottage, but the last keeper made a lasting impression on me. You remind me of him, Mr. Allen," she added, looking at George. "That man told the most wonderful stories. He lived alone, and he spent his free time reading. Luckily for me, he always had a tale ready to share."

"By God's grace, I wasn't alone. I married a good woman. And before she left this earth, she blessed me with Boyd. He and I have kept each other company for a long time, haven't we, son?" As he spoke, George broke the bear claw apart with his bony fingers. The knuckles were swollen with arthritis, reminding Olivia of the live oaks in the forest.

Olivia sipped her coffee. It was neither rich nor strong, but it warmed her. "I lost my mother when I was a young girl. My father raised me for a few years, before my grandmother took over."

"Then you understand the importance of memories," George said. "What's your favorite memory of your mama?"

Olivia smiled. "Our bedtime ritual. Every night, she treated me to a story and a song. No matter how tired she was, my mother never rushed this special time with me. I fell asleep with my mind full of words and music, the scent of my mother's soap clinging to my pillow."

George nodded, clearly pleased by her answer. "I sent Boyd off to dreamland with stories too. I didn't sing though. That might have given the boy nightmares." He cackled softly. "But he now knows this island as well I as do."

The mention of nightmares reminded Olivia of the dead deer. "I took your advice and hung back from the crowd during last night's walk," she said. "I felt like I'd been transported to a primeval forest—to a place that would always strive to return to its natural state. And then, on our way back, we came across the body of a dead deer. An all-white doe."

George's frown was so severe that his bushy brows nearly touched. "Dead? How?"

"She was shot in the breast with an arrow," Olivia said. "Jan Powell was very upset. She muttered something about a curse. Is there a legend about a white doe?"

The room had gone very still. George bowed his head and folded his hands as though in prayer. He expelled a long, raspy breath and then glanced at the fire. His face was etched with grief. "The white deer are the ghosts of the forest. They stand for that which is beyond the power of man. The Indians believed the deer were magical and wouldn't hunt them. Killing a white deer invites a curse. Not just upon the hunter, but upon everyone."

"My husband saw a white deer on the island over forty years ago," Olivia said. "Have they always been here?"

"The legend began up the coast, at Roanoke Island. Long ago, the British tried to make a settlement there. It was rough going. The colonists were plagued by cold, hunger, and sickness. Hope dawned when the first English child was born in the New World. Her name was Virginia Dare. Her skin was white as milk and her eyes were the color of a summer sky. She was a joyful child and loved by all."

George paused to drink some coffee. "A Croatan Indian chief named Wanchese feared the English. After joining forces with another chief, he attacked the colonists. Men and women were slain without mercy. Their homes were burned. A handful of English escaped, including Virginia Dare. Another Croatan Indian gave them refuge. His name was Manteo."

Olivia nodded. She'd been taught the story of the Lost Colony in grade school but couldn't remember all the details.

"Virginia grew in grace and beauty," George continued. "When she reached womanhood, she won the heart of an Indian warrior named Osisko. But another sought her hand, a magic man named Chico who was known for practicing the dark arts. Virginia was a virtuous woman and did not wish to marry such a man, so she refused him." George turned from the fire and looked at Olivia. "Chico vowed that if he could not have Virginia, no man would. He used his powers to change her into a white doe. Osisko could not undo the spell, so he sought out another magic man. This man told him to shoot the deer in the heart with a mother-of-pearl arrow. If his aim was true, Virginia would be a woman once more."

The sadness in George's voice was contagious and Olivia was almost reluctant for him to complete his narrative.

"Unfortunately, another man heard of the white doe. Wanchese, the Croatan Indian who'd murdered Virginia's people, wanted the white deer pelt for himself. He fashioned an arrowhead from a hunk of silver and set out on a moonlit night. Osisko also went out that same night. Each unaware of the other's presence, they came upon the doe as she drank from a pool of clear water. The moonlight shone down on her and she glowed like a star. Just as she raised her pretty head, Chico released his arrow. It struck its mark and in a blink, the deer became a woman. Virginia had only a moment to see the woods, the moon, and Osisko's handsome face before Wanchese's arrow pierced her heart."

Olivia released a mournful sigh. "She died."

George dipped his chin. "The water at that pool became the color of tea and was no longer safe to drink. Many other misfortunes befell the Croatan Indians after the death of the white doe. It's a curse to slay a creature that stands for purity."

"There was a small pool close to the deer I saw last night," Olivia said, almost to herself. "It's as though someone tried to re-create the legend. But why?"

Neither George nor Boyd could offer any suggestions, and Olivia decided that she'd taxed George long enough. She thanked him for sharing what he knew about the white deer and made to carry her coffee mug into the kitchen.

"Let me," Boyd said, taking it from her. He'd just picked up his father's mug and plate when his entire body jerked. The plate and mugs dropped harmlessly on the carpet, but

Boyd didn't notice. He had the heels of his palms pressed against his eyes and was doubled over in agony.

"Mr. Allen?" Olivia stared helplessly at Boyd.

"He can't hear you," George said matter-of-factly. "He's getting one of his headaches. It'll pass, but until it does, nothing exists but the pain."

Olivia collected the dishes and brought them into the dated but tidy kitchen. She washed the mugs, along with the plates and the frying pan soaking in the sink, and then wiped off the counters.

Everything the Allens owned was worn or damaged in some way, but there was a sense of pride about their tired belongings. Each item had its use and was valued. There were no extraneous objects in their house. As Olivia opened cabinets in order to put the clean dishes away, she realized that there wasn't much in the way of food either.

When she returned to the living room, George had his arm around Boyd's waist and was smoothing his son's sweat-dampened hair. "There now, there now," he murmured with the tenderness of a mother calming a fussy infant.

Boyd was in his sixties, but at that moment, he looked as ancient and frail as George.

Olivia met George's eyes, pointed at the front door, and mouthed, *Thank you.*

"Come again, Miss," the old man said. "I liked having a woman in the house again."

"I will," Olivia promised and left the Allens alone in their shadow-filled room.

Still lost in George's tale of the white doe, Olivia drove her golf cart to the island's library. Most of the attendees would be at the Land End Lodge for the panel on historic weaponry, but Olivia wanted to support Emmett by listening to his talk on haunted landmarks. She had two hours to kill before the day's only ticketed event—a lunchtime lecture and Q&A session with Silas Black. Olivia would see Rawlings again at lunch, and she was feeling an enormous sense of relief that they'd agreed to spend some time apart even though they were on their honeymoon because they were two individuals accustomed to a certain amount of solitude.

It didn't take Olivia long to reach the library, which was a charming, single-story yellow cottage with cobalt-blue shutters and doors. Palmettos obscured the ocean from view, but Olivia could hear the murmur of waves in the distance. She parked her golf cart, pushed open the gate of a white picket fence, and paused to take a photo of the book-drop bin, which was a replica of the island's lighthouse.

Like any Southern cottage, the library's front porch boasted a row of rocking chairs, and Olivia could picture vacationers passing a pleasant hour rocking and reading. Overhead, a breeze coaxed a song with no melody from a set of wind chimes made of shells and silver starfish.

Olivia entered the library and was surprised to find so few people inside. Glancing at her watch, she realized that Emmett's presentation wouldn't begin for another twenty minutes, so she decided to browse among the stacks. She was happily meandering through the fiction section when she heard angry whispers coming from the next aisle.

Peering over a row of Jodi Picoult novels, Olivia saw Leigh Whitlow pointing an accusatory finger at Silas Black's history consultant.

Amy, Olivia thought, suddenly recalling the young woman's name.

"I don't believe you," Leigh said in a voice that was half whisper, half growl. "I've seen how he looks at you."

"That's not my fault. I've never encouraged him in that way," Amy replied firmly. Her body was tensed, as though she was on the verge of flight. Considering the waves of anger rolling off Leigh, Olivia couldn't blame the younger woman. "I'm here to do a job, Ms. Whitlow, not to steal your boyfriend. And I love this job, so if I could prove that I'm not romantically involved with Silas, I would. No matter what I say, you seem to have your mind set on something that isn't true."

Leigh folded her arms across her chest and studied Amy. A malicious gleam surfaced in her eyes. "I told Silas to keep his hands to himself, but it doesn't hurt to repeat the warning to you. I've heard the rumors, okay? If I see a shred of evidence that you two are fooling around, I will act. I'll feed the media such choice tidbits about you that you'll want to spend the rest of your life in a cave."

"I haven't done anything wrong, so save your threats," Amy said, her face flushing with indignation.

"Oh? It's amazing what you can discover by spending a few hundred dollars on a private investigator." Leigh's mouth curved into a wicked grin. "I've learned the hard way that everyone has a dirty little secret. I believe yours has something to do with that hunky history professor. Billinger. You accused him of making sexual overtures, but later recanted when questioned by the university's judicial committee." Leigh made clicking noises with her tongue. "I heard the poor prof had to transfer to a different school because of you."

Amy's blush deepened and her posture changed. Instead of preparing to run, she looked ready to lunge at Leigh. "That was years ago! I made a mistake. And I apologized. My past is none of your business!"

"Not just yet," Leigh said sweetly. "But I'll make it *everyone's* business if you cross me. Keep that in mind while you're doing your *job*." Leigh pivoted sharply on her high heels, causing her dark hair to billow out behind her like factory smoke, and strode away.

As Amy watched her go, her pretty face took on an expression of naked hatred. She'd barely turned to leave when someone tapped Olivia on the shoulder and she jumped.

"Is this some new tactile method of choosing a book?" Harris whispered, gesturing at Olivia's hands, which were clamped on to the spines of two Anne Perry novels like a pair of barnacles.

"Actually, I was eavesdropping. I just got a second glimpse of a woman who'd go to extremes to protect her relationship with Silas Black. A woman, as Rawlings said, with a big anger." Olivia told Harris about the exchange and then recanted Leigh's behavior at The Crab Pot.

Harris whistled softly. "This is why I hang out with you. For the entertainment value. Besides, none of the weapons they'll talk about at the lodge are futuristic, and those are the kind I use in my novel."

"Well, I'm glad you're here to keep me company," Olivia said absently, her thoughts still fixed on what Leigh had said about Amy and Emmett Billinger. Had Amy been one of Emmett's undergrad students? Or a graduate student? And was there any truth behind Amy's accusations that he'd made advances toward her?

Harris waved at Olivia. "The golf carts are piling up outside, so let's get a seat."

In the next room, folding chairs were tightly packed together to accommodate the audience. Harris and Olivia chose seats toward the back and watched as Emmett tested a mini projector.

"I should've brought popcorn," Harris murmured and then cocked his head. "Where's Haviland?"

"Hopefully, he's napping at the rental house. I paid a visit to the oldest resident of the island this morning and decided not to take Haviland along. He can survive for an hour or two alone, though he won't like it. I'll have to walk him before the luncheon, and he'll expect me to feed him a five-star meal in exchange for his forced solitude."

"Oldest resident?" Harris studied Olivia. "The guy who got hit by the rock last night? How's he doing today?"

Olivia shared her experience at the Allens'. She was just recounting the story of the white doe when Amy entered the room. The young woman's focus was entirely on Emmett. She nervously worried a loose thread on the hem of her shirt as she approached him.

"Oh boy," Harris whispered. "I sense a drama storm brewing."

For his part, Emmett was oblivious to Amy's presence. Having made the final adjustments to the projector and screen, he walked to the front of the room, placed his note cards on the podium, and was reaching for the microphone when Amy touched his arm.

Emmett stiffened and for a moment seemed at a complete loss. However, he was a true Southern gentleman, so he smiled politely at Amy and extended his hand. Looking extremely relieved, Amy held his hand several seconds too long. She didn't release it until Emmett apologetically tapped his watch. At that point, Amy retreated. She found an open seat on the end of Olivia's row and sat down, her eyes never leaving Emmett.

"Hot for teacher," Harris whispered.

Olivia elbowed him in the ribs and then spent a moment wondering why Amy had come to the lecture in the first place. If she was in Silas's employ, then why wasn't she assisting him instead of fawning over her former professor?

Before Olivia could dwell on this thought, a woman with turquoise reading glasses Olivia recognized from the opening ceremony as the librarian, Marjorie Tucker, dimmed the lights. The audience fell quiet. Emmett introduced himself and began a slide-show presentation featuring the haunted landmarks of the North Carolina coast. The talk encompassed several antebellum homes, two cemeteries, a stretch of forest, an area of swampland, a theater, and a library.

"One of the most famous hauntings occurs on Palmetto Island," Emmett went on to say. The audience, Harris and

Olivia included, was already engrossed. But now, they sat up a little straighter, eager to hear what the professor knew about the local ghost.

The projector flickered and an oil painting of a young woman appeared on screen. She had creamy white skin, dark hair pulled into a tight bun, and large, golden-brown eyes. Her rosebud lips and the delicate fringe of curls around her face were dainty, but her Roman nose and jaw were too pronounced, making her handsome rather than beautiful. Olivia liked the self-possession she saw in the young woman's face.

"She looks like Silas Black's girlfriend dressed as a Jane Austen character," Harris said under his breath.

Olivia nodded in amazement. Leigh Whitlow was a dead ringer for the woman on the screen.

"This is Theodosia Burr Alston, daughter of Aaron Burr. Some of you might recall that Aaron Burr was arrested in 1807 for treason. He was later acquitted and spent several years in Europe." Emmett pushed a button and an image of an early nineteenth-century schooner replaced Theodosia's portrait. "Theodosia took care of her father's affairs while he was abroad. A very well educated and accomplished young woman, she managed to secure safe passage to New York for her father. He asked her to meet him there for a reunion. However, she was delayed by an unfortunate circumstance."

"Didn't her son die?" someone sitting close to Emmett asked.

"That's right. Her son, who was named after his grandfather, died of a fever in June. Grief-stricken, Theodosia wasn't well enough to travel until December of that same year."

Emmett brought up the next image. This one was a photograph of a woman in a pale green dress walking on a beach. It had been taken at twilight from a distance, so the image of the woman was blurry and almost translucent. "Theodosia boarded a schooner called *Patriot*, which sailed from Georgetown, South Carolina. Legend has it that the ship foundered on the Frying Pan Shoals and sank. Another version of the tale blames the ship's disappearance on pirates. Either way, all hands were lost." He indicated the photograph on-screen. "Since then, more than a dozen witnesses claim to have seen a woman of Theodosia's description walking along the beach near Cape Fear. Some think she is looking for her father. Others believe she is searching for her husband or her son. There have been no sightings since the Cape Fear Lighthouse was demolished in 1958. Perhaps the spirit of Theodosia Burr followed that light to shore, and once its beacon was no longer visible, no longer had anything to hold her to this place."

Emmett concluded by encouraging people to visit the maritime museum and was about to take questions when Jan Powell burst into the room. Her eyes raked the crowd until her gaze landed on Amy. Barreling her way down the row, heedless of shouts of protest as people's feet were trampled, Jan grabbed Amy by the shoulders and shook her.

"That son of a bitch bought the land!" Jan shrieked. "He and the seller closed last night while the rest of us were traumatized by the death of the white deer. Did he do it? Did he kill that deer as a distraction? *Tell me!* You tell me so I can—"

Two men pulled Jan off Amy. Jan fought them for a moment and then collapsed into an empty chair and began to sob. "We *are* cursed! *All of us!* This whole *ruined* island." Her voice carried such despair that Olivia felt a rush of pity for the woman. "A thousand years of natural history are about to be filled in, dug up, and paved over. It's all over. Everything I care about will soon be gone. The island is about to become a place none of us will recognize. Its best parts will exist only in our memories."

Jan buried her face in her hands and cried.

Chapter 5

One need not be a chamber to
be haunted;
One not need be a house;

—EMILY DICKINSON

The library was thrown into chaos by Jan's announcement and her subsequent hysterics. Half the patrons were either crying or shouting, and Olivia decided that it was time to go.

"I wanted to say hello to Emmett, but I can catch up with him later." Olivia pulled Harris out of his seat. "The conservancy people in attendance have every right to be upset, and I don't think they feel particularly warm and fuzzy toward outsiders at the moment."

In the parking area, Olivia pointed at her golf cart and frowned. "I'm penned in."

"This is why you should play video games," Harris said. "One of the lessons you learn while gaming is to always park your getaway vehicle in an accessible spot. Tanks, Ferraris, Apache helicopters, golf carts—it doesn't matter. Be ready to leave in a hurry."

"I'll keep that in mind," Olivia said, hopping into Harris's cart.

Harris had just merged onto the narrow strip of road when

people began pouring out of the library. As they raced to their golf carts, Olivia heard one man yell, "Let's get him!"

"I wouldn't want to be in Silas Black's shoes," Olivia said, gesturing at the throng. "They don't look like the peaceful protestors from last night's nature walk, do they?"

Harris glanced over his shoulder. "With those angry expressions, they remind me more of an army of Klingons."

"Can this thing go any faster?" Olivia asked. "They're following us. *All* of them."

"Us?" Harris's eyes widened. "No. Not us. They're going to the lodge in search of Silas. I just hope there aren't any loose torches or pitchforks lying around."

When none of the drivers turned off at Land End Lodge, Olivia's anxiety increased. "They're still behind us."

Harris tapped the rearview mirror. "I know. If this weren't so weird, it would be funny. What kind of mob travels by golf cart? What's next? Clown cars? Ice cream trucks?"

Olivia saw no humor in their situation. She steeled herself as Harris turned down the driveway leading to Lifesaver, and then exhaled noisily in relief when the rest of the golf carts drove by.

After parking his cart, Harris cocked his head to the side and listened intently. "They're going to your neighbor's house. Is Black staying next door?"

Olivia shrugged. "I have no idea. It's a huge contemporary with floor-to-ceiling windows. Someone must be in residence because I've seen beach towels on the chaise lounges, but I haven't run into anyone on the beach."

"We should approach from that direction. From the beach, I mean." Harris jumped out of the cart. "We need to warn whoever might be inside."

"Can you text Rawlings while I get Haviland? He'll want to know what's happening." Olivia unlocked the side door and whistled for Haviland. She heard the click of his nails on the floor as he rushed toward her and smiled inwardly.

It was a sound she never tired of. "Are you ready for some fresh air?" she asked her poodle.

Harris, Olivia, and Haviland hurried down to the beach. The ocean glittered in the late morning light, and the tide was out, revealing a seemingly endless pathway of shells.

"Looks like we're not alone," Olivia said and pointed at the stretch of sand in front of the enormous house next door. Two men stood facing the water. One appeared to be speaking into a cell phone while the other idly traced designs in the sand with a stick.

As Olivia and Harris drew closer, the man with the stick grinned at Haviland and said, "I bet you'd have fun with this, wouldn't you, boy?" He stood up and smiled at Olivia and Harris. "Nice day for a walk. What's your dog's name?"

Olivia told him and then quickly introduced herself and Harris.

"I'm Dirk Johansson." Dirk, who was around Harris's age, had fair hair, glacier-blue eyes, and deep dimples. He jerked a thumb at Silas Black. "I'm named after a fictional character, but this man creates them."

"Were your parents Clive Cussler fans?" Harris asked after a sideways glance at Silas. The novelist and television writer was so engrossed in his conversation that he didn't even look their way.

"Dad loved Cussler's books. With a name like mine, I almost *had* to become an archaeologist." Dirk held up the stick and grinned at Haviland. "Ready to fetch, boy?"

Dirk threw the stick, and Haviland charged after it.

Harris gestured at a series of yellow buoys bobbing in the ocean. "How's it going out there? Are you finding cool stuff in that shipwreck?"

"I believe we will," Dirk said. "We've had some odd setbacks, though. Last week, we lost a small boat—a Boston Whaler—when one of our guys ran into a shoal and split the keel. The thing sank in seconds."

"These waters aren't easy to navigate," Olivia said, staring impatiently at Silas. She wanted to catch his eye so she could tell him about the uninvited guests gathering in his front yard.

"True, but this guy thought he was being safely guided in by someone onshore. Someone with a light. My colleague was the last person to leave the wreck site, and by the time he motored in, it was dark." Dirk spread his hands in a gesture of helplessness. "He thought the light was leading him to the house Mr. Black rented for us on the west beach. Instead, it led him to the reef. We wasted hours recovering our equipment the next day."

"A strange light. A white deer shot in the heart with a crossbow bolt. This is not your typical vacationer's paradise," Harris said.

Dirk tossed the stick for Haviland again and then looked at Harris. "A white deer?"

Harris was about to reply when Silas finally put his phone in his pocket and turned to examine the newcomers. Slapping Dirk on the back, he said, "I see you found a mermaid." Silas gazed appreciatively at Olivia, clearly expecting her to be charmed.

She wasn't. In a cool voice, she said, "You may have a lynch mob forming in your front yard. Jan Powell announced your land purchase in a rather dramatic fashion at the library. More than half of the attendees are on the other side of your house as we speak. And they looked very angry."

Silas shrugged. "What are they going to do? Make me give the land back? I purchased it fair and square. People were able to voice their opinions during not one, but two town hall meetings, but the buyer decided to sell to me anyway. Privately. And he didn't need anyone's permission to do so. Now, I'll make sure the project manager protects as much natural space as he can, but I won't be intimidated into halting this project. Not by the conservancy people. Not by anyone. I didn't get this far by—"

The rest of his monologue was interrupted by the sound of glass shattering.

"What the hell?" Silas whipped his head around to face his house.

Haviland barked in alarm, and Olivia called him to her side and ordered him to be silent. She didn't want him to give away their position. Four humans and a poodle were no match for an enraged gang.

"I think you should both come with us," Harris said. "Olivia's renting a place next door. You can wait inside until help arrives."

Silas shook his fists in the air. "Giving them leave to destroy my house—which is *not* a rental? Not a chance!"

They heard multiple crashes, more glass shattering.

"Don't be stupid," Olivia snapped. "They're throwing rocks at your windows. Who's to say they won't hurl one at your head next? You can fix the windows. A broken skull isn't so easily repaired."

Obviously unaccustomed to being addressed so directly, Silas rounded on Olivia, his dark eyes lit with annoyance. However, he bit back whatever acerbic reply he'd been on the verge of speaking and nodded. "You're right. Dirk and I are grateful for the offer."

Inside Lifesaver, Olivia told the men to make themselves comfortable in the living room. In the kitchen, she filled Haviland's water bowl and prepared some refreshments for her guests.

She was just pouring coffee when Rawlings entered the house.

"Officer Peterson's en route." He pointed to the east, toward Silas's house. "Seeing as you wisely removed Mr. Black from harm's way, I'll wait for the local boys to arrive before heading over myself. It was my hope that the mob's fury would be spent smashing windows, but the noises have changed. I believe the group has moved beyond property damage and is now engaging in home invasion. Peterson needs to arrive before someone decides to instigate an even more violent act, such as arson."

"I'm glad you decided not to ride in on your golf cart and save the day." Olivia gave Rawlings a small smile and loaded the iced coffee onto a tray.

He returned the smile. "I've gotten wiser in my old age. I married you, didn't I?"

In the living room, Dirk was telling Harris about his most unusual underwater finds while Silas paced near the windows like a caged panther. With his dark hair, tanned skin, and sinewy body, he bore a strong resemblance to the big cat.

When Olivia introduced him to Rawlings, Silas shook Rawlings's hand with obvious relief. "A police chief? Excellent. With an armed escort, I should have no trouble reaching the lodge. If we don't leave soon, I'll be late."

"Better late than dead," Rawlings replied evenly. "And I don't have my gun belt, sir. I'm on vacation."

Silas glanced at Harris and then at Dirk. "What about you? Can you get a spear gun or shark prod from the rental house?"

"That's not the way to handle this," Rawlings said before Dirk had a chance to respond. "The local cops are on the way. Once they've successfully diffused the situation next door, I'd be glad to take you to the lodge."

Making no attempt to disguise his irritation, Silas took out his phone and began to type.

"Where are Laurel and Millay?" Harris asked Rawlings.

"I told them to stay at the lodge," Rawlings said. "Millay was inspired by something she heard in the panel, so she's scribbling in a notebook like a madwoman. As for Laurel, she's in reporter mode. When I left, she was conducting an informal interview with George Allen. He's being honored at today's luncheon as the island's oldest resident, and the curator of the maritime museum is surprising him with a slide show. Mr. Sherrill has collected photographs that span nearly one hundred years of Palmetto Island history."

Olivia was pleased to hear that George was being honored. "I hope Boyd's well enough to accompany his father. He had some sort of attack while I was visiting. A migraine, maybe. It seemed pretty severe, and I doubt he can afford medical care. They barely had any food in the house."

"I know that look," Rawlings said gently. "Tread carefully, Olivia. Like the men who supported the land sale because it gave them hope of securing employment, the Allens have their pride."

"I can handle that kind of pride." Olivia gestured covertly at Silas. "It's that kind I can't tolerate."

Officer Peterson and two other officers drove Silas Black to the lodge in a delivery truck. As soon as they were gone, Olivia, Rawlings, and Harris walked to the house next door. Thinking of all the broken glass they were sure to encounter, Olivia left Haviland behind.

While Rawlings exchanged courtesies with the pair of officers assigned guard duty, Olivia and Harris surveyed the damage through the nearest window frame.

"They wrecked the place," Harris said with a trace of admiration. "This could be a cut scene from *Den of Thieves 4*. It took me weeks to create this much virtual detritus."

Olivia took in the slashed oil paintings and the splayed books scattered across the floor. "For a spontaneous, emotionally charged crime, this room looks thoroughly worked over. The contents of the drawers have been dumped out and the bookcases have been emptied." She put a hand on Harris's arm. "Let's see if the sight through that far window is the same."

The next window provided them with a view of a ruined

media room. The leather sectional was cut in a dozen places, and beige foam poked through the rents like cartilage. Several pairs of woman's pumps—Leigh's, Olivia assumed—had been trampled until they were almost unrecognizable.

"Leigh's not going to be happy," Olivia murmured. "No woman likes to see her Christian Louboutin or Stuart Weitzman heels turned into ballet flats."

Ignoring her comment about designer footwear, Harris pointed at the far wall. "Whoa. Do you see that framed *No Quarter* poster that was once encased in glass?" Harris said. "It's signed by the entire cast *thanking* Silas Black."

"No wonder he was upset." Olivia stared at the hundreds of DVDs spread over the rug. Most of the jewel cases were cracked or crushed. "Things are in such disarray that it'll be difficult to tell what's been stolen."

Rawlings rejoined them a few minutes later. "According to those officers, the whole place has been turned over. If I didn't know better, I'd say this was a robbery from the get-go." He gazed around the media room, assessing every detail. "It's been an unusual twenty-four hours, hasn't it?"

Harris tapped his watch. "We should go. If lunch is as unforgettable as the rest of the morning, then I don't want to be late."

In the lodge's main dining room, Millay and Laurel waved them over to a table with a view of the veranda and, beyond that, the blue smudge of the ocean.

Olivia was admiring the room's autumnal decorations—pumpkin centerpieces filled with saffron-colored chrysanthemums and branches of bittersweet—when she saw a familiar face. Seated at the table on the raised dais, where Silas Black had adopted a lord-of-the-manor posture, was Charles Wade.

"What's *he* doing here?" Olivia asked aloud.

The Bayside Book Writers followed Olivia's gaze and were all just as surprised to see the man with Olivia's sea-blue eyes.

At sixty-seven, Charles cut a handsome figure, and the waitresses seemed as intrigued by him as they were Silas Black. With Leigh Whitlow glaring at every pretty woman in the room, it was safer for the servers to flirt with Charles.

As Olivia took her seat, she continued to stare at Charles. Though he was her biological father, she didn't think of him in that way. His twin brother, Willie, had raised her, and she hadn't known Charles until recently. Now he was living in Oyster Bay. He'd acquired Through the Wardrobe, the town's only bookstore, and was doing his best to revive the foundering business while also trying to create a relationship with Olivia.

"Why aren't you marching over to his table?" Millay asked.

Olivia frowned. "I'm not sure I want to know what he's up to. I'll find out after the event. Besides, I'm starving."

As the diners were served bowls of roasted butternut squash soup, the woman who'd managed Emmett Billinger's presentation stepped up to the lectern to the right of Silas's table and switched on a cordless microphone.

"Welcome, everyone. Welcome to one of the highlights of the Coastal Carolina Festival. I'm Marjorie Tucker, head librarian, and I'd love to thank everyone who came out to hear Professor Billinger's fascinating talk on haunted landmarks. Before we get to our program, I'd like to remind you of the afternoon activities. Immediately following our lunch, there will be an extended question-and-answer session with Mr. Black. At five, be at the marina for the Arrival of the Pirates. Finally, we invite you to listen to ghost stories around the bonfire at eight o'clock this evening. Several guests, including our island's oldest resident, Mr. George Allen, will be sharing spine-tingling tales. As noted in your programs, this will take place on the back veranda. Feel free to bring marshmallows for roasting."

"Sweet!" Harris whispered and pumped his fist.

Marjorie paused, quickly scanned the room, and then reluctantly continued. "Most of you have probably heard about the unfortunate actions committed by a certain group of people. I must remind everyone that the sale of the Allen's Creek land has nothing to do with our festival. I also hope that you'll be reassured by the knowledge that the Riverport Police Department will be patrolling the island for the remainder of the weekend. If you have any concerns, please speak with Officer Peterson after our meal." She gestured to the back of the room, where Peterson stood, straight-backed and stern, by a plant stand bearing a jack-o'-lantern.

"To return to more pleasant subjects, don't forget our annual golf cart decorating contest and parade occurs tomorrow. The grand-prize winner will appear in a forthcoming episode of *No Quarter*! Other wonderful prizes—including a basket of novels signed by North Carolina authors like Greg Iles, Lee Smith, Sherryl Woods, and Kathy Reichs, as well as gift certificates to area businesses—will be awarded for specific categories as denoted in your festival program."

Harris squirmed in his chair. "I have to win. I want to be on *No Quarter*. How could Emily resist me as a pirate?"

Millay smirked. "Not every woman fantasizes about peg-legged men with too much facial hair, noxious body odor, and poor grammar."

"Isn't that an accurate description of your last boyfriend?" Harris teased, and Millay kicked him under the table.

"Behave yourselves," Laurel scolded. "If I wanted to listen to squabbling children, I would have stayed home."

The soup bowls were cleared and the salads were served. During this time, Marjorie asked George Allen to stand. After briefly introducing George, she surrendered the microphone to Vernon Sherrill, the museum curator. He provided narration for the slide show, which was called *George Allen's Island*.

The Allens were the only family whose founding father had rowed over from the mainland for a job and had never left. George's father had fallen in love with the place, and after he'd put down roots, so had George. Then Boyd. None of them had ever left. Sadly, the landmarks these men had devoted their lives to were gone. George's father had been captain of the Cape Fear Lifesaving Station. George had kept the beacon of the Cape Fear Lighthouse burning. Boyd had worked at the lumber mill until it closed and then served as a channel pilot, shuttling people from the island to Riverport until the ferry made his job superfluous. The lifesaving station, lighthouse, and lumber mill were gone. Pricey vacation homes had been erected in their places.

Olivia's heart ached for George and Boyd Allen. As both men watched the images flash on the screen, grief darkened their eyes and pinched the corners of their mouths. Olivia realized that the slideshow wasn't a pleasant trip down memory lane for either of them. It was a scrapbook of loss.

To us, they're just images of buildings, but to the Allens, they're the shades of lives they used to live. A past they can never reclaim.

The main course, apple-glazed pork tenderloin with mustard greens and wild rice risotto, was served moments before the slide show came to an end. When the final image disappeared, Marjorie asked George to say a few words.

As he rose unsteadily to his feet, Olivia winced at the sight of his bruise. However, she was even more concerned about Boyd. The younger Allen's face had a sickly gray cast, and he was leaning against the table as though he might fall forward into his food.

"I haven't lived a very exciting life," George began, "but I'd like to think that I gave my best to my Creator, this island, and my family." He locked eyes with his son, and the loving look exchanged between the two men was so powerful that many audience members were moved to tears. "What we have left, in the end, is our own story. It's important to tell it while there's still time. And remember, you don't always have to leave your mark on a place. Sometimes, leaving no footprint is the wisest choice. I thank you for this honor."

For a storyteller, this was a remarkably short speech. While the audience clapped politely, George returned the microphone to Marjorie and eased his body back into his seat. He put a hand on Boyd's shoulder, and Boyd smiled weakly at his father.

As the applause faded, Olivia glanced at her friends. "George really believes in that message. When Emmett was young, George told him that the island fights back whenever someone tries to leave too deep a footprint."

"I guess that's his way of speaking out against the housing development," Laurel said.

"Or against change in general," Millay said. "It has to be hard for him. All the places he remembers are gone. I feel sorry for his son too. When George dies, Boyd will be totally alone."

Harris pushed his plate away. "That whole slide show was a downer. I hope Silas can pump some life back into this event. I'm itching to catch a ferry to the mainland so I can buy supplies for my golf cart."

It didn't take long for Silas Black to reverse the dour atmosphere. He was a humorous and engaging speaker. Olivia found this version of Silas far more likable than the man she'd invited back to her rental house. She was also surprised to learn that Silas had grown up in Ocean Isle Beach, which was less than an hour away from Palmetto Island.

"My folks ran a souvenir shop," he said. "I didn't mind selling Jolly Roger T-shirts or pirates carved from coconuts, but what I really wanted was to bring the stories of these men—mercenaries, rogues, pirates—to life. I wanted to write about men who could not only navigate these unpredictable and lethal waters, but had the skill to capture *other* vessels in these treacherous settings."

Silas stepped away from the podium, his eyes glimmering as he warmed to his subject. "Imagine the thrill of this

hunt! The ship heaving in the swells. The shouting and scur-
rying on deck. The boom of cannon fire and the crack of
splintered wood. These men didn't waste their lives talking
on cell phones. They ventured upon the wild waters and
took life by the throat." He closed his fist around empty air.
"Can any of us claim such a feat?"

"This is why *No Quarter* is so good," Harris whispered
to Olivia. "Black's passion comes through in every episode.
You should watch it."

Silas went on to talk about his books and dropped a hint
that a ghost of a famous pirate would appear in the next
novel. He concluded by giving advice to aspiring writers.

"People say write what you know, but I say write about
what makes your blood race. Write about that, and your words
will become sails filled with a strong wind. Thank you."

The crowd rewarded Silas with boisterous applause, and
then Marjorie thanked him again and turned off the microphone. The luncheon was officially over.

Silas and his entourage were the first to leave the dining
room. Charles Wade stayed where he was, his head bent
over the wine list.

"I'm headed to the Q&A," Millay said. "Anyone else?"

"I think we're all going." Rawlings turned to Olivia.
"Unless you'd like me to wait here with you?"

Olivia shook her head. "I'd like to speak with Charles."

When she reached the table on the raised dais, Charles
Wade was sniffing the contents of his wineglass. Seeing
Olivia, he smiled and got to his feet. After pulling out a
chair for her, he gestured at the bottle of pinot bianco.
"Would you like a glass?"

"I'd rather know what you're doing here," Olivia said,
ignoring the chair.

"Nothing nefarious." Charles patted the chair cushion.
"Take a load off, and I'll tell you how Silas and I were bosom
buddies back in college."

Olivia complied but regarded Charles warily. Though she'd enjoyed working on the bookstore renovations with him, there was still so much about Charles Wade that she didn't know. And she didn't completely trust him. Not yet. He'd built a successful career and amassed a fortune by buying companies, splitting them apart, and selling the pieces. Olivia didn't want anything in Oyster Bay to be split into pieces.

"Silas and I were similar in many ways," Charles said. "We were both from small coastal towns. We both had loans and partial scholarships, and we worked in the cafeteria to cover the cost of our room and board. Those four years were the best of my life. Because Silas and I loved all things related to media, we decided to major in communications. After school, I moved to Raleigh to work for a local television station, while Silas landed a job as reporter. We've kept in touch through the years, so when I heard he was headlining this festival, I gave him a call."

Olivia wanted to believe Charles, but a niggling feeling wouldn't let her accept his words at face value. "Through the Wardrobe's grand reopening is next weekend. I'm surprised that you left the bookstore at this crucial juncture."

Charles laughed. "You've seen through me, which is why you're such a good businesswoman. I do have an ulterior motive, and it's this: I thought I'd spend some quality time with my old friend before he did me a big favor. That's primarily why I'm here."

Ignoring the latter remark, which was both cryptic and puzzling, Olivia studied Charles's face. "What favor?"

"You said it yourself. Our reopening and Millay's book launch is next weekend. What could draw a huge crowd better than a famous North Carolina author and television producer?" Charles grinned. "That's right. After this festival is over, Silas Black is coming to Oyster Bay." He raised his glass. "Millay's release party will be the most unforgettable event in the town's history. Mark my words."

Chapter 6

*When your heart is broken, your boats
are burned.*

—GEORGE BERNARD SHAW

Olivia was annoyed with Charles for having made plans
for the bookstore's grand reopening behind her back.
She knew Silas Black would draw a large crowd and that
his presence would garner tons of media attention, but she
didn't like surprises. She preferred to be made aware of
every aspect of her businesses and investments.

However, she wasn't about to let Charles see that he'd
gotten under her skin, so she politely told him that they could
discuss the subject in great length some other time.

Feeling out of sorts, she decided to skip the Q&A session.
Instead, she drove to the Marina Market. In the privacy of
the manager's cluttered office, Olivia arranged for items
such as bread, milk, eggs, cheese, lunch meat, and frozen
vegetables to be delivered to the Allens' cottage on a monthly
basis.

"I wish to remain anonymous," Olivia instructed the
manager as she added her signature to an order form. She
placed a business card on his desk. "You can reach me at

this number. Please don't hesitate to call if you think the Allens need additional supplies."

The manager, a gaunt man with deep-set eyes and the gruff voice of a chain-smoker, stared at Olivia's check.

"Is that enough to cover several months' worth of orders?" Olivia asked, confused by the manager's apparent hesitation.

"More than enough. And you can trust that I'll make your money stretch as far as it can go," the manager assured her. "I just have to figure out what to tell the Allens when I drop the stuff off. They're not keen on charity. They're not too fond of folks poppin' by either. We all live on the other side of the river, so the Allens don't consider us neighbors. Used to be that George would tell stories at the library, but he only does that once in a blue moon now. I guess a man gets tired of talkin' after so many years."

Olivia considered the problem of getting the Allens to accept the supplies. "Just leave the box on their doorstep with a note saying that it's a gift for the island's oldest resident," she said. "The Allen men are both proud of George's resilience." She paused, recalling how her visit with the Allens had ended. "One more thing. I know it's none of my business, but is Boyd unwell?"

The manager shrugged. "I couldn't say, ma'am. Boyd spends most of his time fishin' and carin' for his daddy. He buys things from my store, but he doesn't talk much." Tucking Olivia's check and business card into the corner of his desk blotter, the manager tented his fingers. "I don't mean to pry, but why are you doin' this, ma'am?"

"I knew a man like George Allen when I was a girl. He told me stories and kept me company when I was lonely," Olivia said. "I moved away and never had the chance to repay him for his kindness. I want to help the Allens in his name."

"Don't you worry, ma'am. I'll make sure they're taken care of," the manager said, apparently satisfied by her explanation.

Olivia left the market in a much better mood and drove back to Lifesaver to walk Haviland. Afterward, she loaded two folding chairs into the golf cart and then gestured for her poodle to hop aboard. "Time to meet the rest of the gang, Captain. We can't be late for the arrival of the pirates. Rawlings probably used crime scene tape to stake out places for us on the dock."

The thought of Rawlings waiting for the first glimpse of a schooner and its black flag made Olivia smile. For the moment, she forgot about the violence from that morning—the tension between Leigh and Amy, Amy's disconcerting connection to Emmett, and the appearance of Charles Wade. Olivia had come to Palmetto Island to make new memories, and the look of wonder on Rawlings's face as the pirates landed was certain to be memorable.

As it turned out, Rawlings had commandeered a large portion of the dock for the Bayside Book Writers. He'd spread two picnic blankets over the rough wood and had adopted the stiff and vigilant posture of a secret service agent. Harris had helped claim the area by stretching his long, lean body across one of the blankets. With his sunglasses on, it was hard to tell if he was awake or had been lulled to sleep by the warmth of the afternoon sun. Either way, Haviland decided to emulate Harris. He stretched out beside Harris and laid his head on his paws.

"I bought refreshments," Rawlings said, coming forward to relieve Olivia of a chair. "Nothing Michel would approve of, but I couldn't resist buying a jar of spiced rum. Check out the pewter mugs." He pointed at a group of five mugs on the picnic blanket. "We get discounts on drinks with these."

Olivia examined the label hanging from the jug of spiced rum. "How to make spiced rum. Place rum, allspice, cloves, cardamom, star anise, cinnamon, nutmeg, orange peel, and one vanilla bean—split lengthwise—in a jar and store in a dark place for 2 days. Strain rum using cheesecloth. Pour and enjoy."

"Sounds good to me," Harris said, sitting up.

Olivia uncorked the jar, inhaled the pleasant aroma of the spiced rum, and filled a cup for Harris. "Where are Laurel and Millay?"

"Hopefully, on that ferry." Harris waved at the incoming vessel. "They decided to participate in the golf cart parade too, and while I did most of my shopping in the hardware store—and don't ask me what I bought, because that's classified—they wanted to visit, like, a billion stores."

"If they miss the pirates, they'll be sorry." Rawlings glanced at his watch.

Rawlings needn't have worried. The ferry docked, disgorged several hundred passengers, including Laurel and Millay, and shut off its engines. Clearly, no one was leaving the island by ferry anytime soon.

Laurel and Millay dropped a handful of shopping bags at the edge of the picnic blanket and gratefully accepted mugs of spiced rum from Rawlings.

"I'm parched!" Laurel declared happily and took a swallow. "Whoa, this stuff has a big kick."

"Better go easy, Mama Bear," Millay teased. "After the pirates entertain us with a few choreographed swordfights and a bunch of lame jokes told in super-bad accents, we'll have a huge barbecue feast. Then, we can finally look forward to the best part of today's events: ghost stories around the bonfire."

Olivia smiled at her friend. Millay was too cool to admit that she was as excited about the arrival of the pirates as Rawlings. "What did you think of the Q&A session? Did you get anything out of it?"

Millay nodded. "Yeah. In fact, Silas gave me a bunch of ideas to promote the next book. It's too late in the game for *The Gryphon Rider*, but what he told me was really useful.

Here's the weirdest part. He also said that he'd be at my inaugural signing." She shrugged. "The guy must have had too much wine at lunch."

"He's probably referring to your Through the Wardrobe launch party," Olivia said. "It looks like you'll be sharing the limelight with Silas Black."

Harris's mug froze halfway to his mouth. "What?"

"Apparently, Charles and Silas were college buddies," Olivia explained. "Charles has somehow convinced Silas to appear at the bookstore's grand reopening."

"But he'll steal Millay's thunder," Laurel protested. "This is supposed to be *her* big debut! *Her* moment in the sun."

Millay held out her hand. "Hold on to your idioms, lady. This is good news. Do you know how many more people will come to Oyster Bay, and thus *see* my book, because Black will be there?" She smiled. "This is actually pretty freaking awesome."

"I guess . . ." Laurel trailed off, her attention diverted by the sight of a tall ship on the horizon.

Rawlings sucked in his breath. His face glowed with wonder, and he suddenly seemed decades younger. "She's magnificent," he murmured, and Olivia had to agree.

Under full sail, the tall ship entered the channel leading to the harbor with incredible grace. From its mermaid figurehead to its stern, the frigate was easily one hundred and eight feet long. Its three masts were festooned with billowing linen-colored sails, and the Jolly Roger flapped proudly from the tallest mast. A pirate standing a hundred feet from the deck, his feet planted on the main crosstrees, raised his sword and released a wild howl.

This must have been a signal for the band at the end of the dock to strike up a tune and the jaunty strains of a sea shanty burst across the water. The crowd cheered and a dozen couples began to dance.

When the ship reached the middle of the harbor, the

spectators were treated to the loud report of cannon fire. Colored smoke billowed from the portholes and flares erupted in the sky above the pirate flag. Haviland, who disliked loud noises of any kind, pressed his head against Olivia's leg, and she soothed him until the brief display ended.

Now that the ship was closing in on the marina, the people lining the docks whooped and hollered. Groups of small children raced about, jabbing at one another with plastic cutlasses. The children wore eye patches and red bandanas, and several had even affixed fake parrots to their shoulders.

"My boys would love this," Laurel said. "I'll have to bring them next year."

There was so much commotion on the dock that Olivia was tempted to back away from the edge, but something off the starboard side of the tall ship's bow caught her eye. A small craft, which looked as insubstantial as one of the dugout canoes she'd seen in the museum, was headed for the frigate.

Rawlings had spotted the smaller boat too.

"A dinghy," he murmured as if to himself.

The afternoon sun was waning, and the luxury motorboats and big yachts moored in the harbor cast shadows across the darkening water.

"It's unmanned," Olivia said, pointing.

Suddenly, the little craft began to glow. It looked as though it was filled with gold. Within seconds, the golden light expanded. It became a bright spot on the water, and Olivia couldn't look away. As she and Rawlings squinted intently, fingers of flame clawed at the air, and the sides of the boat turned black as the fire chewed through the wood.

By now, other spectators were pointing at the boat and shaking their heads in confusion.

"It's headed right for the tall ship," Rawlings said. A deep crease appeared between his brows. "I don't think this is part of the show."

Harris stood on his tiptoes. He had one hand on Haviland's head and had raised the other to shield his eyes against the glare of the waning sun. "That dinghy is about to get crushed. There's no way the bigger ship can turn aside in time. It's hemmed in on both sides by moored boats."

The shouting on board the tall ship changed. Gone were the lively bellows of the pirates in the rigging. The clipped commands of a captain directing his crew reached the ears of those watching in silent fascination. But the sailors' efforts were in vain. The bow of the tall ship split the flaming dinghy with a loud crack of splintering wood. The ruined boat sank within seconds, leaving behind plumes of smoke and a few pieces of flotsam.

"What the hell?" Millay glanced around. "There was a motor attached to the back of the boat that just sank, and I think the tiller was tied so that it would stay on course. Was someone trying to blow up the tall ship?"

Rawlings squinted in the direction from which the small craft had come. "Damn it. I can't see that far. I wish I had binoculars."

"There's nothing to see," Laurel said. "A bunch of moored sailboats. No one's moving around on the decks either."

"That boat had to have come from somewhere," Olivia said. "What we saw was a deliberate action."

The five friends silently watched the tall ship ease into the second ferry berth. One of the pirates leapt onto the dock, brandishing a pistol and sneering with feigned malice, and secured the bowline to a cleat.

A second pirate tied the stern line while four crew members pushed a wooden boarding ramp over the frigate's side. It hit the dock with a thud, and the pirates streamed off the boat. Several women appeared from behind the vendor booths dressed in laced bodices and full skirts. The pirates paired off with the women, and within moments, the couples were dancing down the dock, encouraging members of the crowd to join in.

Soon, the entire marina reverberated with the sounds of music and merriment.

"Would you care for a dance?" A swarthy pirate in a red waistcoat performed a rakish bow and then extended his hand to Millay. "You're the prettiest wench I've seen since we left Barbados."

"Thanks for the tempting offer, but this wench is going to sink her teeth into some barbecued ribs." Millay gave the pirate a dismissive smile and then turned to Harris. "Are you ready to get your pig on? This music is making my head hurt."

Harris looked surprised. "Seriously? How can a fiddle and fife give you a headache when you listen to punk rock to relax?"

"I just want to step away from everything for a few minutes," Millay said. "I feel like we've seen some weird crap since we got here, and I want to take a break to process it."

Olivia couldn't have agreed more.

"But what about the sword fights?" Harris protested. "I heard one of the reenactors had too much rum last year and forgot his choreography. He attacked when he was supposed to feint and nearly skewered his opponent. Ended up nicking the other guy in the side. This place"—he waved with his free arm, encompassing the whole island—"is so unpredictable. To use book talk, it acts more like a character than a setting. It has its own personality."

"Oyster Bay has a personality too," Millay said. "But not like this. Palmetto Island has a *Heart of Darkness* vibe. Not all the time. But we've caught glimpses of it."

"That's what I've been feeling too," Olivia said. "But I don't like admitting it."

The friends packed their gear into their golf carts and walked to the huge tent erected behind the Marina Market. After loading their plates with pulled pork, ribs, brisket, succotash, and slaw, they settled down at a table at the back of the tent.

"The incidents are likely someone's outlandish way of protesting the land sale," Laurel began the discussion while smearing butter on a piece of corn bread.

"How does killing a rare deer and burning a boat get that point across?" Millay argued. "These are theatrical demonstrations like you might find in an episode of *No Quarter*."

Harris stared at her. "Are you implying that Silas Black shot a deer in the heart? Why would he do that? His show is already a hit and he's making beaucoup bucks off the novels and merchandising. If Black didn't end up with the Allen's Creek land, I doubt he'd lose much sleep over it."

"What about Jan Powell? She was so zealous about her cause that I believe she spurred folks into vandalizing Mr. Black's beach house. However, she didn't kill that doe," Rawlings said. "Let's list the oddities that have occurred over the past two days. First, there was the deer." He held up a thumb. "Next, it appears that Mr. Black's house was searched in addition to being trashed." He added another finger. "Now we have an unmanned burning boat added to the mix. What do these three acts have in common?"

Harris reached over and uncurled the chief's ring finger. "You have to count the light on the beach too. The strange light that archaeologist, Dirk, told us about. No one knows where it came from, but someone created a beacon and lured Dirk's crew member to the shoals, causing him to wreck his motorboat."

Olivia shook her head in frustration. "The events don't seem linked at all—other than a general theme of destruction. Killing a helpless animal. Invading a man's home and trashing his belongings. Misdirecting another man on the water in order to sink his boat and cause the loss of his equipment. And finally, threatening the crew on a tall ship by setting fire to a smaller boat." She looked at Millay. "You're right about the theatrical element of these acts. This person wants witnesses. But what is his or her message?"

"Go away?" Laurel suggested. "Leave this place or you'll get an arrow through the chest, or have your belongings damaged, or your boat sunk?"

Rawlings wiped a dollop of barbecue sauce off his chin with a napkin and then stared down at the stain on the white paper. "You might be on to something, Laurel. But *who* needs to leave? And what else will this person do to drive people away? Because I don't think he or she will stop. My guess is that the violence will escalate until their message is made perfectly clear."

"We'd better figure this out quickly. It's only a matter of time before someone is seriously hurt," Olivia said.

The friends spent another thirty minutes brainstorming, but came no closer to unraveling the reason behind the strange occurrences.

"I need to go back to our rental house," Harris declared after draining his glass of sweet tea. "I want to work on my golf cart before tonight's bonfire."

"I'll join you," Millay said. "I'm running a Facebook contest to drum up preorders of *The Gryphon Rider*, and I'd like to interact with my future readers."

Laurel stacked their dirty dishes and tossed them in a garbage bin. "I should check in with Steve and see how he's surviving as a single parent."

Olivia glanced at Rawlings. "Let's take Haviland back to Lifesaver. He's not used to waiting for his supper."

At the mention of his name, Haviland licked his lips and did his best to look particularly hungry.

Muttering something about coddled canines, Rawlings led the way to his golf cart.

"See you at the bonfire!" Laurel called as she drove out of the lot. Millay saluted them from the passenger seat.

Harris followed behind the two women in his own cart. "Don't forget your sticks! I bought *tons* of marshmallows."

Laughing, Rawlings waved. He then leaned against the

frame of Olivia's golf cart and said, "You go first. You'll just race past me in your eagerness to feed Haviland, disregarding the speed limit signs or any other traffic laws."

Olivia turned her ignition key and faced Rawlings with a puzzled expression. "Are there traffic laws on this island?"

But Rawlings's gaze had wandered to the rear of the market, where a man was feverishly scrubbing his hands under a spigot by the shop's garbage bins.

Unclear as to why the scene had captivated the chief's interest, Olivia was about to warn him to step away from her cart when she took a longer look at the man. "It's Emmett," she whispered.

"I know," Rawlings said. "He seems very intent on cleaning his hands. I wonder if they smell like gasoline."

Olivia was about to ask why Rawlings would say such a thing when she saw a red plastic gas container near Emmett's feet. It was on its side and appeared to be empty, though it was difficult to tell in the waning light.

"The burning boat?" Olivia asked in a very quiet voice. "Could he . . . ?" She shook her head. "No. Why would he do such a thing?"

Rawlings didn't answer. He stood without moving and observed Emmett Billinger until the professor completed his ablutions, picked up the empty container, and vanished around the corner of the building.

When Rawlings finally met Olivia's gaze, he didn't bother to hide the suspicion in his eyes. "He might be your friend, Olivia, but you don't really know him."

Though Rawlings spoke the truth, Olivia didn't want to entertain the idea that Emmett was behind the series of unsettling events.

"I'll talk to him later tonight," she told Rawlings. "If he has done these things, I'll be able to tell."

"You should only approach him if I'm with you," the chief answered and retreated, giving Olivia room to drive away.

Olivia headed down the road; glad to be the sole cart beneath the canopy of oak trees. She welcomed the lengthening shadows, for they hid the confusion and unhappiness on her face.

"Nothing on this island is what it seems," she muttered. "Including the people."

Chapter 7

Those are pearls that were his eyes.
Nothing of him that doth fade,
But doth suffer a sea-change
Into something rich and strange.
Sea-nymphs hourly ring his knell.

—FROM WILLIAM SHAKESPEARE'S
THE TEMPEST

George Allen sat in a canvas chair in front of the bonfire wearing the look of an aged ruler who longs to put the heavy crown aside. Boyd was nowhere in sight. It was Marjorie Tucker, the island's librarian, who fitted George with a headset microphone and tucked a water bottle into the cup holder in the arm of his canvas chair.

Olivia was as eager as the rest of the Bayside Book Writers to hear George's ghost stories. When he launched into a tale featuring the capture and subsequent hanging of Stede Bonnet and his crew, she was so entranced that she nearly forgot her mission to speak with Emmett.

"The waters of Cape Fear are fickle," George said, his grizzled voice filling the air. "They can run your enemy aground and split his ships as though they were bits of kindling." He plucked a twig off the ground, snapped it in half, and tossed it into the fire. "Or the tides can rush in and free his ship from where it's stuck on a sandbar. That's what happened to Bonnet. The gentleman pirate never had a chance. He was outmanned. Outgunned. And he'd lost the luck of the sea."

Olivia was seated between Rawlings and Harris. Harris was so engrossed that he burned the marshmallow on the end of his stick. As for Rawlings, his gaze was fixed on George Allen's face, and Olivia guessed that the chief was picturing Stede Bonnet's capture. She could also imagine the grappling hooks and boarding axes in the raised hands of the conquering crew and hear the shouts of rage and dismay from Bonnet's men.

Haviland appeared to be listening attentively as well. Sitting tall on his haunches, his ears were lifted and his caramel-colored eyes followed George closely.

"Come on, boy," Olivia whispered.

Olivia led Haviland into the dunes. The casual observer would assume that Haviland needed a bathroom break, but Olivia knew better than to underestimate Sawyer Rawlings. She needed to move out of Rawlings's line of sight and quickly locate Emmett.

She found him on the far side of the patio sharing a beach blanket with Caesar and Calpurnia.

"May we join you?" Olivia asked.

"Of course." Emmett made Caesar scoot to the other side of a picnic basket. Haviland exchanged friendly sniffs and grunts with both greyhounds and then settled down between the pair.

"I don't have a thing in this basket that could hold a candle to the meal you fed me, but I did bring wine," Emmett said. "May I offer you a glass?"

Deciding that having a drink with Emmett might help to loosen his tongue, Olivia accepted.

"I respect you too much to dance around a prickly subject," she said after they'd both taken sips of their wine. "But I overhead Leigh talking with Amy about falsely accusing you of improper advances when you were both at UNC. You don't have to tell me what happened, but I'm concerned about you."

Emmett didn't reply for a long moment. He stared at the bonfire, his expression revealing nothing. However, his right hand drifted from his lap to the top of Caesar's head. Olivia recognized the gesture. She'd done it herself hundreds of times. Emmett was calming himself by making contact with one of his beloved greyhounds.

Finally, he turned to face Olivia with a frank and open expression. "Amy Holden was one of my most promising graduate students. She had an incredible capacity for recalling facts and data, but she was also able to look at opposing sides of major historical events and find empathy for all those involved. She had a way of seeing into the past as though it were a living thing."

"That sounds like someone else I know," Olivia said.

Emmett smiled. "I saw myself in her as well and perhaps that blinded me to her real reasons for seeking me out after class. I was her advisor, so that explained her persistence at first. But eventually, even this clueless academic began to realize that Amy wanted more from our relationship than was proper."

"She's very pretty," Olivia said. "Many men would have been flattered."

Emmett's gaze slid to the fire again. "My students are kids in my eyes, so I didn't take her seriously. That was foolish. I should have addressed her feelings directly, but I figured it was just a crush and she'd get over it. I ignored her flirtatious body language and accidental touches, striving to maintain an air of professionalism. I think my insistence on decorum made her angry. One night, Amy saw me having a late-night dinner with a female colleague, and she was obviously furious. The next day, she went to the dean of students and filed a complaint saying that I'd made sexual advances toward her and that she'd complied in exchange for high marks in my class."

Olivia felt a surge of hostility toward Amy. "That's terrible!"

Emmett nodded. "I went through hell. I was subjected to countless interviews. My professional reputation was spotless, but Amy was very convincing. Not only that, but my being a lifelong bachelor worked against me. I went from being the unattached man who'd never found the right lady to a lecherous womanizer in the blink of an eye."

"Amy said that she recanted. And apologized," Olivia said. "Not that an apology can restore a tarnished reputation . . ."

Emmett released a long sigh. "She did recant, but things weren't the same for me afterward. There was a distance between my colleagues and myself. They were cordial, yet aloof. I no longer felt comfortable working in the department, so I took a position at UNC-Wilmington. It ended up being a change for the better because I love it there. I have a house overlooking the Intracoastal Waterway, and I bought a little boat."

"Come on, Emmett. You were forced to start over again while Amy went on to graduate and land a job as Silas Black's consultant on one of the most popular shows on television." Olivia reached for the wine bottle and refilled Emmett's glass. "And now she's on this island. She attended your talk. It couldn't have been easy for you to see her again."

"It wasn't," Emmett admitted. "Especially since I thought she'd do something more meaningful with her love of North Carolina history. She only seems vested in helping Black vilify every well-known figure from the Golden Age of Piracy. I hate to think of how they'll skew the stories of this place." He glanced up the beach, and his lips tightened.

Olivia wanted to believe everything Emmett had said about his relationship with Amy Holden. He'd certainly sounded sincere, but Olivia had been fooled by a guileless expression and candid tone before.

"Emmett." She rested her hand lightly on his arm. "Were you at the docks this afternoon? When the pirates arrived?"

Called back to the moment by Olivia's touch, Emmett blinked. "I was. Quite a sight, wasn't it? I try to come to the island for this weekend every year. I rent out my house for the high season because the tourists are willing to pay such a handsome price per week, but I like to spend time here when there's no one else around. The beach during late autumn to early spring is very different. I like being the only person on this whole stretch." He made a sweeping gesture to incorporate the shoreline.

Olivia caught the note of possessiveness in Emmett's voice. "I assume this was the first time the pirate ship plowed through a burning dinghy."

Emmett shook his head in wonder. "That was really strange, wasn't it? But it didn't stop the show, and no one seemed too upset, though I expect the dinghy's owner isn't happy. His boat's now just a bunch of torched kindling." Emmett shrugged, as though the subject wasn't worth discussion, and pulled a bag of marshmallows from his picnic basket. "I'm ready for dessert. How are your roasting skills?"

Better than my interrogation skills, Olivia thought ruefully. This was the moment for her to ask Emmett about his fervent handwashing behind the marina market, but she hesitated. And in that space of silence, Emmett stood up and began sliding marshmallows onto a long metal skewer.

"I've spent decades perfecting my technique," Emmett said, grinning down at her. "Let's get closer to the fire. I have chocolate and graham crackers if you'd care to make a giant s'more."

He offered her his hand.

"I'd better get back," she said, ashamed by how easily Emmett disarmed her. He always seemed so sincere and amiable, and she was reluctant to jeopardize their friendship by asking him the one question she needed to ask. And yet she was annoyed with herself for not speaking up. "Maybe I'll see you and the dogs on the beach tomorrow morning."

"Maybe," Emmett said. "I hope you find something special. Something that will make your visit to this place unforgettable."

With a wave and a smile, Emmett carried his loaded skewer over to the fire.

By the time Olivia returned to her seat, George Allen had finished his story and was taking a minute to rest and drink from his water bottle.

Rawlings turned to Olivia. "What did the professor have to say?"

"I bungled the whole thing," Olivia confessed. "Instead of asking him directly about what you and I saw at the marina, I raised the subject of Amy Holden."

Rawlings winced. "You went straight for the jugular, eh? Not quite the trust-building interview technique I'd recommend, but did you learn anything?"

Relieved that Rawlings wasn't angry with her for sneaking off, she repeated her entire conversation with Emmett.

"I guess the only way to confirm his version of events is to have a chat with Miss Holden," Rawlings said when she was done.

"Which I'm *not* going to do," Olivia replied tersely. "First of all, it's none of my business. Second, what happened in Emmett's past has nothing to do with a dead deer or a burning boat." But even as she spoke, Olivia wondered if that were true. Could Emmett be trying to exact revenge on Amy by framing her employer? As Harris pointed out, the theatricality of the incidents had a Hollywood feel. If Silas took the blame, he might pack his bags and move to another location before he started filming the next season of *No Quarter*.

That's pretty far-fetched, Olivia thought and settled back in her chair to listen to George Allen's next story. When he mentioned the Lost Colony, Olivia knew he was about to tell the tale of the white doe. At the story's end, she scanned the faces around the bonfire to see if anyone reacted to the manner in which the white deer was killed. Though several people were surprised, no one acted suspicious or looked guilt-ridden.

After George was done, Boyd materialized from inside the lodge to escort his father to a golf cart. The second storyteller, Vernon Sherrill, took George's seat and began to speak of Blackbeard's ghost.

The sky darkened.

Olivia ate several warm, sticky, and perfectly toasted marshmallows, and then told Rawlings she was going to walk Haviland by the water's edge.

Away from the bonfire, the night air was crisp and cold. Olivia folded her arms over her chest and stared out over the inky water.

Suddenly, she felt the weight of a warm blanket around her shoulders.

"I picked this place. I'm the one who decided we should spend our honeymoon here," Rawlings said from behind her. "I'm not sure if I chose well."

Olivia leaned back against his chest. "This island has personality. It has depth. And a colorful history. In a way, it's just like us." Rawlings slid his arms around her waist. "Besides, you were looking for inspiration for your book, and this place fires the imagination. Did you get any ideas today?"

"I wrote close to five pages of notes after the panel and Q&A session, and I think the festival is just what I needed to fix the problems with my manuscript," Rawlings said. "Though I have to admit, I enjoyed our time alone more. The last two days have felt . . . crowded. Between our friends, your father, and Professor Billinger, I haven't had you to myself enough."

Olivia was more than ready to retreat to Lifesaver. "Come on, then. We can creep away without a word to anyone."

"And leave our chairs behind?" Rawlings asked in mock horror. "I've stored those things in my garage for years in hopes of using them. I finally get the chance and you want me to abandon them?"

Olivia turned, wrapped her arms around Rawlings's neck, and kissed him.

"Yeah, screw the chairs," Rawlings whispered.

With Haviland loping along behind, the pair headed away from the fire, letting the brilliant moon and a legion of stars light their way home.

Several hours later, Olivia was roused from sleep by the sound of a clanging bell. It wasn't loud, but it was persistent. She sat up in bed and saw that Haviland was awake too. The poodle was staring out the window with such intensity that he didn't hear Olivia approach. When she touched his head, he flinched.

"What is it, Captain?" she whispered.

Haviland whined and continued to gaze down at the beach. He licked his lips and shifted his weight, signs of agitation.

The bell rang again, fainter this time. The sound reminded Olivia of a large ship's bell. It was old-fashioned and lacked the clarity of modern-day bells and horns, which were often automated. However, Olivia saw no lights out in the water.

Following the direction of Haviland's stare, she spotted a smudge of white farther up the beach toward Land End Lodge. Olivia realized that the white object was a dress. It billowed around a woman's legs as the wind from the ocean filled it like a sail.

Or a nightgown, Olivia thought.

She was tempted to step out onto the deck and get a better view of the woman who'd decided to wander the beach in the middle of the night, but she was tired and the bed was comfortable, so after calling Haviland away from the window and inviting him to curl up by her feet, Olivia went back to sleep.

The next morning, she rose with the sun. Leaving Rawlings contentedly snoring, she and Haviland went downstairs. While Haviland breakfasted, Olivia brewed coffee and sat in the sunroom, where she watched yellow seep into the lower half of the sky like spilled honey.

The ship bell still echoed in her mind. It had been a haunting sound to hear in the dead of night, as was the sight of the woman in white.

"Where was she going?" Olivia asked Haviland. "And wasn't she cold?"

Olivia sipped her coffee as the sun slowly rose over the water. When Haviland pawed at the deck door, she put on her sneakers and the jacket Rawlings had left on the sofa and followed her poodle outside. She didn't wait while Haviland busied himself in a cluster of sea oats, but walked down to the beach. She turned west, looking for footprints, but all traces of the woman had been washed away by the waves.

"Was she a dream?" Olivia murmured to herself. "The woman and the bell?"

She passed the lodge and the place where she'd met Emmett's greyhounds. Haviland sniffed at a dozen different scents and didn't seem too interested in any of them until he suddenly let out a sharp bark of alarm. Farther along the beach, Olivia spotted a figure lying in the sand.

As Olivia got closer, she could see that the person was a woman. She was stretched out on her back, staring up at the sky. Her blue lips were parted, and the whites of her unblinking eyes had a blue cast. Her long dark hair looked to have been pulled into a loose bun high on her head, and several strands had escaped, framing her face with loose curls. Her arms and legs were spread like someone paused in the act of making a snow angel.

She was not wearing a nightgown, but a white dress with an empire waist. The dress appeared too small for her tall frame and looked antique. Olivia's gaze swept over the woman's body and then returned to the flaccid skin of the woman's face.

"Leigh Whitlow. What happened to you?"

Olivia reached into the jacket pocket for the cell phone she'd left on the table back at the rental house.

"Damn," she muttered. Seeing no obvious clues around the body, Olivia could think of no recourse but to return to Lifesaver, alert the authorities, and send Rawlings to stand guard over Silas Black's dead girlfriend.

"Where were you going?" Olivia asked the lifeless woman.

Leigh had no bag, no shoes, and no flashlight. The moon had lit her way.

"It was cold last night. Did you leave in a hurry? Were you scared?" Olivia remembered what she'd seen from her bedroom window. "You weren't running. It seemed like you were listening to the ship's bell—following it—but where did the sound come from? There were no boats on the water."

Leigh's corpse offered no answers, so Olivia told Haviland to heel and jogged back to Lifesaver.

Rawlings was in the kitchen, a coffee cup in one hand and a piece of toast smeared with a thick layer of cream cheese in the other. He smiled warmly when Olivia entered the room.

"You went out early. I thought . . ." He stopped midsentence. "What's wrong?"

"Leigh Whitlow is dead," Olivia said. She'd meant to sound calm, but her voice wavered. "Her body is on the beach, about a quarter mile past Land End."

Rawlings scooped his phone off the counter. "I'll make

the call while I get dressed. You'd better leave Haviland here. The locals could show up with K9 units."

Already dialing the Riverport Police, Rawlings rushed upstairs.

By the time Olivia led him to Leigh's body, the morning sun had risen above the waves and the haze of dawn was gone.

Rawlings kept his distance from the dead woman. He stood very quietly for several minutes, looking at her, and then he glanced at the sand around her body.

"No drag marks. No deep depressions to indicate she was carried." Though he spoke out loud, Olivia knew that he wasn't addressing her. Everything but the scene had ceased to exist for him. "I think you drowned. So how did you end up in this posture? Who arranged you like a human starfish?"

Olivia stared at Leigh. She no longer resembled the embittered woman Olivia had seen at the ferry dock or the library. That woman's cosmetics had been applied with skill and care. She'd worn false eyelashes and obviously taken pains with her long hair. This woman's face had been scrubbed clean. With her dark hair pulled back into a bun, she looked younger and far more vulnerable than the person who'd gained fame for being Silas Black's jealous and unpredictable girlfriend.

"Theodosia Burr," Olivia whispered and felt a shiver of horror over the coincidence. "That dress. The hair. The drowning."

Rawlings stopped examining the sand. "Who's Theodosia Burr?"

"The daughter of Aaron Burr. She was lost at sea somewhere off the North Carolina Coast. Emmett mentioned her in his talk on haunted landmarks. He showed us her portrait." Olivia gestured at Leigh's body. "In the painting, Theodosia wore a dress just like that."

In the morning light, the dress didn't glow as it had the

night before. It clung to Leigh's legs in damp, wrinkled folds. Clumps of sand stuck to her bare arms and feet, but there wasn't a grain of sand on her face. It was as though someone had carefully wiped off her cheeks, chin, forehead, and nose before leaving her to face the sunrise alone.

"Over the years, many people claim to have seen Theodosia's ghost," Olivia said quietly. "She walks along the beach, apparently searching for something or someone. And though Theodosia was younger than Leigh when she died, the two women could have been twins. Harris and I both noticed the resemblance right away."

"Another ghost story come to life," Rawlings said. "Maybe we need to pay a visit to the Allens."

Olivia studied his face. "You don't think they had anything to do with this, do you?"

Rawlings shook his head. "No, but I'm hoping George can shed some light on these seemingly random occurrences. I still can't figure out what message the person responsible for these events is trying to send."

"I think it's safe to assume that the message is meant for Silas Black," Olivia said. The dead deer was a warning that the island would seek revenge if he went through with his development. Directing the boat containing archaeology equipment into the shoals undermines the project Black is helping to fund, and putting a burning boat in the path of the tall ship indicates that the perpetrator isn't a fan of pirates. Or of books or television shows featuring pirates. Remember, Black plans to film on this island."

Rubbing his chin, Rawlings fixed his gaze on Leigh's face. "Those acts were done from the shadows. They were both theatrical and cowardly. They were also carefully timed and meticulously executed."

"The culprit is getting bolder. Killing that deer was awful, but . . ." She trailed off, raising her hand to indicate Leigh's inert form. The wind swept in from the water and ruffled the puffed sleeves of the white dress. Once again, the sight reminded Olivia of an untrimmed sail flapping in the breeze.

Your journey has ended, she thought and wished she could close Leigh's eyes.

Rawlings reached for Olivia's hand, and together, they stood silently over the body until Peterson and his team arrived.

Peterson briefly shook hands with Rawlings and then assessed the scene.

"Aw, hell!" he exclaimed as he looked down at Leigh. "We don't find dead bodies on Palmetto Island. The worst that happens here are B&Es in the winter and drunk and disorderlies during the high season. Our first suspicious death and it's a goddamn celebrity!" He rubbed his forehead. "Goddamn it."

"It's a tough situation," Rawlings said sympathetically. "I'd be glad to assist in any way that I can. The footprints closest to the victim belong to my wife. She found Ms. Whitlow while walking our dog this morning."

Peterson grunted.

"I canvased the sand, moving in an outward circle from here"—Rawlings walked closer to the body, made a line in the sand with his foot, and then backed up and repeated the motion—"to about here. I didn't find a thing. No cigarette butts. No drag marks. No foot or shoe prints. I think the killer carried her to this spot from the water, and then used something to clear off his tracks. Either that, or the wind and water did it for him."

"You think she was drowned?" Peterson asked. "Maybe she got wasted and stumbled into the water. Someone else came along and found her floating there, so they pulled her up the beach and laid her down. Maybe this person didn't want to get involved, so they took off."

Rawlings nodded respectfully. He always listened to contradictory theories with an open mind, but Olivia knew Peterson was wrong. She'd seen the bruising on Leigh's neck. The blue oval marks indicating that someone's fingers had dug hard into the soft flesh.

"Someone held her under," Rawlings said. "Look at her neck."

Peterson squatted beside Leigh and cursed. "It had to be a goddamn celebrity." He straightened and started barking orders at his men.

Rawlings and Olivia retreated. As Peterson's men erected a tent over the body, a female officer took their statements. When they were done, Peterson asked for a summary and then looked at Rawlings.

"The handler of our K9 unit is on vacation, so we're calling in backup from the next county. ME's on his way too." Peterson shifted, and Olivia could sense his anxiety. "I assume you've overseen murder cases before, Chief. Anything else I should do before I speak with Mr. Black?"

Rawlings recommended that Peterson send men to all the houses between Black's house and the place where Leigh's body had been left.

"Last night, I heard the ringing of a ship's bell. That's what woke me," Olivia said to Peterson. "If anyone else heard the sound, they might have gotten out of bed and seen Ms. Whitlow. She was walking as though she didn't feel the cold, like she was spellbound. Like she was being lured."

"Her dress is unusual too," Rawlings added. "I'm not up on fashion, but my wife thinks Ms. Whitlow is wearing a Regency-style dress and a hairstyle that would make her resemble Theodosia Burr."

Peterson's eyes widened. "The woman from the ghost story?"

"You're familiar with it?" Olivia asked.

Peterson nodded. "All the locals are. Women dress up as her for Halloween. Put seaweed in their hair. Paint their lips blue. Try to make it look like they've . . . drowned. Jesus."

"We think someone is taking coastal stories—ghost stories—and using them to send a message," Rawlings said and repeated Olivia's theory.

"Silas Black won't leave," Peterson said. "He's not the type to be intimidated."

"A trashed house is one thing," Olivia said. "A murdered girlfriend is another."

Rawlings raised his hand. "Wait a minute. Where *is* Mr. Black staying? His house isn't habitable."

"I don't know," Peterson said ruefully. "But I need to find him. He should be among the first to know what happened to Ms. Whitlow."

"Unless he already knows," Olivia murmured and stole a final glance at the tent on the beach.

Chapter 8

As the ocean so mysterious rolls toward
me closer and closer,
I too but signify at the utmost a little
wash'd-up drift,
A few sands and dead leaves to gather,
Gather, and merge myself as part of the
sands and drift.

—WALT WHITMAN

"Officer Peterson seems a little out of his depth," Olivia said on the way back to Lifesaver. "I hope he does ask you to help."

"Me too. As soon as the press gets hold of the news, Peterson will be pressured into solving this case quickly." Rawlings increased his pace. "Let's call the gang. They can come over for breakfast—or brunch—and we can put our heads together."

Olivia glanced at him. "You don't think Peterson will have cause to arrest Silas Black?"

"I don't," Rawlings said. "When I observed Mr. Black during yesterday's luncheon, he paid almost no attention to Ms. Whitlow. And after the Q&A session, Millay showed me a host of online news articles documenting Ms. Whitlow's jealous rages. I believe Ms. Whitlow committed these dramatic acts to get her boyfriend to notice her, but I doubt they worked. My impression is that Mr. Black didn't feel strongly about Ms. Whitlow one way or another. Perhaps she was an ornament, but he didn't value her."

"What if the only reason Silas and Leigh were together was because she had something on him?" Olivia said. "I overheard Leigh accuse Amy of having an affair with Silas. What if Silas actually *was* having an affair and he decided to kill Leigh to shut her up? The night Silas's house was vandalized, Harris told me that Silas has had multiple affairs. Of course, this is all based on things Harris has read online, but if it's true, then why has Silas continued to keep Leigh close? They're not married. Silas could have walked away at any time. So why hasn't he?"

Rawlings scratched his chin. "You have a point. But if Mr. Black drowned Ms. Whitlow, then why include the ringing bell? Why dress her like Theodosia Burr?" He tapped his temple. "Peterson should try to track down where the dress came from."

Olivia ascended the stairs to the Lifesaver's deck, reached for the sliding glass door, and stopped. "If Peterson doesn't get anything out of Silas, maybe we should talk to someone who's known him for a long time."

Rawlings understood at once. "Charles."

"I'll invite him over for a cup of coffee," Olivia said, opening the door for Haviland.

"Then I'd better take a shower." Rawlings looked down at his sweatshirt and jeans. "Your father will be polished and pressed, while I'm as rumpled as an old sheet."

Olivia got her phone and scrolled through her contact list until she reached the *W*s. She still didn't think of Charles Wade as her father. The father she'd grown up with had viewed his role with reluctance and resignation. Willie Wade hadn't shown an ounce of warmth toward Olivia, but he'd loved her mother and done his best to provide for them. Shaking her head, as though to dispel the ghost of Willie Wade, Olivia dialed the number.

Charles was delighted by Olivia's invitation and promised to arrive shortly. "I'm not far from you," he said. "Silas was able to get me a cottage on the South Beach. I believe you know my neighbor, Professor Billinger. Turns out, he and I are both night owls."

Olivia felt a prickle of unease. "Oh?"

"I introduced myself to him two nights ago when he was out on his deck with those pretty dogs of his. Last night, he left the dogs behind. He was wearing a backpack, so maybe he was on his way to see a lady friend." Charles paused, and Olivia could picture him shrugging. "Should I bring anything? Croissants?"

"Sure," Olivia said absently. "See you soon."

She stood still for a long moment, taking in what Charles had said.

A backpack? Containing what? And where was he going? Was he involved in Leigh's murder?

"No," she said aloud. "He doesn't know Leigh or Silas. He has nothing to gain from . . ." She trailed off, recalling the image of Emmett washing his hands behind the marina. She thought of the empty gas canister and of the possessive tone in Emmett's voice when he spoke of the island. He'd moved away, but he grew up in Riverport. He probably knew all the local ghost stories. "He knew them well enough to step in as a last-minute guest speaker."

"Are you talking to your coffee cup?" Rawlings asked as he entered the kitchen. His hair was wet and slightly tousled, and he smelled of soap and aftershave.

Olivia told him about her brief conversation with Charles.

Rawlings frowned. "Something isn't right about Emmett. I'm sorry, Olivia. I know he's your friend. But red flags are popping up all around the guy. I'll have to mention this to Peterson."

Nodding in unhappy agreement, Olivia trudged upstairs to shower and change.

By the time she returned, Charles was ensconced in a club chair in the sunroom. He had a coffee cup in one hand and was stroking Haviland's head with the other. Seeing Olivia, he smiled warmly. "Good morning. This is excellent coffee. Is it Kona?"

"Yes," Olivia said, accepting a cup from Rawlings.

"The chief asked me to share my thoughts on Professor Billinger." Charles arched his brows. "Why are you so interested in this guy?"

Rawlings shot Olivia a warning look, but he needn't have bothered. "You'll understand in a moment," Olivia said. She sank deeper into the chair, trying to appear as relaxed as possible.

Charles stopped petting Haviland and gestured at the plate of croissants on the table next to his chair. "Would you like one? They're quite good. Homemade by someone in that Marina Market."

Olivia hadn't had breakfast, so she accepted a croissant as well as a jar of raspberry jam. "Forget about Emmett Billinger for the moment. Tell me about Silas. Now that he's part of our grand reopening, I'd like to know what to expect. So would Millay. Will he be gracious about sharing the spotlight?"

"I may have called in a favor to get Silas to come, but that doesn't mean he won't work hard to sell his books, Millay's book, and anything else written by regional authors." Charles folded one leg over the other, resting his ankle on his knee, and rubbed at a scuff on his Italian loafer. "Silas's love for the North Carolina coast was the one thing that divided us in school. I didn't want people to know where I grew up. Most of the kids we met had beach houses where Silas and I lived. The fish they ate on vacation was caught by men like my dad. The T-shirts they bought were sold by people like Silas's parents. I avoided talking about my roots, while Silas bragged about his town and the area's history."

That's a point in his favor, Olivia thought.

"Have the two of you visited each other much since college?" she asked casually. "Has he met your family?"

"Only once," Charles said. "I traveled often on business, which made it easy for me to knock on his door every few years. He lives in California now, but he has more than one vacation home on the North Carolina coast. He just can't stay away."

Olivia spread jam on a piece of croissant. "What do you make of Leigh?"

Charles grimaced. "I don't understand why Silas stays with her. They met during our senior year in college, and she was just as insanely jealous then as she is now. I guess she has good reason. Silas has a wandering eye. And hands."

"I wonder why they never married," Rawlings mused.

Charles shrugged. "Silas isn't the marrying kind. He's always had a girl on the side. I've met several of them."

"It sounds like he deliberately tried to hurt Leigh." Olivia shook her head in disapproval. "Why do people linger in poisonous relationships?"

"Because there's comfort in the familiar," Charles replied softly and pointed at the ring finger of his left hand. His wedding band was gone. "My wife stayed married to me for years, partially out of habit and partially in hopes that I'd change. Perhaps Silas and Leigh have done the same."

Olivia knew that Charles's wife had threatened divorce, but he'd been wearing his wedding ring the last time he and Olivia had met to discuss plans for the bookstore. She reached over and squeezed his hand. "I'm sorry."

"So am I," he said with a sad smile. "Not because she left me, but because I failed as a husband. And as a father. If there's a bright side, the divorce has helped open lines of communication with my other children. It's been a painful process, but it's also been cathartic for all of us to say what we've held inside for years."

"Does this mean you plan to settle in Oyster Bay?" Olivia asked.

Now it was Charles's turn to take Olivia's hand. "For the immediate future, yes. I'm having the time of my life revitalizing this bookstore with you. I couldn't imagine anywhere I'd rather be."

The warmth of his big hand made Olivia feel unexpectedly vulnerable. She glanced at Rawlings, silently conveying the message that she didn't want to string Charles along anymore. Rawlings picked up on her wish.

"Charles, there's something you should know," Rawlings began.

"You have bad news," Charles said, releasing Olivia's hand. "No one ever starts a sentence like that when presenting a person with a winning lottery ticket."

At any other time, Rawlings would have smiled, but his face remained solemn. "I'm afraid my news isn't good. Olivia found Leigh Whitlow's body on the beach this morning. Silas's girlfriend is dead."

Charles gripped the arms of his chair in surprise. "What? How?"

"I believe someone held her underwater until she drowned," Rawlings answered. "The police are probably questioning Mr. Black as we speak. Do you know where he's staying?"

"I should say so. He's staying with me. He moved in after his place was vandalized." Charles drew his eyebrows together in confusion. "But I didn't see a single cop on my way here, and Silas left the house over an hour ago to meet with someone about his show."

Olivia stared at Charles. "Was Leigh staying with you too?"

"She was supposed to have been," Charles said. "But she and Silas had a nasty fight last night and she left, shouting curses over her shoulder."

Rawlings looked pensive. "I'll have to share this information with Officer Peterson. If you don't mind, Charles, we'll wait for him at your cottage. I should warn you now that the police will want to search the premises. They'll be especially interested in Silas's clothes. Whoever held Leigh under the water couldn't have done so without getting wet and partially covered in sand."

Charles nodded gravely and then turned to Olivia. "Does this have anything to do with your sudden interest in the professor's nighttime habits? Was he wandering the beach when Leigh was killed? Because that seems pretty coincidental to me."

The weight of his words sank into Olivia's heart like a stone. Emmett's behavior was most definitely odd.

Not odd. Suspicious, she thought glumly. Emmett might seem sincere, but his actions raised questions. Too many questions.

"Peterson has a ton of ground to cover in a very short amount of time," Rawlings said, getting to his feet. "Olivia, do you remember Emmett's address?"

She met his kind and sympathetic gaze. Though he didn't want Emmett to be involved because that outcome would cause Olivia distress, Rawlings was a cop through and through. He wouldn't consider withholding information from a fellow officer of the law, even to spare his wife's feelings.

"I don't remember the house number, but I remember the name," Olivia said. "Emmett's house is called Shifting Sands."

Charles carried his cup to the kitchen and waited for Olivia by the door.

"This is some predicament, eh?" he asked quietly. "One of our friends might have done something unforgettable." He held open the door. "Stuff like this isn't supposed to happen here. People are supposed to come to places like this to leave their troubles behind. People pay thousands of dollars to spend a few days on this island, hoping to slow down, to stop time from rushing by so quickly, to forget about their worries."

Haviland pushed past Olivia and jogged toward the golf carts. Leaping onto the closest one, he gazed at Olivia, his eyes shining with eagerness.

"People try to run from their problems," Olivia said to Charles as she joined Haviland in her golf cart. "And from their secrets. But they follow us. They follow us everywhere."

A shadow passed over Charles's face. He tried to turn away so Olivia wouldn't see it, but he wasn't fast enough.

"Care to ride with me, Chief?" he asked Rawlings, and the two men set off first.

It took fifteen minutes to reach Charles's rental cottage. A modest, three-bedroom house with a screened-in porch and a plaque bearing the name Sea Haven over the front door, the entire cottage was decorated in blue and white hues. Charles led them into the kitchen, pointed out the ground-floor master bedroom suite, where he slept, and then paused at the foot of the stairs. "There are two bedrooms on the second story. I don't know which one Silas chose, but I'd rather not be there while you rifle through his things."

Rawlings put a hand on Charles's shoulder. "I understand. Would you rather leave? I won't examine anything but the upstairs rooms and the laundry facilities. And the outside shower, if there is one."

"It's on the southeast corner of the house." Charles spread his hands. "I guess I can make myself useful by putting out some food for the cops. I'm no cook, but I can run to the market and get soda and sandwich fixings."

"That's a great idea. Very thoughtful," Rawlings said, clearly relieved that Charles wouldn't be hanging over his shoulder while he searched Silas's belongings.

The moment Charles was gone, Olivia and Rawlings headed upstairs. Haviland came along too. He stopped to sniff every other stair, his tail wagging with curiosity.

"It's convenient that you don't have to secure a warrant," Olivia said. "Is Peterson okay with us doing this?"

"He doesn't know," Rawlings said. "I plan to be very discreet, but I have to seize this opportunity. Try not to disturb anything. Just look for dirty clothing or suspicious items."

Olivia entered the bedroom on the right. Though the bed was made, the seashell quilt was wrinkled and partially obscured by a tote bag, a voluminous handbag, and a pile of fashion magazines. A pair of Louis Vuitton suitcases had been dumped on the braided rug, and a cosmetic case and hairbrush sat on top of the bureau. "This looks like Leigh's stuff," she said to Rawlings, who was close on her heels.

Rawlings poked his head into the bathroom. "No male grooming items. No razor, shaving cream, etcetera. Just a purple toothbrush and a bunch of hair products."

"I don't think Silas and Leigh planned on sharing a room," Olivia said.

Silas's things were in the second bedroom. His clothing was hung in the closet and folded neatly in the drawers. There was no sign of wet or sandy clothes or of anything else that obviously linked him to Leigh's murder.

The moment Peterson arrived, Rawlings pulled him aside to repeat what Charles had told him while Olivia took Haviland outside for a bathroom break.

Emmett's house was visible through a break in the foliage, but Olivia turned away from it. She knew that Peterson—possibly with Rawlings in tow—would soon be headed next door, and she didn't want to witness that scene.

Olivia went back inside the cottage, told Rawlings that she planned to join the rest of the Bayside Book Writers, and drove Haviland to the house where her friends were staying.

"Don't look!" Harris cried as she pulled into the parking nook. "My masterpiece isn't complete!"

Harris threw a piece of plastic sheeting over the front of his golf cart and stood, hands on hips, glaring at her. "Have you come to spy on me? Laurel and Millay said they'd try to recruit you."

"The golf cart parade may not occur at all." Olivia took Harris's arm. "There's been a murder."

Harris cocked his head as though he hadn't heard her correctly. "Say that again. Because I swear you mentioned murder."

"Let's go inside," Olivia said softly. "That way, I can talk to all of you at once."

Laurel and Millay were at the kitchen table, blowing up inflatable fish toys.

"Olivia! I'm so glad you're here!" Laurel gestured at an inflated angelfish. "We could really use an extra pair of lungs. We're running short on time." She pushed a flattened clown fish across the table.

Harris drew a finger across his neck. "Forget about the fish, ladies. The parade might not happen."

Millay stared at Olivia. "What's going on?"

"I found Leigh Whitlow's body on the beach this morning. Just after daybreak," Olivia said and went on to describe the scene.

While Millay and Harris absorbed the news, Laurel fired off a series of questions.

"I'll tell you what I know," Olivia said. "But not so you can whip up a story for the *Gazette*. We need to help the local cops. They've never had a murder on the island before."

"I can write about it later," Laurel promised. "Is Rawlings with the Riverport Police?"

"Yes. They're at Charles's rental cottage. Both Silas and Leigh were staying with him."

Olivia brought her friends up to speed. When she told them about Emmett, they frowned in unison.

"Why would the professor kill Leigh? Has he even met her before?" Harris asked.

"I don't know, but there are plenty of strange and surprising connections. Emmett used to teach Amy Holden. Now Amy works for Silas. Charles went to college with Silas. I don't like all these seemingly random coincidences. Neither does the chief."

With their golf cart decorations completely forgotten, Laurel, Millay, and Harris argued theories and raised more questions.

"Call Rawlings," Harris said when they'd run out of ideas. "Have him ask Peterson if the parade is still on."

Millay rolled her eyes. "Would you shut up about the parade, already?"

"Don't you see? If I win the contest, I'll have a reason to get close to Silas. It'll give me an excuse to watch him and Amy. Maybe chat her up a little." He looked at Olivia. "You'll have to do the same with the professor. You're friends. If the cops don't find out what he was doing walking the beach at night wearing a backpack, then you'll have to get the truth out of him."

Laurel touched Olivia's arm. "He's right. Emmett obviously likes you, so he's bound to be more open with you than with the police."

Olivia wanted to tell her friends that she didn't know Emmett the way she knew them. While she trusted the three people at the table with her life, she couldn't say the same about Emmett. However, the words stuck in her throat, so she called Rawlings instead. When he didn't pick up, she sent him a text.

A few seconds later, she received a short reply saying, *The parade is on*.

She read the text aloud.

Harris shoved his chair back from the table. "I need to get back to work! Olivia, can you give me a hand?"

When Olivia made to rise, Laurel pointed at the clown fish and whispered, "Traitor."

After a lunch of chicken salad sandwiches, which Laurel prepared and served on paper plates, Olivia drove to the marina to meet Rawlings.

"How did it go with Emmett?" she asked anxiously.

"Peterson didn't invite me to sit in on the interview. It was fairly short, and he didn't detain Professor Billinger. Mr. Black was located and is with Peterson now. The police have created temporary headquarters at the library."

Olivia was troubled by the fact that Rawlings was no longer using Emmett's first name. This meant Rawlings viewed Emmett as a suspect.

"Our friends think Emmett will be more forthcoming with me than with the police. They're full of all kinds of ideas, including the possibility that Leigh threatened Amy once too often and that Amy finally snapped."

"A plausible theory, except that Ms. Holden is much smaller and lighter than Ms. Whitlow. It's hard to picture her overpowering Ms. Whitlow and then dragging her body up the beach." Rawlings's expression turned thoughtful. "Then again, Ms. Holden could have had help."

"I wonder if Silas will be released in time to judge the golf carts," Olivia said, gazing down the road, where the parade was expected to appear any minute.

Rawlings jerked his head toward a raised platform where the judges sat. Marjorie Tucker, Vernon Sherrill, and the manager of the Marina Market occupied three of the four seats. The empty chair was presumably reserved for Silas.

As if thinking about the man conjured him from thin air, Silas suddenly materialized on the dock behind where Olivia and Rawlings were seated. Silas waved to Dirk, the young archaeologist, who stood at the wheel of a small motorboat. Dirk flashed a bright grin, saluted Silas, and put the boat in reverse.

The grassy area surrounding the docks was just as crowded as it had been for the arrival of the pirates, but the spectators were facing away from the water. No one but Olivia and Rawlings seemed to have noticed Silas's arrival.

As for Silas, he strode down the dock with a light step and a smile playing around the corners of his mouth.

"He's hardly the picture of a man in mourning," Olivia said to Rawlings.

Rawlings grunted. "If anything, he looks relieved. Lightened of a burden."

Before ascending the raised platform, Silas rearranged his face into a more sober expression. He responded to the words of comfort from all three judges with lugubrious nods and downcast eyes. Marjorie Tucker patted his arm and gestured at the empty chair. Silas sat with slumped shoulders and fixed his gaze on the empty road.

It wasn't long before the first carts came into view. The bystanders gave a rousing cheer.

The leading golf cart had been wrapped entirely in pink paper. A large pig face covered the hood and grill, and the driver was dressed as a piece of bacon. Following behind the pig was a haunted house complete with ghosts, spiderwebs, a vampire in the passenger seat, and a witch at the wheel. The next four carts had been decorated to resemble a Chinese dragon, a tugboat, a fire truck, and Cookie Monster. The group after that contained a puppy with a wagging tail, a pioneer wagon, a flamingo, a locomotive engine, and a whale. The whale's driver, who was surrounded by trash, was a Biblical Jonah.

"I see Millay and Laurel!" Rawlings pointed at a golf cart covered with blue paper, nets, and a dozen different kinds of inflatable fish. A purple octopus made of foam pool noodles held a sign reading, CATCH OF THE DAY.

"I like their fishermen's caps," Olivia said, smiling.

Rawlings grinned. "I can't wait to tell them how attractive they look with those pipes dangling from their mouths."

Millay and Laurel threw small bags of Swedish Fish to the children in the crowd and then drove on to the parking area.

The next cart looked like a car from *The Flintstones* cartoon. Wilma waved to the spectators while Betty pivoted in her seat to blow kisses at the driver of the cart behind them. That driver happened to be a bearded man in a Santa suit. His cart, which had been transformed into a sleigh complete with eight cardboard reindeer, was clearly a crowd favorite.

"That's going to be tough to beat," said Rawlings. "Where is Harris?"

"There." Olivia pointed at the approaching pirate ship.

Harris had covered the entire cart with cardboard, which he'd then painted to resemble wood. He'd also added portholes and cannon holes. The foam cannons held lit sparklers, and a Jolly Roger flew from pillowcase sails. Harris was in the driver's seat, dressed in full pirate regalia. When he approached the judge's platform, he shouted, "Ahoy, me hearties! Show me yer treasure or I'll blast ya to the briny deep!"

Several people standing along the road yelled in approval, but Harris was focused on the judges. "You've no pieces of eight for me, you curs? What a shame. See how I deal with lubbers such as yerselves." Harris stopped his cart in the middle of the road, opened a hatch on the side of his ship, and pushed a cannon through the aperture. A loud *pop!* echoed through the air, and a missile of glitter and confetti soared toward the judge's platform.

The bystanders whooped and applauded in approval. Harris gave a rakish bow and put his golf cart into drive again.

Olivia glanced at the remaining carts and said, "He has a good chance."

"It was clever of him to pick a pirate ship. Silas was definitely amused."

In the end, Harris was declared the winner. He shook hands with Silas, who quickly passed him off to Amy Holden. Amy pulled Harris aside while Silas focused on congratulating the second- and third-place winners.

While they waited for Harris, Olivia and Rawlings walked over to where Millay and Laurel stood by their golf cart.

"I think you should have placed based on your pipes alone," Rawlings told his friends.

"We had fun, and that's all that matters," Laurel said.

Millay glowered at her. "Speak for yourself. I like to win. And what are we going to do with all those inflatable fish?"

"Why don't you use them to decorate the bar?" Olivia teased.

Millay reached up to the roof of her golf cart, pulled a foam octopus leg free, and whacked Olivia on the rump with it.

The four friends were still laughing when Harris joined them.

"Well, Mr. Hollywood?" Millay slung the octopus leg over her shoulder. "Aren't you supposed to be hanging out with Silas?"

"I can't." Harris threw out his arms in a show of helplessness. "The guy just disappeared. Just like that!" Harris snapped his fingers. "Like a freaking ghost."

Chapter 9

*There is more treasure in books than in
all the pirate's loot on Treasure Island.*

—WALT DISNEY

Olivia looked at Rawlings. "What do we do now?"

"We split up," Rawlings said. "I'll go back to Charles's cottage and see if he can find out what happened during Officer Peterson's interview with Mr. Black."

Millay patted her messenger bag. "I'm coming with you. I need to plop down on a sofa for a few minutes and interact with my readers online."

"Don't you mean fans?" Harris asked.

"Seriously, I cannot use that word," Millay said, instantly embarrassed. "I'm a bartender, okay? Silas Black has fans. I have customers. Regulars. Men—and a handful of women—who drink too much, curse too loudly, and aren't overly concerned with personal hygiene."

Olivia smiled. "And yet, Fish Nets is more interesting on a Saturday night than any other Oyster Bay establishment."

Harris glanced over at the raised platform. "I'm going to hang around Amy. Maybe I can get her to have coffee with me. After all, how can she resist this face?" Harris winked at his friends. "Let's regroup at Lifesaver later. Text me if there's any news, and I'll do the same."

"Look at that swagger," Millay scoffed after Harris walked away. "See what you've done, Chief? Ever since you hired Harris, his head's swelled like our inflatable puffer fish." She gestured at the fish in question.

"No one can hold a candle to him when it comes to research," Rawlings said and then turned to Olivia. "Are you going to speak with Emmett?"

She shook her head. "Not right now. I need to figure out how to approach him first. My immediate plan is to track down the museum curator and see if he can elaborate on the Theodosia Burr legend."

"I'll join you," Laurel said. "I can pick up some goodies for the boys in the gift store."

Rawlings examined his watch. "As Harris said, we'll keep in touch by text message. Why don't we regroup at Lifesaver for cocktails around five? Hopefully, one or more of us will have discovered a useful clue by then."

"We'd better find something," Olivia said. "Peterson only had two suspects, and he hasn't made an arrest."

"Not yet," Rawlings said. "But my guess is that he's being very, very careful. This will be a high-profile case within the hour. The only reason the whole island isn't aware of the murder is because people were attending the golf cart parade. However, those with rental houses where Ms. Whitlow's body was found are bound to notice the tent erected on the beach any moment now. Soon, this place will be flooded with reporters, and their presence will make Peterson's job all the more difficult." He paused and gave Laurel an apologetic smile. "I'm not referring to you, of course."

Laurel gave her ponytail a tug. "Maybe you should. My editor will expect me to cover this story. I'm a journalist, and I'm right in the thick of things. I'll have to e-mail at least a teaser article tonight, though I promise not to write anything that would interfere with the investigation."

"I trust you," Rawlings said. "You've always shown excellent judgment."

Buoyed by Rawlings's compliment, Laurel practically skipped as she, Oliva, and Haviland struck out for the museum.

Haviland was also in excellent spirits. He pranced at Olivia's side, his gaze raking the ground in search of a stick or something else that might work in a game of catch.

"We'll play after our museum visit," Olivia assured him. "I bet there are wonderful sticks in the maritime forest."

"Just don't wander off the path," Laurel cautioned. "Jan Powell told us that the alligators are probably hibernating by now, but I paid close attention to her use of the word 'probably.'"

Olivia had nearly forgotten about Jan Powell. "Peterson should speak with Jan too. If someone wanted to threaten Silas Black, to get him to leave, then the head of the conservancy might be that person. How far would she go to protect the status quo, despite the sale of the land?"

"It's worth checking out," Laurel agreed. "Do you want me to send a text to Rawlings? I know you're not fond of texting while walking."

Olivia scowled. "No, I'm not. I can't seem to type and walk in a straight line."

By the time they reached the maritime museum, the text had been sent. However, it didn't look like they'd be gaining entrance to the museum. A CLOSED sign hung in the window.

Olivia stepped up to the door and peered inside. "The lights are on. And the woman I met the other day is standing in the threshold of the gift shop. I believe her name is Rosemary. She looks upset."

"Maybe she heard about the murder," Laurel said, removing her fisherman's hat and tossing it on the seat of the golf cart.

"Only one way to find out." Olivia knocked on the door.

Rosemary jumped in surprise and made a waving motion, indicating that Olivia should go away.

Olivia knocked again and gestured for Rosemary to come closer.

Reluctantly, she took out a pair of keys and turned the dead bolt. After another click, she opened the door a crack.

"I'm sorry, but we're—"

"Closed," Olivia said apologetically. "I don't mean to bother you, but when my friend saw the wonderful things I bought in the gift shop, she was dying to get several items as well. Is it possible for us to make a few purchases without entering the museum itself?"

Rosemary was clearly tempted. Having sat on several museum boards, Olivia knew that small museums relied heavily on donations as well as profits from their gift shops, and the maritime museum seemed in desperate need of funds.

"Christmas is right around the corner," Olivia added. "I'm sure I could find additional gifts for my niece and nephew. We'll be in and out in five minutes."

"All right," the woman capitulated. "But I'll have to lock the door behind you. We've had a theft."

Laurel's eyes widened dramatically. "That's terrible! Were you here when it took place?"

Rosemary shook her head. "No, it happened after hours. Mr. Sherrill reported the crime first thing this morning, but the police *just* showed up. Mr. Sherrill is livid, and with good reason."

They don't know that the cops are busy with a murder investigation, Olivia thought.

"What was stolen?" Laurel asked in a sympathetic voice. "Something valuable?"

"*All* of our artifacts have value," Rosemary said, ushering the women into the gift shop. Her stern face softened a little as she watched Haviland sit on his haunches next to Olivia's right leg. "We don't know what's missing yet," she continued. "Mr. Sherrill and I were trying to take an inventory when the police finally arrived. One item is definitely gone, though I don't know why anyone would steal such a thing."

Olivia and Laurel exchanged glances.

"Does your collection include antique clothing?" Olivia asked, handing Laurel a pirate costume kit.

Rosemary inhaled sharply. "What makes you say that?"

Olivia passed Laurel a second costume kit. Rosemary's eyes followed the movement and then returned to Olivia's face.

"Was it a dress?" Olivia asked quietly. "A white dress with an empire waist?"

Gasping, Rosemary retreated a step. "How could you know that? Unless . . ."

"We had nothing to do with the theft," Olivia hastily assured her. "But the dress is part of a bigger mystery. Can you please take us to Mr. Sherrill? I think he'll want to speak with us."

Laurel glanced down at the pirate costumes in her hands. "Um, should I buy these first?"

Rosemary quickly rang up Laurel's purchases and shoved them in a plastic bag. She then told Olivia and Laurel to follow her and marched through the first two exhibit spaces and through a door marked with a STAFF ONLY sign.

The curator was at the end of a narrow hallway, gesticulating wildly at a very young policeman.

"I'm trying to help you do your job. Amy Holden worked in this museum for three summers when she was a teenager. Don't you see what that means? She'd have known where every item in our collection was stored. She may still have a key to this room. We haven't changed the locks in this building since I've been the curator, and you said there was no sign of forced entry, right?"

The officer jotted something on his notepad, murmured something to Mr. Sherrill, and disappeared through the doorway behind him.

Rosemary cleared her throat and raised her hand in an awkward little wave. "Mr. Sherrill? I'm sorry to interrupt, but these women might know something about the theft."

"At this point, I'd accept help from SpongeBob SquarePants," Mr. Sherrill nearly shouted. "That cop is as green as a Girl Scout. I don't know why they sent him. This is a museum robbery, for Chrissakes!" He glared at Haviland. "And now there's a *dog* in my museum? What's next? A plague of locusts?"

Olivia failed to understand the connection between her well-mannered poodle and a Biblical plague, but decided to ignore the remark. "Could we sit down for a moment? In your office, perhaps? There's something I'd like to ask you as well."

Mr. Sherrill's red face took on a purplish hue. "If you know anything about what happened here, I highly suggest you tell me this minute."

"All right," Olivia said. "I believe it has to do with the legend of Theodosia Burr. My friend and I don't know much about her other than she was lost at sea off the North Carolina coast. Is she connected to Palmetto Island in any way?"

Olivia had correctly guessed that the curator wouldn't be able to resist demonstrating his knowledge, and he told them a story very similar to the one Emmett had shared during his lecture.

"Professor Billinger gave a talk on haunted landmarks two days ago." Olivia jumped in when Mr. Sherrill paused for breath. "He said that witnesses saw Theodosia's ghost on the beach. Do you know which beach? Or what she was wearing?"

"It's always been the South Beach, but . . ." He trailed off and all the color drained from his cheeks. "Our dress."

His eyes blazed. "If someone used it to play a prank, I will—"

"Was the dress from Theodosia's time?" Laurel asked.

The curator looked confused. "Yes. It was given to us by a collector of vintage and antique clothing. While we'd certainly love to own a genuine article belonging to Theodosia Burr Alston, we didn't. This dress was something she, and the ladies of her age and class, would have worn, however."

Olivia was puzzled. "Why give a dress to a maritime museum?"

"It was the donor's wish that we use her collection to create a tableau called The Widow's Walk," Mr. Sherrill explained hurriedly. "Her brother had been lost at sea during World War Two, and she wanted us to honor the women who'd watched and waited for their men to return safely from their sea voyages. We honor her request every Memorial Day weekend. Now, I've been exceedingly patient. Where is our dress?"

Olivia knew that word of Leigh's death would be all over the island soon, so she decided to be forthcoming with the curator in hopes that he'd have a theory concerning the killer's motive. "Somehow, your dress ended up being worn by Leigh Whitlow, Silas Black's girlfriend."

"What?" The word was an exhalation of shock and fury. Mr. Sherrill turned. "That useless cop can arrest—"

Reaching out to grab his arm, Olivia said, "Leigh's dead. I found her body on the beach this morning. She was wearing a white dress. Do you have a photograph of your dress so I can confirm that what I saw matches the one you're missing?"

Mr. Sherrill looked at Rosemary. "Would you?"

"Of course," she said and entered a room at the other end of the hallway.

While they waited, Mr. Sherrill seemed to sag.

"Why has this happened?" he whispered after a full minute of silence.

"I overheard you say that Amy Holden used to volunteer at the museum," Olivia said softly.

The name immediately brought the curator back to life. "*Amy!*" he cried angrily. "Once upon a time, that girl loved coastal history—more than any other young person I knew. But look what's become of her now. If Black told her to leap from a ship into shark-infested waters, I believe she'd do it. And if he wanted her to steal that dress, she'd do it! He asked to borrow some of our artifacts, and I turned him down. So what does he do? He sends his lackey to steal them!"

"Did Mr. Black ask to borrow the dress?"

Mr. Sherrill appeared to be in a daze, and Olivia had to repeat the question.

"What?" he said as though stunned. "No, he didn't. Here's Rosemary. Please look at the image. Is this the dress you saw?"

Rosemary proffered an eight-by-eleven color photograph of a mannequin wearing the white dress, white gloves, and a wig of dark curly hair. A white ribbon held the curls in place, and a strand of pearls encircled the mannequin's slender neck.

"That's it," Olivia said. "Do you have any idea why someone would give that dress to Leigh Whitlow before killing her on the South Beach?"

"What would be the point of making Black's woman look like Theodosia Burr Alston?" Mr. Sherrill demanded. "How was she killed? Is the dress . . . Was there blood?"

Rosemary let loose a whimper, and Haviland searched her face and then shifted uneasily on his feet. He'd sensed the sudden agitation in the air, and it had put him on the alert. He always stayed close to Olivia, but now he pressed his body against her leg, and she stroked his back, trying to convey that she was not in any danger.

"Mr. Sherrill," Olivia began.

The curator interrupted by saying, "Call me Vernon."

After introducing herself and Laurel, Olivia asked her

question. "Can you think of any connection between that dress and Leigh Whitlow?"

The curator ran his hands through his thinning hair. He was clearly on edge. "I don't understand any of this. As of now, I don't know what else was stolen, but the dress isn't as valuable as some of our other artifacts. Why would someone take it, give it to Black's lady friend, and then kill her in it?" His eyes locked on Olivia's. "You said you found her body on the beach. How did she die?"

"It looks like she was held under the water until she drowned," Laurel said and then quickly added, "Though the cause of death hasn't been confirmed. The medical examiner may come up with a completely different ruling."

Vernon glanced at Rosemary. "Most historians agree that Theodosia drowned. A few radicals believe that she survived and lived with the buccaneers who scuttled her ship, but that's very unlikely. I don't know when the legend of Theodosia's ghost began, but there are documents referring to a woman walking the South Beach in either a pale green or white dress. A woman who leaves no footprints in the sand. A woman who vanishes before sunrise."

"Leigh had long dark hair like Theodosia," Rosemary said, her eyes glimmering. The docent had obviously recovered from the initial shock. In fact, she leaned forward on the balls of her feet, eager to hear every lurid detail. Olivia guessed that Rosemary would spread the story of Leigh's murder like an August brush fire the second she had the chance.

"What about a bell?" Olivia looked at Rosemary. "Is that tied to the legend?"

Rosemary nodded. "People who have seen Theodosia's ghost also claim to have heard the ship's bell from *Patriot*, the schooner Theodosia was on when she disappeared, ringing out a death knell for its passengers and crew."

Laurel shuddered. "That's so eerie." She turned to Olivia. "And you heard that bell, didn't you?"

"I did," Olivia said.

Rosemary covered her mouth with her hand and stared at Vernon.

The curator wore a deep frown. "This makes no sense. Why re-create the ghost of Theodosia Burr Alston?"

"Who has access to your storage room, Mr. Sherrill?" Laurel asked.

"Rosemary, myself, and Larry, our other staff member. And as I told that bumbling officer, Larry took a leave of absence to care for his mother. She's having a hip replacement in Mississippi. Larry called yesterday to tell me he'd be back on Wednesday. My office phone has Caller ID and Larry phoned from his mother's house, so I know Larry didn't steal the dress." He sighed in exasperation. "And Rosemary was home with her family. I was also at home. We both live in Riverport."

Olivia hadn't suspected either of them for a moment, but Peterson would undoubtedly run down their alibis all the same.

Suddenly, Rosemary gasped. "The white deer! That's a North Carolina legend too!"

"Yes. And the burning boat in the harbor could represent the tale of the Burning Boat of Ocracoke," the curator said.

Olivia could see that while the museum workers were drawing the same conclusions as the Bayside Book Writers, they didn't seem to have any new information to add.

She studied Vernon. "You wrote a book on the island's history, right? Can you shed any light on these events?"

He shook his head in bewilderment. "My book is about facts, Ms. Limoges. It's about the men and women who shaped this island. To me, theirs is the story of most interest." He shrugged. "I can't imagine why anyone would bring the region's ghost stories to life. They're just legends, after all. To think that a young woman lost her life because of the tales we all grew up hearing is sickening. The person committing these acts is seriously disturbed."

Seeing that there was nothing else to be learned, Olivia asked Rosemary if she could purchase a copy of Vernon's book, and then she, Laurel, and Haviland left.

"That wasn't much help," Laurel mumbled unhappily.

"Other than it gives credit to the theory that Leigh was meant to remind people of Theodosia Burr. Can you text Harris and ask him to research both women? Maybe there's more to connect them other than a physical resemblance."

Laurel pointed at Olivia's golf cart. "I'll text, you drive."

"Go ahead and have a seat. I'll be back in a sec," Olivia said and strode into the Marina Market. She reemerged a few minutes later with a bag containing two pints of clam chowder and a pair of freshly baked rolls.

"Something smells good," Laurel said. "Are we having a midafternoon snack?"

"I bought apples for us, but the soup is for the Allens. While you text the chief and tell him about the robbery, I'll see if George Allen has anything to say about what's happened." Olivia started the golf cart and headed to the Allens' cottage.

She pulled to a stop and glanced over at Laurel. "You and Haviland had better wait here."

"That's fine. It gives me the chance to finish sending messages to the rest of the Bayside Book Writers. I just wish one of them would write back." She stared at her phone screen as though willing a message to come through. "I hope they're having better luck than we did."

"Me too." Olivia told Haviland to stay and picked up the bag containing the soup and rolls. Cradling it in her left arm, she used her right hand to gently knock on the Allens' door.

She waited, but no sounds came from within the small house. She knocked again, a little louder this time, and someone, probably Boyd, pulled back the living room curtain. Olivia saw a flash of a pale face and a dark eye before the curtain was replaced. A moment later, Boyd cracked the door. He stood in the opening, blocking Olivia's view of the interior.

"I'm sorry to disturb you," she said, taking in Boyd's haggard appearance. He looked like he hadn't slept in days. "I brought some soup for your father. I thought he might be tired after last night. There's plenty for you as well."

Boyd managed a wan smile. "That's mighty kind of you. Pop isn't feeling well today, but I'll be sure to let him know that you—"

"Tell her!" George called from somewhere inside the house. "Tell her how the island will punish those who try to change her!"

Olivia felt her pulse quicken. Did George know about Leigh's death? Had he seen or heard something? The only person who was overtly trying to change Palmetto Island was Silas Black. "Should I come inside so he doesn't have to shout?"

Looking a little shamefaced, Boyd shook his head. "You'd better not. He'll get even more wound up. He really needs to sleep. It's kind of you to think of us. It's been—"

"Tell her to mind the warnings!" George shouted hoarsely. "To not get mixed up with those other outsiders!"

Boyd reached for the bag containing the hot soup, and Olivia reluctantly gave it to him. "Are you feeling all right, Mr. Allen?"

"I'm fine!" Boyd snapped and then held up his hand in an apologetic gesture. "I get headaches sometimes, but not today. Thanks again." And with that, he shut the door in Olivia's face.

"That didn't look too hospitable from where I'm sitting," Laurel said when Olivia got back in the golf cart.

Olivia glanced at the cottage. Unlike the other houses on the island, it bore no name plaque. It was a real home inhabited by the island's oldest resident. It wasn't a rental house that saw a steady stream of strangers during the high season and then stood empty for the winter. Like the Allens, the nameless cottage had borne witness to many changes. "Boyd said that his father isn't well. George was shouting from inside the house. Something about how the island will punish people who try to change her."

"It sounds like he knows something!" Laurel cried, causing Haviland to stand up and bark.

Olivia rubbed her poodle behind the ears. "Either that, or he's a very old man who's not himself due to sleep deprivation."

Laurel blew out a puff of air. "After I gave birth to the twins, I experienced that phenomenon myself. You truly feel like you're losing your mind. I was so messed up from consistent lack of sleep that I put a dirty diaper in the produce drawer of our fridge. I noticed it two days later when I opened the drawer to get a head of lettuce. Needless to say, we didn't have salad for dinner that night."

Olivia laughed and drove away.

"It's funny now, but I really didn't feel like myself," Laurel went on in a far more solemn tone. "Many parents who've accidentally injured or killed their infants were suffering from serious sleep deprivation. It turns you into someone else. Someone with fog in the brain. Someone who's slightly insane."

"Are you saying that George Allen is crazy?"

Laurel shrugged. "I don't know what I'm saying, but what if last night wasn't his first night without rest? What if he's been sleep-deprived for a long time and acted on his belief that the person trying to change the island deserves punishment?"

"He's in his nineties," Olivia said, feeling instantly defensive of George Allen. "Can you picture him holding Leigh's head under and then dragging her up the beach?"

"No, but Boyd could have helped."

"That means Boyd also shot the deer, burned the boat,

and flashed the light to misdirect the archaeologist," Olivia said dubiously. "It also means that he broke into the museum, stole the dress, and somehow convinced Leigh to put it on and follow the sound of the ship's bell."

Laurel threw out her hands. "Okay, so it's really unlikely. I'm considering every possibility."

Olivia nodded. "I do think the Allens know something. Boyd was acting very cagey, and George warned me not to get mixed up with the rest of the outsiders, which was strange, seeing as I'm an outsider too."

"Maybe not to him. You showed up at his house the other day bearing food. You listened to his stories and treated him with respect," Laurel said. "He might view you as an ally. As someone who understands what matters to him."

Olivia recalled telling George about the lighthouse keeper she'd known as a girl and how pleased George had been to hear her speak of her hometown and its people. "Perhaps." She gestured at Laurel's phone. "Have you heard from the others yet?"

"Harris was having coffee with Amy at Land End Lodge and only had time to send a quick text saying that they were still talking. I haven't heard a peep from the chief or Millay."

"I guess I'll drop you at your golf cart," Olivia said. "From there, we can head back to Lifesaver and wait for the others."

"Hold on." Laurel raised a finger. "I'm getting a text from Millay. She writes that—oh no!" She clamped her mouth shut and shook her head from side to side.

Olivia hit the brakes and instinctively pressed her hand against Haviland's side. "What is it?"

"Peterson's made an arrest," Laurel said, her eyes filled with sadness. "It's the professor, Olivia. The police have taken Emmett Billinger into custody."

Chapter 10

All writing problems are psychological problems.

—ERICA JONG

Olivia gestured for the phone. "Let me see that."

She read Millay's text and then called her. When Millay answered, Olivia's mouth was so dry that it took her a moment to speak.

"Tell me everything," Olivia demanded without preamble.

"The chief just heard a few minutes ago, but the cops took the professor across the river just after the golf cart parade started. Apparently, Peterson learned something during his interview with Silas that made him believe the professor was his man."

It can't be true, Olivia thought. To Millay, she said, "Did you speak with Charles?"

"Yeah. He's been trying to track down Silas all afternoon to find out what he told Peterson, but Silas isn't returning his calls." Millay paused. "I'm sorry to give you such crap news. Do you want to talk to the chief?"

"Yes," Olivia said, wishing she were with Rawlings right now.

There was a rustle as Millay passed the phone to the chief. "Olivia." His voice was tender. A breath of comfort. "Just because Professor Billinger has been arrested doesn't mean that he's guilty."

"Why would Emmett murder Leigh?" Olivia yelled. She wanted to lash out at someone. Anyone. "He doesn't even know her!"

"That may be irrelevant," Rawlings said quietly. "The fact that she resembled Theodosia Burr might have been all that mattered. When I spoke with one of Peterson's officers, I was told that the professor had wet, sand-covered clothes at the bottom of his washing machine. There was a book about Theodosia Burr on his nightstand. He was out last night for more than two hours. He knows all the ghost stories the crimes have been based on. It doesn't look good, Olivia."

Abruptly ending the call, Olivia got out of the golf cart and began to pace around the grass. She wanted to kick something but had to settle for grabbing a small stick and tossing it as far as she could into the underbrush.

With a yip of delight, Haviland chased after it. Olivia hurled the stick three times in a row, feeling Laurel's eyes on her back the whole time.

Finally, Olivia turned to face her friend. "I have to see Emmett. Would you take Haviland to Rawlings? I'm going to catch the next ferry."

Laurel frowned. "You don't think he's guilty, do you?"

"I don't *want* him to be guilty," Olivia said. "But if it's true, then I need him to explain this madness to me." She glanced at the ground where Haviland had dropped the stick. "I need to know why he did these things."

"And if he convinces you that he's innocent? What will you do next?"

"I'll do whatever I can to help him. He's my friend, Laurel. Unless he proves to be unworthy of my loyalty, he has it." She squatted, pressing her face against Haviland's shoulder. After murmuring softly to him, she told him to jump into Laurel's golf cart. Laurel had just put the key in the ignition when the ferry whistle blew.

Without another word, Olivia raced toward the docks.

Olivia was known by most of the Oyster Bay police force and had always been treated with courtesy and respect whenever she appeared at the station. Here, at the Riverport Police Department, she was a stranger. She couldn't call in favors or make special requests. She was a civilian and an out-of-towner to boot.

The front desk clerk was clearly on edge. A middle-aged woman with glasses and brown hair styled into a severe bob, she juggled phone calls on multiple lines. She briefly spoke to each caller before moving on to the next. Olivia guessed that most of the calls were from members of the press. She knew that the media had gotten wind of the murder because she'd seen half a dozen reporters and cameramen on the ferry landing.

"I'd like to speak with Emmett Billinger," Olivia said.

"Are you his attorney?" the desk clerk asked, giving Olivia the once-over.

Olivia considered lying, but decided against it. "No, but I can contact an attorney on his behalf if he hasn't done so already. I'd just like five minutes with him."

The clerk shook her head. "Sorry, but that's not going to happen."

Olivia put a business card on the desk. "If Professor Billinger has yet to make his one phone call, could you please give this to him? He has two dogs, and with his being in custody, there's no one to take care of them. They're back at his house on Palmetto Island."

The clerk didn't seem interested in Emmett's dogs. "Animal Control will get them. As for this?" She tapped Olivia's card, and then she gestured at the plastic chairs lining the wall. "You can wait if you want, but I'm not making any promises."

Thwarted, Olivia left the station and walked to the coffee shop she and Rawlings had passed on their way to the ferry docks. There were only two customers inside River Brew, and the bored baristas were more than happy to take Olivia's order.

"And you'll deliver those to the police station?" she asked while handing the cashier her credit card. "Along with a selection of sandwiches and pastries?"

"Give us fifteen minutes and we'll get it done," the cashier assured her.

Olivia returned to the police station and took a seat in a plastic chair. The desk clerk had the phone pressed to her ear and her gaze fixed on her message pad. She didn't glance up until two servers from River Brew placed three trays of coffee on the counter.

Putting her hand over the phone's mouthpiece, the desk clerk pointed at the coffee. "What's this?"

"A cure for the midafternoon blues," said one of the servers. "We have food too. Where do you want it? There's enough for the whole station."

The clerk reached for a coffee cup and then hesitated. "Who ordered this?"

The server waved at Olivia. "The lady did. She said you guys were probably in for a long day. Maybe a long night too. We've got coffee, scones, cinnamon rolls, and a bunch of sandwiches. She pretty much cleaned us out. Enjoy!"

The servers thanked Olivia for adding such a generous tip to her credit card receipt and left.

Olivia stared at the opposite wall as though riveted by the public safety announcements. She didn't want to look at the desk clerk for fear that her attempt to get on the woman's good side had completely backfired.

She sat for several minutes, listening to the clerk answer

a dozen phone calls, until a stout, gray-haired police officer entered the lobby from a hallway to Olivia's right.

"You asked to see Mr. Billinger?" he asked brusquely.

Olivia stood up. "Yes. I'm a friend of the professor's."

"And I understand that you're responsible for our River Brew delivery?"

Olivia nodded.

"Ed Fields." The officer held out his hand. "I got a call about you. Officer Peterson told me that Chief Rawlings of the Oyster Bay PD helped out with our investigation. I've met the chief before. Conferences, mostly. He's a good egg. It's because of him, not the coffee, that I'll let you have five minutes with our suspect." He indicated the hallway. "If you'll follow me, I'll take you back."

Olivia indicated the coffee cup Fields was holding. "May I give the professor something to drink?"

Fields paused. "We offered him soda, coffee, and water. He won't take anything."

"He's probably in shock," Olivia said. "He might not want it, but he needs it."

"Be my guest," Fields said and led her into a small kitchen, where five men in uniform were loading paper plates with food.

Afterward, Olivia carried coffee and a ham and cheese sandwich into an interview room and then waited for Emmett to be brought in.

He entered, rumpled and glassy-eyed. He didn't speak. He merely dropped into the chair across the table from Olivia and stared at his cuffed wrists. His shoulders were slumped and he looked utterly defeated.

"Emmett, we don't have much time," Olivia said softly. She slid the coffee cup in front of him and then shot Fields a look of silent appeal. With a grunt, the policeman unlocked the cuffs and hung them from his utility belt.

"Drink this," Olivia gently ordered. When Emmett made

no move to comply, Olivia said, "Drink this, or I'll walk out of here right now."

Emmett blinked and picked up the coffee cup. He took several sips and then cradled the cup in his hands.

"Eat a few bites of this sandwich too." Olivia pushed the plate toward him and waited for him to reach for the sandwich. "Have you called a lawyer yet?"

Chewing mechanically, Emmett shook his head.

"Do you want me to call one for you?"

When Emmett didn't answer, Olivia sighed in frustration. The seconds were ticking by, and she was getting nowhere. "Tell me what to do about Caesar and Calpurnia," she said.

This finally elicited a reaction from Emmett. "They'll need to be walked soon. And fed their dinner. What will happen to them if . . ." He swallowed hard. "Will you take care of them, Olivia?"

Olivia didn't want to mention Animal Control. "Does Peterson have the keys to your house?"

"Yes, but I keep a spare in the duck decoy by the back door for emergencies too." Emmett quickly explained where he kept the greyhounds' food, toys, and treats. "They don't like to be left alone for long. When I'm teaching, a dog walker visits them twice a day. But I'm always there at night. I even let them sleep in my bed. What will happen—"

"I'll see to them," Olivia interrupted. "But you have to do something for me."

Emmett nodded fervently.

"I need to know, Emmett. Did you do these things? Did you shoot that deer? Burn the dinghy?" Her eyes bored into Emmett's. "Did you drown Leigh Whitlow?"

Emmett was shaking his head before Olivia could even finish. "No," he whispered forcefully. "God, no! None of it—it wasn't me!"

"What were you doing on the beach last night?"

"Just looking for inspiration." Emmett spread his hands.

"You'll understand this better than any of *them*." He jerked his head toward Fields. "I've had a major case of writer's block, and I wanted to walk when no one else was around so I could imagine what it was like to live in a different time." He picked up a piece of crust and rubbed it between his fingers. "I'm writing about a period in history that predates the discovery of electricity. The world was much darker then. One might see an occasional flickering candle through a window, but for the most part, the nights were black and silent."

Olivia made a hurry-up gesture. "Go on."

"So I put a bottle of wine, a notebook, and a blanket in my backpack and headed out. I'm often awake late at night. I do some of my best thinking then."

"What are you writing?"

Emmett hesitated before answering. "Historical fiction. A novel about a wealthy North Carolinian merchant. A man with a complex moral code. Devoted family man. Slave owner. A character that readers will both love and hate. I've been working on this thing for two years. It's a far cry from my academic material, and it's hard as hell to write."

"If everything you just told me is true, then why were you arrested?"

There was a shift in the air, and the light that had appeared in Emmett's eyes when he'd spoken of his book dimmed. "They found something of mine near the crime scene, though I have no idea how it got there. I also had a book about Theodosia Burr on my nightstand." He spoke more and more rapidly, desperate to explain himself. "Not only does she fit the time period of my novel, but ever since I was asked to do the talk on haunted landmarks, I've been wanting to read up on her. I thought this was a good time to do it."

Emmett's version of events was so far-fetched that Olivia wasn't surprised that Peterson had brought him in.

"What was found near the crime scene?"

"A bottle opener with an embossed greyhound on the

handle. I have a bunch of them because my aunt gives me one every Christmas." He tossed the crust back on the plate. "I don't remember dropping it. I don't even remember putting it in my backpack. The bottle I had with me was already open. I was planning to finish it off."

Olivia wondered what kind of evidence she could possibly find to corroborate Emmett's story. "Did you write anything in your notebook to prove that you'd been working on ideas for your novel in the middle of the night?"

A small groan escaped from between Emmett's lips. "It'll only damn me more. The man I'm basing my book on was real. His daughter was found drowned in the Cape Fear River, which ran behind their plantation house. Years after her death, the servants claimed to see the young woman's ghost. I was thinking of adding her death, in the form of a murder, to my next chapter. That's what my notes are about."

No one will believe this, Olivia thought miserably. And yet she did.

"You have one more minute," Fields said from where he stood near the door.

Olivia felt panic well up inside her. "Did you know Leigh Whitlow personally?"

"I had never laid eyes on her before this weekend," Emmett said. His voice quavered with desperation. "I swear it."

"You were on South Beach during the time period she was killed. You were drinking. You'd taken notes about a woman's death by drowning. You were reading about Theodosia Burr. And you didn't bring your dogs." This was the detail Olivia had the hardest time accepting. "Why didn't you bring the dogs?"

"I didn't want them to get wet before jumping into bed with me," Emmett said. "I dote on them, but I prefer not to sleep on damp sheets or to wake up with sand in my hair."

Fields removed the cuffs from his belt and advanced

toward Emmett. "Time's up. Place your wrists together, please."

"Get a lawyer," Olivia said without breaking eye contact with Emmett. "I believe you. Okay? I believe you, and I'll do anything I can to help you."

A glint of hope appeared in Emmett's eyes. "You will?"

"You've helped me in the past," Olivia reminded him. "And you and I are friends. This is what friends do for each other."

Fields put a hand under Emmett's right arm and coaxed him to his feet.

"Thank you for taking care of Calpurnia and Caesar. They're my family. Knowing they're with you will keep me going," Emmett said before he was led from the room.

Olivia stayed where she was until another policeman arrived and escorted her back to the lobby.

Thank you, Olivia mouthed to the desk clerk.

The clerk gave her a small, sympathetic nod.

Olivia didn't want her sympathy. The clerk's expression said that she felt sorry for Olivia for being friends with a killer. It was a look that spoke of hopelessness and wasted effort.

Bursting through the doorway and out into the waning afternoon, Olivia began to run. She didn't stop until she reached the ferry ticket office. After boarding the boat, she made her way toward the bow. She stared across the river as the ferry headed east and waited for Palmetto Island to come into view.

"I'm coming for you," she whispered into the wind. She wished the real murderer could hear the determination in her voice.

Olivia watched a pelican dive-bomb into the water, and felt a deep satisfaction when the bird rose up again with a fish trapped in its beak. The fish had time to wriggle once—a flash of silver in a black maw—before disappearing down the pelican's throat.

Olivia drove straight to Emmett's house. Ignoring the yellow seal placed across the front door to warn trespassers against unauthorized entry, Olivia found the spare key in the duck decoy by the back door and entered Shifting Sands by the rear entrance. The moment she was inside, she called Caesar and Calpurnia.

There was no response. No barking. No clicking of nails on hardwood. The house was empty.

Olivia took out her phone, which she'd turned off at the police station, and noticed the string of text messages and missed calls. She dialed Rawlings's number.

Rawlings didn't bother saying hello. "Where are you?"

"I'm back on the island," she said. "Emmett asked me to look after his dogs. Please tell me they weren't taken to the county shelter."

"Your father has them." Rawlings was angry. "Damn it, Olivia. I've been trying to reach you for the past two hours. We all have."

Olivia glanced around Emmett's living room. "He didn't do it, Sawyer. Give me five minutes. After that, I'll meet you and explain everything."

"Olivia—" The note of reproach in his voice was unmistakable, and Olivia had a bad feeling that he knew exactly where she was.

"Please, this is important," she said. "Just tell the others that we'll be spending most of the cocktail hour coming up with a game plan."

Rawlings grunted. "Five minutes, Olivia, and don't take anything from the professor's house. You can't help him if you're in a holding cell."

"I won't," Olivia said and hung up.

She went straight to Emmett's bedroom to see if the book on Theodosia Burr was still on his nightstand. It wasn't, and Olivia assumed the police had bagged it as evidence. What remained, however, were two nonfiction books about a nineteenth-century North Carolina merchant. Flipping through the hardbacks, Olivia spotted photographs of a plantation house overlooking the Cape Fear River. Emmett had also marked the pages detailing the drowning death of the merchant's daughter with sticky notes. On one of the notes he'd written: *Add death to chapter 10. Murder by slave? Servant? Jilted lover?*

Olivia sank down on the bed. She hadn't realized until this moment that a small part of her had doubted Emmett. She'd wanted to believe him, but she'd been deceived by people she cared about before. She also knew that Emmett's story could be sprinkled with just enough truth to throw her off balance. And there was his bottle opener to consider as well. If Emmett hadn't dropped it at the scene, then how had it gotten there?

"That's almost as perplexing as the idea of your gaining access to the museum," she said to the empty room. "How could you possibly have gotten inside and stolen that antique dress?"

Amy.

The name surfaced, unbidden, in Olivia's mind.

She headed for the door. She needed to be with Rawlings and her friends. She needed to tell them everything so they could help her sort her addled thoughts and make sense of her contradictory emotions.

Moving past the kitchen, she caught sight of the empty food bowls on the floor. She paused just long enough to wonder what would become of Emmett's greyhounds should he be denied bail.

But Olivia already knew the answer to that question. She would keep the dogs until Emmett was free to reclaim them.

If *he's set free*, the niggling voice inside her head whispered.

Olivia hurried back to Lifesaver. When she entered the house, Haviland was waiting for her on the other side of the door. He rushed forward, his tail wagging with happiness at the sight of her, and pressed his nose against her hip. It was his canine version of a kiss hello. Olivia put her arms around his neck and held him while listening to the familiar sound of the members of the Bayside Book Writers engaged in animated discussion.

"Home," she whispered into Haviland's ear and then walked into the living room.

Olivia refused to tell her friends what had happened at the station until Rawlings explained how Charles had ended up with Emmett's greyhounds.

Rawlings described how Olivia's father had argued with the officers in charge of securing Emmett's house until they finally relented and granted him custody of the dogs. Charles had even thought to take their food and leashes, as well as a box of dog waste bags, before the officers locked and sealed the house.

Olivia felt a surge of affection for Charles. It was hard to imagine such a fastidious person dealing with dog hair, wet paw prints, or kibble crumbs. Olivia sensed that he'd taken the dogs for her sake and was deeply moved by the gesture.

It took two cocktails for Olivia to describe her visit with Emmett. When she was done, Millay said, "Whoa. That story is almost too crazy to be made up."

Harris studied Olivia. "Do you believe the professor?"

"I want to," Olivia said. "The evidence seems pretty circumstantial to me, so unless the cops find Emmett's prints on Leigh's body—"

"They won't," Rawlings said. "Sand and salt water make

collecting evidence nearly impossible. And though the bruising on the neck was likely created by a man's fingers, I doubt even the state forensics lab can match the marks to a specific individual. Even if they could, it would take a week, or weeks, before the tests were complete. So unless the ME finds traces of Leigh's DNA under Emmett's nails or somewhere in his house, Peterson may not have enough to hold him."

Laurel raised her index finger. "If they can tie him to the museum break-in, he won't be going anywhere. Sorry, Olivia. I'm just playing devil's advocate."

Olivia looked at Rawlings. "The curator was quick to name Amy Holden as the likely culprit. Do you know if the police questioned her?"

"I was with her when the cops showed up at Land End Lodge," Harris said. "Our food had just arrived too. It was such a bummer. I could hardly stuff my face while Amy was being interrogated."

Millay poked him in the ribs. "You're such a gentleman."

"I am. After all, there's no such thing as a delicious *cold* platter of calamari. The whole thing went to waste."

"What questions did Amy answer?" Olivia asked impatiently.

Harris shrugged. "Despite my position with the Oyster Bay Police Department, I wasn't exactly given the same level of respect as the chief. The cops took Amy to a separate room, while I was left with the calamari. When Amy returned to the table, she didn't want to talk. In fact, she just took off."

"Seeing as the cops didn't arrest her, Amy must have convinced them that she wasn't the thief," Millay said.

Rawlings picked up the notebook he'd been using to record plot ideas during the festival and flipped to a blank page. "There was no sign of forced entry at the museum, correct?"

"That's what Vernon Sherrill said. Both he and Rosemary,

the docent, were positive that the robbery was committed by someone familiar with the museum's inventory."

"Are there other staff members?" Rawlings asked.

"The third employee is caring for his mother following her hip replacement surgery," Olivia said. "He phoned Mr. Sherrill from his mother's house in Mississippi, so he's in the clear."

Rawlings scrawled something in his notebook and then stared at the page. Olivia didn't want to disrupt his thoughts, but she was eager to hear what the rest of the Bayside Book Writers had learned while she was in Riverport.

"What did you and Amy talk about before you were interrupted?" she asked Harris.

Harris took a quick sip of beer. "She didn't say so outright, but she definitely has a thing for her boss. She didn't bother to hide her dislike for Leigh either. She said that Leigh never gave Silas any space and that she couldn't understand why Silas hadn't dumped the 'albatross' years ago."

"I've heard the same sentiment from several people, Charles included," Olivia said. "And Silas? Why isn't *he* a suspect?"

"According to your father, Mr. Black was able to supply a credible alibi for the time period in which Ms. Whitlow was murdered," Rawlings said.

Olivia held out her hands. "Wait. Wasn't *Charles* his alibi? Silas was staying at his house. And if Charles was awake late enough to see Emmett leave on his late-night walk, then wouldn't Charles have been the one to confirm Silas's whereabouts?"

"No, because Silas wasn't there. He wasn't in the house at all," Rawlings said. "Your father didn't mention this to us because he felt the matter was private—that it was between Mr. Black and the authorities."

Staring at Rawlings in confusion, Olivia asked, "Where *was* Silas?"

"With Amy." Millay smirked. "After Silas and Leigh had

their little spat, Leigh stormed out and Silas sought consolation in Amy's arms."

"Or so she says," Olivia muttered. "What if Amy is just covering for him? She's obviously smitten with him. Not only that, but he's also her employer. She might be afraid *not* to lie on his behalf."

Rawlings tapped the point of his pen against his notebook. "I agree that it's a weak alibi. I've shared my opinion on the subject with Officer Peterson, but I fear that he may be starstruck. Officer Peterson is far too impressed by Mr. Black's fame and wealth. I believe it's clouded his judgment."

"In that case, *we* need to discover the truth!" Olivia hated the shrill note in her voice but did nothing to suppress it. "If Emmett is innocent, then we must secure his freedom. And if Silas is guilty—"

"Then we need your father's help," Rawlings said softly. "He tried to reach Mr. Black all afternoon but was unsuccessful." He looked at his watch. "The closing banquet starts in an hour. That doesn't give us much time to get ready."

Olivia downed the last of her Chivas Regal and got to her feet. "You're right. We'd better move fast. We only have tonight to catch a killer."

Chapter 11

*Without wearing any mask we are
conscious of, we have a special face
for each friend.*

—OLIVER WENDELL HOLMES

Rawlings whistled when Olivia reached the bottom of the stairs. She wore a floor-length dress with a fitted white halter top and a flowing black skirt. She carried a red beaded clutch and wore bold red lipstick. The festival program had called for the attendees to come to the closing banquet "dressed to kill," in black or white cocktail attire with "a splatter" of red.

"You're stunning," Rawlings said.

She smiled at him. "So are you. Seeing you in your tux makes me think of our wedding." She crossed the room and then turned, displaying her bare back.

Rawlings reached for the zipper pull and slowly closed her dress. The tips of his fingers lingered on the nape of her neck. He traced infinity symbols across her smooth skin, raising gooseflesh along her arms and shoulders. "This vacation wasn't what I'd imagined it would be. I wanted to collect more moments of happiness," he whispered into her hair.

Olivia pivoted so that she and Rawlings stood face-to-face.

"We're not like those couples in the getaway brochures. Some people attract darkness. I know that sounds melodramatic, but I believe that all five of us are such people. That's probably why we gravitated toward one another in the first place. Joining the Bayside Book Writers changed my life. And falling for you made me realize that we can handle the darkness as long as we're together."

Rawlings cupped her cheeks in his hands and then pulled her in for a kiss. After releasing her, he said, "We should be eating, drinking, and dancing. We should be thinking about our writing projects. Instead, we're forming a hunting party." He stepped back to admire Olivia once more. "Or a very well-dressed war party."

Olivia grinned. She was straightening the folds of the red handkerchief peeking from his breast pocket when the doorbell rang.

"The rest of the warriors have arrived," she said and headed for the kitchen.

Haviland bounced in excitement as Harris, Millay, and Laurel entered the house.

"We were just here, you silly boy." Laurel gave Haviland's head a fond scratch and then stared at Olivia. "You're gorgeous. What I'd give to be that tall and slender."

Millay responded to Laurel's remark with a dismissive wave. "We have different weapons in our arsenal, lady. You're the only woman I know who could pull off an all-white pantsuit without channeling Don Johnson in *Miami Vice*."

"Pantsuits are hot," Harris agreed. "Especially with the red pumps. You should snap a selfie and send it to your husband."

"Who says I haven't already?" Laurel replied with an enigmatic smile.

Olivia complimented Millay on her short, formfitting, black-and-white silhouette dress. She'd traded her boots for a pair of black stilettos with silver tips and dyed a stripe of her dark hair bright red. Any other woman would have looked trashy in such an outfit, but Millay managed to make it look chic.

"And you," Olivia said to Harris. "For years I saw you as a grown-up version of Peter Pan. But tonight, you're a ginger-haired James Bond."

Preening, Harris smoothed his white tux jacket. "The red bow tie isn't too much?"

Laurel shook her head. "Bow ties are sexy. You could be the next Doctor Who. They need a ginger Doctor Who. Like pantsuits, gingers are in."

Millay rolled her eyes. "All right, I think we've stroked one another's egos enough. Can we go now?"

Rawlings offered her his arm. "Permit me to escort you to your golf cart."

Feigning annoyance, Millay took his arm. The five friends said good-bye to Haviland and stepped into the chilly night.

Olivia was glad she'd had the foresight to pack a long coat and wasted no time putting in on. Millay pulled a red pashmina from her handbag and grudgingly allowed Rawlings to drape it over her shoulders. She then started up her golf cart and drove off, the ends of her pashmina trailing behind her like ribbons on a little girl's braids. Harris and Laurel were in the backseat, their white jackets glowing in the moonlight. Rawlings and Olivia followed in their own cart.

"I still find it hard to believe that tonight's banquet wasn't canceled. Tell me again what the lodge manager said when you called," Olivia said as the sign for Land End Lodge came into view. A cluster of reporters and cameramen waited on the main road, held at bay by a line of sawhorses and lodge employees wearing reflective vests. They shouted at the attendees, who were momentarily blinded by camera flashes.

"Just that Mr. Black insisted that the show must go on." Rawlings pulled into the parking lot and brought the cart to a halt. "Mr. Black is either very resilient, or he doesn't care that the woman he's been with since college is dead."

Olivia frowned. "You saw his face right before the golf cart parade started. He was relieved, if not downright happy. His only challenge will be playing the part of the grieving lover."

Together, the Bayside Book Writers entered the lodge.

In the dining room, all traces of the autumnal theme were gone. The tables were now covered with black cloths, and red napkin fans sat on white plates. The centerpieces were hollowed plastic skulls filled with purple calla lilies, dark red roses, and Spanish moss.

"It's surreal to see the crime-themed décor after what happened to Leigh Whitlow," Millay said as the group located their table. "Normally, I'd love this stuff, but it's kind of creepy to have a skull staring at you while you eat, considering there's been a murder." She picked up a place card. "Someone's crashing our party."

Laurel examined the card. "Charles Wade? No offense, Olivia, but he might put a damper on our plans."

Rawlings took the card from Millay's hand and put it back on the table. "I asked Charles to join us. He's our only connection to Mr. Black. We need him."

"Maybe we should get the two of them drunk," Harris suggested. "It's a cash bar, but I'm willing to blow some of my hard-earned money if there's a chance that Charles and Black will talk."

Olivia looked at Harris. "You think Charles is hiding something too?"

"I do," Harris admitted sheepishly. "He and Silas have been friends for a long time. You can't maintain a friendship like that without having each other's backs. I'm not saying that Charles is one of the bad guys, but I'd hazard a guess that his loyalties are torn between protecting his college buddy and supporting you. I think that's why he took the professor's dogs. He's playing both sides. That isn't easy to do, and it must be stressing him out."

"Where are you getting this from?" Millay stared at Harris. "Last time I checked, you didn't have a degree in psychology."

Harris tapped his temple. "I used my massive brain to process everything Charles has said since his arrival. Think about it. Why is Silas Black coming to Oyster Bay? Because Charles asked him for a big favor." He glanced at Olivia for confirmation. "Isn't that a direct quote?"

"Yes," Olivia answered.

"Silas came to Palmetto Island because he's ready to start filming the next season of *No Quarter*. The guy has a timeline, and yet, he's willing to stop his work and bop up to Through the Wardrobe for its grand reopening?" Harris smirked. "Even if he's a nice guy, which we're all seriously doubting at this point, why would he be willing to do a signing at an independent bookstore in a small town when he needs to rent warehouse space, hire extras, fly the cast out here, and get the cameras rolling? Every day that he wastes, he's losing money, so why would he waste a single day?"

"Silas must feel compelled to do this favor for Charles. We need to find out why. I like your idea of using alcohol to loosen their tongues, Harris." Olivia started toward the bar.

The five friends read the cocktail menu. The drinks, which had names like Jailbreak, Smooth Criminal, Crime of Passion, and Death Sentence, were various shades of red. Laurel chose the Crime of Passion, a cosmopolitan served in a sugar-rimmed glass. Millay opted for the Smooth Criminal, which was a blend of pomegranate and lime juices, vodka, bitters, and vanilla cardamom syrup. Harris ordered the Jailbreak because he liked the idea of mixing cherries, whiskey, amaretto, and cola. Rawlings and Olivia both asked for a Death Sentence, a cocktail made of champagne, strawberries, and Campari.

Carrying her own drink in one hand and a Smooth Criminal for her father in the other, Olivia returned to their table. As she put the drinks down, she spotted a cop standing by the entrance to the dining room. It was the young policeman from the maritime museum. Olivia assumed that Peterson had sent one of his men to make the guests feel more secure in light of the recent murder. Peterson clearly didn't anticipate further violence, or he would have assigned an experienced officer to the task.

Glancing away, Olivia saw Charles weaving his way through the crowd. "Here comes Charles," she told her friends. "And he has Silas Black in tow."

Charles headed straight for Olivia. "You outshine every woman in this room," he said and leaned in to kiss her on the cheek.

"Thank you." Olivia gave him a small smile. "How are Caesar and Calpurnia?"

"They've been walked and fed, but I don't think they're happy." Charles looked genuinely concerned. "I have very little experience with dogs, and I'm sure they can sense that."

Olivia picked a dog hair off the arm of Charles's tux jacket. "Still, it was really sweet of you to intervene on their behalf. I'm grateful, and I know Emmett will be as well. Do you want me to take them from you after the banquet?"

Charles shook his head. "Silas isn't staying with me tonight, and to my surprise, I enjoy their company. I'm worried that moving them again might distress them even more." He turned and, slinging an arm around Silas's shoulders, pulled him toward Olivia. "I hear the two of you met the other day, but I don't think you realized at the time that Olivia is my daughter. Well, now you know."

Silas took Olivia's hand. "It's obvious that you get your good looks from your mother." He nudged Charles in the ribs and smiled at Olivia. "Charles showed me a photograph of Camille once. She was lovely. She had the face of a classic movie star. Grace Kelly or Kim Novak."

"She wasn't very interested in movies or television shows for that matter," Olivia said woodenly.

There was a moment of uncomfortable silence.

"We're very sorry for your loss," Rawlings said, stepping forward and extending his hand to Silas. "It must be difficult to engage in small talk after what happened."

Silas nodded somberly. "It is, but I wanted to be here tonight. There's nothing I can do for Leigh. The authorities aren't ready to release her body, so I can't make funeral plans, and I didn't want to sit alone in some hotel room across the river feeling sorry for myself. I'd rather be surrounded by people and by noise. It'll be too quiet all too soon."

If you're not staying with Charles and you're not staying in a hotel room, then where are you staying? Olivia thought and searched the room for Amy.

Suddenly, she remembered that she was supposed to be plying her father with drinks. Picking up her own cocktail, as well as the one she'd ordered for Charles, she offered the drinks to the two men. "We'll do our best to distract you," she said, addressing Silas. "After you've wet your whistle, you can tell me what Charles was like when he was a college boy. It's hard for me to picture him in anything but a tailored suit."

Silas laughed, and the mournful look he'd worn seconds ago vanished. "Your dad was a slob. He wore the same clothes for days, his room looked like the aftermath of a hurricane, and he ate like a barbarian. I don't think he used a napkin until our junior year."

Charles mustered a scowl. "I know you enjoy your creative license, Silas, but there's no need to get carried away." He turned to Olivia. "I was a little untidy, but my mind was on other things."

"Women, sports, and drinking my fraternity brothers under the table," Silas said. He'd downed his cocktail and was staring into his empty glass.

"I'm going for refills," Rawlings announced and headed for the bar. Laurel trailed after him but then veered off to speak with Vernon Sherrill. Olivia noticed that Harris and Millay were making their way over to where Amy sat alone at a table in the center of the room. Amy's gaze was locked on Silas's back and she looked on edge. Her hands danced from her flatware, to the stem of her wineglass, to the flowers in the centerpiece. She couldn't seem to stop them from fluttering about.

Is she frightened? Guilty? Or both? Olivia wondered.

By the time Rawlings returned with more drinks, Charles and Silas were caught up in memories of their time at William and Mary.

"What was special about our school was how much both the faculty *and* the students valued history," Silas explained to Olivia and Rawlings. "We didn't just study history. We revered it. The past was sacred. No matter what town you came from, the story of your home—your origins—was important. And when our classmates learned that Charles and I came from locales where pirates once operated, they wanted to know every detail about our seaside havens."

Olivia arched a brow at Charles. "I thought you didn't want people to know where you grew up."

"I didn't," Charles said. "But Silas did the talking for us both. And people loved to listen to him. He even pledged the school's oldest and most influential fraternity. He tried to get me to join, but it wasn't for me. Those guys were from wealthy families who owned beach houses up and down the North Carolina coast. To them, I'd always be a local boy. A fisherman's kid."

Silas polished off his second cocktail and carelessly set

the glass on the edge of the table. "I told him that those guys didn't matter—that we were better than them—but we needed them to get ahead in the world." A zealous glint appeared in his eyes. "I *told* him we'd come out on top in the end." He clapped Charles on the back. "And we did, didn't we?"

A change came over Charles's face. A shadow dimmed the merriment in his eyes. "Some things are better left in the past. Ah, look, our appetizers are being served." He gave Silas a tight smile. "You're welcome to join us, but your assistant appears to be on her own. Where's your usual entourage of underlings and admirers?"

"Getting ready for our first shoot. We'll do background shots this week and more of my people will be flying out from L.A. to hire the extras." Silas suddenly shook his head. "Of course, things might not go as scheduled if I can bury Leigh. She has no family, so . . ."

Charles put a hand on his friend's shoulder. "Come on, man. Let's grab another drink before we eat."

"Excellent idea." Silas chortled. "It might make the food taste better." He winked at Olivia and sauntered off with Charles.

Olivia and Rawlings sat down to plates of shrimp cocktail in a Bloody Mary sauce.

"Did you see how Charles reacted when Silas talked about coming out on top?" Olivia asked Rawlings.

"Yes," he said. "But who knows if secrets from their college days mean anything. We all did stupid stuff when we were younger. That's partially what youth is about."

Olivia considered the series of meaningless affairs she'd had with rich playboy types in her twenties and nodded. She'd traveled around the world attending gallery openings and movie premieres and had been hounded by the media everywhere she went. She'd been a beautiful, reckless heiress then, but those days were well behind her. Smiling at

Rawlings, she said, "It took me a long time, but I figured out what matters in life."

Rawlings brushed the back of her hand with his fingers. "Better late than never."

Their appetizers were nearly gone by the time Harris, Millay, and Laurel returned to the table.

"I've been talking with Vernon Sherrill. The cops have no idea who broke into the museum," Laurel said. "They dusted for prints and only those belonging to museum employees turned up. Both Vernon and Rosemary spent hours going through their inventory. The dress was the only thing taken."

"There's no evidence that Emmett gained access to the museum, so why isn't Peterson looking for other suspects?" Millay stabbed a shrimp with her fork. "Amy and Silas provided each other with an alibi, but that's hardly proof of their innocence. Here's what I think happened. Amy got the dress and gave it to Silas. He convinced Leigh to put it on, go to his beach house, and wait there until she heard the bell. He then lured her out with the bell, killed her, arranged her body, and got into bed with Amy. I have no idea why he did it, or why she listened to him, but I have to start somewhere."

Harris, who'd already gobbled up his appetizer, frowned. "Why didn't the professor hear the bell?"

It was a good question, and no one had a ready answer.

"What I don't like about this scenario is how easily Mr. Black convinced Officer Peterson to back off." Rawlings fell silent while a waiter cleared their plates and then continued, "Peterson is either starstruck or corrupt."

"Corrupt," Laurel repeated and then cried, "The land deal! Peterson might be in on the land deal!"

Olivia inhaled sharply. "Of course. There's a fortune to be made for anyone getting in on the ground floor. Judging from the price of weekly rentals, the housing demand far outweighs the supply, and if Silas's development includes amenities, the owners can charge exorbitant weekly rates."

"It's doubtful that Officer Peterson could come up with enough cash to invest in a project of this level," Rawlings argued.

"Maybe he didn't have to spend a cent," Harris said. "Maybe his *cooperation* was his payment."

The rest of the Bayside Book Writers considered Harris's words in silence. The waitstaff appeared with their entrées— cracked pepper prime rib or pan-seared chicken with a garlic and sherry sauce—refilled water glasses, and then left again.

Olivia had just cut into her chicken when Charles returned.

"The steak is here," he said happily. "Sorry to have left you for so long, but I wanted to be sure Silas was holding up okay." He turned to Harris. "I saw you talking with Amy earlier. How's she doing?"

Harris kept his eyes on his food. "She seemed scared. Unsure of what the future holds for her." He shrugged. "I can't help feeling a little sorry for her."

This clearly surprised Charles. "Why? She's part of a hit television series, she makes great money, and Silas treats her like a queen. For a small-town girl with a history degree, she's done quite well for herself."

Millay glared at Charles. "Harris probably feels sorry for Amy because the media is going to tear her apart. Silas's alibi for the night of Leigh's murder is that he left your place to seek solace in Amy's bed. That makes Amy *the other woman*. No is one ever kind to the other woman."

"Not only that, but many people will doubt her story about Silas's being with her when Leigh was killed," Laurel added. "She's about to be put under a very large microscope, and I think she's just beginning to get an idea of what's in store for her."

"*I* don't believe her story," Olivia said, looking directly at Charles. "I think she's lying. For the record, I think Silas is lying too."

If she expected her comment to elicit a reaction from Charles, she was to be disappointed. He swallowed a mouthful of roasted vegetables and signaled for the waiter. After ordering a bottle of costly merlot, he leaned back in his chair and returned Olivia's stare. "Why would Silas commit murder? He had no motive. Leigh could be a thorn in his side, but he didn't care enough about her to kill her. He'd gain nothing from such an act, and Silas is all about gain. He'd never risk the success of his show by doing something so stupid."

Olivia wanted to argue the point, but the waitstaff began to remove their plates. Charles waved off their offer of coffee and gestured at the wine bottle. "I'm having grape juice for dessert." He glanced around the table. "Anyone care to join me?"

Laurel accepted and Olivia guessed that her friend had done so in order to encourage Charles to continue drinking.

A waitress informed them that dessert was a choice between pumpkin pavé or pirate rubies.

"What's a pirate ruby?" Harris asked.

"Strawberries dipped in chocolate," she said. "The chef named it that in honor of Mr. Black. Everyone on staff is a *No Quarter* fan."

"I'll have both," Harris said, smiling at the waitress. "Mine and my neighbor's." He jerked a thumb at Charles.

While the diners enjoyed coffee and dessert, Marjorie Tucker took the podium.

"I'd like to offer a heartfelt thanks to all the authors and experts without whom this festival could not have taken place. I'd also like to express my deepest sympathy to Silas Black. May you find comfort and peace on Palmetto Island as you begin filming your show." She paused. "And I hope everyone will return to our paradise next summer. If you do, please stop by the library and say hello. Thank you again, and feel free to linger over your dessert. The bar will remain open until eleven."

The attendees applauded loudly before focusing on their food and conversation once more. There was such a sense of closure to the evening that no one noticed Jan Powell until she was behind the podium, the mic in her hands. She wore black pants and a black sweater and looked more like a cat burglar than the head of the conservancy.

"Before you go, I want you all to know that the island won't look like it does now if we don't join together to stop that man's development." Jan pointed at Silas. Her voice was calm, but her eyes blazed. "Our delicate ecosystem will crumble. There will be erosion and the loss of vegetation and animal species. Put your hands up if you've been enchanted by its wild beauty. If you've taken a nature walk or been amazed by our sea turtle program."

Throughout the room, hands rose in the air. Marjorie jumped to her feet and signaled for the young policeman to leave his post by the door and come to her aid.

"People come to our island for its beautiful beaches and incredible views, but they return again and again because it has so much *more* to offer," Jan continued hurriedly. "The natural areas are what make Palmetto Island unique and unforgettable. Don't allow it to become another Myrtle Beach. Another Panama City Beach. This place, *as it is now*, is the real jewel in North Carolina's crown. This northernmost tropical island. A habitat to rare and beautiful plants and animals. *Please.* Call your congressman. Donate to the conservancy. I won't stop fighting, even if it means standing in front of a bulldozer. If a single sight on this island has moved you, then join me in saving it! It's not too late!"

By now, Marjorie and the cop had reached the podium.

"That's enough, Jan." Marjorie's voice could be heard through the microphone.

"I won't stop fighting you!" Jan shouted at Silas as the cop grabbed her arm. "You haven't won! Not you nor your sneaky silent partners!" She used her free hand to point an accusatory finger at Olivia's table.

Olivia and her friends exchanged befuddled glances.

"*Help me*! Help me save the island!" Jan cried before she was hauled away from the podium.

Marjorie apologized for the disruption and then added, "American poet James Whitcomb Riley once said, 'Never allow your energy or enthusiasm to be dampened by the discouragement that must inevitably come.' As you can see, Ms. Powell's energy and enthusiasm are unflagging. May we all apply such devotion to our work and the causes near and dear to our hearts."

"Nice recovery," Charles said, nodding in approval.

Olivia was still processing what Jan said and how she'd pointed at their table. "You didn't come here merely to hang out with your college buddy," she said to Charles, her voice tight with anger. "I can't believe it didn't occur to me before. You've made a fortune thanks to your ability to recognize profitable ventures. You knew all about Silas's development because you're a silent partner. How many times have you been to the island prior to this festival?"

"Just once. Silas asked me to take a look at the property and I did," Charles replied casually. "It's not a crime to make money, Olivia. How many properties do you own?"

"I acquired them mainly to preserve the structures and to create jobs," Olivia snapped. "But we're not talking about my business dealings. Why didn't you tell me from the first that you were involved with the development? And what other relevant details about your relationship with Silas have you opted not to share?"

Charles put his napkin on the table. "I'm sorry that your friend was arrested for murder. I can see that you're upset. However, Silas had nothing to do with the crime. He's my oldest friend and I know the man. He didn't do it." Charles got to his feet and smoothed his tie. "I'm leaving in the morning. There's a great deal to see to before Saturday's grand reopening. Maybe you can't help your professor, but you can still support another friend as she celebrates the release of her first book." He gestured at Millay. "Maybe it's time to look ahead and leave what happened on this island behind."

He wished the rest of the Bayside Book Writers a pleasant evening and walked over to Silas's table. The two men shook hands and exchanged affectionate smiles, and then Charles left the dining room.

"Now we know what Charles stood to lose if Silas went down for Leigh's murder," Olivia told her friends. "A great deal of money. I firmly believe that Charles is hiding something. And not just out of loyalty for his buddy. He's protecting his investment too."

"But what can we do at this juncture?" Laurel asked. "Everyone's leaving tomorrow. We have to be out of our rental houses by noon."

Everyone looked to Rawlings for an answer. "I'll call Peterson as soon as we get back to Lifesaver. It's my duty to confront him about Mr. Black's weak alibi."

"Not only that, but did Peterson bother to ask where Jan Powell was last night? Or has he figured out how the professor managed to get inside the museum without any sign of forced entry?" Millay's frustration was palpable.

Harris nodded in agreement. "Yeah. Those are really good points." He pushed his plate away and watched as the people at the next table stood up to go. "Looks like we've come to the end of a very unusual festival." His eyes met Olivia's. "What are you going to do tomorrow?"

Olivia balled up her napkin and squeezed it between her hands. "After I pack, I'm going to pick up Emmett's dogs. I don't trust Charles anymore. I almost did, but he blew it.

When we get back to Oyster Bay, I intend to spend lots of time at Through the Wardrobe. If Charles knows anything that can exonerate Emmett, I'm going to find out what it is."

Releasing a heavy sigh, Millay waved her arm around the room. "You know what really sucks about all this drama? It's going to follow us. It's going to follow us all the way home."

Chapter 12

The river widens to a pathless sea
Beneath the rain and mist and
sullen skies.
Look out the window; 't is a gray
emprise,
This piloting of massed humanity
On such a day, from shore to busy
shore,
And breed the thought that beauty is
no more.

—RICHARD FRANCIS BURTON

The next morning, Olivia woke to the sound of rain striking the roof. Neither Rawlings nor Haviland stirred when she got out of bed, pulled on a robe, and crossed the room to the window. She looked out on a world that was entirely gray. A thick fog blanketed the entire beach, and Olivia couldn't tell where the land ended and the ocean began. The visibility was so poor that there was no demarcation between sky and sea. Everything was a blur, as though an artist had run a finger through smoke-colored paint, smudging the entire scene.

Olivia wondered how sailors had ever navigated the shoals in such conditions. She tried to imagine how the island must have appeared from their vantage point on deck or high up in a crow's nest. How the sound of a bell ringing in such absolute silence must have created a haunted echo. Did the island send an answering reply, or did it remain quiet, veiled in mystery?

Olivia remembered Leigh walking on the beach, her nightgown glowing like a moon. It was hard to believe that Leigh was now dead. And despite the fact that a woman had been murdered, Olivia was leaving—all of the Bayside Book Writers were leaving—without knowing why someone had brought old ghost stories to life.

Even Rawlings, who'd bluntly expressed his opinion to Peterson over the phone last night, couldn't alter the present circumstances. Peterson claimed that he'd spoken with Jan Powell and that he had no cause to view her as a suspect. And when Rawlings broached the subject of Silas's and Amy's weak alibis, Peterson became angry and ended the call.

Tiptoeing downstairs, Olivia went into the living room and picked up the book of ghost stories. She flipped through the pages, hoping against hope that a clue would jump out at her. When she reached the tale of Theodosia Burr, she stared at the black-and-white drawing of a young woman walking on the beach, her bare feet leaving depressions in the damp sand as her dark hair trailed out behind her. Olivia could almost imagine the wind rippling the woman's dress and whipping her hair around her face. She thought of what Millay had said the night before, about the drama following them back to Oyster Bay.

"Not if I have anything to say about it," Olivia murmured and snapped the book shut. Though she dressed quickly and quietly, Haviland woke and followed her down to the kitchen.

Olivia fed him breakfast and set the coffeepot to brew. While she waited for the coffee, she wrote a note to Rawlings and finished packing the few belongings they'd used in the kitchen. Next, she filled a takeout cup with coffee and left the house with Haviland in tow.

The morning was preternaturally still, as though the fog

had muted all the island's creatures. There was no wind rustling in the undergrowth, and the trees were dark, crooked blurs that only gained definition when Olivia was almost close enough to touch them.

When she pulled into the parking nook of Charles's cottage, Olivia saw light coming from the kitchen window and heard the sound of dogs whining from inside the house. Haviland's ears shot up, but Olivia shushed him before he had the chance to bark.

She knocked on the door and was met by Charles and both of the greyhounds. Olivia took one look at their mournful dark eyes and had to bite back a cry.

"I thought you might show up this morning." Charles moved aside so Haviland could shoot into the house.

Haviland and the greyhounds sniffed and grunted, clearly overjoyed to be in one another's company again.

"I'm going to take them home with me," Olivia said, pointing at the dogs. "It's what Emmett would want."

"All right." Charles headed for the kitchen. "I just made some eggs. I'm not much of a cook, but I scramble a mean egg. Have you had breakfast yet?"

Olivia was about to decline his offer when her stomach rumbled. She decided to sit with Charles and give him one more opportunity to come clean.

"I added a bit of shredded cheddar. Like bacon, cheese makes everything taste better." Charles spooned eggs onto a plate and set it in front of Olivia. "Tabasco?"

"No, thank you." Olivia watched Charles sprinkle hot sauce, salt, and pepper over his own serving of eggs. "I'd like to talk about the grand reopening."

Charles spread a napkin on his lap. "Let me guess. You don't want Silas to come."

Olivia paused midchew, surprised by Charles's acuity. When her mouth was empty, she said, "In my mind, he's a murder suspect. That's not the type of celebrity I want at Through the Wardrobe."

"It's too late to cancel. The press has already been notified. Leigh's death was tragic, but Silas Black is all anyone can talk about. Like him or hate him. Suspect him or not. The line to get into our bookstore will wrap around the block. Thousands of people will hear about Millay's debut novel because of Silas. We're giving her the kind of exposure most people would kill for." Charles immediately held up his hand. "Forgive me, that remark was in poor taste. Despite my *faux pas*, you must concede my point."

It galled Olivia to admit it, but Charles was right. If they refused to host Silas, Millay's sales could suffer.

"Fine," she said tersely. "I can see that nothing will come between you and your bottom line. That's what drives you, isn't it? Monetary gain. Building a relationship with me is secondary. If that were your main priority, you would have told me you were Silas's silent partner."

Charles looked genuinely confused. "Why? I invest in all sorts of projects with a variety of people. I realize that this development will proceed under considerable protest from the wildlife organization, but I'm not ashamed to be involved." He took a sip of orange juice. "I've seen the plans, Olivia. The project manager will develop the land with a mind toward conservation. There will be plenty of green space, and each plot will be allowed only the bare minimum when it comes to tree removal. Silas wants to preserve as much of the natural landscape as possible. He loves this place, Olivia. Why do you think he bought a house here? It's what I keep trying to convey to you. He *loves* the coast. Every town. Every grain of sand. He isn't the bad guy in this scenario."

Olivia lapsed into silence. She was angry with Charles, but she couldn't help but respond to his calm tone and rational replies. "I want to believe you, but I can't. To tell you the truth, your blind loyalty where Silas is concerned has jeopardized the progress you and I were making. You're intelligent. And shrewd. You can't buy his alibi. No one with half a brain could."

Charles released a heavy sigh. "He gave me his word, Olivia. I know that doesn't mean much these days, but Silas and I have been friends for a very long time. No matter how ludicrous his alibi sounds, no matter how damning the rumors against him, I will take him at his word. Wouldn't you do the same if it came to one of your friends?"

Olivia picked up her coffee cup and whispered, "Yes. I'd go to the grave believing what they told me."

"There you have it. We're not that different after all," Charles said and smiled at Olivia. "So can we call a truce?"

Now it was Olivia's turn to sigh. "What about Amy? Could she be responsible? Could Silas be covering for her?" When Charles didn't respond, Olivia grabbed his hand. "Don't you see? I'm leaving Emmett in a jail cell. He might be granted bail, but then again, he might not. This investigation is a media sensation, and those vultures will crucify him before he ever gets the chance to plead his case. I have to find the real killer."

"I understand, and I admire your grit," Charles said. "I honestly can't vouch for Amy. I don't know her from Eve. However, she goes where Silas goes, so if you and the chief want to question her, she'll be in Oyster Bay in a few days."

Olivia stood up and carried her plate to the sink. She washed it and then reached for the frying pan.

"You don't have to do that," Charles protested.

"The cook doesn't clean the dishes," Olivia said, returning to the table to collect his plate. "That's how it works in my house."

Charles joined her at the sink. He smiled at her and said, "I'll dry. We work better as a team."

*   *   *

An hour later, the Bayside Book Writers stood on the ferry dock. Rawlings held the end of Haviland's leash while Olivia gripped Caesar's and Calpurnia's. The greyhounds were highly agitated and only calmed down when Haviland made physical contact, which he did often. It was as if he knew they needed comfort and reassurance.

Olivia turned away from the approaching ferry and glanced back at the old lighthouse. The fog had lifted, but filmy clouds still obscured parts of the island.

"You hold your secrets close," Olivia whispered. As her eyes drifted to the marina store, she saw two familiar figures walk inside.

"Harris, would you take Caesar and Calpurnia for a minute?" she asked. "I just spotted some people I'd like to speak with before we go."

Harris nodded. "Just don't miss the boat. I wouldn't want anyone left behind on a day like this. It's a setting right out of a ghost story."

"I've had my fill of ghost stories," Millay grumbled. "I'm ready to leave them here, where they belong."

Millay's words followed Olivia up the dock and to the store, where she found George and Boyd Allen examining a row of canned soups.

"Hello," Olivia said, feeling strangely awkward and shy around the two men.

Boyd took two cans of potato-and-bacon soup off the shelf. "You're on your way home, then?"

Olivia nodded. "The highlight of my visit was meeting you both. I want to thank you again for sharing your stories. I just wish someone hadn't used those old tales as an inspiration for wickedness."

George's eyes took on a veiled, dream-like expression.

"The island always gets what she wants. We're all just visitors here."

"What does she want?" Olivia whispered eagerly. Was George about to give her the answers she so desperately needed?

"To be left alone," George said, his gaze coming into focus again. "For folks to come, stay for a spell, and then go. Like the signs say, people should leave only footprints. The water can wash those away."

Olivia held her exasperation in check. "But a *person* killed that deer. A *person* set fire to that dinghy. A *person* murdered Leigh Winslow. The island had help. Do you know who helped her?" She put a hand on George's arm. "I know you want to protect this place. It's your home. But my friend has been accused of these crimes, and he's innocent."

"We know, and we were sorry to hear it," Boyd said in a soft, sympathetic voice. "Emmett loves the island too."

"So you haven't seen or heard anything that might exonerate him? Please," Olivia added plaintively. "This is my last chance to help him."

As though on cue, the ferry whistle blew.

"She's pulling up to the dock," Boyd said.

George took Olivia's hand and gave it a gentle pat. "You have a safe journey, Miss. Maybe we'll see you again. Though at my age, a man can never be sure."

Olivia wanted to beg the Allens to talk to her, but they were already headed for the checkout counter. Olivia followed them with her eyes. The store manager, who stood behind the cash register, appeared to be in a deep conversation with Vernon Sherrill. Olivia wondered if she had time to wait for them to finish talking. She wanted to ask Vernon if he agreed with Officer Peterson's assessment that Amy wasn't involved in the museum robbery, but before she could take a step, Silas and Amy entered the store. Silas immediately noticed Olivia and made a beeline for her.

"Your ride's here." He jerked his thumb in the direction of the dock and smiled his trademark smile.

Amy didn't even glance at Olivia. She walked directly to the refrigerator case and began to fill a basket with bottled water and soda.

Olivia stared at Silas, searching his face for a sign that he was hiding something, but his smile stayed in place.

"I'm really looking forward to visiting Oyster Bay," Silas said congenially. "Charles promised—" He faltered as Jan Powell stepped into the store. "Not that shrew again! Excuse me, but I think I'll wait outside. It's too early in the day for a verbal altercation."

Because Jan stopped to say hello to Vernon and the Allens, she failed to notice Silas ducking out the back door.

The ferry whistle blew again, and Olivia knew that her chance to discover any new information was gone.

She hurried to the end of the dock, where Rawlings and Haviland were waiting. Despite the dampness in the air, Olivia and her friends chose to stand near the ferry's stern. They watched the island slowly recede into the distance, and it wasn't long before its coastline disappeared into the mist. Eventually, all they could see was the top of the lighthouse. Its beacon was unlit, and in Olivia's mind, the lack of light was symbolic. To her, the nonfunctioning lighthouse represented a place that offered no safe haven, no shelter from the storm. It was a place that embraced the dark night. The deadly shoals and shipwrecks.

"And secrets," Olivia whispered.

She turned away from Palmetto Island and focused her thoughts on home.

When they landed in Riverport, Rawlings tried to secure a visit with Emmett, but the desk clerk at the police station informed him that Mr. Billinger was meeting with his attorney.

"He's hired one of the best defense attorneys in the state," Rawlings said when he rejoined the others in front of the station. With three dogs in their company, Olivia had deemed it best to wait outside.

"That's really good news," Olivia said. "Emmett now stands a chance at his bail hearing. Did you leave a note for him about the dogs?"

Rawlings nodded. "Let's go. There's nothing else we can do for him right now."

"When should we get together again?" Laurel asked as they turned toward the parking lot. "I don't want to wait until Millay's book launch."

"Me neither," agreed Harris. "Why don't we take you out on Thursday, Millay? We should celebrate your official release day."

Millay smiled at him. "That would be cool, but my parents are coming to town. I'm sure they're hoping that my becoming an author will inspire me to quit my job at the bar, take out my piercings, and trade in my miniskirts for khakis."

Harris shuddered. "You wouldn't."

"You know me better than that," Millay said with a grin.

Suddenly, Olivia had an idea. "Why don't we meet for dinner Friday night? If we invite Charles, Silas, and Amy, we'll have an opportunity to ask them questions on the sly." She looked at Millay. "But only if you're willing. Your book release is a big deal to all of us. I don't want our investigation to detract from what should be one of the most memorable moments of your life."

Millay shrugged. "I would never have made it to this point without you guys, so let's go for it. I want to nail the bastard who committed these crimes, and whatever we do, whether it's writing or catching lowlife scumbags, we do it better together."

Laurel sniffed. "That was beautifully put."

Millay cast a woeful glance at Rawlings. "Is there room in your car? She might be like this the whole way home."

Rawlings laughed. "Between Olivia's luggage and three dogs? Not a spare inch. See you in Oyster Bay."

For the first time, Olivia had to employ a dog sitter. Haviland had always accompanied her whenever she went, but Caesar and Calpurnia weren't adjusting well to their new surroundings and only seemed content when Haviland was around. The greyhounds' anxiety left Olivia no choice but to hire Haviland's favorite groomer to exercise all three dogs twice a day.

Without Haviland hanging out in her office, Olivia felt out of sorts. She found it difficult to concentrate on the many tasks awaiting her at The Boot Top Bistro, but she knew she had to get something done or she'd never catch up. Not only did she have tons of work to do, but her head chef, Michel, was also in a tizzy due to the impending visit of a famously harsh and influential food critic.

"The man eviscerates chefs in print," Michel complained as Olivia tried to balance the budget. "And my food won't be the only thing on the chopping block. He'll rate everything from the cocktails to the starch in the napkins. Last week, he completely ruined a five-star restaurant in Vegas. He wrote that his drink tasted like formaldehyde, the music sounded like monkeys shrieking, and his soup tasted like fish guts mixed with runny eggs. Just thinking about that review is giving me palpitations."

"Well, we can't have that," Olivia said, smiling indulgently at Michel. Her head chef had a penchant for drama.

Michel crossed his arms over his chest. "You clearly don't understand the gravity of the situation. If Jonathan Randolph wants to take us down, he will."

Olivia stood up, took Michel by the hand, and led him back into the kitchen.

"Close your eyes and pretend that you and Shelley aren't

already married," she said. "Imagine you've just met. You're intrigued by her. And a little intimidated. Eager to impress this woman, you invite her to dinner at The Boot Top Bistro. A table for two awaits you in the far corner of the dining room. The lights are dimmed, Ray Charles is crooning softly in the background, and you're hoping to win Shelley's heart with one meal." Olivia waited a moment before continuing. "Now open your eyes and tell me what you'd cook for a woman who knows as much about food as you. A woman who also trained at a culinary school in Paris. A woman with a highly sophisticated palate. What can you prepare to seduce her?"

A faraway look came over Michel's face. "It's autumn, so I'd begin with an artichoke, sweet potato, and pomegranate salad. I'd follow that with a creamy risotto. Parmesan with fresh mushrooms and herbs. There'd be scallops with caramelized spaghetti squash. And then duck. Perfectly crisped, with a sour cherry sauce. And for dessert? It has to be an apple. Poached with coriander meringue. And a side of apple sorbet sprinkled with sugared hazelnuts."

"It sounds like you have the perfect meal for Jonathan Randolph all lined up," Olivia said. "Make a shopping list. You can practice by serving this tasting menu to Millay and the rest of us tomorrow night."

Michel wrapped Olivia in a bear hug. "You're a genius, *ma cherie*!" Releasing her, he snapped his fingers at his staff, who'd wisely kept silent during the exchange. "Look alive, my friends! We're going to dazzle this man. The only thing he'll complain about is that he can't dine at The Boot Top Bistro every week!"

Satisfied that Michel's worries had been conquered, Olivia went back to her office. She managed to finish the budget and had just turned her attention to the supply orders when her cell phone rang. The caller was Emmett Billinger.

"I'm out on bail," he said. "And I'm heading your way."

Olivia felt joy, sweet and pure as honey, course through

her. "Thank God! And the dogs are fine, Emmett. They're at my house. They're okay. They miss you terribly, but they're okay."

There was a long expulsion of breath, and Olivia knew she'd said what Emmett needed to hear.

"I'm still pretty shocked that I was granted bail, but my attorney pressed the point that my DNA wasn't found on Leigh's body and that none of hers was found on me or in my house. He also showed my manuscript to the judge and explained my notes on Theodosia Burr. He argued that there's no evidence of my having broken into the museum or having previous contact with Leigh. My cell phone records show no calls to her. That bottle opener is the most damning thing the prosecution could come up with, but my attorney declared that their entire case was circumstantial. Thankfully, the judge agreed."

Olivia found herself nodding. "As would anyone with common sense."

"But I'm hardly in the clear." Emmett hesitated. "I know I've asked so much of you already, Olivia, but have you made any progress in finding the real killer?"

"Not yet, but we're having dinner with Silas and Amy tomorrow night and hope to get something out of them. We're particularly interested in grilling Amy. She and Leigh didn't like each other, and Amy used to work at the maritime museum. The curator believes she might have had keys to the place."

Emmett made a noise between a grunt and a growl. "That girl's caused me enough grief. If she's responsible for the mess I'm in, I won't handle it well. When she tried to ruin my life before, I responded by moving away. There won't be any escape for me this time if I can't offer up another suspect in my place."

When Olivia spoke again, her tone was low and gentle, as though she were placating a child. "Emmett, you can't be involved. Let me and my friends handle Silas and Amy. After you get Caesar and Calpurnia, you should return to Palmetto Island. Speak with the Allens. I swear they know something, but they wouldn't talk to me. They know you, so you might have better luck."

Emmett snorted. "I'd hardly consider myself lucky, Olivia. Not anymore. I used to lead a charmed life, but that was before Amy Holden became one of my students. If she's responsible for what's happened to me . . ." He trailed off.

"The best way to make this disappear is to think deeply and act carefully," Olivia said. "You have a brilliant mind, Emmett. Use it."

After a long moment of silence, Emmett thanked Olivia for listening and then told her when he expected to arrive at her house.

Later that afternoon, Olivia had the privilege of witnessing Emmett's reunion with his beloved greyhounds.

Caesar and Calpurnia became different dogs the second they saw their owner. They leapt on him and covered his face with canine kisses, yipping in ecstasy and relief. Their tails whipped back and forth with such fury that Olivia half expected the dogs to rise off the ground.

"I can never repay you for taking such good care of them," Emmett said after his dogs had settled down. "I don't know what would have become of them if you hadn't been on the island."

"Rawlings and I have enjoyed their company, and Haviland will be especially sorry to see them go," Olivia said and opened the sliding glass door leading to her deck. "I guess we should let them stretch their legs before the long car ride. Maybe you and I can work a few things through while they exercise." She led Emmett over the dunes and paused when they reached the open beach. "What we're missing is the killer's motive. Why did this person bring North Carolina ghost stories to life? What message did he or she want to convey? And to whom? That's what we need to figure out."

Emmett nodded. "I've had many hours to consider motive, and it seems to me that the Allen's Creek land sale triggered the events. My initial thought was that someone in the conservancy was responsible."

"It wasn't Jan Powell," Olivia said. "According to the police, she had a solid alibi for the night of Leigh's murder. Of course, I don't have much faith in Officer Peterson. The chief suspects that Peterson might be protecting Silas in exchange for shares in the new development, and we'll be sure to ask Silas about that tomorrow night. But let's assume Jan is innocent. Who else would want to drive Silas away? Because I think these acts focus on Silas. The killer chose his girlfriend for a reason."

Emmett stared out over the water. South, in the direction of Palmetto Island. "Maybe it's not about the development. Maybe everything happened because of Silas Black. What if someone wants to stop him from filming on the island?"

"Who would be so opposed to a television show that they'd commit murder?" Olivia asked. "The Allens would undoubtedly object to their history being fictionalized. But could you picture either of them shooting a deer with an arrow or holding Leigh under the water until she drowned?"

Emmett shook his head. "No, but I'm going to speak with them and to Vernon Sherrill anyway. The Allens are the island's only year-round residents, and Vernon knows all the conservancy folks because a portion of their meetings are held in the museum. If these men know anything, I'm going to make them tell me."

They passed under the shadow of the lighthouse, and when they stepped into the sunlight again, Emmett stopped to gaze up at the majestic structure.

"It's a shame they're all automated," he said. "I like the idea of a keeper. Of a man whose job is to keep a light burning for those out at sea. I like the thought of someone watching out for others through the dark and the raging storms. I can almost see a man climbing the stairs to the top over and over again—making sure the light never goes out."

Olivia thought of the lighthouse keeper she'd known as a child. "I think it was both a noble and very solitary existence."

"Except for these two"—Emmett gestured at the greyhounds, who were frolicking along the waterline with Haviland—"I live a solitary existence. But my job isn't noble. I don't save lives. I don't keep people safe." He looked at Olivia and suddenly seemed older and sadder than the man she used to know. "This whole experience has made me question myself. Jail time can be dangerous because there's nowhere to go but here." He tapped his temple.

"Put your midlife crisis on hold, Professor," Olivia softly admonished. "You can buy a sports car and date a woman ten years your junior *after* you've been exonerated."

Emmett threw back his head and laughed. "Ah, it's good to be with you, Olivia." He smiled at her. "Through all this, you've been my lighthouse keeper."

Touched by the compliment, Olivia returned his smile. "Come on. The chief should be home by now, and he's been looking forward to seeing you. We're all on your side, Emmett. None of us will rest until you're safe. And free."

"I take back what I said earlier," Emmett declared. "I am a lucky man. Very lucky. After all, I have the Bayside Book Writers as my champions."

Chapter 13

*A person who publishes a book willfully
appears before the populace with his
pants down. If it is a good book nothing
can hurt him. If it is a bad book nothing
can help him.*

—EDNA ST. VINCENT MILLAY

O livia had ordered enough copies of Millay's book to
give to the staff of The Boot Top Bistro and had asked
her friend to arrive a bit early for her celebratory dinner in
order to sign each copy.

"This will be good practice for tomorrow." Olivia placed
the books in neat stacks along the length of the bar and then
smiled at her friend.

"Too bad I won't be drinking cocktails at the bookstore,"
Millay murmured. She looked at Olivia with dark, unhappy
eyes. "I'm only saying this because the others aren't here
yet, but I'm freaking out."

Olivia was about to present Millay with a gift-wrapped
box, but she kept it hidden behind her back. "Over the launch
party?"

"Over everything." Millay rubbed the cover of one of her
books. "My parents are partially to blame. They spent their
entire visit, which was mercifully short, grilling me about
advances, contracts, sales numbers—you name it. Every

conversation centered on money. How much I'd made so far. How much I could expect to make. What had I spent on promotion? Had my agent negotiated the best deal?" Millay pressed her fingers to her temples. "They sucked all the joy out of the official release day."

Sitting on the bar stool next to Millay's, Olivia tried to hide the resentment she felt toward her friend's parents. "You once told me that they tend to focus on facts when communicating with you. Maybe they just don't know how to express their pride in your accomplishment. They don't know how to speak your language."

Millay smirked. "That's for sure. They never have. And they have all the warmth of a pocket calculator."

"Perhaps their zeal in collecting data was their way of showing an interest," Olivia said. "I don't blame you for being disappointed in how they acted, but they care. They just have a crappy way of showing it."

"If they'd only asked *one* question about the *story*, I would have been cool with the rest of the inquisition." Millay took a generous swallow of her drink. "Forget it. I'm not going to let them bring me down. They're gone now, and I won't hear from them again unless I make a bestseller list."

Olivia shrugged. "Anything's possible. Jenna tells me that your preorder numbers were very strong. She said she hasn't been so excited about an event since she was made manager of the bookstore."

"I keep checking my sales rank on Amazon, but I have no clue what it means." Millay spread her hands in a gesture of helplessness. "Numbers are my parents' field. And I'm terrified to read the reviews, so I haven't. I can't believe how many have been posted already."

"The ones I've seen are very positive, and I'm not surprised. I'm quite familiar with *The Gryphon Rider*, remember? I know how good it is." Olivia put the gift on the bar and slid it over to Millay. "Hundreds of thousands of people believe they have a book in them. Out of all of those people, you completed a manuscript, were signed by an agent, and landed a three-book deal with a major publishing house. You've beaten incredible odds, so don't you dare be glum. I can take modest. I can take flippant, because that's so you, but in your heart, you'd better be proud and happy."

"Is that a threat?" Millay's mouth curved upward.

"Definitely." Olivia pointed at the box. "Open your present."

Millay tore off the gift wrap and removed the box lid to reveal a lime-green fountain pen on a bed of cushioned silk. "Cool color," she said, looking pleased.

"Give it a try." Olivia tapped the top book on the stack. "This one's for Gabe. He's in the kitchen getting lemons."

"I've been obsessing over how to inscribe people's books," Millay admitted sheepishly and then put the tip of her pen to the title page. She'd just started the first letter when she stopped. "Purple ink! Awesome. Thanks, Olivia." Smiling widely now, she wrote, *Fly high and fight hard*, which was the credo of her protagonist's clan, and signed her name with a confident flourish. "That felt good," she whispered and Olivia knew that she was referring to more than just the fountain pen.

Olivia passed her the list of employee names. "I'll leave you to it. I need to check on Michel. I'm sure he's in a complete tizzy."

When Olivia entered the kitchen, she realized that "tizzy" was far too tame a word to describe Michel's condition. The head chef was red-faced, frantic, and loud. He'd tasked the sous chefs with preparing the food for the rest of the diners so that he could concentrate on the special autumn tasting menu, but it was clear that he couldn't stop interfering with their work.

"Michel, you can't play the dictator tonight," Olivia scolded. "You have to focus all your energy on the tasting menu. Trust your staff. They're more than capable of handling the main dining room. Pretend you're cooking for Shelley. Get into the zone."

Michel's shoulders sagged. "I wish I was cooking for Shelley. I've been so preoccupied with this menu, and she's been so busy making chocolate gryphons and wyverns for tomorrow's book launch that we've barely seen each other."

"I keep telling you to take off more than one day a week," Olivia said. "Even if you ended up helping Shelley at the desserterie during that extra day, the two of you could spend more time together. You both put everything you have into your food, but you need to take time for your marriage too."

Michel grinned, and Olivia knew that she'd gotten through to him. "I like the idea of working at Decadence once a week. If I helped in the kitchen, Shelley could take a half day and let her employees handle closing up. I'm going to talk to her about this when I get home. *If* she's awake." Michel turned to his staff. "You are now invisible to me. I am devoting all my attention to my tasting menu. Do not get in my way, and I won't get in yours."

The sous chefs shot Olivia a grateful look just as Rawlings poked his head around the edge of the swing door. "Everyone's here," he said.

"*Bonne chance!*" Olivia shouted before leaving. From her office, Haviland chimed in with a single bark, and the entire kitchen staff laughed.

"They sound merry," Rawlings said and kissed Olivia hello.

Olivia smiled at him. "I'm feeling strangely optimistic too. Emmett's been released—albeit temporarily—Millay's debut novel is on bookstore shelves across the country, and we have another chance to question Silas and Amy."

Rawlings gazed at her, his eyes filled with warmth and affection. "Yes, but we have to treat our dinner guests with kid gloves if we want them to open up. If either of them sense that we're interrogating them, our big chance will be blown."

"In other words, I should keep my mouth shut?" Olivia asked playfully.

"Just be the gracious hostess," Rawlings said. "Let me take a crack at Ms. Holden. For whatever reason, she seems to be attracted to father figures. According to the rumor mill, her parents disapprove of her entering into a romantic relationship with Mr. Black, as do other people who knew her when she was younger, including Vernon Sherrill. She used to intern at his museum, remember? If I show interest in her career and express approval in Mr. Black, she might confide in me."

Olivia nodded in agreement. "What about Silas?"

"Laurel's in charge of Mr. Black. Not only is she pretty and charming, but she's also a reporter. She plans to get Silas to talk about the new season of *No Quarter* and to tap into his love of history. Once he loosens up, she'll ask what happened the day you saw Mr. Black and Ms. Holden at the maritime museum."

"That was the day Vernon refused to lend Silas certain artifacts," Olivia said, recalling the scene with clarity. "The curator was rude to both Silas and Amy. Perhaps it was all the motive Amy needed to steal the antique dress."

Rawlings touched the tip of Olivia's nose with his index finger. "Perhaps."

"We shouldn't keep our guests waiting." Taking Rawlings's hand, Olivia drew in a fortifying breath, and together, she and Rawlings left the kitchen.

By this time, Silas, Amy, and Charles had joined Laurel at the bar. Gabe was busy serving them drinks while Millay continued to sign books. A small crowd of curious patrons had gathered around her.

"You should come to her launch party tomorrow," Silas informed them. "I'll be signing my books, and Ms. Hallowell

188 · Ellery Adams

will be signing hers. It's going to be an unforgettable event. Not only can you witness the unveiling of the state's coolest bookstore, but anyone purchasing one of our novels will also receive a piece of chocolate from the town's desserterie."

"Chocolate *and* books? Count me in!" a woman declared.

"I heard we need to get there early," someone else said. "People are coming from all over the region to visit *our* bookstore."

Charles walked up to Olivia and smiled. "He's quite the salesman, isn't he?"

"He is," Olivia said. She was determined to get along with her father despite the lingering feeling that he was keeping something from her. They'd met several times throughout the week to discuss the launch party, and judging by the media coverage the event was already receiving, it was going to be an incredible success.

"I dropped by Through the Wardrobe before collecting Silas and Amy from the B&B, and Jenna told me that *The Gryphon Rider* is doing very well," Charles said. "Loads of favorable reviews and tons of buzz on the social media sites. Jenna thinks Millay stands a strong chance of hitting the *New York Times* list and of having a true breakout book—a book that starts off with a bang and just keeps gaining momentum."

Olivia liked the sound of that. "For Millay's sake, I hope that proves to be true."

Glancing around, her gaze fell on Silas. The famed writer and television producer, who'd brought a box of *No Quarter* T-shirts for Olivia's employees, was chatting with Gabe. Without missing a beat, Gabe poured a drink into a martini glass and served it to Amy with a bright smile. Rawlings took the bar stool next to Amy and asked Gabe which beers were on tap.

"Should we order a bottle of wine?" Olivia asked Charles, knowing how much he enjoyed perusing the restaurant's wine list.

While Charles tried to decide between several of the costlier cabernets, Harris and Laurel gestured for Silas to follow them to one of the bar's seating areas. After settling in the comfortable club chairs, the trio talked and snacked on handfuls of cocktail peanuts.

Charles placed his order with Gabe and then turned back to Olivia. "The chief told me that your professor was released on bail. I'm glad to hear it."

"I just hope it isn't a stay of execution," Olivia said, feeling her jovial mood slip a fraction. "Without another likely suspect in the picture, the police will do all they can to strengthen their case against Emmett."

Charles indicated Silas with his thumb. "Are you planning to give him the third degree tonight?"

"Not at all," Olivia said. "I'm going to sit next to you and talk business. I have several ideas for future bookstore events."

Visibly relieved, Charles smiled. "Excellent. I can't wait to hear them."

Olivia waited until her guests had finished their first round of cocktails and were well into their second before catching the hostess's eye.

The hostess dipped her chin in acknowledgment, showed an elderly couple to their table, and then walked into the bar.

"Your table is ready whenever you are, Ms. Limoges," she announced.

"I think our published author should lead the way," Olivia said, indicating Millay.

Millay grabbed Harris by the elbow. "I'll walk behind you, so that Olivia's customers won't wonder who let the riffraff in."

"I'll only go first to keep the men from ogling you," Harris replied. "If I don't, their wives will catch them staring, marriages will be ruined, and waiters will end up with crappy tips. Stick close, okay?"

Laughing, Millay obliged.

"Silas? Amy?" Olivia beckoned her guests. "Laurel will escort you to the table. I'm going to ask Charles for his advice on wines to accompany our meal."

Rawlings paused for a moment to wink at Olivia before following Amy.

By the time Olivia and Charles reviewed the tasting menu and Olivia passed Charles's recommendations along to a waiter, the rest of the party had already been seated.

As planned, Amy was positioned between Silas and Rawlings. Silas was immediately drawn in by Laurel, but Amy clearly didn't mind. She seemed to have developed an easy report with Rawlings, and Olivia guessed that Rawlings was playing up his roles of aspiring writer, bumbling artist, and history lover while going out of his way to make Amy forget that he was a police chief.

The first course was served and Michel's sumptuous food went a long way in relaxing the entire group. By the end of the second course, Silas was talking louder, smiling wider, and gesticulating enthusiastically. Amy, on the other hand, had her head bent toward Rawlings like a flower tilting toward the sun. She spoke quietly, casting shy smiles at the chief, and seemed to be basking in his attention. Her eyes glimmered with pleasure and the flush in her cheeks deepened with every glass of wine she consumed.

While watching her guests out of the corner of her eye, Olivia discussed tomorrow's launch party with Charles. After that subject was spent, she proposed seasonal menu ideas for the bookstore's eatery, the Biblio Tech Café.

The café was new to Through the Wardrobe. When Charles purchased the failing bookstore, he also bought the abandoned warehouse building next door and renovated both spaces. Half of the bookstore looked exactly as it had before. The books were displayed in antique wardrobes, lending the space a magical, lost-era feel. However, when

Olivia stepped through the massive stainless steel wardrobe that divided the bookstore from the café, she felt like she'd left behind the library of an English country house for a chic bistro in SoHo. The newly renovated space was sleek, modern, and still inviting. The exposed brick wall was covered with oversize posters of book covers, and every table featured electronic screens promoting a range of interesting titles.

Patrons of Biblio Tech could enjoy the usual coffee drinks and a selection of artisan sandwiches. Charles had wisely included a small stage and projector screens in the design plans, giving local musicians a place to perform and encouraging organizations to rent the café for meetings. The front of the room featured a huge display window and a wall-length bar. The bar had numerous outlets, and it was Charles's hope that people would bring their laptops to the bookstore and work while having coffee or a bite to eat.

Olivia loved the idea that Through the Wardrobe would merge two worlds. On one side were books, magazines, a large children's section, and comfortable chairs. It was a reader's paradise. On the other side, customers could hear live performances, savor a delicious meal, and learn about exciting new releases by viewing the screen on their table.

"Prepare yourself, Olivia," Charles had said several weeks ago. "Through the Wardrobe is going to be the town hot spot. This will be one independent bookstore that does more than just survive. It will flourish. Mark my words."

As a waiter cleared their salad plates, Olivia looked at Charles and saw him in a fresh light. He had, in truth, saved the bookstore. The place was dear to her, and she felt such a surge of gratitude toward him that she suddenly grabbed hold of his hand.

"Considering you've hated Oyster Bay for most of your life, you've done a great thing for its residents. If the bookstore had gone under, we'd have lost more than a shop. Part of the town's soul would have died too." She shrugged self-effacingly. "I know I'm waxing poetic, but a person needs a place filled with books. People need to take them off the shelf, feel their weight, smell their pages, and examine their covers. The quiet joy of browsing in a bookstore is one of life's greatest pleasures. The soft music, the coffee-scented air, the rounded depressions in the chairs where countless readers have lost themselves in a story. Whispered conversations, the squeak of a bookmark spinner being turned, the gentle rustle of pages. Paradise."

"I should have had you write the press release," Charles said, squeezing her hand. "I saved the store for you. And for Camille. I've never known two people more enamored with books and stories than you and your mother."

"She would have loved it," Olivia said.

Just then, a waiter cleared his throat behind Olivia's shoulder. "Ms. Limoges, you have a phone call."

Olivia reclaimed her hand and scowled. "Inform whoever it is that I'm not available. We're in the middle of dinner."

The waiter lowered his voice so that only Olivia could hear. "The caller asked me to tell you that it's urgent. His name is Emmett Billinger."

Olivia nodded. "I'll take it in my office, thank you." As she got to her feet, she touched Charles on the arm. "Be right back. Some drama in the kitchen."

"It's not always easy being the boss, but you're a natural." Charles raised his wineglass in salute.

Rawlings, who was still deep in conversation with Amy, glanced up just long enough to meet Olivia's eyes. She flashed him a brief smile and then wove her way through the dining room with as much dignity as she could muster. Her every instinct told her to hurry, but she fought her body's urge to rush until she passed through the swing doors and into the kitchen.

Shutting her office door so hard that she startled her

sleeping poodle, Olivia snatched the cordless phone from its cradle. "Emmett?"

"I'm sorry, Olivia. I know you're having dinner, and I know that I could jeopardize things by interrupting, but I had to call." Emmett sounded winded, as though he'd just finished a fast sprint.

"What happened? Are you all right?"

Emmett took a gulp of air. "I've been running around the parking lot at the ferry dock, looking for my car. It's not here. That's why I'm calling."

Olivia was confused. "I don't understand."

"Damn. It's definitely gone." He exhaled noisily. "Okay, I'm heading to the police station, and I'll explain as I walk. Not that I ever wanted to step foot in there again, but—"

"Emmett!" Olivia said sharply.

"Sorry." Emmett was instantly contrite. "I drove straight back to Palmetto Island from your house. This morning I started talking to people. Members of the conservancy, museum employees, the people working at the lighthouse gift shop, the manager and employees of the marina store. The restaurant staff. Having discovered nothing useful, I invited George and Boyd Allen to my place for an early supper."

Olivia sank into her chair and pressed the receiver against her ear. She could tell that Emmett was still moving and could feel her anxiety rising with his every breath. "And? How did it go?"

"It was a weird evening from the start. They both kept saying how sorry they were that I'd been arrested. However, when I said that I'd soon have to plead my case in court and could use their help avoiding a jail sentence, they went quiet." Emmett paused. "I'm going to sit on the bench outside the station even though it isn't that warm. I have to finish talking to you before I go in. Maybe I shouldn't go in at all. Maybe I'm losing my mind."

"Let me be the judge of that," Olivia said. "Go on."

"Well, George started talking about what the island wanted and how the island resisted change. I wasn't too surprised by this because he said similar things when I was a kid. I thought he was old even then. Part of the reason why he seemed ancient was how he always acted as the island's mouthpiece."

Olivia was unaware that she was shaking her head. "George is in his nineties. If he wanted to stop any changes from occurring, Boyd would have to carry out his wishes."

"I don't think Boyd is healthy enough to have committed those acts, Olivia. I've seen sick people before. If I had to guess, I'd say he has cancer."

Closing her eyes, Olivia was transported back to the Allens' gloomy living room. She remembered the black-and-white photographs and the stacks of old newspapers in vivid detail. The past was preserved in that space, and both of the Allens had devoted their lives to keeping the island's history alive. "George said that his son has headaches, but I think it's more serious than that," Olivia agreed. "Migraines. Seizures. I'm not sure. What I do know is that the Allens have motive, if not the means. They're against the development, and they clearly disapprove of the way Silas presents coastal history."

"That's true, but can you see either of them shooting that deer? Or killing Leigh?"

Olivia admitted that she didn't think it possible. "All right, then," she said, feeling a fresh bout of frustration. "Tell me the rest of your story."

"At one point during the day—and I don't know when— someone entered my house and took my car keys," Emmett said. "I left them in the kitchen by the phone. I was out all day questioning people, so I don't know when it happened, and the deck door was unlocked. Caesar and Calpurnia were with me. They're still too upset to be left alone."

Coldness spread through Olivia's chest. She recognized the familiar sensation. It was dread. "And your car is gone?"

"It's been stolen." Emmett's voice was tight with worry. "The only explanation I can come up with is that I unknowingly spoke with the killer today. I made him or her nervous or angry or what-have-you. Now they've either fled or . . ." He trailed off, waiting for Olivia to fill in the blank.

"Or they're coming to Oyster Bay," she said. "Is that what you believe?"

Emmett hesitated. "I think Silas is the target. I think he's been the target all along."

"If that's true, then why not wait for him to return to the island?" Olivia argued, though she'd voiced the same theory about the crimes focusing on Silas.

"I've tried to put myself in the killer's place, and the answer to your question seems clear enough," Emmett said. "Silas will be surrounded by hordes of people when he returns. On-set security, assistants, actors, cameramen, grips, makeup artists, etcetera. Over the next few weeks, he'll hardly ever be alone."

"Whereas he's vulnerable here. With us." Olivia cast a wild glance around her windowless office. The coldness in her chest seeped into her limbs, and she was desperate to move. To act. "I need to tell Rawlings. Report your missing car to the cops, and I'll call you back later. When I know we're all safe."

After begging her to be careful, Emmett hung up.

Olivia put down the phone and rushed out of her office. She didn't bother walking gracefully through the dining room, but hurried toward their table. Before she was halfway there, Rawlings was on his feet. Olivia waved for him to follow her to the side of the hostess station. When they were out of sight of most of the diners, she grabbed the chief's arm.

"We might be in danger," she said and repeated what Emmett had told her as quickly and succinctly as possible.

Rawlings reached for his cell phone and headed for the front door before Olivia finished talking. She continued with her hushed narrative until they stepped outside, where they both scanned the street and parking lot.

"What's the make and model of Emmett's car?" Rawlings asked when Olivia was done.

"Damn, I forgot to ask." Olivia felt incredibly foolish. "I'll call him back."

Rawlings shook his head. "No, I'll have Officer Cook contact the Riverport desk clerk. If Emmett's inside the station reporting the theft, he might not answer his phone."

"What should we do, Sawyer?"

"We should treat this very seriously," he said, his eyes moving slowly over the parked cars. "Mr. Black and Ms. Holden will stay with me in town tonight. The killer will expect them to be in a hotel, so they'll be safer at my house."

Olivia nodded. "Then I'm staying with you. As is Haviland."

"That won't be necessary. I'll put a car with two officers outside the house, and I'll keep watch from inside." Rawlings brushed her cold cheek with his fingertips. "If the killer is after Silas, then I want to put as much distance between you and him as possible."

Olivia gazed at the shadowy trees and shrubs that created a natural barrier between The Boot Top Bistro and the main road. "The Allens know my name. I told them about growing up next to a lighthouse. If they can't find Silas, they might come looking for me. *If* the Allens stole Emmett's car. I still don't think either one of them is physically capable of these crimes."

Rawlings said nothing for a long moment. He stood and listened. His jaw was clenched, and his body was tense. "Our dining companions should be done with their entrées by now," he finally said. "Let them continue with their meal. I don't want to move them until Cook arrives. Go into the kitchen and lock the back door. Keep your cell phone on you. After I text you, calmly lead our friends and guests through the kitchen and outside."

"I don't want to leave you out here by yourself," Olivia said though she knew he'd been armed the entire evening.

Rawlings removed his handgun from its holster and clicked off the safety. "This is what I do, Olivia. Go inside, please."

When she didn't move, he smiled at her. "I'll be all right."

Nodding solemnly, she reached for the door. She paused for several seconds, her fingers closing around the brass handle, and glanced back at Rawlings. They exchanged a long and tender look.

And then Olivia left him to face the shadows alone.

Chapter 14

Writing is both mask and unveiling.

—E. B. WHITE

Olivia explained the situation to her friends and guests over dessert. Her voice was calm, but her gaze kept straying to her cell phone.

"I'm *from* the North Carolina coast," Silas blurted. He seemed more offended than afraid. "How can they view *me* as an outsider? *My whole life* has been defined by the history of this state. This is ridiculous."

No one responded to his outburst.

Harris, who'd only taken a bite of his dessert, frowned at Olivia. "Why does the professor blame the Allens for stealing his car?"

"Emmett doesn't know who took it for certain, but George and Boyd were at his house for dinner last night, and he thinks they'd do anything to defend the island," Olivia said in a low voice. "Either way, the chief is concerned for Mr. Black's and Ms. Holden's safety, so we're going to do exactly as he says."

Charles sighed. "I was hoping we could put that horrible business of the ghost stories behind us."

Millay shook her head. "I knew it would follow us here. Something prompted the killer to act, and I think it was the sale of the Allen's Creek land. The ghost stories were just stories until that deal became publicized." She spread her hands. "I'm sorry to be blunt, Silas, but I believe your business venture started all of this."

"But the debate over the land went on for months before the purchase was finalized," Silas argued. "There were numerous town hall meetings and plenty of press coverage. The land was surveyed, investors visited the island—I've been twice in the past year. If someone wanted to take a shot at me, they didn't have to wait."

"But the sale didn't become public until the day the deer was killed and put on display," Harris said. "That can't be coincidence."

"Did the Allens have a claim on that land?" Laurel asked Silas. "It does bear their name."

"No," he answered firmly. "The creek was named after George's father, but he never owned a square foot of land near its banks. In fact, there are no deeds connected to the Allens other than the cottage they currently live in."

Olivia turned to Charles. "Then who owned the land? It's a done deal, so there's no need to protect the seller's identity any longer."

Charles shrugged. "His name is Bill Henley and he lives out-of-state. His family has owned the tract since his father, Bill Senior, tried to turn Palmetto Island into a vacationer's paradise in the sixties. Back then, the endeavor failed, so Bill Senior sold the marina and hotel outright and loaned the Allen's Creek land to the wildlife conservancy. There was a clause in the loan stating that Bill's heirs could reclaim the land at any time. Bill Senior passed away a year ago, and Bill Junior decided that he wanted to see his father's vision of an island resort come to fulfillment. However, he didn't want to take on the project himself, so he decided to sell the land to someone who would develop it."

"So how did you become involved?" Olivia asked Silas.

"Bill and I were fraternity brothers. We're also neighbors on Palmetto Island," Silas said. "Knowing I'd be interested in investing in a development, he reached out to me. I brought Charles on board and the rest is history."

Olivia glanced at Charles and saw a wary look in her father's eyes. It was the same look she'd seen on the island. The one that told her that Silas and Charles shared a secret.

Before she could let Charles know that she was on to him, her cell phone vibrated. She read Rawlings's message and slowly rose to her feet. "Please get your things and follow me into the kitchen. Officer Cook is waiting by the back door."

Charles gestured at one of the wine bottles, which was half-full. "Too bad I'm driving."

"You're not," Olivia said firmly. "The chief has arranged for another officer to take you home."

Laurel touched Millay's arm. "I'll take you and Harris. Other than the glass of wine I had before dinner, I've stuck to water. That makes me your designated driver. Besides, you're now a star, so you need a chauffeur."

"And your minivan's just like a limo," Harris teased. "It has a TV and lots of cup holders."

Olivia led her friends through the dining room and into the kitchen.

The staff paused in the midst of chopping, steaming, sautéing, and cleaning to stare at the interlopers.

"Excellent meal, Chef," Charles said, clapping an astonished Michel on the back. "One of the best I've ever had."

While Olivia fetched Haviland from her office, the rest of the Bayside Book Writers complimented Michel until his chest puffed with pride.

"I am very grateful for the praise, but this is highly irregular." He waved his arm around the kitchen. "Normally, the chef visits the dining room."

"We wanted to thank you, but we also needed an escape route," Silas said placidly. "Stalkers. Happens all the time."

Baffled, Michel looked to Olivia for an explanation. Not wanting to cause him unnecessary worry, she said. "As a precaution, the chief has assigned two officers to keep an eye on the restaurant. They'll be outside until you lock up. There's no cause for alarm."

Taking Silas by the elbow, she practically pulled him to the exit door. At the same time, she called for Haviland to heel. She didn't want her poodle darting outside with armed policemen waiting on the other side of the door.

Olivia cracked the door and was relieved to see Officer Cook's familiar face. He told her to send everyone out.

"Let's go," she ordered and gave Silas a little push.

Unable to resist a dramatic exit, he glanced over his shoulder and saluted the kitchen staff. "If I die tonight, I die having dined on excellent food. Good night and thank you!"

Officer Cook, who was clearly displeased by Silas's cavalier attitude, bustled Silas and Amy into the backseat of his cruiser. With his hand on his holster, he scanned the parking lot before waving the rest of the group outside. Another patrol car was idling behind Cook's, and a third was closer to the street. Two officers were searching the property on foot. They swept their flashlight beams over the parked cars, and the light refracted off windows and rearview mirrors.

In these brief seconds of illumination, Olivia's imagination ran wild. Dry cleaning hanging from hooks became a man hiding in the backseat, and every shadow between every car turned into a killer, crouched and waiting to spring.

Olivia stood with Cook and watched Laurel's minivan pull out of the lot. Charles was settled in the patrol car behind Cook's, and Haviland was shifting uneasily by Olivia's side. It was time to go.

"Where's the chief?" Olivia asked.

Cook pointed. "In his car. He wants to leave last—to make sure no one's following us to his place." He opened the passenger door for Olivia. "Don't worry, ma'am. I'll be watching the house all night. No one will come anywhere near you."

Reassured by Cook's confidence, Olivia got in the car. Haviland sat on her lap, his nails digging into her thighs and his nose pressed against the window. Olivia used her sleeve to wipe away the smudges he made. She wanted to be able to see every car that passed by.

"What's the make and model of the stolen car?" she quietly asked Cook.

"A silver Ford Explorer with a custom roof rack for kayaks and canoes." He recited the license plate number. "It's an Adopt a Greyhound plate. Has a dog outline and a red heart on the left-hand side."

"Of course it does," Olivia said and held Haviland a little tighter.

Olivia tried to sleep but couldn't. Amy had gone to bed soon after arriving at the chief's house, and Rawlings and Silas were in the living room, speaking in hushed tones. Haviland was curled up by Olivia's feet, his steady exhalations a familiar and comforting sound.

Olivia's mind refused to quiet. It wasn't fear that kept her awake, but the unanswered questions swirling around and around in her head like a whirlpool.

A blade of moonlight snuck through the gap in the curtains and painted a white line on the duvet cover. Every so often, the wind would nudge the bushes outside the window and shadows from the crape myrtle branches would fracture the light.

The crooked shadows reminded Olivia of the island's maritime forest. Her mind leapt from image to image. The lighthouse, Land End Lodge, the Allens' sad cottage. She'd never sensed malice in George or Boyd. To her, they were tragic figures. Men who dwelled in the past and had little hope or joy in the future. Olivia remembered how affectionate George and Boyd were with each other. She recalled George's bone-deep weariness and Boyd's weakness and pallor. It was impossible for her to accept the idea that they'd taken Emmett's car keys, crossed the Cape Fear River, and were headed to Oyster Bay. For what purpose? To bring another ghost story to life?

From the living room, Olivia heard Silas laugh.

She turned on her side, putting her back to the window, and closed her eyes. She pictured herself on that first ferry ride when the deckhand had told her about the quarantine platform. She remembered the brown pelicans diving into the water and the small boats dotting the water around them.

Suddenly, she sat up.

"Boyd had a boat. He caught fish and crabs to sell to the island's two restaurants. He had a boat." Getting out of bed, she slipped one of Rawlings's sweatshirts over the T-shirt and boxer shorts she'd taken from his dresser, and tiptoed into the living room.

Seeing her, Rawlings jumped to his feet. "Did you hear something?"

"No." She briefly laid a hand on his chest, silently assuring him that all was well. "I can't sleep. The same questions have been running on a loop in my head, but then a new thought floated to the surface when I started thinking about boats."

Silas, who had a tumbler of whiskey in his hand, peered at her from under heavy lids. "At two in the morning?"

Ignoring him, Olivia sat down next to Rawlings. His right hand rested on the arm of the sofa, inches away from the end table where he'd placed his sidearm. Olivia took his left hand and pressed her palm against his.

"Whoever broke into the museum was either already on the island or had access to a boat," she said, noting the exhaustion on Rawlings's face. The lines between his brows and bracketing his mouth looked deeper, but his gaze was still sharp and alert. "Whoever killed that deer needed a boat too. That man from the conservancy—Brett, I think—was adamant about the doe not being from the island. Every island deer was tagged and tracked, so the white doe must have been *brought* to the island. By boat."

Rawlings had a faraway look in his eye and Olivia knew that he was reviewing the details of each crime.

"The killer could have used a boat to lure Ms. Whitlow along the beach. He could have played a recording of the ship bell while quietly motoring in the shallows. Though this seems like a great deal of trouble to go through to replicate the sounds of a ghost story. And why would Ms. Whitlow follow the sound of the bell in the first place? I keep coming back to the question," he mused to himself. "But if the killer did use a boat, any hull marks could have been erased by the incoming tide by the time you found Ms. Whitlow the following morning."

"Boyd Allen has a boat," Olivia said. "Though I have no idea what kind or where it's kept. From what I understood during our visit, the boats in the harbor are all luxury yachts or motorboats owned by vacationers. Since no one other than the Allens lives on the island, there's no need for anyone to own a permanent mooring. But what about the people who work on Palmetto Island? Does Jan Powell or someone else who was passionately against the sale of the Allen's Creek land also have a boat?"

Silas groaned. "Not *her* again!"

"She supposedly had a solid alibi, but I wonder . . ." Olivia leaned toward Silas. "Is Peterson involved in the development? Has he been promised a kickback of any kind?"

"In exchange for what?" Silas's tone was glib. "Covering up my involvement in Leigh's murder? I know you think I'm somehow culpable. Charles told me."

The words were a knife-twist in Olivia's heart. How could her father be so duplicitous? "Your alibi is too convenient."

Silas shook his head. The movement was very slow, as though he was under water. He suddenly seemed drained of all energy. "I didn't hurt Leigh. Not physically, anyway. I hurt her in every other possible way during our time together, but I haven't so much as touched her for weeks." He took a swallow of whiskey and winced. "You don't really believe I'm a murderer. If you did, we wouldn't be having a cordial chat in the police chief's living room."

"You've done something wrong," Olivia insisted. "Charles knows what it is. You and he share a secret, and I believe that secret set these events in motion. If not, we wouldn't be sitting in the police chief's living room."

"Touché." Silas polished off his whiskey and saluted Rawlings with the empty glass. "I'm turning in. Thank you for watching over us." He walked toward the hall and then paused. Glancing back at Olivia, he said. "To paraphrase the Bard, I plan to sleep despite the thunder. I hope you will too."

Eventually, Olivia did. She sat with Rawlings for another hour, but after that, he convinced her to go to bed. She'd barely hit the pillow when she was pulled down into sleep like a stone dropped into a dark, deep ocean.

Through the Wardrobe was buzzing when Olivia arrived. Charles unlocked the front door, and together, they walked into the café, where they found Jenna giving a pep talk to the employees. When she was done, she yielded the floor to Rawlings.

"You'll see a significant police presence at this event," he told the staff. "Our primary purpose is crowd control, but we're also on the lookout for two men who may have malicious intent toward Mr. Black. Officer Cook will distribute photos of these men." He waited a heartbeat. "If you see either of these men, alert an officer immediately. Do not approach them."

"What'd they do?" one of the café workers asked as Cook began to distribute the candid shots of George and Boyd Allen that Harris had luckily captured during the Legends of Coastal Carolina Festival.

"At this point, we have no evidence that they've done anything unlawful or will appear today at all," Rawlings said. "We're viewing them as a possible threat as a precaution and wanted you to be aware of the situation. Thank you for your cooperation."

It had taken Rawlings half a dozen phone calls to the Riverport Police to learn that the Allens were not at home, nor had anyone seen them in the past twenty-four hours. So while he told the bookstore and café staff that the police presence was just a precaution, Olivia knew better. Rawlings and his men were on high alert.

Olivia, who'd hoped to corner Charles and demand that he tell her what he and Silas had to hide, was soon swept up in last-minute prep for the launch party. The bookstore phone rang nonstop, employees positioned signs and tied balloon bouquets to chair backs, and police radios contributed to the overall din.

With only minutes left until it was time to unlock the front doors, Millay and Silas mounted the stage in the back corner of the café. They sat behind a sturdy library table, coffee cups and pens at the ready. Both authors were smiling widely, and for a moment, Olivia stood still and reveled in Millay's happiness.

Millay caught her staring. "Not you too. I've had plenty

of gushing from Laurel already. She's in the restroom wiping off mascara tracks for the second time today."

"Just enjoy yourself, okay?" Olivia said. "And know that I'm extremely proud of you." She gave Silas a pointed look. "Make sure to send your fans her way."

"She'll sell out before this event is done. I guarantee it." Seeing Amy enter the café, Silas waved her over. "You ready, honey?"

Amy smiled and nodded, and Olivia was struck by the effect Silas's use of an endearment had on the younger woman. Amy's face glowed, and she hummed softly as she adjusted one of the stanchions that would keep Silas's fans in an orderly line.

Unless she was playing a part, Amy's blushes and shy glances convinced Olivia that the romantic relationship between Silas and Amy was new. Amy might have harbored feelings for Silas for a long time, but Olivia got the sense that Silas hadn't returned those feelings until recently. Very recently.

Could the night he spent with Amy—the night Leigh was killed—have been the first time the two of them were together? Has Silas been telling the truth about that night all along? If so, then who stole the dress from the museum, and how did this person convince Leigh to wear it and walk the beach at night, following the sound of a ship's bell?

When Charles appeared in the doorway separating the bookstore from the café, a pair of gold ceremonial scissors in his hand, Olivia knew that she'd have to put these questions on hold. After wishing Millay luck, she joined Rawlings by the front door. He finished speaking into his radio, slid it into the holder on his utility belt, and looked at Olivia.

"Still no sign of the car?" she asked softly, concerned by his haggard appearance. Rawlings was too old to be pulling all-nighters.

He shook his head and Olivia moved closer to him. "When this is over, I'm taking you straight home."

"I'll drink to that." He smiled and raised a coffee cup to his lips. "I'm riding high on a double espresso. The barista knows his stuff. Your father does too. This place is going to do very well."

Charles beckoned to Olivia. "It's time to charm the members of the press, Olivia."

Rawlings gave her a goofy wink and stood to the side as she and Charles cut through a length of blue ribbon. While Olivia posed for photographs, she noticed the queue of customers waiting to enter the store. There were dozens of men dressed as pirates, and it seemed like half the crowd wore *No Quarter* T-shirts or baseball caps.

She laughed out loud when she spotted Harris in a green Gryphon Clan T-shirt. He walked slowly, pulling a red wagon piled high with folded shirts and enticing the crowd to choose between the Gryphon and Wyvern Clan shirts. Harris had designed and ordered the T-shirts as a surprise, and Olivia couldn't wait to see Millay's face when the first person wearing a shirt based on characters from *The Gryphon Rider* asked her to sign their book.

Despite the festival air both in and outside the bookstore, Olivia was unable to relax. She kept scrutinizing the customers, especially the males. She took in every face, continuously watched the doorway leading into the café so that no one slipped by unnoticed, and checked in with Rawlings every twenty minutes or so.

"No sign of them yet," he'd say, keeping his gaze on the line of people waiting to enter the store. "How are things going for Millay?"

"Really well," Olivia would answer.

In truth, Millay was connecting with everyone she met. Even those who'd come for the sole purpose of meeting Silas found themselves lingering at Millay's end of the table. Her stack of books quickly shrank, and Jenna had to pull more boxes from the storeroom. Silas's books, which were available in both hardcover and paperback reprints, were also disappearing from the table and waterfall displays in the front of the store. Wherever Olivia looked, she saw customers with a Through the Wardrobe shopping bag in one hand and a coffee cup in the other. All the café tables were occupied, as were the reading chairs in the original part of the shop.

Someone tapped her on the shoulder, and she turned to find Charles holding out a plate with a pumpkin scone. "I have two forks. Come on, put your feet up for a second."

"There's no place to sit."

Charles laughed. "I reserved seats at the window bar."

After signaling Millay that she'd be back shortly, Olivia followed Charles to the bar in the front of the café. An employee, who'd been saving their seats for them, quickly wiped off their chairs and then moved off to clear empty coffee mugs from a nearby table.

"I can't believe how many people are still out there." Olivia gestured at the crowd on the other side of the window.

"The event is officially over in thirty minutes," Charles said, dividing the scone in half with the side of his fork. "Silas and Millay will be out of books by then. I thought Jenna had ordered more than enough, but I underestimated Silas's draw. The chocolates Shelley made are gone, as are the T-shirts Harris designed." He pushed the plate closer to Olivia. "Eat something. You look like you need a sugar pick-me-up."

Absently, Olivia raised her fork and speared a piece of pastry. The scone was warm and incredibly moist. She tasted comfort in every bite and could easily imagine how delightful it would be to spend an hour in the café with a cup of tea, a scone, and a book.

"After this turnout, we'll be able to lure other big-name authors to Oyster Bay," Charles said brightly. "We can put them up in the bed-and-breakfast, host a ticketed dinner at The Boot Top Bistro—turn every signing into a major social event. If we get a response like this each time, the bookstore will become a regular stop on author tours."

Olivia nodded. "If we're going to have high-stress events, we'd better make sure the employees are well paid and well prepared. So far, I've been very impressed by the café staff. They've been as efficient as machines, while being exceedingly friendly at the same time."

"The manager is from New York. He's used to running things at breakneck speed, but he also understands that Southern hospitality requires plenty of smiles and small talk. The guy was dying to exchange his shoe-box apartment for a house, a yard, and a more temperate climate. He would have taken the job at half the salary." Charles glanced around the café and sighed in satisfaction. "But I took your advice and offered everyone a bit more money than I'd originally intended."

Olivia gazed out the window. "It's a shame this day ended up being tainted. I wanted it to be perfect for Millay. Even though she's been incredibly busy, part of her must have been expecting something to happen. She's probably studied every face, just as I have. Just as Harris, Laurel, and Rawlings have." She looked at Charles but kept her gaze soft. "Please. If you know anything about Silas—anything from his past that could have initiated this mess—please tell me. He's your friend. I get that. But don't I matter too?" She waved her hand around the room. "What about what we're trying to build together?"

Charles's expression immediately became closed off, distant. He lined up the two forks on the empty plate and made to stand.

"Please," Olivia repeated.

Just then, Jenna appeared behind his shoulder. "We've sold out," she announced gleefully. "Millay's books are totally gone, and there are only a handful of Mr. Black's hardcovers left. I'm taking orders from people and promising to ship copies with signed bookplates so as not to lose sales, but our computers are running super slow." She looked at Charles. "Didn't you say that you knew a way to make the spinning rainbow wheel of death disappear?"

"I most certainly do," Charles chuckled, clearly relieved by the interruption. "I'll be right there." He then turned back to Olivia. "Silas will return to Palmetto Island in the morning. He'll have plenty of film people to protect him, and you and I can focus on what we're doing here."

Olivia's anger flared. "A woman died. There's no return to normalcy in the wake of a murder. Murder creates its own kind of shrapnel. It flies out in all directions, injuring everyone in its path. I've seen the damage it inflicts. We can't just pretend nothing happened. We have a responsibility, Charles."

"Yes," he agreed unconvincingly. "And right now, mine is to help Jenna."

"Damn it," Olivia muttered when Charles was gone. She carried the plate to a busing station and returned to the author table. Both Millay and Silas were on their feet, stretching and drinking thirstily from their water bottles.

The event had come to a close more quickly than Olivia had anticipated. She looked out the window and found that there were no more customers waiting to get into the bookstore. She could also see that the sky had gone from a dull gray to a murky charcoal hue, as though the empty sidewalk had given night permission to fall.

Rawlings entered the café and, after seeking Olivia with his eyes, waved at her before heading over to where Silas stood talking to a group of teenage girls. Rawlings pulled Silas aside and seemed to be relaying instructions to him. Silas nodded, shook Rawlings's hand, and then signaled for Amy to gather their things.

Olivia waited for the group by the steel wardrobe.

"We're taking Mr. Black and Ms. Holden out through the back door," Rawlings quietly explained. "It'll be easier to guard them at the B&B, especially now that it's getting dark."

Suddenly, Rawlings's radio crackled and he held it up to his ear.

Olivia, close on his heel, heard two words. "Victims" and "paramedics."

Rawlings swung around and raised his hand. "Stop," he commanded sternly. "Wait here." Putting his hand on Olivia's shoulder, he squeezed her hard and said, "You too. I mean it, Olivia."

Seeing the mixture of fear and sorrow in his eyes, Olivia knew she couldn't obey. She knew that following him would cause her pain, but she couldn't stop herself. She had to see.

Casting a frantic glance around the café, she noticed Millay chatting with a barista. She hurried into the bookstore and spotted Laurel and Harris speaking with Dixie and Shelley.

Trailing after Rawlings, she made a mental catalog of the people she cared about. They were all present. All safe.

All but one.

Charles. The name reverberated through her mind. *Charles. Charles. Charles.*

She was unaware that she was whispering his name over and over as she followed Rawlings through the children's section and into the storeroom. She didn't know that she was chanting it like a prayer until she came to a halt at the back door.

She only stopped speaking when she saw the blood.

So much blood.

Her dazed murmur became a scream.

Chapter 15

~~~~~~

He did not wear his scarlet coat,
For blood and wine are red,
And blood and wine were on his hands
When they found him with the dead.

—OSCAR WILDE

The scream turned into a strangled cry as Olivia clamped a hand over her own mouth.

Rawlings tried to pull her away, but she wrested her arm free and knelt beside Charles's body. A police officer pressed a folded cloth against Charles's stomach, and Olivia could see that it was already saturated with blood.

"Paramedics are en route," another officer said.

"Get clean dishcloths from the café!" Olivia shouted to him without looking away from Charles's ashen face.

Charles was lying in the stockroom, a few feet from the back door. The door was ajar, and when Olivia shot a brief glance through the opening, she saw more officers clustered around another body.

Only the victim's legs were visible, and it took Olivia's brain a moment to register that the black skirt and camel-colored ankle boots belonged to Jenna.

"No, no, no," she whispered. Not knowing where else to look, she focused on the officer trying to stop Charles's abdomen from bleeding. "What happened?" she asked him. "Was he stabbed?"

"Yes, ma'am. It's a nasty wound, I'm afraid."

Olivia put her hand on Charles's forehead. It felt simultaneously cold and clammy. She gently pushed a strand of damp hair off his brow, and he groaned. He opened his eyes, though not all the way, and peered at Olivia from beneath heavy lids.

"Jenna," he croaked.

"Shhhhh." Olivia continued stroking his hair. "Don't try to talk. Help is coming."

Someone proffered a wad of dish towels to the officer tending to Charles, but Olivia grabbed them. "Let me," she told the officer.

Clamping his fingers around her wrists, he forced her to push the fresh towels against the wound. Olivia was sickened by the deep gash in Charles's belly and terrified by the sight of so much blood, but she didn't flinch.

"Apply firm pressure." The officer positioned Olivia's hands so that both of them covered the towels. "Use your body weight."

Olivia wished she could pour her strength into Charles's body. With every passing second, he seemed to be weakening, to be growing paler and less substantial.

She searched the area, her eyes passing over half a dozen police officers. "Where are the damned EMTs?" she yelled, her voice shrill with fear. "Rawlings!"

He came in from outside at once. "They're here. They're just backing in. Hold on, Olivia. Keep holding on."

"He's running out of time!" she cried, and then she saw that Charles's lips were moving.

Keeping her arms taut, she leaned over, putting her head as close to his lips as she could without releasing any of the pressure she was applying to his wound. "Dad," she said for the very first time. "You're going to be okay."

The policemen near the door parted, allowing the paramedics through.

"The secret," Charles murmured. "The cup . . . Silas . . . took it. Long . . . time ago."

"That's what this is all about?" Olivia asked. She hated the way Charles's words were faint whispers of breath. They sounded like a deathbed speech. And though she didn't want to hear them, she had to know. "A cup?"

Charles, too weak to nod, blinked his eyes once, and then closed them.

"Ma'am, we've got this." An EMT touched Olivia's arm, indicating she should move.

Numbly, Olivia backed away. She watched the paramedics apply an oxygen mask and a blood pressure cuff to Charles. He turned his head to the left and right, his fingers stretched, searching.

"I'm here," Olivia said loudly as he was loaded onto a gurney. His skin was chalk white. "I won't leave you."

She started to follow the paramedics to the ambulance, but Rawlings caught her by the shoulders. He tried to block the door, to keep her from seeing Jenna. "Cook can take you to the hospital."

"No, I need to be with him." Olivia twisted away. The urgency to be with Charles was overpowering. She had lost too many people already. She felt that if she could just stay with Charles, he would stay with her.

She took two paces forward and then stopped.

Jenna was lying on the ground, injured. Or dead.

A paramedic was pressing a thick wad of gauze against the delicate flesh of her neck.

In the disco flashes created by the ambulance light bar, Olivia met Jenna's glassy stare. Just when Olivia was on the verge of crying out, Jenna blinked.

She wasn't dead. She was in shock. Olivia guessed that Jenna had been stabbed, or cut, in the neck. She'd probably lost a great deal of blood and needed to be rushed to the hospital as quickly as Charles.

Suddenly, Olivia became disoriented. The lights confused her. There was too much noise. Too many colors. She tried to walk, but her legs wouldn't respond.

And then Rawlings had his arm around her waist. He led her to the closest of the two ambulances and helped her inside.

Feeling nauseated, Olivia found Charles's hand and clasped it. Nothing else made sense but the feel of his flesh on hers.

"He's in custody. It's over," Rawlings said from what seemed like a great distance. He spoke other words too, but they failed to penetrate the fog in Olivia's head. Before she knew it, the ambulance doors slammed shut and they were moving.

Olivia bobbed back and forth in the cabin, deaf to the siren's shriek, the abrupt turns, and the bursts of acceleration. She felt like a buoy cut from its mooring line, set adrift in rough seas. The only thing keeping her from going under was the hand in her hand. There was a pocket of warmth where her skin met her father's, and she focused on this fragile tether with everything she had. The warmth meant that her father was with her. The warmth meant that he was not letting go.

A nurse had given Olivia a pair of scrubs and showed her to the women's restroom.

"You can put your clothes in here," she'd said, handing Olivia a red plastic biohazard bag.

When Olivia hesitated, the woman had smiled kindly. "If there's any news, I'll come get you. Until then, you should change and have some caffeine. You can only help if you stay strong."

Olivia obediently put on the scrubs, stuffed her bloodstained clothing in the plastic bag, and was now drinking hot chocolate from the vending machine.

The waiting room was cold and quiet. Olivia huddled into her thin sweater and wished she'd taken the blanket the EMT had offered her, but she'd been too fixated on her father to respond.

My father, she thought in surprise.

Charles Wade hadn't raised her. He hadn't known her as a child. And yet she carried his genetic code. If someone were to unroll her like a blueprint, he'd be there, visible in the lines and corridors.

And since Olivia had already lost the man she'd thought of as her father, she didn't want to lose her second chance at being someone's daughter.

She finished her drink and cradled the empty cup between her hands and mulled over what Charles had murmured about a secret until Harris, Millay, and Laurel entered the waiting room.

Laurel had a blanket tucked under her arm, and Harris carried a takeout tray of Starbucks.

"There you are." After draping the blanket around Olivia's shoulders, Laurel rubbed her back in wide, circular motions. "You're freezing." She gestured at Harris. "Give her a coffee."

"I added shots of whiskey to all of them," Harris said. "We need to warm up from the inside. I feel cold right here." He pressed his fist against the center of his chest.

Millay sat down next to Olivia and jerked her head at the OR doors. A bold red plaque reading NO ADMITTANCE was attached directly to the wood. "How's he doing?"

Olivia followed her gaze. "He's lost so much blood. That wound . . ." She shook her head. "And Jenna. God. Jenna. She's back there too." She looked at Laurel. "Was it the Allens?"

"It was Boyd," Millay said. "He'd been hiding in the store since yesterday."

Laurel shuddered. "He must have slipped in when one of the employees brought something out to the Dumpster or a delivery was being made. There are so many boxes in the storeroom that he just hid behind them, in the far corner. There was no reason for anyone to go back there."

"Why would he attack Charles and Jenna?" Olivia was unable to process what she was hearing. "I thought the Allens were after Silas."

"We don't understand it either," Harris said. "But the chief is with Boyd now. He'll get answers from him."

Olivia took a sip of coffee. The woody, slightly metallic taste of whiskey coated her tongue and burned her throat. It also woke her from her stupor. She drank some more, allowing the heat to sear through a layer of shock. "This is more than a shot, Harris, but it's just what I needed. Thank you."

A chorus of voices echoed down the hall and, suddenly, Rawlings appeared in the waiting room. He and one of the hospital security guards held a short conversation, and then he joined the rest of the Bayside Book Writers.

"Why are you here, Chief?" Harris asked.

"Boyd collapsed," Rawlings said, squatting down in front of Olivia. He put his hands on her knees and searched her face. "Are you okay?"

She shrugged as though to say she couldn't possibly answer such a question. "Charles and Jenna are both in surgery. I've been told that the wound in Jenna's neck missed the artery. As for Charles, he's lost a great deal of blood." Olivia struggled to keep the panic from entering her voice. It was there, on the edge of each word. "Has Boyd been admitted too?"

Rawlings nodded. "He wasn't right when we arrested him. He was so weak that he couldn't stand, and he had a seizure at the station. I don't even think he was aware that we Mirandized him."

Olivia wasn't sure she could handle any more surprises. "I can't believe this."

"What about George?" Laurel asked. "Did you find him? Or Emmett's car?"

"Not yet." Rawlings stood with a grunt. "Cook is leading the investigation. Because Charles is my father-in-law, it would be a conflict of interest for me to take charge, which is why I'm dealing with Boyd. Cook is doing everything by the book. He has a team searching for George Allen and a second team collecting evidence and securing the scene at Through the Wardrobe."

Flashing on the image of Jenna's glassy stare, Olivia pulled the blanket tighter across her chest. "Has Jenna's family been notified?"

"Yes," Rawlings said quietly. "They're on their way."

"Meanwhile, Silas, who is responsible for all that's happened, is just fine and dandy." Olivia shook her head in frustration. "Charles was trying to tell me about Silas's secret, but all he managed to say was 'the cup' and 'he took it long ago.'"

Harris frowned pensively. "Took? Or stole?"

"If there's a secret attached to this cup, I doubt Silas got it as a Christmas gift," Millay said. She looked at Harris. "Time to whip out your phone and start researching. We're not dealing with the Riverport cops anymore. You work for the good guys, remember?"

"That might be the nicest thing you've ever said to me." Harris smiled at Millay and reached for his phone. His index fingers flew across the screen, and then he blew out an exasperated breath. "This connection's too slow. I'm better off using my desktop at home. I've modified my Wi-Fi, and I also have access to all the databases from there."

Olivia nodded. "You should go."

"I'll come with you," Millay said. "I can follow any leads using your laptop." She shot an apologetic glance at Olivia. "I hate places like this, but I'd stay for you."

"No," Olivia said. "You should go with Harris. And Millay? I'm sorry your launch ended the way it did."

Millay's eyes darkened with anger. "Are you kidding me?

You and Charles gave me the release party of my dreams. If he doesn't come out of there okay"—she pointed at the operating room doors—"I'll kill Boyd Allen myself!"

"We need Mr. Allen to live," Rawlings said very gently. "Unless we find George, Boyd is the only person who can explain this madness."

"Screw that. He can go right ahead and die," Olivia said savagely. "If Charles survives, he'll tell us about the secret, or we can hold Silas down and beat it out of him!"

Laurel tossed her empty coffee cup into the trash bin. "She has a point, Chief. Why should Silas be treated with kid gloves? Leigh's been murdered. Jenna's in surgery, and Charles might be fighting for his life in the next room." She gestured at the double doors. "If Silas had answers all along—a secret that created a chain reaction—then he shouldn't be allowed to drive back to Palmetto Island and start filming as if nothing ever happened."

"You're right, which is why Cook is interviewing him as we speak," Rawlings said. "Ms. Holden is being interviewed as well. We're not on Palmetto Island or in Riverport. We're in Oyster Bay, and two of our own—for Charles Wade *is* one of us—have been gravely injured." He looked at each of the Bayside Book Writers in turn. "Just because I sound calm doesn't mean that I'm not raging inside. If Mr. Black's actions, past or present, determined what happened at the bookstore today, then he will answer for it. I promise you."

His words hung in the air for a long moment.

Millay nodded and said, "We'll call if we find anything."

As soon as Millay and Harris had gone, Olivia turned to Laurel. "You should go too—be with your family. I know you also have an article to file. I'd rather you write about Jenna and Charles than anyone else."

"They're both going to be okay. Charles is going to pull through. You'll see." Her eyes wet with tears, Laurel hugged Olivia and then walked briskly away.

An hour later, a female doctor appeared in the waiting room.

"Are you with Charles Wade?" she asked.

Olivia got to her feet. "I'm his daughter," she answered. Rawlings put his hand on the small of her back, steadying her.

"Your father's abdominal wall was penetrated, and an area of his intestines sustained injury. We were able to successfully clean and suture the wound, and he's being taken to the post-op recovery room. He lost a great deal of blood, and whenever a patient sustains an abdominal penetrating trauma, we need to be on guard against infection." She paused to make sure Olivia was following along.

"What comes next?" Olivia asked.

"An abdominal CT scan. This is to be certain that there weren't what we call occult injuries. These are injuries that are not apparent during initial presentation. I didn't see this type of injury when I was operating, so the scan is more of a precaution. We'll run several tests on your father over the next few hours. Because of the seriousness of his injury, I'm keeping him in the ICU."

Despite the amount of detail the doctor had given her, Olivia was still unclear as to her father's condition. "May I see him?"

"Later tonight, maybe," the doctor said and then offered a reassuring smile. "Your father obviously takes good care of himself. That made my job easier. If all goes well over the next twenty-four hours, we can hope for a full recovery."

Olivia finally let go of the breath she'd been holding. "Thank you. And what about Jenna? She came in the same time as my father."

Rawlings briefly explained their relationship to Jenna.

"She's stable," the doctor replied. "We're expecting her to make a full recovery."

With her messages delivered, the doctor handed Olivia

off to a nurse, who supplied her with phone numbers for the ICU desk and a piece of paper outlining visiting hours and rules.

Olivia slipped the paper into her handbag and turned to Rawlings. "I should feed and walk Haviland while Charles is in the recovery room. It'll take me a while to get home and back here again."

"He would have liked how you called him your father," Rawlings said. "You should do that again when he wakes up." He dug in his pocket and pulled out his badge wallet. "I need to get an update on Mr. Allen's condition. After that, I'll probably head into the station. I'll keep checking in with you, okay?"

Olivia put her arms around Rawlings and sighed. From the moment she'd seen Charles on the floor, she'd been holding herself as tightly as a fist, but now she dared to let go a little. Closing her eyes, she rested her head against Rawlings's shoulder. Together, they spent a quiet minute listening to the waiting room music, the hum of the fluorescent ceiling lights, and the echo of rubber-soled shoes in the hallway.

Eventually, Rawlings pulled away and placed his car keys in Olivia's open palm. "You'll need these," he said, kissing her lightly. "Talk to you soon."

She watched him approach the nurses' station, opening his badge wallet as he walked. Though part of her wanted to stay and hear what had become of Boyd Allen, she most longed to be with Haviland. Just thinking of him waiting for her at the kitchen door had her quickening her pace.

She planned to feed him and then force herself to eat a little dinner. Afterward, she and Haviland would go down to the beach. Olivia wanted the salt-laced air to whip her hair and to sink her feet in the damp sand. She needed to hear the rush of the breaking waves and for the water to run over her hands, washing her clean.

* * *

The sky was lit by an enormous moon. It hung low on the horizon and was as gleaming white as a restaurant dinner plate. Olivia remembered how her mother used to look up different moon names in the *Farmer's Almanac*, so after feeding Haviland, she pulled her own copy off the cookbook shelf and flipped to the section on moons.

"The full moon in October, which rises one month after the Harvest Moon, was called the Hunter's Moon by certain American Indian tribes," she read over the sound of Haviland's gulping. "This was when the leaves were falling and the game was fattened. It was the time to hunt and fill storehouses for the winter. This moon was also known as the Travel Moon." She paused to stare at the next line. "And the Dying Moon."

Unwittingly, memories from Palmetto Island, from the felled doe to Leigh's lifeless body spread out on the beach like a starfish, flooded her mind. And her thoughts were already overwhelmed by traumatic imagery from the bookstore. Slamming the almanac shut, Olivia pulled on a coat and took Haviland outside.

She brought her phone along, hoping that Harris would send a text saying that he'd solved the riddle of the cup, and tried to focus on Haviland.

Her poodle raced along the waterline, releasing some of his pent-up energy in short bursts of speed. He barked at shadows, snapped at eddies of wind-blown sand, and then doubled back to Olivia. He'd let her pet him once or twice before leaping away again, glancing playfully over his shoulder as he ran.

He darted past the lighthouse, his ears flattened. Sand shot out from under his paws, and his black body nearly merged with the night.

Olivia, whose attention was divided between her poodle and the moon's reflection on the water, grew calmer. The empty stretch of beach and the endless, gentle rolling of the ocean made her feel like she could breathe again.

She walked briskly to the Point, a jetty that stuck out into the water. This jetty lacked the unsettling atmosphere of Cape Fear. She thought of the toy pirate coin she'd found before Leigh's death and wondered what message the ocean had been trying to send her in the coin with the snarling face.

After gazing over the water for several minutes, Olivia shouted for Haviland and turned back toward home. She was approaching the lighthouse when she saw a glint of moonlight on metal in the dunes. She veered to the right, confused by the bulky shape peeking out from behind the base of the lighthouse. Suddenly, there was a flash of red, and Olivia realized that the moon was reflecting off a taillight.

"A car," she murmured. For half a second, she wondered why someone would park on the sand, but then, another thought quickly replaced the first.

Emmett's car.

She could see the outline more clearly now. It was definitely a silver SUV.

"Haviland. To me!" Olivia ordered. Fear made her voice high and shrill.

Sensing her mood, Haviland was instantly alert. His body tensed and he sniffed the air in search of the threat.

Olivia pulled out her phone and called Rawlings. When her call went straight to voice mail, she left a hurried message and then dialed Harris's number.

"I'm glad it's you," Harris said excitedly. "I think I found the mystery cup."

"Harris," she whispered. "I'm at the lighthouse. Emmett's car is here."

There was a brief hesitation as Harris took this in. "Don't get close, Olivia," he pleaded. "Go home and call the chief."

"I tried to reach Rawlings, but he didn't answer, so I'm calling you."

"Millay and I are heading over. She'll drive while I get in touch with Cook. Is Haviland with you?"

Olivia reached out to touch her poodle. She couldn't count the number of times she'd been grateful to have him by her side, and this was certainly one of them. "He's here. We'll meet you at my house."

After putting the phone back in her pocket, Olivia stood still and listened. Other than the wind rustling through the sea oats and the sound of the waves, there were no other noises.

Moving closer to Emmett's SUV, Olivia watched Haviland carefully for signs of alarm, but he appeared completely at ease.

Olivia peeked through the passenger window and saw the keys dangling from the ignition. She also saw that the passenger door hadn't been closed all the way. Carefully stepping away from the car, she used the flashlight mode on her phone to shine a light on the sand. There was a line of footprints heading from the passenger side toward the lighthouse.

"George," Olivia whispered, stooping to examine one of the prints. It was elongated, as though the elderly man had staggered through the sand.

"Stay close," Olivia told Haviland.

Her fear had dissipated. Instead, she felt a hollowness in the center of her chest. Someone had attempted to kill Jenna and Charles today. Leigh Whitlow was already dead. The unsuspecting woman had been lulled outside in the middle of the night to be drowned in the cold water. And Olivia had the sensation that there would be more death before the night was through.

The closer she got to the lighthouse, the stronger that feeling became.

Haviland began to growl. It started as a low rumble deep in his throat, and his gait became tentative. As Olivia coaxed him forward, his growl grew louder and his lips peeled back, revealing his teeth.

A figure rested against the base of the lighthouse. The dark shadow of a man sitting in the sand, his legs stretched out before him, his head slumped over his chest.

"Shhh," Olivia murmured to Haviland. Her hands were shaking, and the tremble began to move up her arms.

"George?" she whispered, directing the phone's flashlight beam on the man.

She let the light touch him for only a moment before turning it off.

"George," she repeated mournfully.

She didn't need to get any closer to know that George Allen was dead.

Olivia sank to her knees and let an inexplicable wave of sorrow wash over her. This man, who'd been overlooked by the world for more than ninety years, had met his end on a distant beach. This man, who'd been a stranger to her until recently, had reminded her so much of the old lighthouse keeper she'd known as a child. This man, who'd had no one but his son to keep his company for most of his life, had died in an unfamiliar place. Alone.

Olivia knew that she should have been relieved to find George dead. After all, he was somehow involved in the ghost story reenactments. He was likely an accessory to murder. And yet, against all logic, she grieved for him.

Tears slipped down her cheeks and dropped to the sand. She let them fall unchecked, gazing at George through her blurred vision. Haviland whined and licked her hand. She pulled him to her and made soothing noises.

After several minutes, she dried her eyes and stared at the ocean. She wondered how George had gotten to the lighthouse and how long he'd been here. Olivia hadn't taken a walk on the beach yesterday, so George could have been waiting out here for over a day.

The thought sickened Olivia.

She guessed that George had come to this place to die. Because it had a lighthouse. And because Boyd was out of time. George and Boyd had made their plans to go after Silas. Boyd had hidden in the bookstore, and somehow, George had driven the car to the lighthouse. Both men had decided that they would never return to Palmetto Island.

You were both dying, Olivia thought sadly.

"Your island isn't too far away. It's there, just to the South," Olivia told George in the soft voice of a mother soothing a child woken from sleep by a nightmare. "The same ocean surrounds its shores. The same tides pull the water on and off the beaches. Your home—your snug cottage with the photographs of your wife and of Boyd when he was a little boy—is right below that beautiful moon. See it? It's also called the Hunter's Moon. And the Travel Moon." She glanced over to where George Allen sat. In farewell, she whispered, "I hope you found your way back."

Chapter 16

~~~~~~

*I am a man of substance, of flesh and
bone, fiber and liquids—and I might
even be said to possess a mind. I am
invisible, understand, simply because
people refuse to see me.*

—RALPH ELLISON

Olivia walked home without looking back.

Now, sitting at the kitchen table with Millay and Harris, she wondered how it could be only eight o'clock when it felt like midnight.

"I don't know why we didn't think of this before," Harris was saying. "We should have known better."

Olivia rubbed her tired eyes. "Known what?"

Harris folded his hands and looked at her. "You grew up here. What's the single most popular ghost story told in these parts?"

Without hesitating, Olivia answered, "The legend of Blackbeard's ghost. It's mainly because Ocracoke Island is just across the Pamlico Sound. Not only that, but Blackbeard also lived near the town of Bath. You've read Rawlings's manuscript. His whole story is about the missing treasure supposedly hidden somewhere along the banks of the Neuse River. But what's the connection between Blackbeard, Silas, and my father?"

"I'm sure this is a familiar tale, but Blackbeard's final battle occurred off the coast of Ocracoke. Virginia's governor, Spotswood, wanted Blackbeard dead. The famous pirate was chased, his ship was fired upon, and, after a fierce battle, his crew was eventually overpowered. Blackbeard fought several men at once and suffered a terrible wound—a slash in the side of his neck."

"Like Jenna," Olivia murmured, her stomach turning in disgust.

Harris nodded reluctantly. "I hate to go into this when everything's so fresh, but we have no choice."

"Go on," she prompted.

"When he finally died, Blackbeard had been shot and cut multiple times. His death becomes a ghost story the moment the victorious lieutenant chops off Blackbeard's head and hangs it from the bowsprit of his ship."

Olivia made a gesture of impatience. "Yeah, yeah, and Blackbeard is still out there searching for his missing head."

"That's the part the kids like to focus on," Millay said. "But there's a lesser known legend about Blackbeard's missing head. This one is just as gruesome, but much more intriguing."

"According to several historical documents, Blackbeard's head was exposed to the ravages of weather for so long that the jawbone was lost," Harris said. "Not only was it displayed on the ship's bowsprit, but Governor Spotswood also hung it from the town gates as a trophy. Later, the head was supposedly dipped in silver and fashioned into a drinking vessel." Harris stood up, grabbed a bowl from Olivia's cupboard, and returned to the table. "Imagine a skull inside this ceramic shell. Without the jawbone, you'd have depressions here and here for the eye sockets. If you held it by the sides with each hand, you'd have a—"

"Cup," Olivia finished for him.

Millay pointed at the bowl as though it was the actual

artifact. "The men who wrote about seeing this cup or having actually drunk from it weren't novelists. They didn't embellish. They were lawyers and government officials. But their description of this cup was very similar. They all used the words 'silver,' 'vessel,' 'skull-shaped,' and they mentioned the phrase engraved on the cup's rim."

"'Death to Spotswood,'" Harris said. "Variations of the spelling occur, but the most common is death spelled, 'D-E-T-H,' and Spotswood's name with an *e* added to the end."

Millay opened Harris's laptop and turned it so the screen faced Olivia. "Men have been searching for this cup throughout this century. The last credible sighting occurred in the 1920s during a meeting of William and Mary College fraternity members, which took place at one of Blackbeard's former haunts. Since that time, the cup was purportedly sold to a private collector, but it was X-rayed and proved to be a fake. Other cups have shown up at auction and were donated to museums. None of them has been the genuine article."

"Forty years ago, a misshapen cup of unknown origin was stolen from a small maritime museum in the town of— wait for it—Ocean Isle Beach. It had never been put on display and had been cataloged as originating from the estate of John Spotswood. John was Governor Spotswood's son. The same Governor Spotswood who hung Blackbeard's skull on his wall."

Olivia's fatigue ebbed a fraction. "Ocean Isle. That's where Silas grew up."

"This whole Blackbeard's cup thing is like the old shell game," Millay said. "You have three shells, and a ball is hidden under one shell. Someone mixes up the shells as fast as they can and you just have to keep your eye on the shell you think the ball's hidden under, but your guess is never correct. It's like someone practiced the art of misdirection in order to keep the real cup for themselves. And Harris and I think that person was Silas Black."

Confused, Olivia stared at the image on the computer screen. It was a black-and-white engraving of Blackbeard's head, bound with nautical rope and hanging from the bowsprit. The pirate's famous dark beard had been partially shorn, as had his long locks of black hair. His eyes appeared to be squinting, and his mouth yawned to the side in anguish, astonishment, or both.

"So let's say Silas stole this rare artifact," Olivia said. "Why would a theft that occurred decades ago suddenly compel the Allens to commit acts of violence? Because Silas showed up on their island? How would they even know that Silas had taken the cup? I had a clear impression that neither man left the island if they could help it. Their world was very small."

Harris pulled the computer toward him and began to type. "I don't think they had a clue about the cup. But Vernon Sherrill did. He was the curator at the museum when the cup was stolen."

He pivoted the laptop again, showing Olivia a newspaper article describing the disappearance of the artifact from the museum's storage area. The piece ended with the voluntary retirement of the curator, a Mr. Vernon Sherrill.

"I'll be damned," Olivia whispered.

"Vernon is also a graduate of William and Mary College," Millay added. "And we dug up a number of rumors speculating that the skull cup was being used in fraternity rituals. Bonding ceremonies and crap like that. A couple of sources stated that drinking from the cup served as a reminder of what happens when one disregards the law, while others claim that the inscription—'Death to Spotswood'—warns of what befalls those who stand against the men of William and Mary. Way back when, Spotswood and the president of William and Mary were adversaries." She shrugged. "Either way, the cup has always been the stuff of legends. There are no photos of it. No X-rays. No official documents. If it ever existed, there's no proof. So either the cup has always been with this fraternity, or the one those boys have been drinking from for decades is a fake and the real deal somehow ended up at a small museum in Ocean Isle, North Carolina. Until Silas Black stole it, that is."

She fell silent, allowing Olivia to absorb the bizarre details.

"Leigh Whitlow is dead. Jenna is recovering from a serious wound. Charles is in the Intensive Care Unit. Over a cup that may or may not have been fashioned from Blackbeard's skull? Come on." Olivia's voice betrayed her disbelief. "I love this state. I treasure its history, but I can't—"

Her cell phone rang. Seeing Rawlings's name on the screen, she scooped the phone off the table and answered it.

"I'm sorry," he began. "I couldn't pick up earlier because I was talking to Mr. Allen's neurologist. Boyd will never leave this hospital. He has brain cancer. A tumor, and it's very advanced. Cook just reached me. He told me about George. Are you all right?"

Olivia held out a finger to her friends, signaling that she'd be back in a minute and walked into the living room. Standing in front of the large windows overlooking the ocean, she said, "I know that George was twisted inside. I know that now. And yet I'm sad for him. I don't like that he spent his whole life being invisible. I don't like that he was dispensable. No one should matter so little."

"He mattered to Boyd," Rawlings said.

"That's true," Olivia said. "And what did Boyd get in exchange? He got trapped. George whispered to him about the island's history, about its stories, until that cursed place was all Boyd knew. He had no friends. No lovers. No family other than his father. He became as invisible as George. The only thing that mattered to him was pleasing his father. And championing his home."

"It's interesting that you should use that word," Rawlings

said. "'Championing.' Boyd has been telling the nurses that the island speaks to him. That only he can hear its voice."

Olivia looked at the ocean, following the flash of the lighthouse beam as it pierced the darkness. "Is he crazy?"

"I suspect the whispers have come from his father, but the neurologist says the voices Boyd Allen hears are most likely the result of the tumor. It's possible he's had hallucinations too. Especially at this advanced stage. It's clear that Mr. Allen has suffered multiple seizures over the past few weeks, and his vision is impaired." Rawlings hesitated. "I believe he mistook Jenna for Silas because she was standing near a cardboard cutout of Mr. Black sent to Through the Wardrobe by his publisher. Both Charles and Jenna had opted not to use the display as it seemed over-the-top, and Jenna had decided to move it to the recycling bin. In the dim light, Mr. Allen thought he was actually attacking Mr. Black. He thinks he's accomplished his task and can die in peace. Unfortunately for your father, he just happened to be in the way when Mr. Allen sprang from his hiding place."

A fresh surge of anger coursed through Olivia's body. "So let me get this straight. Boyd either murdered his own father or left him on a beach to die, after which he spent the night in a storeroom so he could attack Silas with what? A pirate's cutlass?"

"Yes. We have the weapon in evidence. And Cook isn't certain yet, but the ME thinks George Allen died from carbon monoxide poisoning. It looks like Boyd ran a hose from the exhaust pipe back into the SUV. Once his father was gone, he carried him to the lighthouse."

Again, Olivia was almost too furious to speak, but if she wanted justice, she had to control her rage. "Where did Boyd get the cutlass? Did Vernon Sherrill give it to him? The same way he procured the white dress?"

Rawlings grunted in confusion. "I'm not following you."

Olivia returned to the kitchen. "Harris found a connection between Silas, a missing pirate artifact that happens to be a cup, and Vernon Sherrill. Here, I'll let Harris explain everything. I'm still trying to work through some things in my head, and I need a minute."

After passing the phone to Harris, Olivia waved Millay into the living room. The two women collapsed onto a sofa and stared at the cold hearth.

"Do you mind if I make a fire?" Millay asked and went to kneel before the fireplace.

Olivia almost smiled. "There isn't much to do. They're gas logs. Do you see that switch at the base?"

Millay pressed the button. There was a hum, a whoosh of air, and then the flames sprang into life. Millay stayed on the floor, her eyes fixed on the bluish flames in the heart of the fire.

"What if Boyd and George Allen were just pawns?" she asked quietly. "They're simple men who led simple lives. Everything that happened has been complicated."

"My thoughts have headed in that direction too," Olivia said. "Vernon as puppet master. I remember when I first saw him and Silas together at the museum on Palmetto Island. At first, Silas acted chummy because he wanted to borrow artifacts for his show, but Vernon was openly unfriendly from the get-go. He wasn't nice to Amy either. He clearly disapproved of her association with Silas."

Millay turned away from the fire. "But why would losing his job all those years ago incite Sherrill into committing murder now? He was hired to curate another small coastal maritime museum almost immediately after his *voluntary* retirement from the Ocean Isle Museum. I'm sure he was embarrassed and angry, but to re-create those ghost stories? That took tons of planning. And energy."

"It speaks of obsession," Olivia agreed. "I think Vernon has been comparing himself to Silas for longer than we can imagine. For instance, Vernon is also an author. His book has probably sold in the hundreds while Silas's titles have sold millions. Silas is rich and famous and has legions of fans. If he stole that cup, forcing Vernon to step down from his position, he instigated Vernon's cycle of invisibility. I believe that's the common thread between Vernon and the Allens. The curator, the lighthouse keeper, and the boatman. At one time, they were useful, vital members of society. And then, through no choice of their own, they were forced to retire or their positions were phased out."

"As the years passed, only visitors came to Palmetto Island," Millay said. "There was no community. That's something Vernon lost when he left Ocean Isle Beach. He had status in that town. The article Harris found mentions how respected Vernon was among the community members. I guess being the curator of the Palmetto museum didn't open doors for him in Riverport. The museum is fairly decrepit."

Haviland padded into the room and stretched out on the rug. He yawned and then eyed Millay expectantly. With a smile, she scratched him on the neck and belly and then abruptly stopped, her fingers caught in his black hair.

"So did Vernon get his hands dirty?" Millay asked. "George couldn't manage the physical stuff required to re-create the ghost stories. But could Boyd do it all on his own? And I still don't see how Leigh Whitlow fits into any of this."

"I don't know either. All I can say is that Boyd isn't much stronger than his father." Olivia told Millay about the debili-tating symptoms of Boyd's cancer.

Haviland raised his head and Millay resumed her scratch-ing. "If Boyd's vision was impaired, then how did he drive from Riverport to Oyster Bay?"

Despite the heat of the fire, the skin on Olivia's arms broke out in gooseflesh. "He couldn't have."

Millay stole a glance at the tall windows. "He's here, isn't he? Vernon's here."

"He must be." Olivia slowly got to her feet. She felt as

though she were in a waking dream. Her head was heavy, and her thoughts were slow and somnolent.

"Harris!" Millay shouted, startling both Haviland and Olivia. "Get in here, pronto! We have a problem! Are you still on with the chief?"

Harris appeared, his open laptop balanced on his forearms. "No, he just got back to the station and had to talk to someone. As far as problems go, we have bucket loads of them. After hearing the tail end of your conversation, I sent a group text message to Cook and the chief. *If* Vernon realizes that Boyd got the wrong man—sorry to put it that way, Olivia, but I'm too stressed to be delicate—then our crazed curator will probably try to take out Silas himself."

"*If* he's in Oyster Bay," Millay said. "Too bad we'd have to ask those useless Riverport cops to check on his whereabouts."

Harris looked thoughtful. "They've been ripped apart by the media over how Leigh Whitlow's murder was handled. Peterson in particular. So the powers that be might be eager to polish their tarnished image. I'm going to call down there and tell them what happened here. We need to work together now."

Before either woman could respond, Harris was already speaking to someone at the Riverport station. Five minutes later, he ended the call with a triumphant grin. "Two officers are en route to Vernon's apartment. They're also going to contact the other museum volunteers. Maybe they know something that can help us."

"Good work," Olivia said.

"Now what?" Millay asked.

"I'm going to see what else I can find out about Vernon." Harris took a seat at Olivia's desk and focused on his computer again.

The fire crackled and threw shadows on the walls. Haviland groaned and stretched in lazy contentment while Olivia and Millay listened to the soft sound of Harris's fingers moving over his keyboard.

Eventually, Harris broke the silence. "There's not much on the guy. He doesn't exist on social media. He owns next to nothing. An old boat and an even older car. He's rented the same one-bedroom apartment in Riverport for the past twenty years. He's never been arrested. Not even a moving violation. Pays his taxes. According to this"—he tapped his computer—"he's practically a ghost."

Millay got off the floor, went into the kitchen, and returned with a bottle of beer. She took a long pull from the bottle and stared at the fire again. "Aren't we making some major assumptions about this guy? For instance, how would Vernon know that Boyd failed to kill Silas unless he was watching from inside the bookstore Dumpster or something? And here's another question. How did he get back to town after leaving Emmett's car at the lighthouse? Did he thumb a ride from one of Olivia's neighbors?"

Harris shrugged. "That SUV has a big cargo hold. He could have had a bike or moped back there. I'll call Cook and ask him to check it out."

Olivia tried to picture Vernon pedaling into town just before daybreak, a hooded sweatshirt obscuring his face and a bag with supplies strapped to his back. Was it possible?

"Vernon can't get to Silas anyway," she said to no one in particular. "Isn't he safely tucked away in an interview room at the station?"

"I'm not sure," Harris said after a moment's pause. "He told Cook that rumors about the skull cup have been attached to several William and Mary grads, which is true enough, and refused to admit to stealing from the Ocean Isle Museum." He raised his phone to his ear. "With two active crime scenes and a suspect in the hospital, we're spread too thin." He jerked to attention, his eyes sliding away from Olivia's. "Cook? That text I sent about Vernon Sherrill? Yeah, I think there's more.

He might be in Oyster Bay, hoping to take a shot at Silas Black. I know I acted without authorization, but I went ahead and asked the guys in Riverport to visit his residence." He paused to listen. "Are Silas Black and Amy Holden still at the station?"

Without waiting to hear the answer, Olivia retrieved her own phone and dialed Rawlings's number. "Where are you?" she demanded when he picked up.

"Driving Ms. Holden to The Yellow Lady," Rawlings said, referring to the bed-and-breakfast Silas had commandeered for the weekend. "Actually, she's in the lead car. I'm taking up the rear."

Olivia stiffened. "Vernon Sherrill could be waiting there."

"Yes," Rawlings said. "Which is why we'll take every precaution."

"Where's Silas?"

Rawlings chuckled dryly. "Spending the night in a holding cell. Not quite as comfy as the Captain's Quarters at The Yellow Lady, but it's for his own protection. We gave him a choice, and he chose wisely. Ms. Holden won't be staying in the main inn either. It's too big to guard, and we don't have the manpower. After I get her settled in the guest cottage, I'll rejoin Cook at the station."

"What can we do?"

"I'm glad you asked," Rawlings said. "If Vernon Sherrill is the mastermind behind the ghost story reenactments, then he's most likely gone through all this trouble not just for revenge, but to publically one-up Silas Black. To be the greater storyteller. To dramatize these old ghost stories better than Silas ever did on his television drama. And to do this, he needs to complete his work with a breathtaking finale—the death of Silas Black—by mirroring Blackbeard's murder. Is that what the three of you believe as well?"

Olivia darted a glance into the kitchen. Harris was pressing his phone to his ear with his left hand while typing with his right. "Yes. It explains why Boyd had an antique cutlass in his possession."

"What I'd like you to do is to try and put yourself in Mr. Sherrill's place. Mr. Allen's attack failed, so what do you do now? How and when do you strike? Because you have *one* chance. There's no room for error." Rawlings paused to listen to chatter on his police radio. "We're pulling into the inn now. I'll get back to you later."

"Be careful," Olivia whispered, but Rawlings was already gone.

Millay, who'd overheard Olivia's side of the conversation, arched her brows in question. "Should we call Laurel?"

Olivia nodded. "Only because she'd be furious if we didn't. But tell her to stay home. She can think from the safety of her house."

The three friends took their seats around the kitchen table again. Millay read different versions of Blackbeard's death out loud while Harris took notes. Olivia tried to focus on Rawlings's assignment, but the anger she'd been trying to tamp down was steadily overpowering her thoughts.

"Olivia?" Millay snapped her fingers. "Are you in there? You look like you want to punch someone."

"It's Charles," she said tightly. "If he'd mentioned this damned cup earlier, Leigh would still be alive. Jenna wouldn't be injured. Neither would he."

Harris grabbed Olivia's hand. "It's down to us to put an end to what started with that deer, and I know what might help. Think back to your trip to the maritime museum on Palmetto Island. Which pirate weapons were on display? Even if you don't know what they were called, try to describe them to me."

Olivia nodded, glad to have something to focus on other than her anger. "The displays were both organized and eye-catching. One case contained blades. Daggers, dirks, swords, cutlasses." Her voice took on a dream-tinged quality as she reconstructed the exhibits in her mind. "Another held boarding weapons such as grappling hooks, axes, and some kind of pike. There were quite a few firearms as well. I don't remember the names of all the guns, but there was a set of flintlock pistols, a blunderbuss, and a much longer gun that looked like a musket."

"That was probably a matchlock," Harris said, examining a website on pirate weapons. "I think Vernon is carrying this beauty." He tapped on the image of a flintlock pistol.

"Because after Blackbeard received that nasty gash in the neck, he was shot," Millay said, pointing at a line in Harris's notebook.

"Exactly. Plus, the fighting took place on deck, at close range," Harris said. "That would call for the flintlock pistol. Vernon had access to a pair. Assuming one of the guns is in working order, which might be a stretch considering their age, I'd say that's his weapon of choice."

Having no knowledge of pirate weapons, Olivia and Millay had to defer to Harris's opinion on the matter.

"So we've deduced that a maniac with an antique gun is planning to put a lead ball into Silas Black. That's just peachy," Millay said. "What are we supposed to do now?"

"What we always have to do," Olivia said. "Wait for the chief."

An hour later, Rawlings entered the house. Haviland met him at the back door, barking sleepily and giving him a cursory lick on the hand before returning to his resting place in front of the fire.

Rawlings sank into a chair at the kitchen table and waved off Olivia's offer of coffee. "If I have another cup, I'll float away." He leaned back and sighed. "I just came home to rest for a few minutes. Wash my face, put on a fresh shirt, have a sandwich. Unless the three of you figured out where he's hiding, my men and I will be driving through town in shifts looking for Mr. Sherrill." He smiled at Olivia. "This has all the makings of a very long night."

"I'll come with you," Harris volunteered and then turned to Millay. "Come on, I'll drop you off at home first. The chief can pick me up from my place."

"Good," Rawlings said approvingly. "I already called Laurel and told her to stay put. I know she has a police scanner next to her desktop."

After Harris and Millay left, Olivia carried the coffee cups to the sink and rinsed them with hot water. She let the water run until the steam fogged the window, so she was unaware that Rawlings had come to stand behind her until she felt his arms around her waist. "Maybe you should wait to see Charles tomorrow," he said softly. "Check in with his nurse by phone instead. You've been through enough today."

She shook her head. "I won't sleep anyway. I'd just lie there, rehashing the day's events or picturing Vernon hiding in random places throughout town. In alleyways. Under docks. Construction sites." She turned off the water. "He could be anywhere, Sawyer."

"Yes," Rawlings agreed and held Olivia in silence for a long moment. "Officer Peterson called to confirm that Mr. Sherrill is not at home. He hasn't collected his mail for two days, and he also entrusted the museum to his docent. I spoke with her earlier. She said that although Mr. Sherrill rearranged the pirate displays right before he left town, she's not sure if any of the weapons are missing. She's going to check the remaining items against the inventory and call me in the morning."

"Can we actually trust that Peterson did his job this time?" Olivia's tone was derisive.

"He apologized for what he realizes was shoddy police work. It's too late, of course, but I feel for him. He was too green. Too starstruck by Silas. You'd better believe there's going to be a shakedown because of what happened on Palmetto Island." Rawlings stepped away from Olivia and passed his hands over his face. "Such an enormous fallout over a goddamn cup."

"That's what I thought too. Initially. But it's not about the cup," Olivia said. "It's about being seen. George. Boyd. Vernon. They've been seen now. They're not invisible anymore."

Rawlings eyes grew glassy. "Maybe they wanted to be ghosts. Specters. Haints. To become a part of local lore the way they never could have in life. Maybe they believed their deaths were the only things left that mattered. The only time they'd be seen and not forgotten. The only way to right a lifetime of wrongs."

"In that case," Olivia said, feeling a current of cold air sneak into the room, "Vernon is prepared to die. But not tonight. Not under cover of darkness. He wants to fire that pirate pistol—to take out his enemy in front of witnesses. He wants to become a legend."

Rawlings turned his gaze to the window. Patches of steam still clung to the panes, but the darkness waiting on the other side seemed to have crept closer. To have grown denser.

"People always think of dawn as a peaceful time," he murmured. "Birds stirring. A gentle awakening. But a poet I admire, George Bradley, described it very differently. He wrote a poem about the sound of the sun. It's an explosion we don't hear. Roiling gases raging. A burning sky. Every morning, an Armageddon. Tomorrow's dawn will not come on slippered feet. I have a feeling it's going to be full of cracks and shouts. And violence." His fingertips brushed the holster on his hip, and he drew in a resolute breath. "I cannot let Mr. Sherrill have the storied ending he so desperately craves."

Chapter 17

The river is within us, the sea is all about us.

—T. S. ELIOT

Olivia let Haviland out once more before kissing him on the nose and giving him a small pile of treats. She left the house while he was still crunching away.

The trip to New Bern took forty-five minutes, and by the time Olivia appeared at the ICU nurses' station, her mind was as drained as her body. She didn't want to think anymore. She wanted to sit in a hushed room beside Charles's bed and be still.

"Your father was awake and talking earlier, but he's asleep now," a nurse whispered to Olivia outside Charles's room. "His temperature started climbing around seven, so we've been pumping him with fluids and trying to keep him quiet. The more he sleeps, the better."

Olivia was immediately concerned. "If he has a fever, doesn't that mean he's fighting an infection?"

The nurse nodded. "Abdominal wounds are tricky, and a fever is common after surgery. We'll just have to keep an eye on him." She smiled. "You're lucky Dr. Boardman was on rotation today. She's one of the best general surgeons in the state." She poked her head into the room. "You can go in now. I'll be at the desk if you need anything."

Olivia put her coat and bag on the recliner in the corner of the room before approaching the bed. Her father seemed to be sleeping comfortably. She stood over him, her gaze slowly traveling from his face down the length of his arm to where the tube from the IV bag entered the swollen vein in the back of his hand, when he opened his eyes.

"Olivia," he croaked.

She put her palm to his forehead. It was too warm, and his hairline was damp with sweat. "No talking," she gently admonished him. "I'll stay with you, but only if you promise to go back to sleep. You have a fever, and you need rest."

"I'm sorry," he said. His voice was a dry rasp. "I should have told you. I'm sorry, Olivia." He spread the fingers, wordlessly asking for contact.

She slid her hand under his, careful to avoid the IV line, and sat on the edge of the bed. "Close your eyes," she whispered. "If you do, I'll hum you a French song Camille used to sing when she was happy. You might even recognize it. It'll give you good dreams, and you'll wake in the morning feeling much better."

Olivia began to hum "La Mer" while lightly tracing the veins on the back of her father's hand. She thought of how they flowed through his body like tiny rivers—dozens of tributaries rushing into the sea of his heart. His blood flowed through her body too. Would that help Olivia forgive him for what he'd done?

She was suddenly caught in a terrible moment of déjà vu—of the night she'd sat vigil at Willie Wade's deathbed. She'd held his hand too. She'd been with him as his life had ebbed like the retreating tide.

The notes of her mother's song stuck in her throat. Charles stirred, and fearing he'd come fully wake again,

Olivia swallowed and continued the soft song. She wanted him to live. And in that moment, she knew she would forgive him. He was the only parent she had left, and they'd lost enough time as it was.

When the nurse entered the room, Olivia put her finger to her lips. The nurse nodded, checked the IV bag, placed a blanket on the arm of the recliner, and left.

As the minutes ticked by, Olivia's head grew heavier and heavier, and her back began to ache from perching on the edge of the bed. Very slowly, so as not to disturb her father, she eased off the bed and settled on the recliner. She covered her legs with the blanket and told herself that she'd just rest her eyes for an hour. As soon as her father's fever broke, she'd drive back home.

She woke hours later to the sound of a man's voice close to her ear.

"Good morning, sunshine."

Olivia turned her head to find Silas Black crouching beside her. He held out a takeout cup from Starbucks. "You look like you could use this more than me." He put the cup down on the side table and stood erect. "I've been up for ages already." Jerking a thumb at Charles, he whispered, "How's the patient?"

Olivia's eyes were full of grit. Her tongue felt like cotton, and her neck was stiff and sore. The morning light streaming in through the rectangular window was too bright, and Silas's presence was both intrusive and unwelcome.

She took the water pitcher from Charles's nightstand and poured herself a glass. As she drank, she noted how fresh and well rested Silas looked. His vitality reminded her of Jenna. Jenna, who cheerfully rang up sales at Through the Wardrobe. Jenna, who hosted every children's story hour and loved to moderate book clubs. She'd spent the night in the hospital because her neck had been cut, and that wound had been meant for Silas Black.

"Get out," Olivia hissed in quiet fury.

Silas blinked at her in surprise. "What?"

"Your secret killed one woman and nearly killed a second," Olivia's voice was a harsh whisper. "It almost killed my father. I know he shares in the blame, but not equally. Why don't you save Vernon Sherrill the trouble and drink some drain cleaner from Blackbeard's skull? Better yet, there's sure to be a supply of bleach in a nearby maintenance closet. You can help yourself to a bottle on your way out. You're good at taking things that don't belong to you."

"Charles told you?" Silas gaped at her for several seconds before dropping into a wooden chair across from the bed with a disappointed sigh.

Afraid that her anger would wake her father, Olivia turned away from Silas. She retrieved a comb from her handbag and pulled it roughly through her tangled hair. She focused on the sound of Charles's steady breathing and was comforted by the fact that color had returned to his face.

After a few minutes, she put her comb away and dug around in her purse for a pack of gum. "He didn't tell me. He only gave me a hint," she whispered to Silas. "Harris pieced the rest of the puzzle together. Other than how Leigh fit in. We couldn't figure that out. Obviously, she knew you'd stolen the cup, and somehow, that knowledge chained the two of you together."

"That's right. I served a decades-long prison sentence with that woman." Silas spat out the words. "I paid and paid for what she had on me. Which, before you ask, was a videotape." He snorted. "I was already done with Leigh when she caught me. It was the summer after our college graduation, and I'd moved back to my hometown while I looked for a job. I was putting the moves on the woman who managed the gift shop at the museum because I knew the cup was there. I'd drunk from a fake one the summer before—so had Charles—but I figured there had to be a real one, so I tracked the items Spotswood left his children and found it."

"Amazing that you were able to do that when no else could," Olivia said disdainfully.

"I know," Charles said. "It was purely by chance. The cup donated to the Ocean Isle Museum was mistakenly listed as being made of pewter, which was quite common for the time, but Blackbeard's cup was silver. I thought the mistake might be deliberate, and I was right. I had it tested by an archaeologist friend of mine. I have the real cup," he added smugly. "I've only shown it to two people, including Charles."

Olivia gave him a flat stare. "How did you get it?"

"One night, I slipped something in the gift shop gal's drink, used her keys to get inside the museum, and the rest is history. No sign of breaking and entering. No proof of the theft. It was beautiful. Except that I had no idea Leigh was following me. Or that she had a camera. Damn that woman."

"She filmed you stealing the cup."

Silas nodded miserably. "Yes, and though the footage was probably crap—I was wearing black and had a baseball cap covering part of my face—she also had a key to my apartment because we didn't actually break up until July. That night, I celebrated my victory by drinking from the cup. She filmed that too, of course, though I was too drunk to even know she was there. She showed me the footage later. She stashed copies everywhere as insurance and held that video over me for half of my life. I bought her everything she wanted. Clothes, jewelry, cars. But I wouldn't marry her, and she didn't force me to. She wanted that to be my choice. I refused. Still, she wouldn't go away. Even when I blatantly slept with other women, she stayed."

"She loved you," Olivia said. "She probably hoped that, just by sticking around, you'd eventually change your mind. She was murdered because of your crime. She paid, and so did Jenna and my father." Olivia unwrapped a piece of gum and pinched it hard between her fingers. "You knew Vernon Sherrill was behind the ghost story reenactments. You could have put a stop to them after the dead doe was found."

Silas shook his head. "I didn't know. I'd completely forgotten the man. His name vanished from my head years ago. And I definitely didn't remember what he looked like."

"This is why Vernon hates you," Olivia said sorrowfully. "You ruined his life. And yet you could pass him on the street without recognizing him."

"It wasn't until after Leigh was killed that Charles suggested that this whole mess might be about the cup. I thought he was being ridiculous—that he was tossing theories into the wind. But when Officer Cook showed me old newspaper articles from when the cup was stolen and I saw Sherrill's name, I knew Charles was right." He shrugged. "So I'll agree to be bait or whatever the cops want, but I won't admit to the theft. Not ever. That cup is mine. The Graveyard of the Atlantic was my playground. I am a son of the Carolina coast."

"Then why don't you see that it's the *people* that make a place memorable?" Olivia asked. "It's not the relics that matter. Your stories sell because the characters resonate. Your television show is successful because the characters resonate. Your love of history shines through. If you realize that history is about *people*, then why are you so callous about the ones you meet?"

"Like Sherrill? Or the woman who ran the gift shop? Or Leigh? Come on." Silas's tone was dismissive. "The cup is priceless. Blackbeard is *inside* it, for Chrissakes. It symbolizes everything I love about my home. From the time I started working in my parents' shop, I saw what people bought. Anything to do with pirates. Ghost stories. Legends. Tales of freedom and adventure. I planned to make a living off those things. I was working on my first book when I took that cup. It was my Holy Grail. My talisman. I knew that if I had it, there'd be no stopping me, and I was right."

Olivia stared at him in disbelief. "You thought the cup possessed some kind of power?"

"All I'm saying is that it was meant to be mine."

"It's not the only artifact you've stolen, is it? That shipwreck off the coast of Palmetto Island? Aren't you funding it so you can have first dibs on the finds?"

Silas shrugged. "It's not uncommon for the benefactor to receive a gift. Once those pieces are in a museum—"

"You can't get your hands on them," Olivia interrupted coldly. "That's why you don't support museums. Only underwater digs."

"It's not like there isn't an entire antiquities market for these items. And that's just the legal one. Better *I* should own these pieces of local history than some Chicago banker or California vintner. What do they know of our coast? We grew up here. We live and breathe its stories. We deserve to own these things."

Olivia's phone, which had been set to vibrate, began to buzz from inside her handbag. She searched for it without taking her eyes off Silas. "Your arrogance sounds more Hollywood movie producer and less small-town souvenir shop boy to me. You have no remorse whatsoever. I nearly lost a friend yesterday. I nearly lost my father. Because of you."

"Father? Are you talking about me?" came a weak voice from the bed, and Olivia dropped her phone back into her bag and bolted from her chair.

"I'm sorry," she whispered, taking Charles's hand. "Did we wake you?"

Charles smiled at her. "I've been hoping you'd call me that one day."

"I'm still angry with you," Olivia said, pulling her hand away to check his forehead. It felt cool to the touch. Pleased, she pushed the nurse call button. "And I don't understand why this man deserves your loyalty." She pointed at Silas without turning. "He's a thief. He uses people and then discards them. And he's an egomaniac."

Looking to where Silas stood at the foot of the bed, Charles said, "That egomaniac saved my life. One night, back in school, I'd had too much to drink. I was showing off, probably for some girl, and I walked out on a frozen lake that wasn't quite frozen and fell through the ice. I couldn't pull myself up. I started sinking. Silas jumped in after me. He almost died getting me out. I owed him, Olivia."

Stunned, Olivia put a straw in a water cup and held it up to her father's lips. He drank greedily and then let his head fall against the pillow with a sigh.

"Good morning!" A different nurse from the one who'd been on duty the previous night entered the room. She had a blood pressure cuff under her arm and moved to the opposite side from where Olivia stood to check Charles's vitals.

Moving behind Olivia, Silas gave Charles an affectionate pat on his blanketed foot and said, "You must have a thick hide under those Brooks Brothers suits."

Suddenly remembering her phone and just how long it had been since she'd spoken with Rawlings or asked after Haviland, Olivia turned and reached for her bag. That's when she caught sight of a man standing in the doorway.

It was Vernon Sherrill.

She caught a glimpse of his triumphant sneer as he raised a pistol and pointed it in her direction.

What happened next seemed to take place underwater.

Vernon shouted, "Black!" and Silas sprang forward as though he meant to duck behind Charles's bed.

Next, there was a deafening report followed by a flash of sparks and a billow of smoke.

Olivia opened her mouth to scream, but no sound came out. And then she was falling.

Her next sensations were of dozens of lunar-white stars exploding in her field of vision and of a great weight pressing down on her. Then, for just a second, she felt the coolness of the floor against her cheek.

After that, there was only darkness.

"She's coming to," a woman said, and Olivia found herself face-to-face with the surgeon who'd operated on her father.

"Don't try to move," the doctor ordered, deftly slipping a pillow under Olivia's head. "You may have suffered a concussion. Can you tell me how many fingers I'm holding up?"

"Three," Olivia said. From her position on the floor, she could only see the doctor's face and the recessed lights in the ceiling, which were far too bright. Dizziness swept over her, and she fixed her gaze on the doctor's ID tag and took several deep breaths. She needed to focus, but there was so much noise in the room. Too many voices. Footsteps. The rapid-fire sound of camera clicks. And the smells. Sulfurous gunpowder. Ammonia. There was something sticky under her left arm. She spread her fingers and felt a residue in the spaces between, like her hand had become webbed.

It must be blood, she thought.

"What happened?" she asked in a shaky voice. She felt blind down on the floor. But she also knew that if she moved, the entire world would drop out from under her and she'd fall back into the blackness again. "Dad? Are you all right?"

Dr. Boardman put a steadying hand under Olivia's elbow. "He's fine." She turned to look at someone over her shoulder. "We should run a scan on her. Chief, can we carry her out?"

"I'll lift her," Rawlings said, instantly taking the doctor's place.

Seeing his face, Olivia felt the tilting sensation in her head abate a little. She gripped his arms, noting that he wore a jumpsuit over his clothes.

The hospital room was now a crime scene.

How long had she been out?

She tried to twist her head to the left, but Rawlings shifted his body to block her view. "Be still and listen," he whispered. "Vernon Sherrill is dead. I had to shoot him because he reloaded and was taking aim to fire a second round. Mr. Black is in surgery. You can hear the rest later."

Rawlings asked Cook to help him lift Olivia over the bloodstains by the foot of the bed. The men stepped carefully, doing their best to avoid the mess there and in the doorway. Olivia averted her eyes.

Refusing a nurse's offer of a wheelchair, Rawlings carried Olivia to an exam room.

Sitting on the bed, Olivia gave Rawlings a plaintive look. "I feel dazed, but I'm coming out of it. Can you talk to me for a few minutes?"

He scooted his chair close to the bed and took her hand. He then released it again and went to the sink to soak a towel in warm water. As he cleaned Silas's dried blood off her skin, he talked. "Cook was trying to call you. To warn you. I moved as fast I could, but I wasn't fast enough. None of us were. Hospital security. The New Bern cops. We all realized Sherrill was at the medical center too late."

Rawlings dried Olivia's hand with the edge of the bedsheet and threw the stained towel in the sink. He then enfolded her hand in his. Olivia looked down at their clasped hands and thought of how she'd held her father's the night before. Of how she'd traced the veins and thought of rivers.

She exhaled very slowly. "Vernon had a boat. He had a boat all along. That's how he brought a deer from the mainland. It's how he set the dinghy on fire. It's how he lured Leigh with the ship's bell and left no trace at the crime scene. It's how he got here from the lighthouse. He had a boat."

Rawlings looked at her in surprise. "Yes. Emmett's SUV had a tow hitch, and Mr. Sherrill had a boat and a trailer. He dropped George Allen off at the lighthouse and backed the trailer into the water at low tide. He sank the trailer, parked the SUV behind the lighthouse, brushed the tracks off the sand, and left the beach by boat. It's not a long trip from Oyster Bay to New Bern by water. He took Goose Creek to one of the smaller branches and then walked five blocks to the medical center. The local cops have already located the boat."

"Vernon knew that Silas would come to see Charles," Olivia said. "Why didn't we?"

"Because Mr. Black was *supposed* to be at The Yellow Lady," Rawlings replied in a strained voice. "He was driven to the inn early this morning, where he was told to pack and wait for further instructions. Instead, he borrowed the proprietor's car—and by 'borrowed,' I mean he left a hundred-dollar bill and a note saying that he'd be back in a few hours—and took off."

Olivia sighed. "He wanted to make sure Charles wouldn't tell anyone about the cup."

"No matter how rare or wrapped in mystique, Black's treasure is just a thing. He coveted that secret at the expense of many lives." Rawlings shook his head. "I had to kill a man today because of what Black did all those years ago." He stopped speaking and swallowed hard. "I didn't want it to come to that."

Olivia felt Rawlings's pain and wished she could ease it for him, but he would have to carry the burden of having taken Vernon Sherrill's life alone. All she could do was offer him solace. "I know," she whispered softly. "And Silas has been stealing relics for years. Artifacts that belong to everyone. Pieces of our history. He believes he has a special claim to them, but we must put an end to this."

"I'll get in touch with my FBI buddy," Rawlings said, clearly consoled by the idea of taking action. "He'll connect me with someone at the art crime division. They'll have to move fast, though. Silas Black is a slippery eel."

"He's not going anywhere for the next few days. Vernon Sherrill saw to that." Olivia managed a wry smile.

Rawlings leaned over and kissed the back of her hand. "I can see you're feeling better. Thank God, Olivia. I've never been so scared. Standing out in that hall, I didn't know what I'd find—"

"Don't," she said. "None of this is your fault. Or mine. I know they need you back in that room, and my father will want to be reassured that I'm all right. After a hot shower, a cup of coffee, and some time with Haviland, I'll be as good as new. Can my statement wait? I want to go home."

"Only if the doc gives you permission."

Knowing Rawlings didn't need another thing to worry about, Olivia submitted to an examination. And though she had an impressive contusion, the doctor wasn't overly concerned. She reviewed the symptoms and warnings signs of a concussion, gave Olivia a pamphlet on the subject, and said she was free to go.

After calling a cab, Olivia stopped by her father's new room to tell him good-bye until she returned to visit the following day. She kissed him on the cheek, told him to rest, and went outside to meet her cab. She told the driver she'd appreciate a quiet ride home and was grateful when he nodded and tuned the radio to a classical music station.

When he pulled up to her house, she shoved a wad of bills into his hand and jumped out of the cab. On the other side of the door, Haviland was waiting for her. Olivia dropped to her knees on the kitchen floor and released the fear she'd been holding inside in a single choking sob. Shaking, she let her tears slide down her cheeks and drip from the point of her chin into Haviland's hair.

Her poodle whined and alternated between frantically licking her cheeks and sniffing her face and hair. He smelled blood and knew something wasn't right. His agitation allowed Olivia to regain control of her own emotions.

"I'm sorry, boy," she said, trying to soothe him. "I'm okay now. I'm just so glad to be home. I didn't mean to upset you."

She opened the door to let him out, but he wouldn't leave her side. She finally coaxed him to take a quick trip to the bushes near the driveway, and then they both returned inside.

"Let me take a shower, and after that, we'll go for a walk. A slow one."

Olivia indulged in a very long shower. The hot water and steamy air felt glorious. She washed and dried her hair, and then pulled on a thick, soft sweater and a pair of jeans.

She fed Haviland and was just wondering what to make for herself when there was a knock at the door. Laurel stood outside, cradling a takeout bag from Grumpy's Diner.

"Dixie said you'd be needing her special brand of comfort food."

"She's right, as usual." Olivia smiled as Laurel entered the kitchen. "Nothing in my refrigerator looks the least bit appealing."

Laurel put the bag on the table and began unloading its contents. "Grumpy made you a tomato-and–goat cheese omelet with home fries. Sit down and eat while it's still warm. I'll brew some coffee."

The food was delicious. Laurel sat with Olivia while she ate, and was too considerate a friend to ply her with questions. Laurel simply kept her company.

"I hadn't realized how hungry I was until I started eating," Olivia said after polishing off the last potato. "Thank you for bringing this."

The two women stood up and Laurel gave Olivia a brief hug. "You probably need quiet after everything that's happened. Will you call me if you need anything?"

"I will. I take it you'll be working all day?"

"Yes, indeed." Laurel's gaze grew distant, as though she were picturing her to-do list. "Tomorrow's edition of the

Gazette will include an article describing how this madness finally came to an end." She jiggled her keys in her palm, hesitating. "But what I didn't include in the article was the news that Jenna won't be coming back to Through the Wardrobe. She hasn't told anyone yet, but she's leaving Oyster Bay. After what happened, I can't blame her, but I'm devastated. Do you know how many of her story times I've attended? Or how many books she's put into my sons' hands? She was a friend, Olivia. The boys and I will miss her so much."

Olivia touched Laurel's arm. "I will too. And I'll try to talk her into staying. I'll just have to convince her that Through the Wardrobe wouldn't be the same without her. If she needs to take a long leave of absence, she can take it. Her job will always be waiting for her."

Laurel nodded. "That sounds good."

When Laurel was gone, Olivia threw a wool blanket over her shoulders and took Haviland down to the water's edge. She was too tired to walk far, so she settled in the dry sand and watched her poodle trot up and down the beach. He wouldn't leave her side for long. He kept coming back to where she sat to nudge her leg or lick her hand.

"I'm all right," she'd whisper tenderly, feeling better the longer she sat outside, being with Haviland and breathing the salt-laced air.

Soon, Rawlings would be home. Tonight, after he rested for a bit, they could light a fire in the copper fire pit on the deck and watch the nightfall. As the daylight faded and the stars sparked into existence, they could sip their drinks and hold each other's hands. They could sit in companionable silence, listening to the water and the wind. They could begin the process of healing. Together.

Chapter 18

Only from the heart can you touch the sky.

—JALAL AD-DIN RUMI

The following Saturday, the Bayside Book Writers met at the lighthouse keeper's cottage. If it had been a typical meeting, they'd have shared a meal before discussing the chapter up for review. Over glasses of wine, beer, or, in Olivia's case, Chivas Regal, they'd discuss the work in question for at least an hour. Afterward, the five friends would socialize until Millay had to leave for her shift at Fish Nets.

Tonight's meeting was different from the start. Instead of ordering food, everyone had brought his or her favorite dish to share.

"This is going to be a carb overload," Harris said, setting a bowl of mashed potatoes on the counter. "Hm, I smell bacon."

Rawlings pointed at the oven. "The ultimate comfort food."

"No way," Millay argued, pointing at her own casserole dish. "That would be chicken and waffles."

"I made mac and cheese," Laurel said. "With tons of extra cheese."

Olivia gestured at the pot of the stove. "If you're looking for fruits or vegetables, don't look there. It's shrimp and grits."

"I'll have my fruit in the form of crushed grapes, thank you very much," Laurel said, running her hand through her hair. "It's been a helluva week. I'm glad we're not critiquing a chapter, because I don't think I could handle it."

Her friends nodded in silent agreement.

Jenna's announcement that she was leaving Oyster Bay to move closer to her parents had left them all feeling like they'd lost someone dear to them the night of Millay's book launch. Though Jenna loved the town and Through the Wardrobe, she no longer looked at either with the same eyes since being attacked. And because no one could blame her for being frightened, the five friends had taken turns hugging her and wishing her the best. Olivia had also told her that she'd always have a job should she wish to return and had made certain that Jenna's last paycheck contained a few extra zeroes.

The Bayside Book Writers had left Jenna's house that late Friday afternoon to start their weekends on a melancholy note, the gray skies and cold drizzle doing little to lighten the morose atmosphere. And though the rain had stopped around midnight, the damp air had permeated every space, leaving the streets of Oyster Bay nearly deserted throughout the next day.

"Let's get some hot food in our bellies," Rawlings suggested now. "I'm ready to thaw out from the inside. I've felt numb for days."

Olivia knew exactly what he meant.

"Me too," Harris said. "And bacon makes everything better. Right, Haviland? You know I'm going to slip you a piece on the sly," he told the poodle sotto voce.

Carrying loaded plates into the cozy living room, the

friends ate and exchanged small talk. The room grew warm, and Olivia could feel the tight knot in her core slowly unravel in her friends' company. She refilled their glasses and lit the candles on the coffee table. She watched the light soften their faces and listened to their voices and knew that they were all being comforted by more than just food.

"I saw Emmett in town today," Laurel said, turning to Rawlings. The two of them shared the sofa while Harris, Olivia, and Millay occupied three of the four club chairs. "I guess you returned the man's car. After the ordeal he's been through, we should have taken up a collection for dinner at The Crab Pot or a weekend at The Yellow Lady."

"Charles Wade has something bigger in mind," Rawlings said and looked at Olivia. "Why don't you tell them?"

Olivia shook her head. "It's too soon."

Millay scowled. "Come on. Now you have to spill."

"As soon as he feels up to traveling, my father's going back to New York," Olivia said. "Not permanently, but he has things to deal with there. Not only that but . . . well, he feels guilty. He's not ready to face the people of Oyster Bay after what happened. He believes they'll learn that he shared in Silas's secret and will blame him for Jenna's injury and resignation—that he'll be viewed as an outsider again."

"Running isn't going to help his situation," Millay said. "People would learn to forgive him if he stuck around."

"That's what I told him, but he's going." Olivia picked up her tumbler and swirled the caramel-colored liquor around the bottom of the glass. "And he made other unexpected decisions from his hospital bed. For instance, he offered Emmett a job."

Harris, who'd raised a piece of bacon to his lips, let it dangle in the air. "Doesn't he already have one?"

"Being arrested under suspicion of murder wasn't exactly a boon for his professional reputation," Olivia said. "Remember, this is the second time Emmett has had to refute false allegations. He left his position at the University of North Carolina in Chapel Hill because of Amy, and the powers that be at UNC-Wilmington are hinting that they'd be delighted should Emmett suddenly resign. Even though Emmett is clearly innocent of any of the crimes he was suspected of having committed, including murder, he's tainted by association."

"That's unfair!" Laurel protested. "Emmett loves history. He loves teaching too, doesn't he?"

"Charles correctly surmised that Emmett might be in need of a major change, so he arranged for a limo service to collect Emmett and drive him to the hospital. My father wanted to have a conversation with Emmett about fresh starts. That's what he offered. And Emmett accepted. He's bought out my father's half of the partnership in the bookstore. For a very low price, I might add. This is Charles's way of making amends, I imagine. Anyway, Emmett is relocating to Oyster Bay and is to become the new manager of Through the Wardrobe."

The rest of the Bayside Book Writers sat in stunned silence for a long moment.

Finally, Millay said, "He'll be a good fit. I can't picture him using the puppets, but he can hand over the story-time responsibilities to a more qualified staff member. As far as scheduling author events, organizing the store, and talking to people about books, he's the right guy for the job. He'll be animated without being pushy. Passionate but not creepy. He's the perfect blend of cool outdoorsman and nerdy professor, bow tie–wearing bibliophile and rugged, dog-loving bachelor. I like him."

"Me too," Harris said with a grin. "He'll help the store, and the store will help him."

Laurel elbowed Rawlings in the ribs. "What do you think, Chief?"

"What?" Rawlings asked innocently. "You mean, do I

mind having a man obviously smitten with my wife living and working in the same town? A man she'll have to meet with on a regular basis to discuss budgets and bookings and such?" He shrugged. "Strangely, I don't mind a bit. It feels right. I just hope Charles doesn't stay away too long. He was just beginning to find his roots again."

Olivia put down her glass a little too roughly. "It's in the Wade nature to take off when things get messy. Charles knows I'm angry, but I'll get over it."

"It's not just you he's running from," Rawlings said gently. "He lost his best friend. Silas blames Charles for everything."

Laurel drew in a sharp breath. "That's right! The seizure was made public today."

Rawlings nodded. "The FBI released a list of the stolen antiquities recovered from Mr. Black's California residence. The majority came from underwater archaeology expeditions, but the skull cup was there as well. It has yet to be confirmed as a match to the one taken from the maritime museum in Ocean Isle Beach. There's also been no mention of Blackbeard. As of now, it's simply being referred to as the silver drinking vessel, but it has been sent to the Smithsonian for additional tests."

"That's awesome," Harris said. "It's like a scene straight out of an Indiana Jones movie. I can totally imagine the cup being packed into a crate and wheeled into some government storehouse, never to be seen again."

Olivia arched a brow. "Why? It's hardly the Ark of the Covenant. Or do you think it holds some mystical power? Silas believed it was his talisman. His Holy Grail."

"That's ridiculous." Harris scoffed. "Look. I love the guy's books. I love his show, which may be canceled since Black is undoubtedly headed to prison, but Silas Black is a megalomaniac. Whatever punishment he gets won't be harsh enough because it won't bring Leigh back. And it won't undo what happened to Jenna or Charles. And he doesn't care about any of them. He'll only be pissed off about having his stuff taken away."

"Except that it was never *his* to begin with," Laurel pointed out. "And Leigh witnessed it all. She wasted her life hanging on to a guy who never wanted her." She frowned. "What I still don't get is how Boyd coaxed her into wearing that dress and walking the beach in the middle of the night."

Rawlings took a sip of beer and then gazed at his bottle with a pensive expression. "Like everything else, re-creating the Theodosia Burr scene was a team effort between Boyd Allen and Vernon Sherrill. At least, this is the conclusion we've had to draw from Mr. Allen's testimony. The testimony of a dying man who is lucid for shorter and shorter periods of time."

"He killed a woman. He shot that deer. I shouldn't feel sorry for him. So why do I?" Laurel asked.

"Because he never stood a chance. His dad pulled and pushed him, shaping him like a lump of clay," Millay said. "After Boyd's mom died, there was one person in his life. George Allen should have packed up and left Palmetto. Started over someplace new and given himself and his son a chance, but he stayed on that island and watched the world go by. Boyd grew up without friends or family. He grew up knowing only his dad's embittered whisperings. The stories, repeated on an endless loop, of how the Allens had been wronged."

Rawlings made a noise of assent. "Until one day, the curator of the island's museum, a man the Allens had come to know and respect, tells them about Silas and the stolen cup. The three men already share a passion for history and coastal lore. They also share what Olivia identified as a desire to be seen, to be memorable, if only once."

Harris, who'd eaten eight strips of bacon, wiped his fingertips on a napkin and glanced at Laurel. "I read Vernon's testimony. No matter what kind of childhood the guy had, I don't pity him. Not when I think about how he manipulated Leigh Whitlow. He knew that Leigh still loved Silas. He knew that she kept hanging on to the hope that, one day, he'd love her in return. Not only had he kept tabs on his enemy through the years, but he also stole Leigh's diary. He snuck into Silas's beach house while it was being vandalized. Through the diary, he learned that although Silas had been with plenty of other women, Leigh felt seriously threatened by Amy. Amy was young, smart, and loved the things Silas loved."

Millay held out a finger to stop Harris. "*Was* the vandalism a ploy to search for the cup? I thought it was instigated by the conservancy folks."

"Vernon stayed in the shadows, shouting stuff to incite the crowd, but he didn't enter the house until he could get in unseen. He did a quick search for the cup and then left. He didn't expect to find it in a vacation house, but he had to look. Anyway, he swiped Leigh's diary while he was prowling around."

Olivia collected the dirty dishes and carried them to the sink. "Where's the diary now?"

"It was burned in the Allens' woodstove," Rawlings said. "But after Mr. Sherrill read it, he asked Ms. Whitlow to meet him at the museum. He showed her an antique pistol and claimed that it once belonged to Blackbeard. He told her that he wanted to leave the island but didn't have enough money to buy property elsewhere. He said that no one else had a clue that the weapon was in the museum's collection, and that he was willing to sell it to her at a reasonable price because he knew that her boyfriend was a fan of Blackbeard. He also showed her documents supposedly proving the pistol was Blackbeard's."

"Leigh must have been suspicious of such a sweet deal." Millay scoffed. "Didn't she recognize Sherrill?"

Harris frowned. "Nope. Silas stole that cup decades ago,

and all Leigh cared about was dazzling Silas—knocking the man's socks off so that he'd forget about Amy."

"I think Leigh knew how Silas felt about Amy before Silas did," Olivia said. "From what he told me, he wasn't aware of his feelings until the night he and Leigh had their big fight."

"Leigh was a desperate woman, there's no doubt," Harris said. "Vernon told her that George Allen would deliver the pistol to Leigh on the beach that night. Leigh was to place all the cash and jewelry she had inside a lantern and give it to George. An unthreatening old man, he was a good choice. Vernon also asked Leigh to wear the white dress as a special favor. He then went on to tell her a moving tale of how George had waited his whole life to see the ghost of Theodosia Burr. He explained that George's time was running out and showed Leigh a picture of Theodosia. He pressed the point that she could fulfill a dying man's wish by simply wearing the dress."

"What a manipulative bastard," Laurel muttered.

"Yeah," Harris agreed. "He even told Leigh that if she didn't speak, George would believe she was an actual spirit. All she had to do was drop the lantern and pick up the case with the pistol and go. He instructed Leigh to follow the sound of the ship's bell to George. I'm sure Leigh found the entire thing bizarre, but she wasn't a bad person, and she figured she could make two people happy that night—George and herself—so she agreed."

Laurel snorted. "Why would any reasonable person agree to such an offer?"

"George Allen was in his nineties," Rawlings said. "To Ms. Whitlow, he would have seemed harmless. In her mind, this was her last chance to win Silas back."

"I'm with Laurel," Olivia said from behind the kitchen counter. "Following a series of random acts of violence, why would Leigh subject herself to such a dangerous situation?"

Rawlings and Harris exchanged a knowing glance.

"What?" Millay demanded. "You guys can't pull that inter-departmental crap. *We're* the real team, and you know it."

"Leigh had a knife with her. She put it inside the lantern as a precaution but was never able to use it." Harris looked down at his hands. "By the time she realized the figure on the beach wasn't George, but Boyd, it was too late. Vernon claims that Boyd did the drowning himself. Vernon landed his boat, helped Boyd arrange Leigh's body, and then tossed Emmett's bottle opener into the sand. Vernon had lifted it from Emmett's picnic basket earlier that night. He'd waited for Emmett to leave the bonfire area to take the dogs on a walk. The Allens hadn't been in on the frame job. They weren't at all happy about it, but they weren't about to turn on Vernon at that point in the game either."

Olivia exhaled slowly, angrily. "Emmett went through hell because of that damned bottle opener."

In the corner of the room, Haviland groaned in his sleep and rolled over onto his back. His paws twitched in the air as he chased his dream prey.

Harris joined Olivia in the kitchen. Prying the sponge from Olivia's fingers, he said, "Let the dishes soak for a while. Have another drink instead."

Taking his advice, Olivia refilled her tumbler, dropped two ice cubes in the glass, and resumed her seat. "At least Silas will serve time for antiquities theft. I just hope Amy doesn't wait for him. Enough people have wasted their loyalty on that loser."

"I'll drink to that," Millay said and knocked the rim of her beer bottle against Olivia's tumbler.

Harris filled the sink with soapy water and flopped back onto the sofa. "Speaking of waiting for people, I have some serious cleaning to do at my place. Emily's flying in on Monday."

"Is she staying long?" Rawlings asked.

Harris's cheeks flushed a dark pink. "If all goes as planned."

Millay kicked Harris's heel with the toe of her boot. "Are you two upping the ante?"

"I want her to move in with me," Harris said, his words coming out rapid-fire. "She's the best thing that's ever happened to me. A parallel position to the one she has in Texas has come open here. She'd annihilate the competition if she applied for the job. We talked about her moving, and she said she'd think about it. We're going out to dinner Monday night to talk about it some more." He shrugged helplessly, boyishly, and Olivia couldn't stop smiling as she observed the dreamy look in Harris's eyes. "If all goes well, she'll be in Oyster Bay by Christmas."

"In that case, I hope all goes well," Laurel said. "I just adore that girl!" She turned to Millay. "Now, if we could just find you a—"

"Don't even start," Millay said with a glower. "You sound like my mother, and that is *not* a compliment. Besides, I'm fulfilled, okay? I don't need a yin to my yang or whatever. I'm dating, I'm working, I'm writing."

Laurel's hand flew to her mouth. "I can't believe it! With all this talk of murder, the investigation, Emmett's coming and Charles's going—we haven't focused on your book. Have you heard from your editor? How were the first week's sales?"

Millay dug the heels of her palms into her eyes. "You're going to find out eventually, so I might as well tell you." She removed her hands, but kept her gaze fixed on her boots. "On Wednesday, my editor called to say that *The Gryphon Rider* hit the *New York Times* Bestseller List. It was just the extended list," she added hastily while glaring at Laurel. "Do not scream."

Laurel's mouth hung open.

"You close that maw this instant," Millay ordered. "Do not shriek, cheer, bounce, or clap, or so help me, I will punch you." Her voice wavered as she uttered this last threat.

Olivia studied Millay with concern. "You're not happy about this news."

Millay shook her head. She was on the verge of tears.

"You think you earned that spot because of publicity and not talent." Olivia spoke very quietly. "That Silas's notoriety and the attack at the bookstore got you those sales."

"Yes," Millay whispered. "It's all wrong."

Olivia gestured at Harris's laptop bag. "May I?"

"Yeah, sure," he said, fumbling for his computer. He opened the lid, typed in his password, and swiveled the laptop around so that the keyboard faced Olivia.

She brought up a website and began to read. "'Hallowell's debut novel kept me reading through the night. Her characters were complex, her plot was riveting, and Tessa is a heroine that women of all ages can identify with. I can't wait for the sequel.'" Without giving Millay a chance to interrupt, she read another review. And then another. And another.

"Okay!" Millay finally shouted. "So a fifteen-year-old from Nebraska likes my book. What's your point?"

"What's *your* point?" Olivia closed the laptop with a soft laugh. "Didn't you write the novel for the fifteen-year-old from Nebraska in the first place?"

Millay stared blankly at Olivia and then slowly, something shifted in her dark eyes. She sank back against the sofa cushions with a sigh. A weight seemed to lift from her as she gazed into the middle distance. "Yes, I did."

"Olivia's right," Laurel said. "You've already gained a significant fan base, so if your sales stay strong, or even gain momentum, it'll be because a buzz is building among readers. And that buzz will have nothing to do with Vernon Sherrill or Silas Black. Got it?"

"Wow, you used such an even voice just then that I almost mistook you for a journalist," Millay said, flashing Laurel a wry grin.

Laurel hit Millay in the face with a throw pillow. "Next time, we'll let you sulk, Miss *New York Times* Bestselling Author."

"That's *Ms.* to the likes of you. Make sure you print it correctly. My parents will want to dip that article in fourteen-karat gold and hang it on the living room wall. At last, they'll have proof that their daughter does more than open beer bottles and pour shots of whiskey."

Harris looked at Millay. "Will you quit your job at Fish Nets?"

"No way," Millay said. "Those men and women might not be the cream of society, but they're like a big extended family to me. They tell me jokes and stories. They talk about their day. Sure, they drink too much and become maudlin and get in fistfights, but they never do any real harm. Besides, the place is a treasure trove in terms of writing material. My customers are tough. They've weathered some serious storms in their lives. It's easy for me to picture them as blacksmiths or wyvern riders. I get new ideas almost every shift."

"I'm glad you're not quitting," Harris said. "I don't think I can take any more changes."

Millay elbowed him. "Says the guy on the verge of a *major* commitment."

Laurel examined her watch. "Speaking of commitments, I'd better get going. We have a full day tomorrow. Church, a soccer game, Cub Scouts." She sighed. "If I didn't have this time with you guys, I'd lose my mind. I'm serious. The four of you are my mooring line."

Millay closed her eyes and pretended to cringe. "Is she going to hug us now?"

"Yes," Rawlings said, opening his arms. "Come on in, Laurel. I'm ready."

The next morning, the sun rose boldly over the water, throwing canary-yellow streaks into the sky and bathing the damp sand in a golden glow. Olivia sat on the back deck, wrapped in a cotton shawl, and sipped her coffee. The sun felt glorious on her face, and she knew it wouldn't be long before one season gave way to another and she'd miss the sun's warmth on her skin and hair. Haviland too seemed to sense the transience of the mild day. He stretched out on the sand at the base of the deck, wriggling on his back, snorting in pleasure.

Olivia finished her coffee and went inside to fill a thermos. She found Rawlings at the kitchen table, the Sunday paper spread out before him.

"I turned straight to the comics," he said, smiling up at her. "I don't think I'm going to read the heavy stuff today."

"Why don't you come on a walk with me?" Olivia asked. "It's beautiful out."

Rawlings took off his reading glasses and set them on the paper. "Are you sure? You usually like to go alone."

"Usually, but not always," she said. "I'll even share my coffee with you."

Getting to his feet, Rawlings pulled Olivia close. "Now, *that's* love."

"It is," she agreed and kissed him.

With Haviland trotting alongside, Olivia and Rawlings struck out for the Point. They walked toward the narrow jetty of land dividing sea and sky, shading their eyes against the sun's glare.

The surrounding light, which reflected off the sand and the water, was such a dazzling white, and shimmered with such mirage-like brightness, that it was impossible to tell where the sea ended and the sky began.

It was a light that bathed everything in radiance. It was a light that, for a brief moment in time, banished all shadows.

Olivia and Rawlings stayed on the Point for a long while. They stood in silence, holding hands. They gazed into the distance, fixing their eyes on the blue blur of the horizon.

And when the light finally shifted, they turned and headed for home.

AUTHOR'S NOTE

Many of you may have guessed that the setting of the first half of this novel is based on North Carolina's Bald Head Island. I didn't use the actual name because the existing island isn't big enough to accommodate a festival of a significant size, and I also wanted to add a library and some other fictitious elements to the setting. However, it might interest you to learn that Bald Head Island was once known as Palmetto Island. In 1916, a developer by the name of Thomas Frank Boyd bought the entire Smith Island complex—Bald Head Island, Bluff Island, Middle Island, and some marshland—and called it Palmetto Island. So in truth, the "fictional" name I use in *Writing All Wrongs* is a throwback name.

Bald Head Island has a fascinating history, and if my novel has sparked curiosity about its past, then I'd highly recommend a wonderful reference book on the subject, *Bald Head: A History of Smith Island and Cape Fear* by David Stick.

As for the ghost stories mentioned in *Writing All Wrongs*, these are fairly common tales told around North Carolina campfires or whispered in the dark during slumber parties.

The tale that is anything but common is the legend of Blackbeard's skull cup. This is a true mystery and one that I find quite fascinating. I stumbled on the subject by accident several years ago when researching another Books by the Bay novel. Rumors surround this rather gruesome artifact, and I read a firsthand account written by a North Carolina judge by the name of Charles Harry Whedbee, in which the judge claims to have seen and held the cup. Sadly, Judge Whedbee is no longer living, but if you'd like to learn more about his experience, pick up his book *Blackbeard's Cup and Stories of the Outer Banks*.

Dear Reader,

Thank you for spending time with Olivia Limoges, the Bayside Book Writers, and the rest of the colorful characters of Oyster Bay, North Carolina.

If you're looking for another cozy and captivating read, I'd like to invite you to visit a rather unusual and intriguing small town. Havenwood, the fictional hamlet featured in my *Charmed Pie Shoppe Mysteries*, is located in an isolated corner of northwest Georgia. Home to heroine Ella Mae LeFaye, a pastry chef with an uncanny ability to enchant the food she makes, Havenwood is filled with quaint shops, delightful eateries, and a population of magical residents.

In the next installment of the *Charmed Pie Shoppe Mysteries*, Breach of Crust, *Ella Mae agrees to help a high-society mother-daughter club celebrate their annual retreat and produce their centennial cookbook by teaching them the fine art of pie making.*

Everything seems as sweet as peach pie until one summer night, Ella Mae finds the president of this elite society, the Camellia Club, floating in Lake Havenwood, and she suspects the Southern belles she's agreed to instruct aren't as genteel as she originally thought. In fact, one of these ladies might be a murderer.

To whet your appetite, turn the page for a preview of the next Charmed Pie Shoppe Mystery, Breach of Crust, coming April 2016 from Berkley Prime Crime.

Thank you for reading and supporting cozy mysteries!

Your Friend,
Ellery Adams

Ella Mae cut a wedge of black-bottom peanut butter pie and slid it onto a plate. Wiping away an errant crumb with the edge of a paper towel, she garnished the surface of the peanut butter mousse filling with a drizzle of melted chocolate and then piped three neat polka dots of chocolate directly onto the white plate. Setting the pastry bag of chocolate aside, she reached for a bag filled with whipped cream and piped two peaks in between the chocolate dots. She'd just put the plate on a server tray when Reba pushed through the swing doors leading from the Charmed Pie Shoppe's dining room into its kitchen.

"You won't believe this," she said, pulling a red licorice twist from her apron pocket and dropping on the stool next to the worktable.

Ella Mae shot her a wry grin. "We live in a world where people have magical powers. My aunt Verena knows when people are lying. Aunt Dee can infuse her metal animal sculptures with sparks of life. Aunt Sissy can influence people with her music. My mother can make plants grow by humming to them. And what about you? How many fiftysomething women could win a mixed martial arts championship with one arm tied behind their back? I can believe in all sorts of things."

Reba's expression turned wistful. "I've always wanted to try cage fightin'. It looks like so much fun."

"You know it wouldn't be a fair fight," Ella Mae scolded the woman she'd known all her life, the woman who'd been a second mother to her. "It'd be like watching a cat toy with a bird with a broken wing."

"I guess so. But what about among our kind? It could be a whole new source of entertainment. Just imagine! Saturday-night fights in groves across the world. You could watch me . . ." She trailed off, looking horrified. "I'm sorry, hon. I don't know why I keep forgettin' that you can't enter a grove anymore. I still can't wrap my head around that."

Ella Mae pointed at the wedge of pie. "Why don't you tell me what you came in here to tell me so you can deliver this to our customer? It's almost closing time."

Reba searched Ella Mae's face as though expecting to find signs of regret or pain etched into her smooth skin, but Ella Mae had learned to accept what had happened to her earlier that spring. She only wished her friends and family would make their peace with the fact that Ella Mae was no longer magical. Their constant scrutiny and deliberate avoidance of certain subjects was driving her crazy.

Brandishing the pastry bag of whipped cream, Ella Mae narrowed her eyes and said, "Spit it out, Reba, or I'm going to pipe a Santa Claus beard on your face."

"Whipped cream and red licorice do not mix." Reba held up her hands in surrender. "Well, here's somethin' you don't often hear, but the lady who ordered this piece of pie will only taste one bite of it. After that, she'll put her fork down and push her plate away."

Ella Mae, who was headed to the sink with a mixing bowl and several utensils, abruptly froze. "How do you know?"

"Because I've watched her do the same thing for the past hour and a half. She orders a piece of pie, takes a bite, lays down her fork, and then has a few sips of water. She dabs her lips with her napkin, as prim as the Queen of England, and raises her index finger to signal me—like I'm supposed to come runnin'. When I get to her table, she orders another slice." Reba looked thoroughly put out. "Ella Mae, after I deliver this pie, she'll have ordered every pie on today's menu."

"She's probably a food critic." Ella Mae shifted the bowl to one hand and used her free hand to push a strand of whiskey-colored hair from her brow. "I hope you've been patient with her, Reba."

Reba made a dismissive sound. "She could trash us on the front page of the *Atlanta Journal* and it wouldn't matter. The Charmed Pie Shoppe will have a loyal customer base for as long as you live and breathe, Ella Mae. Not only did you save the people of Havenwood, Georgia, but you saved plenty of other folks as well. Why do you think we have lines out the door every day? And our catering side has taken off too. Every bride within a hundred miles wants a pie bar at her wedding."

"Our popularity isn't what defines us," Ella Mae said, depositing the bowl in the sink basin. "We must treat every customer as though they were our very first. Bring that lady her pie with service and a smile. If she only eats one bite, that's her choice."

Scowling, Reba grabbed the serving tray. "It's a damned waste. Just because you don't enchant your food anymore doesn't mean that it isn't incredible. No one should be sampl-in' the whole menu like this without even takin' notes. My inner alarm is goin' off."

Ella Mae had learned to pay close attention to Reba's instincts. "Is she the last customer in the dining room?"

Reba nodded.

"Send the rest of the waitstaff home," Ella Mae said. "If this lady has an ulterior motive, she can make it clear to us privately."

Reba's eyes gleamed, and Ella Mae knew her friend was probably envisioning smashing chairs over the customer's head or body slamming her into a café table.

"Just let her enjoy her pie first!" Ella Mae called after Reba, but the only reply she received was the swinging doors flapping in Reba's wake.

Shaking her head in resignation, Ella Mae loaded mixing bowls, pots, pans, and plates into the dishwasher. After cleaning the cooktop and prep area, she took a moment to stand and gaze out the window above the sink. It had been a frenzied week, and she was looking forward to having both Sunday and Monday, which was also Memorial Day, off.

Tomorrow, she and Hugh Dylan planned to take their dogs on a hike in the mountains. They were also going to swim in one of rivers that fed into Lake Havenwood. It was only May, but the Georgia summer heat was in full swing, and Ella Mae couldn't wait to submerge in the cool water. After spending a day in the wilderness, she and Hugh would attend the Memorial Day cookout and concert at Lake Havenwood Resort. There would be food, fireworks, and live music. And maybe, just maybe, Ella Mae and Hugh could stretch out on a blanket under the stars and hold hands like they used to. Back before they'd been forced to keep secrets from each other. Before another woman had come between them.

That's in the past now, Ella Mae thought firmly. *We're starting over. He and I are a fresh piece of dough rolled out on the worktable. We're not the lovers we once were. Nor can we settle for being the friends we've been since childhood. We have to create something new.*

Ella Mae ran the dishrag over the spot on her palm where there was once a burn scar shaped like a clover. The scar was gone now. It had disappeared the same time Ella Mae had poured out all of her magic to defeat a powerful enemy and save her town. She had lost the symbol that marked her as the Clover Queen, but she'd never wanted to rule over anyone. All she'd ever wanted was to prepare delicious food for people. To bake pies in a brightly lit kitchen, filling the warm space with the aroma of melted butter, cinnamon, roasted nuts, sugared berries, and so much more.

"Are you reading your own palm, Ms. LeFaye?" asked one of the college students Ella Mae had hired for the summer.

Ella Mae smiled at the pretty blonde and the two other servers standing behind her. "You caught me gathering wool, Maddie. Enjoy your time off, everyone. You all worked really hard this week, and you deserve a break."

"So do you, ma'am," said Royce, the young man in charge of deliveries. "I hope you have good weather for your picnic tomorrow."

"Me too," Ella Mae said and bid good-bye to her employees.

Reba reentered the kitchen with her serving tray and the remains of the black-bottom peanut butter pie. One bite had been taken from the slice. Two at the most.

"The lady customer would like to speak with you," Reba said. "Here's her card."

"Beatrice Burbank, Camellia Club president," Ella Mae read the white lettering on a field of black. The card was thick, elegant, and expensive. Other than the design of a camellia flower in one corner, it was unadorned. "What's the Camellia Club?"

"No clue," Reba said. "But this woman is a cool cucumber. When I told her we were closin' and asked her to settle up, she said she'd make it worth our while to stay open a few minutes longer. When I told her we weren't interested, she got up, walked up to the counter, and put a hundred-dollar bill in the tip jar."

Ella Mae sighed. "I've had my fill of pushy women, Reba. I don't care if her wallet is stuffed with hundred-dollar bills. I'm ready to call it a day, and I'm going to march into the dining room and tell President Beatrice Burbank as much."

Beatrice got to her feet the moment she saw Ella Mae. She smiled graciously and extended her hand, as though she were welcoming Ella Mae to her establishment and not the other way around. "Ms. LeFaye, it is a pleasure to meet you. I haven't tasted such a wonderfully fresh tomato tart since my grandmother was alive. I had to pay my compliments to the chef in person."

Despite her determination to dislike the stranger, Ella Mae felt herself softening toward Beatrice Burbank. "That's very kind of you, Mrs. Burbank, but—"

"Please call me Bea. I know I'm old enough to be your mother, but 'Mrs. Burbank' is so terribly formal, and I'm hoping that by the end of our conversation, you and I will be on our way toward becoming friends." She indicated the chair opposite hers. "Would you sit with me for just a few moments? I have a proposition for you."

Ella Mae knew she should be wary. Beatrice was much like her business card: rich, elegant, and understated. She wore a blush-colored skirt suit with a gold camellia stickpin on the coat lapel over an ivory silk camisole. Her silvery blond hair was gathered into a low chignon, and her nails were polished a subtle pinkish beige hue. Her voluminous handbag, in contrast, was a vibrant turquoise, as though she wanted to convey that she had a playful side to her as well.

"I'd be glad to sit for a spell," Ella Mae said politely. She'd been raised in the South, and it wouldn't do to be discourteous.

Bea seemed unsurprised by her response. "I tried every pie on your menu. The tomato bacon tartlets in the cheddar cheese crust, the ham and grilled corn, and the chicken potpie. I particularly liked the herb crust on that savory delight." She put her hand over her heart. "But your desserts. Oh my, Ms. LeFaye. You have a gift. I promised myself one bite of each pie. One bite of strawberry-rhubarb crisp. One bite of lemon-mascarpone icebox tart, brown-butter raspberry pie, and black-bottom peanut butter pie. But I took two of the last one. I just couldn't stop myself."

Ella Mae was about to thank the older woman again when Bea held up a finger to forestall her. "I'm not here merely to praise you. In fact, I'd like to hire you. I came to Havenwood to finalize the details of the Camellia Club's annual retreat. This year, we'll be renting a block of rooms at the Lake Havenwood Resort. But we'll also be renting kitchen space there."

This caught Ella Mae's attention. "Oh?"

Bea nodded enthusiastically. "Every decade, the Camellia Club publishes a cookbook of dessert recipes. This year, because we're celebrating our centennial, we've decided to go all out. We're hiring three of the best chefs in the South. Actually, 'best' isn't the right word. We've sought out the most innovative, creative, and hip pastry chefs to teach us what makes an unforgettable dessert." She paused for effect. "Maxine Jordan, the founder of From Scratch, an organic bakery in Charlottesville, Virginia, came aboard in March, and we secured Caroline James from Carolina's Cakes of Raleigh last month. All that remained was to find a champion pie baker. I've traveled from Texas to Maryland tasting pies, tarts, crisps, and cobblers. I had no idea that I'd find a pie virtuoso practically in my own backyard!" She laughed merrily. "I'm from Sweet Briar, as are all of the members of the Camellia Club."

Ella Mae had heard of the town. Not far from Savannah, the scenic riverfront community was filled with historic homes, gorgeous gardens, and quaint shops. Sweet Briar was larger than Havenwood and had more restaurants, movie theaters, and nightclubs. It also boasted a thriving art scene and real estate prices that would intimidate anyone without a trust fund.

"And you'd like me to give you and your club members a crash course in pie making during your annual retreat?" Ella Mae asked. "When is it?"

"The first week in August," Bea said, pulling an envelope out of her handbag. "I realize that I'm asking you to step away from your business for several days in order to instruct a group of women you've never met before, but I can assure you that every penny of profit that the Camellia Club makes from our cookbook sales goes toward a worthy cause. This year, we're raising funds for a young lady who was badly burned at the Georgia State Fair last fall. The dear girl was making funnel cakes when a vat of hot oil overturned, splattering her arms, chest, and face. Her family can't afford her medical care, and we've offered to help."

Ella Mae's hand flew to her mouth as she tried to stifle a gasp. Her aunt Dee had suffered terrible burns that spring, and the memories of the fire came rushing back to her now. During that horrible night, her aunt was admitted to Atlanta's Grady Burn Center, where she'd undergone multiple surgeries, and many weeks later, she'd returned home to her animals and sculptures. Had it not been for the intervention of several brave and selfless people, she could have died in her burning barn, but she would never again be the same person.

Bea touched Ella Mae lightly on the arm. "Are you all right, my dear?"

"My aunt was the victim of a terrible fire not too long ago. She survived, but she will always bear the scars." Ella Mae pointed at the envelope. "Is that a contract?"

"Yes. I thought I'd leave it with you," Bea said. "If it's to your liking, you can sign it and drop it off at the resort. I'm staying through Monday." She gathered her handbag and stood to leave. "I think you'll find the remuneration acceptable, and I know all of the Camellias would be thrilled to have you as a mentor. You, Maxine, and Carolina would truly be our Dessert Dream Team."

After promising to examine the contract and respond to Bea's proposal before she left town, Ella Mae walked her guest to the door.

"I don't know what it is about this place," Bea said as she stepped out onto the front porch. "Every detail of this pie shop—from the fragrance of the flowers in the garden to the fresh herbs in the garnishes and the ripeness of the fruits in the dessert tarts—is magical. No wonder it's called The Charmed Pie Shoppe."

With a smile and a wave, Bea walked down the flagstone path, crossed the street, and got into a gleaming white Cadillac. As the sedan eased away from the curb, Ella Mae noticed a glittery camellia decal affixed to the rear windshield.

"All she needs is a wand to complete the fairy godmother look," Reba said from behind Ella Mae. As usual, she'd appeared without a sound. "I heard what she said about the cookbook profits, but is her bibbidi-bobbidi-boo act genuine?"

"I'm not going into this blindly." Ella Mae held out the contract. "I'll read this over carefully."

"Why bother?" Reba asked, putting her hand on her hip. "I can see she's already won you over."

Ella Mae shrugged. "What if she has? I love the idea of working with Maxine and Carolina. They're serious up-and-comers, and both of them have been experimenting with dessert recipes for people with food allergies. That's something I've wanted to explore as well. Also, Carolina just started shipping her cupcakes nationally. I'd love to talk to her about how she handled that kind of expansion. Her shop isn't any bigger than ours."

Together, the two women reentered the café. Reba closed and locked the front door and then turned to Ella Mae.

"What about these Camellia Club gals? Do you really think it'll be a barrel of laughs teachin' a bunch of debutantes and their mamas? What if one of them breaks a nail? You'll have to call the National Guard."

Ella Mae gave her friend an imploring look. "I need this, Reba. I need to grow as a chef. Without magic, I have to keep honing my skills. There are no shortcuts for me anymore." She glanced at the framed four-leaf clover hanging over the cash register. "I don't want people to come here because of what I used to be. I want them to come because of what I am. A top-notch pastry chef. The best pie maker in the South."

Reba nodded in understanding. "Okay, then. But I'm comin' with you. Someone will have to keep these high-society sugar queens in line."

And with that, she hit a switch on the wall, killing the lights and inviting the late afternoon shadows to flood the dining room.

Ella Mae watched Hugh Dylan leap from a rock into the middle of the river with a jubilant holler. His dog, a Harlequin Great Dane named Dante, jumped in after him. Chewy, Ella Mae's Jack Russell terrier, raced along the bank, barking wildly.

"You can go in, boy." Ella Mae made shooing motions with her hands.

"Why don't you both join us?" Hugh asked, floating on his back and staring up at the cloudless blue sky. "After that long hike, the water feels amazing."

Ella Mae couldn't help but wonder if Hugh missed being able to hold his breath for twenty minutes. Like her, he'd once possessed special abilities. He could see underwater and swim like a dolphin. And like her, he'd lost his magic and didn't seem to regret the loss.

Pulling off her sweat-soaked Dr Pepper T-shirt and

cutoffs, Ella Mae tossed her socks and tennis shoes aside and waded into the water. Hugh was right. The river, fed by the mountain's underground spring, was refreshingly chilly. Ella Mae's skin immediately broke out in gooseflesh.

"You can't stand there like that!" Hugh chided her playfully. "Take the plunge!"

Smiling, Ella Mae dove into the water. She surfaced, momentarily shuddering over the cold, and then swam over to where Hugh was treading water. "Chewy! Come on!" Ella Mae called to her dog.

When her terrier continued to bark in agitation, Hugh paddled to the nearest rock and slapped it with his palm. "Here, Charleston Chew! Here, boy!"

With a joyous yip, Chewy bounded over the rocks until he reached Hugh. After licking him on the cheek, he barked once at Dante and hopped into the water.

"I guess he needed a formal invitation," Ella Mae said and laughed.

She and Hugh rested on the largest rock while their dogs splashed about in the shallows. When she wasn't watching them, Ella Mae followed the path of water droplets trailing from Hugh's dark hair to his cheek and jawline. When one gathered at the base of his chin, she raised her finger and caught it. At her touch, he looked at her, a question in his lagoon-blue eyes.

In answer, she moved closer to him and slid her arms around his wide, muscular back. His kiss was both familiar and strange.

"I feel like I'm cheating on my longtime girlfriend with an exciting and exotic creature," Hugh said when they broke apart.

"That woman is gone," Ella Mae said. "You're left with the girl next door."

Hugh arched his brows. "No one would call you that." He took hold of the hand that had once been marked by the clover-shaped burn scar and ran his fingertips across her water-puckered skin. "You might not bear the mark of a queen, but you're still undeniably regal, Ella Mae. When you enter a room, everyone turns and stares. It's impossible not to. It would be like shutting your eyes just as a shooting star blazes across the sky."

Embarrassed by the compliment, Ella Mae flicked water at him. "They're really looking at you. The big, tall fireman with the beautiful blue eyes."

"Right," Hugh scoffed. "I smell like a kennel and have a farmer's tan because I've been spending too much time doing paperwork at Canine to Five." He twisted one of Ella Mae's damp curls around his finger. "Let's escape whenever we can—try hard to be alone together—just like this. Tonight will be fun, but it won't be the same. When we're with other people, I feel them watching us. I can sense them wondering about us."

Ella Mae nodded. She'd experienced the same sensation. "That's because we don't belong among the magical and we'll never fit in among regular people. Not after what we've seen and done. We still have scars, Hugh. They're just on the inside now."

Hugh kissed her palm. "I don't care about being outsiders. As long as we have each other. I don't need anything but you."

"And some sunscreen," Ella Mae said with a smile. "Your nose is turning red."

That night, Ella Mae left Chewy with her mother, who promised to take the little terrier inside the main house before the fireworks began. Chewy wasn't afraid of much, but he didn't care for the loud bangs and explosions that accompanied pyrotechnics displays.

"Until the show starts, I'm going to let him have the run

of the garden," Adelaide LeFaye said. "The first of the lightning bugs have arrived, and Chewy loves to chase them. It's my hope that he'll be so tired by the time the first rocket whistles into the sky that he won't even notice."

"I might be half-asleep myself," Ella Mae said. "After a crazy week at the pie shop and a day of hiking and swimming, I'm beat. Still, I wouldn't miss this evening with Hugh for anything. I also have a contract to deliver to a special guest at the resort."

Her mother listened as Ella Mae told her about Beatrice Burbank's proposal. "It sounds fun," she said when Ella Mae was done. "But maybe you should have Reba research this Camellia Club before you sign anything."

Ella Mae held up the sealed envelope. "I did the research myself. The Camellias are a philanthropic organization—a group of mothers and daughters who get together to discuss books and attend garden parties, cooking classes, and art exhibits. They raise money for college scholarships and other charities. They're good people. Besides, I don't have to be on the lookout for enemies anymore. That part of my life is over."

Ella Mae's mother shook her head. "Your childhood nemesis is still at large, and Loralyn Gaynor is bound to seek revenge against you. You were instrumental in her father's arrest, and because of your influence, her mother made peace with our family. Loralyn is undoubtedly holed up in some luxurious locale, plotting. She's dangerous, Ella Mae, and you have no idea how, or when, she'll come after you." Cupping a clematis bud in her hand, Ella Mae's mother said, "Things are not always as they appear on the outside. What color do you think this flower will be?"

Peering more closely at the bud, Ella Mae answered, "Pink."

Closing her hand gently around the bud, her mother hummed very softly. She then withdrew her hand and Ella

Mae watched as the bud slowly unfolded, revealing purple petals edged with pink. The purple hue was so dark that it was nearly black.

"People are not always what they seem at first glance," Adelaide said softly. "You should know that by now."

"Point taken," Ella Mae said and gave her mother a kiss on the cheek. "I'll be careful. But not tonight. Tonight, I just want to eat, dance, and watch the sky fill with rainbows of light."

After asking the front-desk clerk at Lake Havenwood Resort to deliver the envelope to Beatrice Burbank by the end of the evening, Ella Mae walked through the lobby and out into the carnival atmosphere on the back lawn. She spotted Hugh speaking with another volunteer fireman at the cotton candy booth and waved. Hugh said good-bye to his friend, grabbed Ella Mae by the hand, and pulled her toward the food tent.

"I was worried that I might not have enough energy to be a good date tonight, but then I saw you and all the cells in my body came alive," he said, smiling at her. "I plan to dance to every song the band plays tonight, so you'd better fuel up."

Ella Mae did. She and Hugh loaded their plates with pulled pork, smoked brisket, cheese biscuits, grilled corn, and pickled tomato salad. After a dessert of banana pudding and s'more cheesecake bars, they danced on the terrace overlooking the lake.

During one of the band's short breaks, Ella Mae glanced around in search of Bea, but she didn't see her anywhere. As the sky darkened, and the master of ceremonies announced that it was almost time for the fireworks show to begin, Ella Mae gave up on finding her.

"I can't believe we never ran into Bea," she told Hugh.

"Maybe bouncy houses and barbecues aren't her style. You described her as being elegant and polished, so she probably ate in the dining room and will watch the fireworks display from her balcony while sipping a glass of sparkling wine."

Ella Mae laughed. "I bet you're right. And where's our special spot?"

"It's a bit apart from everyone else," Hugh said with an impish glimmer in his eye.

Sliding her arm around his waist, Ella Mae grinned up at him. "It sounds like the perfect place."

It was very late when Ella Mae returned to her little guest cottage behind her mother's house. She hadn't felt this happy or optimistic in months, and though she was physically exhausted, she was too wired to go to bed.

Chewy must have been woken up by the sound of Ella Mac's car, for she could hear his muted barking coming from Partridge Hill's kitchen the moment she turned off the ignition. Ella Mae rushed to let him out before he could wake her mother. Together, Ella Mae and her terrier wandered through the fragrant garden, across the dew-covered lawn, and down to the dock stretching like a finger into the lake.

When they reached the end of the dock, Ella Mae sat cross legged on the rough planks and listened to the water lap quietly against the wood. Chewy nestled beside her and put his head in her lap. Ella Mae stroked the soft fur on the top of his head and gazed over the water at the resort.

She smiled, recalling how Hugh's face had lit up with wonder during the fireworks show. And of how he'd kissed her during the finale. At that moment, she'd sensed the brilliance of the lights in the sky overhead, but it was nothing compared to the sparks of heat she felt between herself and Hugh. They were forging their new beginning. Tonight marked the first of many memories they would make together.

After a time, Ella Mae whispered to Chewy, "All right, boy. Time to go."

As she stood, she saw something floating in the water. It was hard to see clearly because the moon had ducked behind a cloud, but when it shone unobstructed again, Ella Mae cried out in surprise and horror.

The thing floating in the water was a body.

A woman's body.

Ella Mae reacted quickly. She pushed the small rowboat kept on the dock into the water and leapt into the craft. Using the oar to push herself away from the dock, she paddled toward the body.

It only took a second for Ella Mae to know that the woman was beyond saving. Her upturned face was just below the surface, and her pale hair looked like a tangle of watergrass. Her dress, the shade of a water hyacinth, billowed around her legs and bare feet.

She wore a single piece of jewelry. A gold camellia stick-pin was fastened to the upper-left breast of her dress, just above her heart.